THE RICH LIST

BEN SAXON

SIMONSTONE
PUBLISHING

Simonstone Publishing
71-75 Shelton Street, Covent Garden,
London, WC2H 9JQ
www.simonstonepublishing.co.uk

1 3 5 7 9 10 8 6 4 2

A CIP catalogue record for this book is available from the British Library.

ISBN (Hardback): 978-1-7384044-0-7

Typset by Amie McCracken

Printed and bound in Great Britain by Clays Ltd, Elcograf S.p.A.

For my dad, who shares my love of reading.

Prologue

Hogan squinted as his eyes adjusted to the dazzling January sunshine after two hours inside the florist's. On previous trips to similar establishments, he'd locate an expensive bouquet, pay, and leave the store within minutes. In comparison, choosing wedding flowers dragged. However, finding time for this, even during a complex investigation, pleased Katie and made it all worthwhile. His fiancée stepped onto the crosswalk, turned, and ran back, dropping her bag and throwing her arms around his neck.

"Thanks for being understanding."

He slipped a hand through her blonde curls and held her close. The smell of lavender lingered from the sprig he'd added earlier.

"You sure you can't stay?"

"It's only two days. You'll be fine. You can think of names for our new pets." Katie smiled, tiny dimples appearing on both cheeks. She glanced back to the Cadillac across the street. "I'd better go. I'll phone you from LAX."

"Okay, be safe," he called as she hustled to make the lights.

Hogan nodded at State Senator Thomas Mitchell, who stood holding the door to the vehicle opposite. The guy was a class act; he'd make a fine congressman. He raised a hand in return. Katie's sunglasses caught the reflection of the late-afternoon sun as she waved and ducked into the car in one fluid motion. Hogan watched while the sleek black vehicle waited to slot into the flowing traffic, which after a short delay, it did.

Then, it exploded.

1

CURSING HIS RACING mind, Hogan admitted defeat. He flicked on the light, illuminating a worn punching bag awaiting his frustration. After he'd worked it until breathless, an ice-cold shower pounded away the sweat from his muscular frame. Once dressed, he clipped his watch onto his wrist. Not that it was much use; it hadn't told the time in close to three years. Stepping out into the darkness, he expected to arrive at the office as the first slivers of daylight caressed the Californian sky.

Balancing a breakfast burrito and coffees, Hogan approached the tower of ugly concrete modernism housing the FBI's city HQ. Function over design had been the government's priority in the late sixties. The Bureau rarely shared federal buildings, but LA's real estate costs stymied any move. He caught the rising murmur of traffic from the nearby 405 as a security officer yanked open the door.

The mirrored elevator accentuated the shadows beneath his cobalt eyes and made him glad he was alone. The doors slid open, and he exited into the Criminal, Cyber Response, and Services Branch. In total, it occupied four of the Bureau's nine floors. He continued beyond his cubicle in the Criminal Investigation Division to the corner office. Assistant Director in Charge Carla Ryan raised a hand in welcome as he eased a coffee onto her desk. She almost lived here since her bitter divorce. As she reached for the drink, her straightened chestnut hair inched forward, framing a set of frown lines embossed on her forehead. Her appearance was as immaculate as her customary navy suit. Driven and well respected throughout the Bureau, she'd been one of the youngest women ever to make ADIC. She suffered neither fools nor bullshit.

They got along. At least most of the time.

She didn't wait for his weekly question.

"Still nothing from Peterson—but the clock's ticking and we're pushing for a definitive answer by the end of next month. My gut feeling is he won't return, and we'll decide on a new special agent in charge then." She raised her cup. "Thanks for this."

Hogan nodded and trudged back to his cubicle. As he gnawed on the burrito, he cursed the approaching deadline. He'd hoped Peterson's situation would remain unresolved for longer. He had to find a career-making case. One that forced consideration for the SAC role, and repaired his damaged reputation.

The department filled up as elevators disgorged agents who'd suffered longer, more stressful commutes. Hogan began working through his orderly stack of mundane case files and welcomed the distraction of Lisa Vance appearing at his desk. A smidgen over five foot six, she was tough, whip-smart, and fun to be around. She wore an irrepressible smile below her small, crooked nose—broken so often she'd stopped getting it fixed. If anything, it added character to her striking features. She'd always had his back, even during the darkest months following Katie's death.

"This is Michelle. She's starting with us today." Vance turned to the rookie alongside her. "If you're worried about remembering all the names, Hogan here can help. He once memorized over one hundred faces and names in ten minutes when he won the US memory championships."

"Wow, really?"

Hogan side-eyed Vance as he offered his hand.

"It was a long time ago. It's not as impressive as it sounds."

"He's modest, too. It comes as standard with the British accent," Vance joked, as she guided her new colleague to the next introduction.

The rest of the day proved as slow and uneventful as Hogan's hour-long drive back to Venice. For once, he squeezed his ancient red Jag XJS into a spot near his second-floor one-bedroom apartment on Westminster

Avenue. He'd moved here a decade back, partly because the location name triggered happy memories of his childhood in London. He'd stayed due to the favorable rent since helping the landlord's son out of a nasty scrape. As he climbed the stairs, his neighbor's cat darted behind their swelling rooftop cactus collection. The contrast to his bare exterior was stark.

His kitchen table had gained two new items since the morning: a terse note from Megan and a spare set of keys he'd offered for convenience. She'd perceived this as commitment, an error he wouldn't make next time. Perhaps he'd not been ready to date again. With a resigned shrug, he opened the fridge and grabbed a Pacifico beer and leftover Chinese food to heat up.

Stepping back into his sparse living room, he raised the bottle at the sizeable fish tank in the corner.

"It's back to three of us again."

The starfish and seahorse offered no reaction behind the polished glass. He observed them in a contemplative silence only broken by the ping of the microwave.

2

KIROV SWUNG THE stolen Ford F-150 onto the empty Malibu Lagoon parking lot. As the engine cooled, he reached for the midnight-blue hardback book on the passenger seat. He selected a chapter to read from the Jules Verne classic—a routine he followed without exception before starting an operation. Phileas Fogg was calm and collected regardless of the challenges his journey around the world presented. A few minutes later, he closed the book, his mind empty of distractions and his heartbeat slowed. In his extensive experience, his profession always demanded composure.

From the truck's bed, Kirov pulled a Yamaha SeaWing II underwater scooter, snorkel and mask. Perching on its edge, he slipped into his wetsuit and slung a waterproof bag over his shoulder.

The moonless night afforded extra protection as he ran the few hundred meters to the water's edge. Beyond the imposing fence to his right, occupied residences punched patches of light onto the deserted private beach. He powered through the murky ocean before pivoting to run parallel to these. At the spot exactly level with one property, he turned and headed back to the shore. Upon reaching it, he followed a blind spot corridor between security cameras either side of the target's home. Reassured by silence, he removed gloves from his bag and climbed the metal stairs to grab a quick view through the towering glass window. In the center of the room, a man waved his arms from left to right—a virtual reality headset strapped to his face.

Kirov had surveilled this property for the last few months. The billionaire owner only used it when visiting LA on business. His permanent home in San Francisco had on-site security. The evenings he spent in

Malibu followed a predictable pattern. His bodyguard would check the property before leaving. Jay Chopra would then drink and play VR games until 1:30 a.m. A few weeks earlier, Kirov had read an insufferable "day in the life" article in which the tech giant claimed to need only four hours' sleep. It featured a picture of a monotone wardrobe that the owner explained reduced time-wasting choice.

Perhaps the latter was why Kirov had been commissioned to kill him.

The assassin peeled off his wetsuit and toweled his lean body dry. After climbing into a Tyvek forensic suit and adding a cap to avoid stray hairs, he resembled a crime scene technician from one of the ubiquitous TV cop shows. He lifted himself from the sand to wipe his feet, slipped into soft running shoes and added shoe covers. The final item he recovered from the bag before he strapped it to his back, was a SIG Sauer P226 with a fitted suppressor. Moments later, he climbed to the back entrance, unconcerned by the camera focused on the steps. The door responded to the code he entered and clicked open. He slid inside. Chopra struck out at virtual foes, unaware of the real one. Kirov grabbed the man's right shoulder, forced him back three steps and swept his legs. Gravity and physics ensured catastrophic damage as Chopra's head smacked into the edge of the kitchen island. He didn't get the chance to see what had hit him. After waiting a minute, Kirov checked for a pulse as a small pool of blood advanced from beneath the shiny white VR headset. He found none. His extensive research and preparation had paid off. He always had a backup plan, but a gunshot wound would have made the next killing he'd planned more difficult.

The empty granite top meant extra work to stage the scene. He placed a new bottle of gin, tonic, and a glass from the well-stocked liquor cabinet next to the body. He added an ice bucket set and pressed the fingers of Chopra's right hand against each item. After moving them all to the kitchen island, he mixed a drink and added ice until it was full. Taking one more ice cube, he rubbed it against Chopra's bare foot, before leaving it to melt next to his knee. He stepped back, making sure the scene and story that the gamer slipped on a melted ice cube added up. It did, for now, so he made for the security room to execute the most complex part of his task.

It took Kirov over two hours to brute force the passcode system to the local server on the house security—Poseidon Gate. He'd modified some THC Hydra software for this crucial part of the plan. Once inside the network, he checked the exit log, then installed a beautiful, simple piece of custom-written malware. It would run in server memory only, leaving no forensic footprint and delete all records between 10:45 p.m. and three a.m. then self-destruct. The program was set to start at four a.m. when Kirov would be long gone. It would prove no one entered the property before Chopra's demise. Next, he headed out of the front entrance and across the narrow courtyard to recover the tiny camera he'd concealed in the lemon tree last month. It pointed at the pin pad for entry. Now he could return to the security room to loop external security footage. It would cover the time since before his arrival, and for the next hour. Satisfied he'd covered his tracks, he returned to where Chopra lay and pushed his gloved fingers forward and upward into the melted ice water. It mimicked a slip pattern. After one final sweep of the property, he snapped the crime scene photos requested by his employer and left through the balcony door. Fifteen minutes later, he licked the sea salt from his lips, pulled onto the Pacific Coast Highway and disappeared into the night.

3

As he neared the office, Hogan's cell phone rang. He tapped the answer icon, his greeting immediately interrupted by his boss.

"Forget coming in, head to Malibu. The governor demanded our presence at an address—I'm sending it now."

He caught the edge in Carla's voice.

"Whose is it?"

"Jay Chopra's."

Malibu proved a traffic friendly destination at this early hour. Carla's follow-up message confirmed a beachfront location and the discovery of the owner's body. The LA County Sheriff's Department had control of the scene. As he parked, his intrigue grew—everyone had heard of Jay Chopra, and he was one of the world's richest men.

Hogan entered an understated courtyard, flashed his badge, and stepped inside the property. An officer directed him down a hallway to the spacious room where the body lay. He immediately speculated a broken neck or fractured skull had caused Chopra's death. His lopsided head suggested an impact of considerable force. The pool of congealed blood wasn't large enough for the deceased to have bled out. He also still had a VR headset strapped to his face. As Hogan bent down, a man sneered in a faux-English accent designed to mimic his own: "It's okay, everyone—Sherlock Holmes is here to solve the mystery."

He didn't look up. It had been a few years, but Detective Butch Karlson was still a prick.

Ignoring the comment, he surveyed the blood-smeared kitchen island. He turned to Medical Examiner Irene Hall, crouched opposite.

"What do you think?"

Karlson didn't allow her the chance to reply. "*I think* he slipped and smashed his head on the island—simple as that." He pointed to a small pool of water next to the dead man's right knee. "See, even a billionaire can die in the dumbest way."

"Irene?" Hogan persisted.

She raised her gloved hands. "Hey, you guys can speculate. I'll tell you *how* he died after I get him back to the morgue."

"There's no sign of an intruder?" Hogan asked, finally acknowledging Karlson, who'd gained weight since their last encounter. His maroon suit creased in protest as he lumbered forward, sporting a smug grin. He knew more and couldn't wait to share.

"The doors were shut front and back, same with all the windows. They're on one security system, which shows none were opened until the bodyguard returned early morning. And when he departed last night, Mr. Chopra was very much alive."

"So he claims."

The detective's bloated red face turned puce. "Why the hell are you here? This ain't FBI jurisdiction, even if this was a homicide, which it's not."

"When the governor calls my boss at dawn, that travels downstream fast—especially when it involves a generous campaign donor. Where's the guy that found him?"

Hogan was over six foot, but the guy Karlson called over could play center for the Lakers.

"Mr. Matthews, can you briefly repeat your story *for the agent's benefit?*"

The giant rubbed the back of his neck and looked down at the two of them.

"Uh-huh, as I explained to the officer, I brought Mr. Chopra home around ten. Now, he always stays here when he's in LA on business, and I take care of him." He had a low, soulful voice, like a downtown jazz club MC. "I checked the property and the security interface too—

everything was cool. Mr. Chopra suggested I enjoy an evening with my girl—she's over in Rancho Park. He was good like that. I was due back at six a.m. sharp to drive him to his breakfast meeting at The Peninsula."

Hogan stroked his trimmed beard. He caught no hint of deception.

"When I returned this morning, I got no response—now you gotta understand that Mr. Chopra insisted upon punctuality. So I waited a little while, then tapped in the code and entered to find him like this. Then I called you guys," Matthews finished, grim-faced.

Karlson's expression said: *I told you so.*

The bodyguard misconstrued it as accusatory, blurting out, "Hey! Tanisha will confirm I was with her, and the surveillance logs will show me leaving and arriving."

"We've checked them already, and your story matches up, at least for now. But that might only be until we get the approximate time of death."

"We can get the exact time of death." Hogan's eyes fell on the controller still strapped to Chopra's thumb.

"Oh yeah, and how do you suggest we do that, genius?"

"It'll be the point the game stopped," Hogan explained with school-teacher patience. He set off across the empty expanse of pristine white marble floor beyond the body. Aside from a painting of two burnt-orange squares, the room's walls were bare. Despite this abstract decoration, the property lacked soul like most unfrequented homes. Light streamed through the vast windows, which provided spectacular shimmering ocean views. He asked Matthews for the code to the door, punched in the ten digits, and walked out onto the balcony. Clear air filled his lungs as the temperature climbed toward the seventies, and sunlight danced across the rolling surf below. As he started down the steps to the caramel sand, a dog walker approached. Tanned and healthy, he personified a wealthy Malibu retiree.

Hogan called out, "This is a private beach, right?"

"Sure is. Fences either side, cameras too. You looking to buy this place?" The man eyed Hogan's smart suit.

"A little outside my price range," he answered, playing along. The man gave a sage nod and continued his slow meander, his Labrador padding behind.

Hogan glanced at the camera trained on the steps, then returned inside and closed the heavy door. He crossed the open space again. Why had Chopra been so close to the kitchen island? He approached it to examine the items on top. A curved bottle featuring an ostentatious chrome stopper with "Sharish Gin" etched upon it rested near the corner. The glass beside it was full. A half-empty bottle of Fever-Tree tonic sat next to a plate of sliced lime and an ice bucket containing water. He checked the liquor cabinet and freezer, then took a few minutes to commit the entire scene to memory. He'd found building a mental journey of images he could walk back through often more valuable than the standard crime scene photos. He also couldn't rely on receiving evidence reports from the LA County Sheriff's Department.

Matthews still loomed in the corner of the room.

"All this normal?" Hogan tilted his head at the countertop, his instincts questioning the scene.

The big guy nodded.

"Mr. Chopra enjoyed a drink or two. He used that and gaming to unwind. Man, I can't believe this."

"Had he made a drink before you left?"

"No, he hadn't."

"Could you show me where the security is?"

They walked down the main corridor and entered a boxy room on the right. No art or marble here—just an impressive array of hardware emblazoned with the name *Poseidon Gate*. A bald detective sat hunched in the only chair, viewing the digital camera playback. He grunted a welcome. A parallel screen displayed the front door activity logs, including an entry at 6:10 a.m. that morning and one 10:16 p.m. exit the previous evening. Law enforcement arrived at 6:32 a.m. It verified the bodyguard's timeline. Hogan pulled up the back door logs. Aside from his recent exit, nothing else showed from that past week. Two guys from the ME's office shuffled by with a squeaking gurney as he squeezed past Kojak and out of the room. He walked out to the courtyard. Irene Hall stood beneath a lemon tree, lighting a cigarette. The wrinkles around her mouth deepened. She exhaled citrus-tinged smoke and offered a shrug.

"For the record—I've always found your English accent sexy."

Hogan chuckled. Irene was old enough to be his mother and they went back years.

"Could you let me know when you have the autopsy results?" he asked. Her report should prove whether this was, in fact, a tragic accident.

Karlson's corpulent frame lurched into view before the ME could respond.

"We don't need your help; run on back to Wilshire. Didn't you nearly get fired for sticking your nose into your girlfriend's death?"

Hogan's quick two steps forward caused his antagonist to shuffle back with surprising speed. Irene cocked her head. She was right—he should know better. He swallowed his anger, spun on his heel, and headed to his car. The scene supported accidental death, but not completely. It could be he'd walked away from the murder of the decade.

4

THE DRIVE BACK to Wilshire took Hogan twice as long as his early-morning ride up to Malibu. The on-ramp to the 10 resembled the opening scene of *La La Land*—minus the cheerful song and dance, so he looped back to Olympic Boulevard. He spent the stop-start journey refining his memory palace from Chopra's property. To create this, you chose a familiar place. On this occasion, he picked his office. You stored the information there, using vivid images—the more outrageous, the better. In this case, Poseidon sat on Hogan's desk, holding a trident and two pink radio alarm clocks flashing 6:10 and 10:16. It was an image your mind wanted to store. Everything stuck when you walked back through your creation; it helped to repeat this to ensure extended recollection. World champions still used this method, but Hogan remained surprised how few people knew about it, or its value. With dedication, anyone could learn how to do it.

He was eighteen when his mum died. As he struggled with grief, he became frustrated about how few special moments with his mother he could recall. It began to eat him up inside, so he started studying memory and learned he could train his brain to remember any information. Everything was possible and had a special technique, from numbers to names and faces. It became a welcome distraction, and when he moved from London back to LA at age nineteen, a borderline obsession. He spent hours a day training his brain—it helped with the pain and loneliness. Once he got to Stanford, a professor, amazed by what his new student could do, encouraged him to train for the US Memory Championships. He did, and to everyone's surprise, including his, he won it.

Stanford wanted him to continue to the world championship, but by then, Hogan needed to move on and start enjoying college life. As he did, he continued to test his brain in new ways and extend its capabilities when time allowed. It became a good side-hustle for prop bets in bars as he performed feats others thought impossible. It also proved invaluable in his studies and admission exam for the FBI. Later, applying these abilities to investigations helped him become a rising star in the Bureau. But then his life was shattered in one moment, and darkness followed.

As Hogan approached his desk, Carla—as if ordained with a sixth sense predicting his arrival—popped her head out of her office and curled a finger. He joined her in the minimalist room with alabaster walls. Scandinavian furniture added to the calming ambience, but it rarely lasted.

"So, what's the deal with Jay Chopra's death? I've heard it looks like an accident," she asked. Carla's ability to acquire developing information was legendary in the Bureau.

"Everything seems to indicate that is the case."

"Seems?"

"Yeah…I mean, there is no obvious evidence to the contrary; if the autopsy comes back benign, then it appears to be a tragic accident. Unusual, bizarre, even, but still—"

"Good, we don't want to be dragged into this. I explained to the governor earlier this isn't our jurisdiction, and that was before we knew specifics."

"Only…" Hogan began as his boss's face darkened, "something about the scene doesn't feel right. I'll figure out what that is, and I can follow up and check—"

"No!" The interjection cut through the air. Carla sighed and softened her tone. "Look, I know you want—shit, even need a big case to make your own, but you can't force this to be it. I'm sure the LA County Sheriff's Department is more than capable of reaching the right conclusions. Also, the press will go fucking crazy over this. Trust me—we don't want to be involved."

Hogan snorted and leaned forward to protest, but Carla's eyes flashed. "That is all, Special Agent."

The message was clear—leave the case alone. Hogan stepped out of her office determined to do the opposite.

Awaiting news from Irene Hall, Hogan's day dragged. He offered terse responses about Jay Chopra's death to inquisitive colleagues who'd swung by his desk. He'd also spent an unhealthy amount of time on Zillow looking at the Chopra property and others nearby. He couldn't comprehend how a four-bedroom home would need seven bathrooms, but it appeared commonplace in Malibu. Media speculation accompanied lurching aerial shots of the house on TV. Hypotheses ranged from suicide on CNN to foul play on Fox News. The LA County Sheriff's Department promised a press conference the following morning.

His patience expended, Hogan called the ME's office, but her assistant informed him Irene was still busy. As he grabbed his jacket to leave, Jared Miller stalked toward his desk; to gloat no doubt. Their mutual dislike extended back to Quantico. Miller's shifty eyes were a little too close together, his copper hair trimmed like a wannabe marine—he wore an expensive but unfashionable suit. The soles of his shoes were rumored to be packed for an extra inch.

"Shame about Chopra's accidental death," Miller announced in a voice suggesting the opposite. "Working a billionaire's murder *would* have been massive."

Hogan feigned insouciance. "Oh, it would've been hard to claim jurisdiction. LA County would have fought tooth and nail. I've plenty going on and the Walter Hicks case will drop any day now."

"Of course. Big win, huge..." Miller responded while dispensing a patronizing shoulder tap. With a shrill laugh, he bounded to join two waiting lackeys. What the hell would he do if this fucker got the SAC job and became his superior?

Quit, most likely.

He allowed time for the group to get a suitable distance ahead, then made for the elevators.

Once he reached Venice, Hogan didn't head home, but instead to Abbot Kinney Boulevard and Blue Star Donuts to collect a box of bribery for the next day. The sidewalk thronged with hipsters and cooler tourists escaping the tackier boardwalk. He joined the queue of phone-wielding Gen Z's and sighed as others sashayed from the store and uploaded their purchase to social media. Sharing the minutiae of your life (and diet) had zero appeal. He'd deleted his social media apps two years ago, and his mental health had benefited.

Back at his apartment, he scrounged a meal of rice noodles with a few forlorn vegetables. His job wasn't conducive to regular grocery shopping. He began formulating a plan for the next day. Carla would suspect he wouldn't leave the case alone—it wasn't in his nature. So, he'd need Lisa Vance to run interference, while he got answers.

5

IRENE HALL'S MESSAGE interrupted Hogan's morning news scroll.

Autopsy completed late last night—no signs of foul play. Press conference with preliminary findings is scheduled for midday. Free for a late lunch if you wanna head over to discuss.

He swore and tapped out a quick reply—he'd be there for lunch. He wasn't quitting yet.

Detective Butch Karlson wore a better-fitting suit for the televised press conference. It unfolded as Hogan expected: no indication of foul play, suspected tragic accident, no evidence of suicide, and no signs of drugs in the preliminary toxicology. They reiterated that the cameras and security system showed no exit or entry, forced or otherwise, until the bodyguard returned to discover the body. The time of death proved he wasn't involved. The overflowing press contingent clamored for more info, and it was promised in due course. The undersheriff turned and left remaining questions in his wake.

Hogan located Lisa Vance in the break room. She was demonstrating a complicated jiu-jitsu choke hold on a wide-eyed colleague.

"Hey, I'm heading over to see the Citibank fraud team. I'm not sure when I'll be back."

Her piercing green eyes scanned the box he held as she released the unfortunate agent.

She leaned in close. "And you're taking donuts?" She flicked open the box and shoved one into her mouth.

"I'm off to see Irene Hall about Chopra, but if anyone asks, you know what to do."

Vance's dirty-blonde ponytail bounced in the affirmative, as she demolished the snack. Fellow agents speculated how she could eat so often yet remain so slim, but most had no idea how hard she trained on the weekends. They bumped fists, and Hogan escaped before he lost any more donuts.

It was a straight run on the 10 to the LA County ME-Coroner's Department over in Boyle Heights. Hogan's twenty-seven-year-old Jag still ran well. His ongoing fear of expensive repairs ensured he nursed it around the city.

He'd bought it five years ago, fulfilling a dream sparked by the poster that had graced his wall as a young boy. And for a fraction of what it retailed for back then. A Spotify playlist filled the vehicle with late nineties songs. Fellow agents mocked his lack of knowledge of contemporary music, but he didn't care—nostalgia created comfort but other memories less so. The paradox of tragedy was that it left you with moments too painful to recall, too painful to forget. As usual, traffic sucked. Everyone in LA spent an unhealthy portion of their life staring at license plates which often featured slogans. It was a "Golden State" and "In God We Trust" kind of day, but upon reading "It will take years for your dreams to die" on a Chevy Tahoe's plate, he stopped.

They could die in a matter of seconds.

He switched lanes and instead contemplated soccer betting strategies for the weekend.

Hogan messaged his arrival to Irene from the steps of the ME-Coroner's building. The century-old redbrick conveyed charm and character the

Bureau's Wilshire office lacked. A young vaper passed by trailing sweet cherry smoke as Irene appeared—a cigarette already balanced on her lower lip as she fumbled for a lighter.

"Do you ever think of quitting?" Hogan gestured toward the youth.

"Nah, when you see as many accidental deaths as me, you kinda trust to fate."

"Ah, which is the reason I'm here. Where do you want to head?"

"Mexican okay?"

"Good with me."

"I was thinking about La Chuperia all morning... Trust me, the nachos are excellent."

As they set off walking, Hogan speculated how anyone could work up an appetite while handling dead bodies.

Irene heaved open a graffitied door to reveal a moody neon-lit restaurant interior. They selected a corner table, away from the speakers and their offbeat Banda soundtrack. Spicy onion and seared pork aromas filled the air as Irene ordered for them both and got onto the autopsy without delay. A devastating fracture in the third and fourth cervical vertebrae had killed Chopra instantly. His skull also showed damage from the same impact with the kitchen island. The VR game's metadata retrieved by the forensics team indicated Chopra stopped playing at 10:53 p.m. This matched Irene's time of death estimate and Karlson remained fixed on the fact that Chopra had slipped. Irene agreed—the injuries were consistent. She passed Hogan the report.

"How about this bruise on his right shoulder?" he asked, pointing to the autopsy description sheet.

"That's anybody's guess, but it's been judged too small to be consequential."

He read on, and when he got to the list of stomach contents, he stopped.

"No alcohol was found in the stomach?"

"Uh-huh," she answered. "But if Chopra hadn't taken a gulp before, well, you know..."

"If I've made my first fresh G&T, I'll have a good drink of it right away. I thought he must have been on his second already, but from your report, obviously not." Hogan closed his eyes and pictured the glass on the kitchen island—it had been full. Who goes to the trouble to make a drink, then immediately straps back on a VR headset that stops you from consuming it? This was strange, and strange bothered him.

"People are different," Irene offered. "I don't think there's anything here—I'm sorry."

Hogan stayed silent, walking through other mental images from the scene. A waitress eased a towering stack of nachos onto the table, breaking his concentration. They proved as good as promised.

His lunch partner met his gaze when they finished.

"You're still not letting this go, are you?"

Hogan shook his head. "I can't. There's something not right here."

He bade Irene farewell and drove the short distance to the forensics lab. After signing in, he waited until the genial Lab Supervisor Bob McCourt appeared, grinning as he approached. Tufts of white hair sat astride his oversized bald head—like a cartoon mad scientist.

"Hey. How you doing, buddy? It's been a while."

"All good, Bob, any more kids since I last saw you?" Hogan teased.

McCourt laughed. "We have quit at five!" He mimed a snipping motion near his crotch. "How can I help you today?" He eyed the box of donuts. "Blue Star—it must be important."

"It's the Chopra forensics—I want info on the bottle and glass."

McCourt fidgeted as he stepped in closer.

"That's LA County's case. Butch Karlson will flip if he finds out I shared any details. They want this wrapped up with a pretty bow ASAP."

"Why the rush?"

"I hear the family is satisfied the death was accidental. They want to quash salacious speculation and that kind of money talks. Plus, they don't want people to know about the game he was playing when he died."

"What do you mean?"

"It's called *Battle Princess*; you fight your way through a castle and at the end, you rescue the damsel in distress."

"Sounds okay."

McCourt blushed. "Then you claim your prize in a pretty graphic way."

"I'm guessing he hadn't completed the quest."

"As he was fully dressed, I guess not. A well-known porn star plays the princess."

"Of course she does," Hogan replied. The idea made sense, as there were lots of lonely gamers out there. Chopra had been single and, by all accounts, a little odd. Still, it wasn't a detail you'd want to be remembered by.

A few seconds of silence elapsed as McCourt shifted his weight between his feet.

"C'mon, Bob—no one will know the forensics are for me."

His friend's head shot left to right. "Okay, listen—I'll stay later tonight and check what we have and call you."

"Thanks, Bob—and I'll still owe you," Hogan added, thrusting the box of donuts into his friend's hands.

Crawling along the highway, Hogan checked in with Vance.

"All cool here. Carla asked after you, but I covered your ass. Any luck with Irene?"

"Maybe, but I'm still chasing down another Chopra lead. If you could send me the update on Hicks before you leave, I'll scan through it. Are you fighting this weekend?"

"I sure am, some trash-talking Brazilian. She'll get dealt with like the rest. Have a good one, hope the bribe pays off—I mean, it should, those donuts are so damn tasty."

Hogan laughed. "You too, good luck in the fight." Although knowing Vance, she wouldn't need it.

Hogan perched on a bar stool, picking at the label of his beer bottle, waiting for McCourt to call as happy hour fueled the growing hum of conversation.

"Bob—what we got?" he asked when his cell phone ended the wait.

"The only prints on the glass and the bottle belonged to Chopra. The contents came back all normal—the gin was gin, the tonic, same. I guess this isn't the update you were after?"

As he digested the news, a chiseled Hollywood hopeful began mixing an elaborate cocktail opposite. He'd hoped for at least a small anomaly.

"Hogan?"

"Yeah, sorry, Bob. Not really. Thanks for looking into it anyway."

"No problem, have a good weekend, buddy."

The barman launched a bottle into the air and caught it behind his back.

"Wait!" Hogan cried, drawing a few surprised looks from around the bar. "Can you check one last thing?" he asked, before explaining what he needed. The technician moaned about working even later but agreed.

One hour passed, and Hogan started another nervous beer when his cell phone lit up.

"Soooo, I checked the chrome cap for prints as you requested," McCourt began.

"And?"

"No fingerprints at all, not from Chopra or anyone."

"So how does he open this bottle of gin without leaving prints on the cap?"

"That's a damn good question."

6

HE AWOKE TO a light shining in his eyes and a man asking if he could hear him. Disoriented, Hogan sat up and looked out onto the street. His memory came flooding back. He stood, shrugged off the paramedic and staggered toward the Cadillac's mangled remains. Blood began to stream down his face. He screamed Katie's name as his world started to spin, and he fell to the floor, into blackness.

Hogan's eyes sprung open. He should have saved her, he told himself for the thousandth time. If only he'd insisted she didn't take that trip. He'd learned to control the devastating memories of that day during waking hours. If he didn't, dark thoughts would consume him. But when he slept, it was a different story. Hollowness racked his body. He instinctively touched the crescent scar above his left eye as he locked the pain back in its mental prison. He checked his phone. Five a.m. On a fucking weekend, too.

He repeated the post-nightmare routine like an automaton: punching bag, cold shower, coffee. As it brewed, he made an omelet and smothered it in HP sauce. The traditional British condiment triggered recollections of his mum's famous breakfasts. As he ate, he thought about Chopra. The lack of fingerprints and untouched drink meant something but what exactly? Another thing bothered him; Chopra's place had been immaculate—the guy thrived on order. So, would he drop an ice cube and leave it? Of course, he could have missed it, but it added further doubt. Still, he'd need a lot more if he planned to risk Carla's wrath.

The Rose in Venice was a brisk ten-minute walk from Hogan's apartment. It was a fashionable spot, with brushed concrete floors and lights entwined in hanging plants. He'd been coming here most Saturdays for the last sixteen months.

A mass of auburn hair framing pretty porcelain features popped up from behind the café counter as he entered.

"Hey, Hogan. We needed more pasta straws." She plonked down a carton. "We're plastic-free now."

"Nice one, Amber. Can I grab my stuff and have the usual?"

"Sure thing—I'll bring everything over."

"Cheers." He headed to the privacy of his reserved corner table to begin his Saturday regime. Shortly after moving from LA to London, Hogan had got into soccer, or as he was soon corrected—"football." He'd grown up supporting his mum's favorite team—Tottenham Hotspur—and kicked a ball around daily with his brother, Scott. These days, however, soccer was about making the extra monthly money he needed, betting and trading on Premier League matches, and why he was here.

Amber appeared with an americano, almond croissant, iPad Pro, and laptop. He stored them here as a precaution against anyone discovering his sports trading activities and income. "Let me know if you need anything further, and don't work too hard," she said, spinning with a smile. Hogan had never elaborated on what he did here, or elsewhere.

"Thanks, Amber, will do," he replied, frowning at the finger-shaped bruises on her arm. But she was halfway back to the counter before he could inquire further.

He connected the laptop to Wi-Fi, and NordVPN, chose an IP address in London and clicked open Betfair. This UK betting platform allowed you to bet against and accept bets from other gamblers across hundreds of soccer markets. Meanwhile, the iPad enabled him to livestream the three p.m. games in England.

The next few hours were the usual blur of placing bets and taking them from other bettors on these matches. Hogan only bet and traded the correct score during games, known as "in play." A few Lakers fans at work had argued that "soccer" had too few goals to be exciting. Hogan disagreed, but the relative lack of scoring had allowed him to develop an exploitative strategy. He'd start by betting on 0-0, then move to 1-0 if either team got a goal. Once the score had remained unchanged for a decent period, he would take bets for the exact amounts he'd staked at shorter odds. His brain could juggle complex calculations to the point where he knew the margins of profit within seconds for each open position. His mind thrived in high-pressure situations. Mental athletes learn to deal with stress like physical ones.

At first, trading didn't go to plan. Two games saw a flurry of early goals and Hogan cut his losses at a few hundred dollars. But he stayed in the zone, choosing his moments with bet sizing to match and turned it around, cashing out several positions for profit. By the final whistle, he'd banked a crucial fourteen hundred dollars. But the high didn't last. His positive emotions gave way to the nagging unease that all this was illegal and enough to cost him his job, or more. This part of his life he kept from almost everyone and never bet on his laptop or phone elsewhere. But he had to make the extra cash each month—his dad needed him. He returned the computers and walked out into the parking lot and an argument.

Amber stood crying as a muscular blond guy in his early twenties snarled in her face. He wore a pastel blue polo and cream slacks, likely stocked at the same preppy shop. He took a step back when he realized they weren't alone.

"Everything okay?" Hogan asked, his gaze fixed on Amber's companion.

"We're all good, mister," Preppy answered.

"I'm asking her." Hogan flicked his eyes left.

Amber gathered herself. "It's fine—this is my boyfriend, Chad. 'Sjust a little argument about something silly."

"Okayyy, then," he replied, making it clear he thought it wasn't.

Chad dropped an exaggerated kiss on Amber's cheek, smirked, and swaggered away to an idling blue Corvette.

Amber mumbled something and hurried back inside. Hogan had always hated bullies—he and his brother had learned to fight back early at school. Reminiscing on happier times, he began the short stroll home.

Back in his apartment, he dropped frozen shrimp and mussels into the two feeding station slots. The starfish plucked a leg from the glass in languid appreciation while the seahorse flittered upward—it could eat up to eight times a day.

He should buy one for Vance; they'd get along.

Car keys in hand, he embarked on the second half of his Saturday routine. He'd made this weekly journey to Culver City for over two years, and it never got easier.

Hogan passed under a sandstone arch emblazoned with Paradiso Care and across a porch flanked by yucca plants. The serene entrance was more country club than dementia nursing home.

The receptionist flashed a lipstick-stained smile and eased across the visitor book. He signed in as she buzzed the door.

"Have a nice visit."

"Thanks, it's another lovely day." Why did he default to British small talk when on edge?

Her thick eyebrows rose once in response.

He walked down the hallway to a door featuring a picture of his father in happier, more lucid times, gave a light tap and walked in.

His dad sat in a lilac satin chair, the same two buttons fastened on his faded orange cardigan. *Roman Holiday* played on the TV, with Audrey Hepburn's beatific face lighting up the screen—a sharp contrast to his father's, who looked up and smiled.

"What a lovely surprise! Thanks so much for coming to see me."

Always the same welcome.

"Of course! It's great to see you, Dad," Hogan said, kissing his forehead and pulling over another chair. "Enjoying the movie?" He pointed at the screen. "It's a classic."

"Oh," his father mouthed like he'd just noticed the TV. "I don't know."

After his mother passed away, Hogan's relationship with his dad suffered. It had been a difficult time for the family. His choice of career after Stanford didn't help. And despite his success and promotions, his father harbored doubts. Then his goal to make SAC took a big hit after Katie's death, and now his dad could never comprehend any future achievements.

The next hour was tough. Hogan asked questions but received blank looks or monosyllabic replies. He filled the silence with banal updates on his life. He avoided mentioning his brother; it was better that way. After checking for hoarded cookies, he kissed his dad and promised to visit again soon.

"How soon?"

"Tomorrow," he lied, knowing shortly his dad would have forgotten he'd even been there. After thinking he should have stayed longer, he hurried from his guilt to the main exit. As he reached it, the Paradiso manager, Mrs. Malkin, intercepted him with a thin smile.

"How was your father?"

"Same as usual. He's comfortable, which is what counts."

"That's good," she responded with feigned enthusiasm and forced an envelope into his hand. "Here's the overdue invoice for next quarter; you know our policy."

"I'll sort it. My dad is going nowhere," Hogan snapped as he punched in the keypad numbers harder than necessary.

He took a moment of solitude in his car and placed the brown envelope on the passenger seat. He didn't need to open it to know $31,333 was due. He still needed to find another twelve grand in the next six weeks, and there was no legal way to make it.

7

KIROV PANNED ACROSS the Mojave Desert. Flat and featureless, this spot was perfect. The cerulean sky contained a few hazy clouds scattered above the distant rust-tipped mountain tops. He returned to his car, an Imperium VX, which, like most other electric vehicles, was powered by the Decker Battery. It was the brainchild of the next man he planned to kill. Quinton Decker had accelerated electric car adoption with his five-hundred-mile range batteries. His aviation industry solid-state prototype was allegedly mere months away. His company's strapline: *Changing the Climate on Pollution*, was a frequent rallying cry for action to counter global warming.

And now, somebody wanted him dead.

Kirov powered up the MCD-MissionLink and waited for the signal to connect to the ThinkPad alongside it. He'd spent time in inhospitable parts of the world, where satellite internet hotspots were essential, and kept the equipment. As his phone also connected, it pinged with a new message. It had one app and no numbers stored. Kirov considered any non-business relationships unnecessary risks and distractions. He tapped the Signal icon—his messaging service of choice—knowing it could only be Silver. Ever since his first client seventeen years prior, Kirov had assigned each one a code name chosen from characters in *Treasure Island*. He still cherished the battered copy given to him as a young boy, when he'd been plain Lukas Vilkas.

The bedroom door creaked as Lukas's grandmother entered carrying a pile of books.

"I think your English is finally good enough for you to have these," she announced, placing them on his desk. "You must take good care of them; I've had some of these since childhood."

Lukas reached across and started reading the titles: Treasure Island… The Three Musketeers…Around the World in Eighty Days. *The titles sounded mysterious and promised adventure.*

"Thank you, Grandma!"

"You deserve them for your hard work." The wrinkles around her twinkling gray eyes creased as she smiled. "Don't stay up too late," she added, heading out of the room.

Over the next few months, Lukas devoured the books. He dreamed of traveling to distant lands and enjoying loyal friendships like d'Artagnan and the musketeers. It did get lonely out on his grandmother's isolated farm, but with these heroes for company, it became the happiest period of his life. Then the KGB colonel visited for the first time, and everything changed.

Kirov returned to the moment and read the message from Silver:

I'm impressed. Your reputation was right to precede you. I have fulfilled the second payment. Do you remain confident in eliminating the next target?

Kirov typed out a quick reply:

Receipt confirmed. Like everything in life, you get what you pay for. Second target planning is well underway. I foresee no issues. You'll know when it happens.

The response appeared almost immediately:

I've no doubt. I'll be in touch after that.

Kirov didn't reply. Conversations ended quicker this way, and that suited him fine. He left the app and checked the balance of one of his offshore accounts. It had grown by a healthy three million dollars following the first stage of what promised to be his most lucrative job. Silver hadn't confirmed the total number of targets, only that the payment would double for each. He derived two facts from this: they would get harder, and if successful, he would get much richer. Providing any suspicion of foul play in Chopra's death remained just that for a little longer, he would be content. After this, any discovery otherwise would matter less. If this trial worked as planned, he should have already eliminated the next target.

Kirov pushed the button to ignite the engine and removed the ThinkPad and MissionLink from the Imperium. With a few keystrokes he powered up the software he'd connected to the main control panel. Crouching on the dusty desert floor, he tapped the trackpad and watched with satisfaction as the vehicle began to pull away. After a few hundred meters, he diverted it to the left and accelerated further. He brought the Imperium to a stop, before repeating the process at a greater distance, with the same results. Complete control of this car was at his fingertips. Once he gained access to Quinton Decker's Imperium to install the same modifications—the billionaire would be as good as dead.

8

HOGAN HAD DEVELOPED numerous theories on how Chopra could have opened the gin and left no prints. Perhaps he used a washcloth or was OCD, like a few of Hogan's fellow computer science majors back at Stanford and wiped the chrome cap afterward. It was too thin to run by Carla. As it turned out, he was summoned to her office mid-morning.

As he closed the door, Carla's eyes narrowed like a lurking crocodile's. It wasn't going to be pretty.

"I was clear about Chopra last week?"

"You were," Hogan deadpanned.

"Only someone requested further forensics Friday. When this came to light, Bob McCourt insisted he got a call from the sheriff's department, though he mysteriously can't remember from who. Do you have any idea? As the lead detective is adamant it wasn't them and suggested speaking to you." The accusation sucked the air from the room.

"I got the message loud and clear—this is LA County Sheriff's investigation. Butch Karlson probably saw an opportunity to throw shade my way." Hogan shrugged. "We don't get on. Our paths crossed on a case years back, and it didn't end well."

He owed McCourt big-time—he hoped he hadn't got too much blowback.

"You better have, because if I discover you're still poking around against my *explicit instructions*. Well…" Carla added menace to the final word.

He nodded as he rose from the chair.

"You nearly wrapped the Hicks case?" she asked before he could escape, fixing her stare in his direction again.

"Getting there, hoping to tie it up this week."

"I'm expecting that to happen. You've done a good job rebuilding your reputation this year. I knew you could, so don't go fucking it up now."

Hogan hadn't been disingenuous—the Walter Hicks case was progressing well. Over the last few weeks, they'd had his Inglewood home under surveillance. The scam involved recruiting high-end restaurant waiters to swipe customer cards through a skimmer. These captured details were transferred to fake credit cards. Other crew members of the card-cloning ring then withdrew money from casino cash kiosks requiring no PIN. And by the time the financial institutions realized they weren't funding a gambler's losing streak, it was too late. Hicks got sloppy, though. Historical usage on several cards occurred at one French bistro, and the waiter led them to Hicks. It was time to bust the entire gang.

Entering the kitchen, Hogan discovered Vance attacking a bagel smothered in cream cheese. She sported a bruise over her left eye.

"Did you win the fight?"

With her mouth half full, she threw him a look to say, *What the fuck do you think?* Then finished chewing.

"Yeah, the fight got stopped—first round, rear-naked choke. My opponent got one lucky shot in before that."

"After which, I'm guessing you had to make her pay."

"You know me too well," she answered, grinning.

Armed with drinks, they moved to Hogan's desk. He dug out the relevant Hicks file and handed a sheet to his colleague as he updated her.

"I've assigned the final team for Friday. Inglewood PD is providing perimeter support."

"Looks good to me. You want me to make copies?" Vance began scanning the names.

"No, it's all cool. I'll sort it. You sure all the suspects will be there?"

"Damn straight, they will! Hicks shares the dough and issues new cards every Friday lunchtime."

"And you're sure we don't need SWAT? I can't afford for this to go south. Not now I have everything back on track."

"To take down a bunch of waiters?" Vance rolled her eyes. "We'll be okay, Hogan. I doubt any will be armed unless it's with a corkscrew. They won't know what hit them." She threw a quick combination to demonstrate this, then danced away like Muhammad Ali.

Jared Miller's grating voice interrupted Hogan's battle with the copier's paper tray. He was showcasing his new Rolex to a huddle of junior agents. It was a gift from his well-connected daddy—a DC lobbyist. Hogan's eyes shifted to the Omega Speedmaster on his wrist. It was still frozen at the time shrapnel had cracked the face on that terrible January afternoon. It had been a birthday present from Katie, and he still wore it every day.

"Soooo the prosecutor is *convinced* we're going to get unanimous verdicts."

Hogan scrunched the paper he held. Miller loved to boast about the "Angels of Death" bust. His task force had made over forty arrests, seized $7.6 million of methamphetamine, and helped clear four homicides. It was a career-making case, and the smug bastard knew it. Hogan struggled with the self-promotion that came with ease to agents like Miller. He'd put this down to his personality's more reserved English side. His mum had considered bragging as unforgivable as bad manners. As he tried ramming fresh paper into the tray, Miller glanced back and flashed a shit-eating grin of certainty that the SAC job would be his.

9

INTENDING TO TAKE his mind off work, Hogan headed to his best friend's new pad in Santa Monica. Andrew Neem, or "Nemo" to everyone since their first year on the Stanford boxing team, was doing great. He'd entered the cybersecurity game with near preternatural timing and built the pre-eminent boutique firm on the West Coast. His contracts ranged from large multinationals to secretive government agencies. Acronyms and initialisms like the NSA and CIA had proved valuable in opening even more doors to new business.

The cab dropped him outside a seven-story apartment block with discreet Foster & Partners signage. Beneath the shadow of one of Ocean Boulevard's ubiquitous palm trees, he entered a pristine lobby. A beautiful blonde welcomed him and called the private penthouse elevator. After a short ride, the doors opened to the familiar giant grin of Nemo and a smothering bear hug. He was the opposite of the archetypal computer geek. Six foot four with Popeye forearms, blond-streaked hair, and a booming voice—he made a memorable impression in an industry dominated by introverts. His confidence was complemented by fierce intelligence. On release from Nemo's clutches, his friend's wife, Francesca, glided over and kissed each cheek. Her beautiful Mediterranean features hinted at aristocracy—a rumor she neither confirmed nor denied.

"Time to show you around our humble abode." Nemo bowed and swept out his right arm toward the hallway.

The place was extraordinary and lifted Hogan's spirits. He could never understand people who failed to enjoy a friend's success, instead becoming embittered and jealous. The tour ended on an expansive ocean view terrace with a sizeable "Yaya and Wenge" table in the center. This, like many of the designer furniture brands, had passed over Hogan's head. At least the penthouse had an equal number of bathrooms and bedrooms. His guide announced her return to one of the latter to work on a new layout.

"It's been like this all week," Nemo groaned. "Man, talk about indecision." He flipped open a fridge behind him, grabbing two beers. "So it's over with Megan then, huh," he stated. "And we were only just getting to know her."

"Yeah, she complained as she tried to get closer, I became more distant. Megan had no interest in a relationship that wasn't…progressing…" Hogan started tailing off.

"You can take your time, dude. You won't struggle for dates with that pretty-boy face and killer accent—just like at college. Plus, single life allows more opportunities for beers with me."

They clinked bottles, but Hogan wasn't sure he'd ever be able to commit to someone again. What if he lost them like Katie? He changed the subject.

"So, listen. I ended up at Jay Chopra's the morning after he died, and I wouldn't mind your opinion on a few things."

"Woooah, you were on the case, at his place? I've been following it on the news; that's pretty cool, dude." Nemo sat forward, excited.

"I didn't get the chance to get that involved, however…" He filled his friend in on the details of the case and his lingering doubts.

"Still, it kinda sounds like an accident," Nemo responded, after Hogan finished. "And no one else could have been there when he died?"

"It doesn't appear so. I mean, his bodyguard had swept the house before leaving around 10:15 p.m."

"Could he have killed Chopra and left, or given the code to the door to someone?"

"They looked at him, but he's got a solid alibi with his girlfriend. The town car is on various traffic cameras driving to her place in Rancho Park. Chopra died at 10.53 p.m. I also thought about the code to the doors, but I struggled for a motive. Anyhow, they weren't reopened until morning, so no one could have entered or left. The property has this fancy security system called Poseidon Gate."

"We have the same here—it's a good piece of kit. So the logs didn't show anything else after the driver departed?"

"Yeah—exactly. The County Sheriff's Department checked. It showed nothing until the bodyguard entered at six fifteen the next morning. By then, Chopra had been dead for over seven hours."

"And they checked the backup sent to the cloud?"

It was Hogan's turn to sit forward. "What do you mean?"

Nemo shook his head from side to side, smiling.

"If my work has taught me one thing, you gotta check the backups. Each day at midnight, the system syncs any daily activity to Poseidon Gate's cloud for every client. Only the entry logs, mind you, not the video footage. Client privacy is as important as security to this company. You wouldn't know this unless you owned it as it's an extra layer of backup. So if an intruder gained entry and killed Chopra, then wiped the local data in situ or if it was corrupted later in any way after then—"

"It could already have been sent to the cloud!"

"It's still a long shot, as they'd have needed serious hacking skills."

"But if the data is different, it changes everything."

Hogan flipped over his pillow as he fought insomnia. He closed his eyes and returned to Chopra's house and back to the spot where the billionaire had slipped, supposedly on a piece of ice. He clicked through the timings again and remembered Chopra hadn't made a drink before Matthews had left. He was dead thirty-seven minutes later. Hogan hurried to his freezer and hunted for a larger chunk of ice, similar in size to the cubes in the tray he'd seen at Chopra's. Walking through the memory palace he'd constructed from the scene. He located the image of two of the seven dwarves from Snow White: Doc and Sleepy, sitting on an air conditioning unit that rested on Vance's desk. They each symbolized a number. He walked to his thermostat and moved the dial to seventy-two degrees. After a while, he removed the ice cube and placed it on the tiled kitchen floor.

When his phone alarm beeped, Hogan returned to the kitchen and crouched. He could see the ice was only half-melted. Enough to slip for sure, but Chopra had slipped with such force that he would have sent what remained from the piece of ice skidding across the room. Another pool of water would have formed elsewhere, except it hadn't. Hogan had walked that entire room, and there had been nothing. And if the slipping story didn't add up, someone else must have been there.

10

IN THE SLEEK lobby of Poseidon Gate Security, Hogan sipped coffee and watched the receptionist scroll away on his phone. It disappeared as a clipped voice announced, "Special Agent Hogan," as if they were separate, unconnected words. The source appeared into view and extended a manicured hand.

"Douglas J. Wilder, COO, so sorry to keep you waiting."

"No problem at all. Thanks for the early appointment." As they shook hands, Hogan struggled to match the smile beaming from the tanned face. He placed the executive at around fifty years of age, and the gray hair suited him. The deep crease lines around his eyes suggested a serious golf habit.

"Let's head to my office." Wilder launched into a brief history of Poseidon Gate and its rapid success as they walked.

Hogan disliked people who inserted an initial into their name. Movie moguls had popularized this, convinced it added gravitas. Now they were everywhere—like it provided a substitute for a personality. He zoned back into the conceited company summary.

"…and with over sixty clients from the entertainment industry, we cherish discretion," Wilder announced as they entered a stylish office with views over Beverly Hills.

He eased into an egg-shaped leather chair and placed his palms on the desk. "How can we help?"

Hogan summarized what he wanted, not mentioning the client's name—though it was obvious whom he meant. Wilder's smile never wavered, but his contracting eyes betrayed him. He offered a considered reply.

"Our relationship with law enforcement is of paramount importance to us. The police commissioner is even a golfing buddy, but I'm sure he would understand our current stance."

"Which is what exactly?"

"That the security of our clients' data takes precedence."

"Even when they're dead?" Hogan's frustration got the better of him.

"You'd still need a warrant." Wilder rose, clasping his hands together. "And then, of course, we'd happily furnish you with the requisite information."

Back at Wilshire, Hogan sat racking his brain for a judge that would be both helpful and discreet. Wilder could make life difficult if he came up empty after serving a warrant. He needed probable cause and plausible deniability but was drawing a blank on both. Vance's appearance at his desk ended his musings. The towering presence of Devon Ranger joined her. The three of them had worked a few successful cases this year, and they'd both stuck by him during darker times. Ranger had the powerful build of an Olympic sprinter, which his dad had almost been before a famous switch to the inaugural Jamaican bobsled team. The consultation on the movie that followed was the catalyst for his father's move to LA. Ranger usually exuded an innate calmness that often hid his playful personality. As a trio, they were well balanced and Spartacus-level loyal.

"We need to be in place by eleven a.m. tomorrow," Vance stated.

Hogan replied, "I'll meet you there." Ranger rested a snow-shovel-size hand on his shoulder.

"First round of beers tomorrow night is on you. We're overdue a celebration together." He had a soft, gentle voice. Not that anyone would ever dare tease him about it.

Well, maybe Vance.

"Okay, okay," Hogan raised his hands in mock surrender. It would be nice to toast the end of a successful case; at the start of the year, it was a feeling he had all but forgotten. Vance tipped her head at a small group of agents assembling around a TV. They joined them as one guy ramped up the volume. The chyron along the bottom of CBSN Los Angeles news stated "Chopra Press Conference" as the undersheriff host became audible.

"As a result, we have definitively ruled out foul play. Our condolences again to Mr. Chopra's family at this difficult time, and we ask you to respect their privacy.

Not much chance of that.

"I want to thank my team for their professionalism in handling this high-profile case." Hogan clenched his jaw as the camera panned left to Butch Karlson.

"And now I'm happy to take any questions."

Both the mundane and the more salacious questions received perfunctory responses: no one else could have been inside the property at the time of death; suicide had been ruled out; toxicology was clean; it was a tragic accident. The conference ended, and agents traipsed back to their desks. Carla threw Hogan a pointed stare before returning to her office.

Hogan swung by the In-N-Out drive-thru on Washington for a double-double and fries. Once home, he demolished the burger and washed the meal down with a few Pacificos. He started skimming through Jay Chopra's obituaries for clues about why someone would want him dead. The latest one was from the *LA Times*:

In his freshman year at MIT, Chopra conceived the idea that would make him a billionaire by the age of twenty-six. Amici became popular fast. He dropped out of college shortly after, and VC money poured in as it grew into a global behemoth.

Hogan skipped a few paragraphs.

...and Chopra supported the Democratic party with generous donations to candidates across California and beyond.

He amassed his $140 billion fortune at an unprecedented age and focused on philanthropy early on. New AI research departments at MIT and Stanford now bear his name. The money for these came with a condition that places were offered to the smartest candidates both in the US and globally. Chopra's parents were Indian immigrants, something his impassioned talks loved to reference. He wanted others to have the opportunities he did.

The tech wizard often sparred with climate change deniers, pointing to the drastic Californian weather events within his lifetime. He helped fund the rebuilding of Paradise after a wildfire destroyed the entire town.

Jay Chopra planned for his benevolence to continue from beyond the grave, although never so early. He was a prominent member of the "sunset philanthropy" group of billionaires, including Quinton Decker and Hugh Fairfax. Along with Chopra, they've vowed to give away the bulk of their fortune before or straight after their death.

Following his tragic passing, his mother, Brinda Chopra, confirmed the dispersal of an initial forty billion dollars across seven global charities and local foundations.

Chopra fostered his enigmatic status—his private life was well guarded, and he rarely dated. He topped eligible bachelor lists but claimed Amici was his true love. His company was rarely out of the headlines, however. As its personalized data on users grew, so did its capacity for misuse. Elections could be swayed by abusing the social network's all-encompassing advertising reach. Several countries in the Middle East had attempted to ban their products, accusing them of fomenting unrest and leading to dangerous cultural changes. The Saudi Arabian Crown Prince blamed Amici for the growing movement to advance women's rights in the kingdom. China prohibited the company from operating anywhere in their territories, and Russia engineered social media blackouts during unrest.

Chopra faced domestic criticism for his crackdown on fake news and misinformation prevalent across all Amici properties. Despite opposition from first amendment supporters, he argued censoring conspiracy theorists and anti-vaccinators, was critical.

His views created powerful opposition from politicians and beyond. With them emboldened, Amici faces an uncertain future without Chopra at the helm. Questions about the voting rights attached to his shares, and the proposed new CEO, are two issues that have hammered the company's stock price since he died.

Hogan scrolled down to the final paragraph and an accompanying red-carpet picture of Chopra and his mother. He bowed his head and imagined her devastation.

In the months following Katie's death, Hogan was desolate. Work, which he'd loved and excelled at, became a trial. He sleepwalked through his days. Over time, he became frustrated with the LAPD's lack of progress. After butting into their investigations once too often, he faced a final warning to stay away. He continued to investigate in his free time but to no avail. The scant leads grew colder. As time passed, he withdrew to a dark place—fueled by Xanax, and he fucked up a straightforward case at work. He found vivid memories of Katie a blessing and a curse. He continued to hide away from friends. But they didn't give up on him. When his dad's worsening dementia threatened to push him over the edge, Nemo stepped in. On his insistence and dime, he took leave at a world-class rehabilitation facility for three months and mentally reset. Over time, he rebuilt his life.

Leaning forward, Hogan placed his laptop on the table and rubbed his temples. He was certain the lack of prints on the bottle cap, and the ice cube experiment added up to something. And if a killer had disguised the murder as a convincing accident, they were a professional—which had broader implications. The case would be massive. Poseidon Gate's servers could prove an intruder had entered the property. If he couldn't get anything from them, the rest was supposition and wouldn't be well received. He'd struck out on friendly judges that could help. He would have to use one that wasn't. And only one thing would get him to sign a warrant: blackmail.

11

THE SPECIAL EDITION Imperium VX eased into its reserved spot in the shadowy underground garage at Decker Batteries' HQ. The eleventh richest man in the world climbed out, and his bodyguard eased the gull-wing door back into place.

Kirov tracked them walking away from the VX. He was familiar with both, having surveilled them for weeks once everything was in place for killing Chopra. He slouched another inch in his black Imperium. License plate recognition software had instructed the shutters to rise when he'd arrived earlier. The head of marketing was currently in Japan, and producing a copy of his plate had been easy.

Tapping the keys on his ThinkPad, Kirov connected to his target's Imperium radio ID, which the car broadcasts. When Decker's bodyguard clicked the fob to lock the vehicle, it sent an encrypted code based on a secret cryptographic key to the car's radio. This triggered the security and enabled the immobilizer. Kirov captured this code and then clicked the ProMark radio he held to spoof the fob again as Decker and the bodyguard reached for the elevator. He now had both codes he needed, but they were still part of a forty-bit cipher. He activated a program to run these against the connected G Drive. He needed this extra hardware as the selection of possible matches comprised six terabytes of data.

Within seconds, he established the correct codes for his cloned fob to mimic the target's and open the vehicle. He added them to it and closed the program down.

Kirov activated a signal jammer for the surveillance cameras. He estimated he had two minutes minimum before security made it down to investigate. They'd wait to see if it was a glitch. He'd confirmed their location on the ninth floor, and it was a distance to the elevators. This should buy him enough time. He strode toward Decker's car, tapping the fob. After the satisfying click of the Imperium opening, he slipped inside and eased the door shut. He had the autopilot computer interface panel off in under thirty seconds—beating his record in practice. He was about to add a customized piece of hardware when the door locks deactivated. His eyes shot up to the rearview mirror to see Decker's bodyguard approaching. Kirov whipped his gun from his waistband and scrunched down into the driver's seat. He never once took his eyes from the bulky figure now two meters from the vehicle's rear. He primed himself to roll out and start shooting. They'd realize the car was a target, and he'd never get near it again, but he had to strike while he retained the element of surprise. As he slipped his gloved fingers around the door handle, the bodyguard stopped level with the trunk and lifted it. Kirov held his breath as an item was removed. A hefty clunk followed. The side-view mirror provided a view of the man carrying a box back to the entrance to the elevator. As he reached it, the door locks clicked once more. Kirov exhaled—that had been too close, but random events could upend even the best planning. Now every second counted in a race against security. His hands remained steady as he completed the installation and reattached the panel interface. He glanced back to the elevator entrance—it was still empty. He tapped the button to deactivate the locks, eased from the Imperium, and jogged to his own. He drove toward the exit. As he disengaged the signal jammer for the surveillance cameras, a security guard stepped into the garage. With everything back working, the departing car would raise no suspicion. Everything was in place for Friday and Quinton Decker's final journey.

12

HOGAN WEAVED THROUGH lawyers calling tardy clients and defendants enjoying their last cigarette of freedom, up the Stanley Mosk Courthouse steps. The portentous statue of justice dominating the wall above the entrance wouldn't approve of what he planned.

Judge Guillermo Ramirez had spared five minutes before he sat for the day. It should be all Hogan needed. He found the judge's location on the building guide and rode the elevator to the fourth floor, where a stern secretary escorted him into his chambers. Sandalwood and bergamot emanated from a diffuser on a bookshelf with rows of leather-bound law books. Judge Ramirez waddled in and eased his considerable frame behind an imposing oak desk.

"How can I help, Special Agent?" Ramirez growled, looking at his watch.

"I'll get straight to the point, Your Honor. I need a warrant with the utmost discretion. One if anyone comes asking about but lacking proof, you'll deny was ever issued."

"And you figured I would help? You have the wrong judge, Special Agent. You should leave right now."

Hogan didn't move. "I don't think I do. We both know what happened with your brother; I was on the surveillance team on the case."

"So, you'll know I was exonerated of any involvement. You planned to threaten me with *this*?" Ramirez escalated to full contempt-of-court mode. The only thing missing was a gavel.

"No, Your Honor. The work was comprehensive. It included following you for a few weeks across the city and, on one occasion, to a specific

45

location off Hollywood Boulevard." Ramirez slumped, his face turning from crimson to off-white in seconds. "Out of respect, and at my discretion, we omitted it from reports. We were aware of the impact this could have…"

Ramirez composed himself and straightened up—his eyes full of actual contempt.

"And you figure *I* return the favor?" he spat.

"No favor, just your assistance and discretion on this matter."

"And if you need some *judicial* help again…?"

"You have my word I'll look elsewhere."

Ramirez froze; his lips pinched. He reached a decision.

"The warrant will be waiting at the front desk by the end of the day. I never want to see you again unless it is in my courtroom. Pray for your sake that never happens."

Hogan's stomach churned as he drove away from the courthouse. If Carla caught him delving into Chopra's death, he could kiss goodbye to the slim chance of making SAC and the sizeable pay raise it brought. He had to get the extra cash; without it, he'd struggle to keep his dad at Paradiso during the English soccer off-season. He'd already taken out a loan to cover the shortfall during the previous summer. If it all went wrong, he'd have to leave the Bureau and seek a higher-paying private sector role. The idea filled him with dread. He glanced at the brown envelope on the passenger seat. *What else would he be willing to do to stay?*

At the staging post for the Hicks raid, Hogan found team members pacing the sidewalk. Vance assembled them and reiterated the plan with her usual blend of accuracy and levity. After a final weapons check, they were good to go.

The breach team approached the run-down house, fanning out to cover any potential points of egress. Ranger strode to the door, announced their arrival, and drove a Thunderbolt CQB ram into it with extreme prejudice. Vance and Hogan rushed through the splintered frame, weapons drawn, as other agents followed them in. Nine suspects occupied tatty chairs and sofas, all shocked and complying with the overwhelming show of force. There was no Hicks, so Hogan followed Vance to check the other rooms. They cleared the first two and stepped into the larger bedroom. His colleague had moved around the unmade bed when the wardrobe door burst open, and Hicks emerged with a baseball bat. He pulled it back to aim a swing at her head, but didn't get the chance. Hogan exploded across the room, smashing a fist into the man's jaw with such force that he bounced off the wall a few feet away. Hicks slumped to the ground as Vance spun around, Glock in hand.

"Only corkscrews, yeah?" Hogan teased. Vance started laughing as she knelt on the back of the dazed Hicks to cuff his hands.

The early part of the afternoon featured one-sided interviews until one suspect agreed a deal to testify and to share all the fraud details. It should be a slam dunk from here. Hogan savored the success he'd taken for granted in his early years as an agent. Never again.

Leaving Ranger and Vance with the new star witness, he gave Carla the positive news and hurried to the exit. He could make the courthouse by six p.m. if he got lucky with traffic.

For once, he did.

Hogan signed the night porter's clipboard and received an envelope.

Next, he completed a slow crawl down to the Poseidon Gate Security offices; more out of hope than expectation that at this hour, he would get any success. He waited in reception, fielding Vance's exasperated messages from The Nickel Mine. He tapped out a reply promising he'd join the celebrations soon. As he did, a man in a gray suit and matching pallor approached.

"Kurt Rogers, customer liaison." The limp handshake brushed Hogan's fingers.

He reciprocated the introduction and raced through what he needed. Rogers immediately began shaking his head and pushed up the glasses sliding down his narrow nose.

"I'm afraid only a director could get that level of data access, even with the warrant. I'd suggest coming back Monday morning—there'll be someone happy to assist you then."

"It really can't wait," Hogan insisted. "Can you please call Mr. Wilder and see if he can make himself available sooner for a *federal inquiry*." The emphasis on the last two words had the intended effect. Rogers fumbled out a cell phone and walked a few yards away. He returned, grayer if possible.

"Mr. Wilder will meet you here tomorrow at midday. He can spare no more than thirty minutes." Rogers' intended smile came out as a grimace. He turned and shuffled away.

Hogan imagined Wilder rearranging his tee time for tomorrow through gritted teeth. If this gamble didn't work out, there would be hell to pay.

The Nickel Mine hummed with the weekend buzz. The interior was schizophrenic: part sports bar, part London gentleman's club. Hogan edged past the packed shuffleboard table to where a burgundy Chesterfield sofa housed Devon Ranger and Vance. The latter was conducting an animated conversation with the rookie, Michelle.

"Hey, about time. Where the fuck have you been?" Vance shouted.

"I had some things to sort. I'll explain later," Hogan replied, then offered to head for a round of drinks to avoid further questions. Ranger had located him a chair on his return.

"Ask him," Vance urged, nudging the recruit.

"How do you do the memory stuff? Lisa claimed you can memorize a pack of cards in less than two minutes, but that seems impossible," Michelle said.

Hogan had fielded this question countless times over the years. People were usually surprised by the response. He shifted forward in his seat.

"I thought so too when I first started it. Your brain doesn't store lists of words or similar information well but is great with spatial awareness. In essence, the trick is to create incredibly memorable images and locate them in a familiar space. This is what we call a memory palace." Hogan reached for his beer, then continued. "Think of it as a personal repository for information, only one fueled by your creativity." He grabbed the cocktail menu, studied it for less than a minute, and handed it to Michelle.

"Prepare to be amazed," Vance announced and turned to Hogan. "You ready?"

He offered an upturned thumb and rifled through the list of twenty-three cocktails as Michelle held the menu in silent amazement. She even clapped at the end.

"So, in this case, I walked into my childhood home, and Steve Martin was in my hallway holding a bottle of vodka. Then I continued into the front room where a well-dressed elderly man danced with a doctor in a white coat. As I turned, a huge gold bell rested on an Italian flag. Vodka Martini, Old Fashioned, Penicillin, Bellini, you get the idea," Hogan explained.

"That's very cool," Michelle replied.

He shrugged.

"The Hemingway was easier, of course. The Gimlet, not so much. There are loads of different techniques for other stuff, but I reckon it is time to concentrate on the real drinks."

Vance downed her remaining wine. "Sounds good to me; who wants what?"

13

KIROV SAT READING in his Imperium on 17-Mile Drive, which snaked its way through an upscale neighborhood of Carmel-by-the-Sea.

Routine was an assassin's best friend. Planning became straightforward if your target repeated elements of their life. Quinton Decker was one of those people. Every other Friday, he would leave his Mountain View office early, collect his daughter and visit Aubergine restaurant. After, he'd drop her back with his estranged wife—a mile from where Kirov now waited—and continue to a penthouse in Monterey.

Phileas Fogg had just acquired an elephant when the GPS tracker built into Decker's car's software flashed to indicate movement. The wait was over. He placed the book on the passenger seat and watched the rearview mirror until the special-edition Imperium VX approached. He eased behind it onto the otherwise empty road. It was the kind of place the aging wealthy residents hit the sack early, even on weekends. As he tailed the vehicle, a sharp bend in the road became visible in the distance. He hit a button on his open ThinkPad. This activated the software attached to the control panel and triggered the autopilot. The bodyguard driving could not take back control, no matter what he did. Kirov forced the car to accelerate, and it pulled away from him. Perfect. He kept the speed increasing, then, as the road met the bend, instructed the Imperium VX to careen left. It sailed through a flimsy wooden barrier and disappeared over the cliffs beyond. Kirov checked the road was still empty, pulled up a few meters from the shattered fence, and walked to the cliff edge. The silver beams of the full moon spilled across the mangled remains of the car embedded in the boulders far below. Neither occupant could have survived the devastating crash. Pounding waves showered the rocks beneath the wreckage and had masked the sound of impact.

Driving away, Kirov allowed himself a moment of self-congratulation. Everything had gone to plan. The scene would only stand up to so much scrutiny, but it might look like an accident or an outlandish driver suicide. The autopilot system would prove otherwise, but only if the digital footprint of his actions survived the crash.

Two targets down, and in days, an additional six million dollars would hit his offshore account. And when Silver messaged again, it would be the name of the next person to die.

14

THE TABLET DISPLAYED a match between Liverpool and Manchester United. With one hundred bucks on a 0-0 draw at 17-1, Hogan needed precise timing. He gripped his coffee mug as the seventieth minute of the game approached. For the plan to work, at that point, it would still need to be goalless. This time, the score obliged, and he traded out this bet and sat back, seventeen hundred dollars in profit. He raised his eyes to the ceiling in silent thanks.

When he set off for a delayed restroom stop, he spotted Amber darting behind the counter.

"Thought you must have been off today."

"Nah, I overslept and trying to atone for lateness now." Amber held up a worn washcloth. Hogan wasn't surprised; she worked two jobs to help support herself at UCLA. He'd had to do the same at Stanford, his scholarship only going so far. That empathy, coupled with over a year of Americanos and friendly chats, left him feeling like a big brother; and as protective.

"What happened there?" He raised his eyebrows and pointed a single digit at Amber's bruised eye. The makeup job was good, but still not enough.

"Oh, it's nothing; I caught an elbow at soccer practice. It looks worse than it is." Amber looked down and swallowed.

Not from Chad? Hogan wanted to say. "I'll let you get back to work," he replied and walked away.

By the end of the morning's trading, Hogan was two thousand dollars closer to paying the Paradiso Care Home bill, or still ten thousand away. It depended upon how you viewed these challenges in life.

He arrived at Poseidon Gate with time to spare. No bored receptionist to greet this time, only a rotund security guard for company. Wilder breezed into the lobby at midday, dressed for golf. As they walked to the executive's office in silence, he tried not to betray his growing discomfort. Spinning the egg chair to face the desk, Wilder sat with a wan smile.

"I'm surprised to see you again after Thursday, Special Agent. The county sheriffs seemed conclusive in their findings. Yet here you are with a warrant no less." The executive reached across and took the thin sheet of paper to check its veracity and, Hogan suspected, the judge's name. Once satisfied, he continued. "Which couldn't wait until Monday and impinges on my weekend." Wilder began tapping the keyboard of the large iMac dominating his desk.

"Okay, so it's Wednesday the twenty-seventh of October you want to look at, right?" Wilder looked across the desk for confirmation. "Perfect golf weather, if I recall, I played a round with the mayor." The subtext here: you're wasting my time. While the judge would keep quiet, if the man opposite escalated this via other channels, it would get back to Carla. It would make it his word against Wilder's—not good. Why would this upstanding business owner have a reason to lie? The man opposite scrolled the mouse, then turned the screen.

A single manicured fingernail tapped the first line of data.

"Nothing all day until ten p.m., when the front door is opened." This made sense. The bodyguard collected Chopra from Van Nuys Airport that morning to drive him to meetings. This was them arriving at the property.

"Then an exit from the front door at 10:16 p.m.," Wilder explained, then froze. His mask of composure slipped, and his head began to twitch from side to side. "This can't be right—the back door opened at 10:52 p.m."

Hogan's heart pounded as he asked, "Can you check the local server data here too?"

Wilder brought up a new screen and in a hushed tone, announced, "There's nothing on that server after 10:16 p.m. until six ten the next morning."

"How do you explain the conflicting data?" Hogan kept his voice level as excitement gave way to relief. He'd been right all along.

"I...I don't know. Unless someone gained access to the system and changed the local files. But the safeguards against this are..." Wilder squirmed and looked up to the ceiling, incredulous. "This must be an error," he finished without conviction.

"We both know it isn't." Whoever entered through that back door killed Chopra.

Wilder deflated as the reality of the situation set in.

"Erm, whaa-what's going to happen next—our reputation could take a hit," he stammered.

Hogan reveled in the sudden change of circumstance as his brain clicked into action.

"We'll need a copy of the files of both servers, also confirmation if any other data anomalies exist between them for the previous two weeks—cameras, entries, exits...you get the idea. Can you create a cloud log-in for me to access this data?"

"Of course, of course—anything you need, Special Agent."

"Let's keep this strictly between us until Monday too."

Wilder couldn't be more obsequious now. "Definitely. Only too happy to help."

After a few strokes on the keys, he scribbled down details and handed them over, composure returning to his voice when he spoke. "I hope you can keep us out of the public domain."

"We'll do our best." No need to kick the man while he was down.

Hogan made a quick call on the way back to his apartment. When he arrived, a white 1966 GT Convertible Mustang sat illegally parked outside his place. Nemo hopped out, holding a six-pack of Pacifico and a giant bag of chips. After popping the beer caps, Hogan returned from the kitchen to find his friend's nose inches from the fish tank.

"I love watching these guys—they seem so calm." Nemo rose and scanned the apartment. "Man, I know your pictures packed are away, but you gotta get some more stuff in here."

Hogan shrugged. "I know." He passed across a bottle and tapped his against it. "Anyhow, you were right on the money with Poseidon Gate, the local server logs were changed."

"Shit! *No way?*"

"Yeah, and I need to know how they did it before I take this to Carla."

"Sure thing, dude." The big guy had loved this kind of challenge ever since they'd met. If authorities had discovered the systems his friend hacked back in college, events might have gone differently. After grabbing his laptop, Hogan opened the cloud link to Poseidon Gate, logged in, and explained what he'd discovered that lunchtime.

Nemo's fingers danced across the keyboard for thirty minutes until he broke the silence, looking up with a low whistle and slow nod.

"I'm positive the person responsible didn't know the local system synced daily with Poseidon Gate at midnight. And if they discovered this once they'd logged in to the local server—it would have been impossible to change. The central cloud server at Poseidon Gate would take my best people days to crack. Don't get me wrong, whoever did this was good, excellent even. They gained complete access on a local server level to install software. This wiped data of their arrival and departure—leaving no digital footprint. I can't prove what they did; only that the logs are different. You've either got one ingenious killer or a pair of guys with different skill sets working together. I can write a breakdown if that helps?"

Hogan began framing a reply when his phone rang—it was Carla. He swore and tapped the green phone icon in trepidation. Had Wilder called someone? A stream of information interspersed with expletives greeted him. After his boss ended the call, he turned to a concerned Nemo.

"I've got to get on the next flight to San José—Quinton Decker is dead!"

15

THE SCREECH OF metal scraping stone announced the Imperium wreckage's journey to the crime lab had begun. Hogan continued bracing against the freezing wind and rain as a crane lifted it from the boulders below. He cursed he wasn't prepared for this inclement weather. After Carla's call, he'd chucked a few items in a bag, and Nemo had raced him to LAX. A warm coat wasn't included. Vance sidled up, holding out a hot drink.

"Thanks. Did you find us somewhere to stay?"

"Yup. We're booked in at the Hyatt, Monterey, near the crime lab. It's also near this great sandwich place an officer told me about," Vance replied with a wink. They walked from the cliff edge toward the accident investigation team. Hogan checked with them about the distance between where the Imperium had crashed and the cliff's height. As he juggled mental calculations, a helicopter swooped, shooting the images that would dominate the following week's news. Carmel PD had sealed off the road much farther down, where press trucks had accumulated since mid-afternoon.

Hogan bent down to examine the tracks left by the Imperium.

"So, there are no brake marks, and he would have been traveling over ninety when he hurtled over the edge, given where the car ended up."

"Then it was deliberately driven off the cliff."

"For sure. You wouldn't hit that speed on this stretch of road unless you had a death wish."

"Which the driver must have had."

"Or it was something else entirely. You know me and coincidences."

Vance smiled. "I do. So, where do we start?"

He pointed at the mass of twisted steel rising through the rain.
"With that."

"Shit, Hogan, you have been busy," Vance proclaimed. He'd spent the last hour filling her in on all the intricacies of the Chopra case. He'd kept his progress secret, so she wouldn't be complicit if it headed south. His previous conversation in this corner of the Hyatt bar had been more fraught. He'd finally shared everything he'd learned from Poseidon Gate and his other suspicions with Carla. She'd been pissed he'd defied her and chewed him out as a result. Once she'd calmed down, grudging respect for what he'd discovered followed, and they'd discussed the implications of Quinton Decker's death. Her instincts had screamed this was part of something bigger, hence ordering them straight up there. If anything, she believed in coincidences even less than him. Two mysterious billion-aire deaths in the space of two weeks was unprecedented. She'd prom-ised to help cut red tape, so tomorrow, when the wreckage examination took place, he'd have full jurisdiction. He was to call the second he had an update.

"Thank God I was right. Can you imagine Carla's reaction otherwise?" Hogan replied. Vance mimed a severe shiver, then checked a message on her phone.

"The Imperium technician will be on-site at ten a.m. I'm told he's the best they have."

Hogan drained his beer—he needed to sleep. "Meet at breakfast?"

"Hell yeah, I've already scoped out the menu."

16

HOGAN PACED THE sterile conference room on the ninth floor at Wilshire, finalizing preparations for his briefing. Late Sunday evening, they'd discovered Decker's compromised autopilot console had led to the catastrophic crash. The technician from Imperium had explained the intricacies as Vance and Hogan had watched on, fascinated. It had only taken forty-two hours from that moment to form a task force, a Bureau record for a case of such scope. The door flew open, and Carla swept in. The shadows under her eyes matched his own.

"I'll call people in, okay." She wasn't asking.

He nodded.

She would oversee the task force, and he would run point as lead investigator. Without his work on Jay Chopra, they'd be much further behind. Carla turned and shouted for everyone to enter.

Hogan moved in front of whiteboards plastered with images, timings, and arrows crisscrossing maps. As he did, thirty agents, and a contingent of law enforcement from Malibu and Carmel, filled the room. Many faces were familiar: Miller aloof at the back; Vance bobbing her head in encouragement from the front row. Others weren't, as they'd drafted agents from the San Francisco field office. Carla stepped forward, and silence fell.

"Most of you know some details, but Special Agent Hogan is the best equipped to get you all up to speed. Please save any questions for after he has finished." Carla moved aside, leaving him with the floor.

"Welcome, everyone. I'll aim to be concise, but please bear with me." He took a deep breath and launched into his scrupulous brief. "As you know, nearly two weeks ago, Jay Chopra was found dead in his Malibu home. At that time, considered accidental." He glanced in the direction of Butch Karlson before continuing. "However, new evidence that came to our attention last weekend suggests foul play. Late Sunday evening, we received confirmation Quinton Decker was murdered."

A murmur of chatter began. Hogan waited for the excitement to subside.

"Firstly, in the case of Jay Chopra, we're confident a person or persons unknown gained access to his home, killed him, and staged the scene. The property's security system was compromised and manipulated by a skilled hacker. Our priority is to ascertain how they gained internal access."

The packed room had started to heat up. Hogan dabbed at a rivulet of sweat rolling down his forehead, turned to the board, and pointed to an enlarged image of a mangled car.

"Last Friday evening, a silver VX Imperium containing Quinton Decker and his driver crashed at Pescadero Point. That's just north of Carmel-by-the-Sea." He moved his finger to the map below. "So far, we have no witnesses, but vehicle data confirms this occurred at 10:07 p.m. We have proof the main autopilot console was hacked, which means the suspect accessed the vehicle before the murder. A high level of technical ability was required to achieve this. You'll notice parallels with the expertise applied in Chopra's suspected homicide." He dabbed his brow again. The room was silent as the audience hung on his every word. It was disconcerting and exhilarating.

"The killer or killers intricately planned Decker's murder. Also, given the tight timeline, Chopra's death concurrently. We don't yet have physical evidence linking the two killings, but the similarities suggest a connection. When the world's second and eleventh richest men are murdered, we must face two stark possibilities: it's the same perpetrator or perpetrators, and this could be part of something much bigger."

Hogan extrapolated on details pertinent to each case, then made way for Carla.

"Okay, listen up. We need concrete evidence to be certain the cases are connected. Until then, this task force will run two simultaneous investigations. Incoming intel will filter through the leadership team headed up by Special Agent Hogan, is that understood?" Collective nodding ensued. "Jared Miller will be handling Chopra's death"—Carla bobbed her head in his direction—"and Karyn Alson will lead the Decker investigation." A keen-eyed woman with black curls and dark features raised a hand in response. She was a SAC up in San Francisco and her excellent reputation preceded her.

"Hogan's team will handle all the crossover and connections pointing toward potential suspects or motives. They'll refine data as we receive it. I hardly need to stress the importance of quick results. We have significant resources available, so please use them. We will be briefing the press later today. It will be a media frenzy, but no further information except what I sanction must leave the Bureau. This goes for social media too. In this era of fake news, I suggest you avoid either posting or consuming information connected to the case. If anyone is unclear on this, I'll be happy to repeat it."

Carla gave the assembled agents her death stare, then marched from the room.

17

CARLA HAD AFFORDED Hogan the perk of handpicking his team. Vance and Ranger were automatic choices. The case would need special financial skills, so analyst Joseph Chung completed the table quartet. Slim and bespectacled, his shy demeanor contrasted with his taste in loud shirts. He wasn't much taller than Vance and even younger. Either his hairdresser harbored a grudge, or his mum still cut his hair; the smart money was on the latter. Chung was a precocious talent in the Bureau, and Hogan had fought hard to get him. The analyst was midway through his introductory briefing.

"We have two forensic accountants at our disposal, and they're both excellent," Chung explained. "Between us, we'll do our best to find links between the deceased. We'll start by examining share trading before both deaths, which saw plunges in respective company values when the news broke. If someone had shorted Decker Batteries and Amici, they would have made a killing." Chung immediately put his hand to his mouth.

Vance spluttered. "No shit!"

"Sorry, poor choice of words, but if they'd taken a position on the value decreasing, they would have realized significant profits."

"Thanks, Joseph." Hogan turned to Vance. "Okay, you're up."

His colleague removed gum from her mouth, wrapped it in paper, launched it into the bin, and began her update.

"Both of the deceased were avid supporters and significant donors to the Democratic party, backing a large array of candidates in previous elections and helped to fund the last successful presidential campaign—"

"It's unlikely that's a motive, don't you think?" Ranger interrupted.

"Yeah, I do, but it is one initial connection regardless. This whole situation is a *little unlikely*," Vance responded with a sideways glance. "They both spoke out on climate change, arguing the lobbying power of big oil companies was a major contributor to the lack of policy progress. They polarized the usual keyboard warriors on social media. These days—it's either unfailing support or vitriolic hatred."

"Perhaps it was a killer troll—" Ranger began his usual routine of teasing Vance. She flashed him a look, suggesting it would be wiser to keep quiet.

"Okay, listen." Hogan raised his hands. "We can discount neither link, but both connections are superficial. There needs to be more substance behind a motive for killing both. Also, why these two, and why now? The next election is some time away, and the climate change argument has been raging for years." He indicated for Vance to continue.

"They were both sunset philanthropists."

"What does that mean?" Ranger asked.

"That they vowed to give away most of their fortune to charitable causes by the time of their death or immediately afterward. There's a bunch of billionaires doing the same."

"Oh, yeah, I think I saw something about a malaria charity in line for a ten-billion-dollar payout from Chopra's estate."

"That pretty much sums it up—several charities and foundations will receive enormous windfalls. Boatloads of dollars for worthy local and global causes."

"Did one of the charities off them?" Ranger proffered, only half joking.

"It won't do any harm to check." Hogan shrugged. "Let's see who the Decker estate beneficiaries are and if any stand out."

"I'll do that," Vance shot back, volunteering for the easy task and beating Ranger to the punch. "You snooze, you lose, big guy."

Ranger sighed before he began to speak.

"I spent most of yesterday palming off cases, so I don't have much else to offer. I mean, they both drove electric cars and bemoaned the yearly Californian wildfires, but I doubt they've been killed for that. Sorry that's all."

"It's fine, Ranger. The last two days have been difficult for us all. It's what we do from now that will count," Hogan replied, meeting his colleague's eye. "I'll follow up with counterintelligence. We need to explore how bad actors from overseas could have orchestrated these killings. Although tantamount to an act of war, certain countries have the personnel to pull off this kind of mission. Russia, North Korea, and China spring to mind. But could they do so without leaving any trail? That's what we must explore. I've asked SAC Jeff Bailey to brief me with an update once he has one."

Hogan drained his cup and turned to the door. "Time for me to go and join Carla to speak to the press. Wish me luck—I'm going to need it!"

18

Kirov flicked off the TV, disappointed but not too surprised the autopilot control panel in Decker's car hadn't been destroyed. The deaths were now reported as homicides. The press conference confirmed the FBI would be handling the investigation. They'd announced an intruder had entered the Chopra property, so Kirov must have missed something with Poseidon Gate. It didn't matter now. They'd run into a series of dead ends. Unfortunately, his next target would scale their close protection team. And as a result, prove a substantial challenge. This couldn't be avoided. Silver had messaged his satisfaction and appeared to take malicious delight in the death of Quinton Decker. Kirov had also received the name of the next person to die. He wasn't as notorious as his previous victim, but wealthier.

Kirov led a normal lifestyle to avoid undue attention and rented average-priced properties in several US cities. He could leave any at a moment's notice. Aside from a penchant for rare whiskey, only one other passion required significant funds to support. It was a book collection he'd started two decades ago. The home he would retire to thousands of miles away would have a secure, custom-built library. Now, because of Silver, the most expensive book should be obtainable. It would take pride of place alongside all the books his grandmother had given him—he'd never parted with one, no matter what.

Lukas tried to shut out the sounds from the other room and transport himself to another world. Whenever the colonel visited his grandmother, he'd grab

Alice's Adventures in Wonderland *and escape into the story. He imagined himself alongside Alice, meeting and talking to various strange characters. It helped him get through those difficult evenings.*

But this night was different, his grandmother's objections were stronger, and the Russian was angry. Lukas recognized some words he'd learned watching Russian cartoons, but when the screaming started, he panicked. He grabbed his door handle, forgetting his grandmother always locked it, insisting it kept him safe. There was a heavy thud, and the screaming stopped. Lukas yanked the handle again, but the door was old and strong. A car door slammed outside as Lukas pulled the window up and contemplated the jump to the ground below. He landed and rolled as their chained dog barked at the vehicle speeding away.

It took three of them to prize Lukas off his grandmother's cold, lifeless body. Later, when they explained he couldn't stay, he didn't understand. But when the car arrived the next day to take him to the orphanage, he realized he had no choice. They tried to take the bag of books off him, talking about space and other issues, but he clenched his fists and vowed to fight. Finally, they relented.

When they arrived at the orphanage, the driver wished him good luck. Later, he realized why—they would be the only kind words he would hear in his six years there.

When he'd first started reading his grandmother's books, he'd wished he was the hero—like Jim Hawkins, or Tom Sawyer. But during that first winter, shivering under his ragged blanket, he began to identify with the antagonists. They helped him get through the isolation he felt—compounded by living in a place devoid of empathy. It was their cunning and indifference to the harm of others that appealed to him. He saw the stories through the prism of their eyes. Cardinal Richelieu, Long John Silver, and Fernand Mondego, all possessed a ruthlessness he came to admire.

After winning a few victories in vicious fights over his possessions, the other kids gave him a wide berth. He was willing to die to protect the books— which became his only companions. He began plotting revenge for the day he finally left. And when that came, Lukas knew he was changed forever.

Kirov picked up the midnight blue hardback, walked across his San José apartment and added it to his cabin luggage. Prepare, kill, disappear.

Repeat.

19

HOGAN ARRIVED AT his desk at six a.m.—an objectionable hour for a Saturday. Even Carla wasn't in yet. Thirty minutes later, she marched past his cubicle and indicated for him to follow. As they entered her office, she removed a framed photo from her bag and added it to her desk. It featured Carla with a forced smile in the sunshine with her two sons.

"Disneyland in August," she offered, sitting down, adding, "too busy and damn expensive." She hated vacations, so Hogan never inquired about her rare trips away.

"Director Sullivan checked in late yesterday, and his feedback on Wednesday's press conference was positive. You handled your questions deftly, and for now, it seems we're ahead of the curve." Carla stopped, frowned, and edged the photo forward before continuing. "We have no exposure to the Chopra investigation fuckup, which is good, but this honeymoon will last days at best, so let's use this time to keep ahead. Given the media scrutiny, we must be extra careful about what we share."

"Understood. I'll reiterate this to my team."

"I assume the task force is coordinating as planned. Do you lack any resources? I'm continuing to get extended support from Quantico and Clarksburg."

"All good so far. We're looking at every possible connection between the two victims and are still compiling all the information. The LA County Sheriff's Department was initially sore but shared their evidence yesterday. We're working through potential motives for the killings to identify where the assassin may attempt to strike next."

"And you remain confident he will?"

"The killer framing Decker's death as a possible driver suicide suggests so. He executed an elaborate plan. He's not done yet."

"Then we can't afford to miss a thing. Your maverick work proved correct on Chopra, but this is major league."

Carla reached into a tray, grabbed the top piece of paper, and slid it across the desk.

"I've another task for you. Hugh Fairfax has contacted Director Sullivan and requested a visit." She rolled her eyes. "He wants to know if there is anything extra he can do regarding security. He suggested early tomorrow afternoon—the details are all there." Hogan glanced at the North Beverly Park address—where the real money lived.

"Why me? Could someone else not do it?" He didn't fancy pandering to Fairfax because the billionaire clicked his fingers—even if he was the richest man on the planet.

"To be honest, he's a bit of an Anglophile, and anyway, you have the most complete summation of the case so far. Did you have plans?"

He sighed. Carla knew he couldn't refuse. "How much can I share?" He didn't want information ending up in the press.

"The bare minimum. I've heard he can be disarmingly cunning, so keep your wits about you."

20

As HIS SUIT jacket swayed on its hook, Hogan pulled onto the private road leading to the Fairfax residence entrance. His dad hadn't registered his unusual visiting attire that Sunday morning, but he noticed little these days. He'd stayed longer to assuage his guilt of missing two consecutive Saturdays and was thankful to avoid Mrs. Malkin as he left.

Hogan had spent the previous evening reading about Fairfax. A teenage Olympic swimmer, he'd taken that competitive edge into business and built one of the world's biggest companies. His interests ranged from railroads to technology. Seen by many as a genius, his purchases of shares and companies could move markets. He'd targeted fast-growing sectors with repeated success. In recent years he'd expanded into the renewable energy sector with several high-profile acquisitions. Rumors were circulating that he planned to launch a secretive new venture. At the last count, his net worth had hit $209 billion. The $165 million he'd plowed into Fairfax Mansion was a mere drop in the ocean.

At the end of the meandering road, two thick-necked security guards toting AR15s greeted him. They checked his ID, then the steel gates parted. It was like driving into an English country estate. Gardens full of sculptures and lazy pathways lined the sweeping driveway leading to a formidable mansion. He pulled up in a circular courtyard framed by lofty firs. Scissor-trimmed bushes lined the granite pathway leading to steps to the main house, where a butler and valet waited. The latter opened his car door. Hogan climbed from his dated Jag—a vintage E-Type would be appropriate here. The vast property had two wings running off a grand arched entrance with thick oak doors that wouldn't look out of place on Windsor Castle. They swung open as he approached, allowing another butler to welcome him.

"If you could follow me, sir," he announced in an English accent straight out of *Downton Abbey*.

"Of course," Hogan replied, adopting an inadvertent posh inflection.

The butler showed him into a spacious library toward a plush armchair. Hogan accepted an offer of tea, sat, and surveyed the room. It featured floor-to-ceiling tomes in seaweed green and cinnamon brown. He began trying to spot any he'd read. As the distinctive aroma took him back to childhood library visits, a man entered and strode toward him.

"I'm Hugh Fairfax. So good to meet you. I appreciate you coming. Sorry to keep you waiting; I've just finished my daily two-mile swim—it keeps me trim." He patted his flat stomach and extended his hand. It was bony, but the grip firm. Even in his advancing years, he was tall and emanated an aura of power. His smile was friendly, the accent difficult to place.

"Special Agent Hogan."

"I recognize that accent." Fairfax gestured back to the armchair and lowered himself into one opposite. "My great-grandfather was from England. Love the place." His style and interior design suggested as much.

"My mother was too, and I grew up there, but I was born here in LA."

"Well, I won't hold that against you." Fairfax smiled, then adopted a conspiratorial tone as he leaned forward. "It's sad about Jay, he was a nice guy, a little weird, but most of those tech guys are. It's well documented I had no love for Quinton Decker, but what happened is shocking. Any theories yet on who may be behind this?"

"Nothing definitive. We're looking at motive, business connections, and political leanings, but I can't share more."

"Well, like those guys, I'm a sizeable Democratic Party donor, but even in today's polarized political landscape, for someone to kill them for that…"

Hogan remained impassive.

"In fairness, that's one link, sir; it could be a motive that hasn't even occurred to us yet—it is early days. You should exercise extreme caution until we find who is responsible."

"I'm taking no chances. I've hired twenty extra security staff, it's a small price to pay. Anything else you would recommend? I'm in an uncomfortable situation with no obvious solution." Fairfax's lips tightened, and his stare became distant.

"Avoid any routine. Also limit or cancel public engagements and refrain from traveling to any residences that are not secured in advance." Hogan assumed Fairfax had several properties; from what he'd read, all billionaires did.

"I won't be leaving here for now. I have everything I need." The older gentleman's expression became resolute, but then he glanced left, and his face lit up. A golden-haired girl in a lemon floral dress ran across the library straight into Fairfax's open arms. "Speaking of which, this is my granddaughter. Audrey, please say hello to our guest."

"Hello, nice to meet you." She stepped forward with a curtsy and a hundred-watt smile. Hogan, charmed, offered a bow, as a voice cut across the room.

"Audrey! What have I told you about not disturbing Grandpapa when he has guests!"

The owner of the voice walked into view. Fairfax winked, which only set the young girl off giggling.

Hogan imagined Audrey's mum made an impact in every room she entered. She was tall like Fairfax, with straight blonde hair that brushed her shoulders. Her deep-blue eyes appraised the situation.

"This, my dear, is Special Agent Hogan," Fairfax said, then extended his arm. "This is my wonderful daughter, Marissa."

Praying his most expensive suit didn't look rumpled, Hogan rose to shake the outstretched left hand, noting the absence of a ring. Close up, her flawless skin shone.

"Nice to meet you, Marissa." His posher inflection returned as he held her gaze.

"And you, Special Agent," she replied with a quizzical look that suggested she wanted to say something else. Instead, she apologized for the intrusion and grabbed Audrey's hand, who turned and winked as she left the room.

Hogan spoke with Fairfax for a while longer. As he deflected more questions on the case, he sensed the steel in the man opposite and guessed he'd make a formidable adversary. They shook hands again, and he promised to be in touch with any updated advice. The same English butler ghosted into the room to show him out. Halfway to his waiting car he heard footsteps and turned to see Marissa hurrying toward him.

"I'm glad I caught you," she panted. "My father may try to downplay his concerns, but he's been worried sick since the murders. If there is anything else…" She appeared to lose her line of thought. "I mean, I… Audrey…we both adore him. If something were to happen…"

"He should be fine. He has first-rate security, and if he cancels any engagements…" Marissa's eyes flickered on his English enunciation of security. Her disarming beauty broke his train of thought.

"Well, I guess that's reassuring," she responded with a light sigh. An awkward pause followed before she spoke again. "Do you have a card if I spot anything suspicious?"

Hogan fumbled one from his wallet and handed it over. She offered a warm smile, tapped the card on her palm, then turned and walked back to the house.

He watched her all the way.

21

A RETURN TO his sparse apartment seemed less desirable after Fairfax's opulent mansion, so Hogan drove straight to Jay Chopra's Malibu home. The task force had pieced together a timeline for the assassin and suspected he'd pushed and tripped Chopra, the granite island doing the rest. On-street camera footage had ruled out the killer entering through the front door. Jared Miller's team had yet to pinpoint an alternative.

Hogan was glad he'd memorized the door's ten-digit code from his first visit, it saved a call into the office and alerting Miller he was there. The human brain struggles to retain numbers over seven digits long without repetition. Back when he was competing, he'd developed a method involving the seven dwarves (and three invented ones), to rapidly remember strings of digits. He walked through his memory palace for Chopra's—spotting the dwarves in various places in the kitchen at Wilshire and punching the digits in order—Sleepy 2, Doc 7, Bashful 3, Bashful, 3, Shouty 9—until the door opened.

He crossed the main living area, pausing by the Rothko. He didn't "get" art, but a few years back had investigated a forgery ring and learned about the market. It would be destined for some fancy gallery. He repeated the code and process at the back door and continued onto the glass-fronted balcony. The wind began to whip at his jacket as he descended to the beach. The killer must have studied Chopra's LA routine, which included surveilling the apartment. Hogan wanted to understand how. He inched backward toward the ocean, all the time staring up. Upon reaching the water's edge, his angle of vision only provided a restricted view into the apartment. The beach was private, with access only from the beachfront residences themselves. Surveillance footage from adjacent properties on the night in question had yielded nothing. The intruder had overwritten Chopra's front and rear camera recordings. For privacy, these videos never hit the cloud at Poseidon Gate. The person gaining entry to Chopra's had secured the door's code in advance, but how? And how had he avoided cameras on his approach? Hogan scanned the mishmash of architectural hubris and ended on a pile of rocks in front of a sturdy fence with a jagged top. This marked the closest boundary of the beach to his right. He hurried back to the steps, through the property, and out to his car—he had a theory he wanted to confirm.

After a circuitous route skirting Perenchio golf course, he arrived at Malibu Lagoon State Beach. He squeezed into the busy parking lot and followed a sandy path to the public beach. A brown pelican glided by before coming to rest on the lagoon edge. A pair of nearby bird-watchers tracked its journey. The incongruity of his smart suit elicited a puzzled look as he said hello and walked onto the beach. Upon reaching the boundary separating the private beach, Hogan noted a camera dead level with the fence and one on the first property after it. Analysts had reviewed footage from every residence on this section of the beach and found nothing. He gazed back to the ocean, where a young couple were kayaking parallel to the coastline. This made him shudder—he hated the water, his fear dating back to childhood. As they progressed with surprising speed, his theory crystallized. He pulled out his phone and snapped a few pictures. The only suitable viewing angle into Chopra's pad would be out on the ocean. The killer could have accessed the property via the strip of beach beyond its back entrance. To do so would have required a kayak, small craft, or submersible. Hogan spun back around to where the bird-watchers still stood. The suspect must have used a vehicle. He sprinted back to the lot.

A teenager leafing through a Superman comic manned the sun-faded hut by its entrance.

"Do you have cameras?" Hogan demanded.

"Huh?"

He repeated the question.

"Oh, yeah, right. We have a couple," the youth said, pointing to the left corner of the lot. "And there's another when you drive in," he added, nodding straight ahead.

"Where does the feed go?"

The boy shrugged. "Head office, I s'pose."

He made the boy retrieve the address before asking one last question.

"How long do they keep the recordings?"

Another shrug. He'd visit the boy's boss tomorrow. If his theory proved correct, he could lay eyes on the killer.

22

SURE-PARK OCCUPIED the second floor of a squat brick building in Westchester. As he waited for the manager, Stuart Trimble, Hogan marveled at the towers of files fighting for space on every available surface.

A man with a bushy mustache, more Groucho Marx than Magnum P.I., sloped into the room and circled behind the desk. His right eye twitched as he offered help. Hogan explained the footage he needed and waited as Trimble shuffled sheets of wrinkled paper, then stopped. He began tapping on his aging computer.

"Did you say you had a warrant?"

"Do I really need one? I can get one if you insist," Hogan added, with the right balance of indifference and menace.

"Ah, um, no. I'm, ah…I'm sure it will be fine. I think we have what you need. I'll be back in a moment." He returned five minutes later with a small box labeled *USB drives*. "These cover each camera for the last eight weeks." He began to edge it across the desk.

"Thanks for your help, sir. We do appreciate it a great deal."

"Will we get these back once you're finished with them?" Trimble still gripped the box.

"Of course," Hogan lied, taking the box and the choice away from him.

Hogan swept through the office straight to his desk and plugged the USB for the corresponding week of the murder into his laptop. He advanced the playback until ten p.m. on the day of Chopra's death and sat glued to the screen as the minutes ticked by. At 10:29 p.m., a dark Ford F-150 pickup pulled into the empty parking lot. The familiar exhilaration from a case breakthrough coursed through his body. A person opened the rear tailgate, removed some equipment, then slipped into a wetsuit. A cap was pulled right down, obscuring their face, and they always kept their back to the camera. They hurried past the crooked beach sign and out of shot. They were familiar with the parking lot surveillance layout. The suspect was of above-average height and moved with feline confidence. He was almost certainly male, and alone.

The killer hadn't left Chopra's property until after midnight, so Hogan skipped ahead to allow for the security system hack. At 2:07 a.m., the figure reappeared and pushed the same equipment into the bed of the Ford F-150. Hogan zoomed in on the frozen image of the back of the man's head as he closed the tailgate, then whispered:

"I'm coming for you."

23

By Wednesday morning, Hogan had a clearer picture of the events leading up to Chopra's murder. Teams of analysts at Wilshire and in the Biometric Technology Center in Clarksburg, West Virginia, had pored over the footage. The Criminal Justice Information Service, which included the BTC, was the finest on the planet. Hogan had visited the campus earlier that year. Despite standing only three stories high, the flagship building had over one thousand windows. The futuristic design reflected the sunlight, and the work inside. The Bureau always embraced new technologies to apprehend criminals, and these would be employed to find their latest suspect.

The jabber of chatter from fellow task force members filled the conference room as Hogan tweaked the whiteboard layout. New pictures and arrows demonstrated his latest discovery. Entering last, Carla closed the door and indicated for him to proceed.

"I wanted to bring everyone up to speed with a major new lead in Jay Chopra's death." Hogan pointed to the enhanced images of the man in the wet suit. "We're certain this is the individual who killed Chopra. Now, of course, these currently offer little scope for identification. What we did send to the FACE Services Unit also drew a blank. But the helpful folks in the BTC have kindly summarized feedback on key physical characteristics for the killer." Everyone sat transfixed—they had a figure to associate with the murder. "They're confident the suspect is male, five eleven to six feet, and around one hundred and eighty pounds. He's physically fit, likely no older than fifty or younger than thirty. His feet are a size ten, and he has no discernible limp or other noticeable impairments." Hogan paused as people scribbled down the details, then moved to a silhouette of a man's head and shoulders with a question mark above. It could be construed as childish, but Vance had been right—it would work fine for illustrative purposes. All the physical attributions and assumptions were written below. "We'll continue to build out our profile here. I know there are ten people in this room this matches, but it's a start." There was a light ripple of amusement. "And the entire CJIS division stands ready to help." He opened a new set of images.

"The suspect conducted two other evening reconnaissance missions when Chopra visited the property. He used the same Ford F-150, attire, and camera angle precautions. We know he used an underwater scooter, but we don't have clear enough images to identify the manufacturer. His wetsuit is plain and unremarkable, and the vehicle has cloned plates from Illinois. We tracked the F-150 each time on the ALPR, which captured it heading south on the PCH before it turned off at Bundy Drive. After this, we have nothing. We need to identify this vehicle's original owner. It's a new-model black Ford F-150 and most likely stolen. It's one of the most common vehicles on our roads, but the killer chose it for that reason." Hogan paused for a moment. "It's also notable that the appearance of accidental death in the case of Jay Chopra ensured persons, such as Decker, weren't aware they could be at risk. This again suggests this suspect"—Hogan pointed to the grainy security camera image—"is responsible for both murders. We must find a link to prove it. I know SAC Alson's team is progressing with Quinton Decker's killing, but she'll explain more."

Alson summarized her team's progress tracing Decker's Imperium's locations in the weeks before the crash and when it was compromised. The initial focus was on Decker's multiple residencies. They'd also caught a break with the surveillance footage on 17-Mile Drive. Another Imperium with cloned plates had been captured on camera, and they were confident the driver was their killer. The hunt for the origin of this vehicle had begun in earnest.

Alson finished up, and everyone rose from their chairs. As people filed out, Carla stopped beside Hogan and said, "Nicely done. I'll brief the director on the progress." He nodded in response as she hurried from the room. Only then did he catch the cold, bitter stare from Jared Miller beyond the doorway.

Hogan began mentally reviewing his update when his cell phone rang with a number he didn't recognize. He tapped the green button and said his name.

"Hi, it's Marissa Fairfax," came the hesitant response.

"Ms. Fairfax, how can I help?"

"I wanted to see if you were free for lunch. There's something I've found that may be useful to your case."

"It's pretty crazy here, but I could grab a quick bite for lunch near my office on Wilshire if you can make that work?" Hogan offered, attempting to sound casual.

"That's fine with me. I'm over in Beverly Hills, so not too far from you—I checked."

He suggested a place, and they agreed to meet at one.

Hogan's pulse quickened as he walked the two blocks to Fundamental. She might have useful information but could have explained it over the phone.

Marissa sat at a corner table perusing a menu. She wore a white silk blouse, open at the neck, revealing a dainty silver necklace. A small Chanel bag hung off the edge of the chair. She radiated effortless beauty and broke into a wide smile as he approached. It creased the corners of her eyes, a deeper blue than he remembered. After exchanging greetings, Hogan settled into the seat opposite.

"The food here is usually decent," he stated.

Marissa hesitated, then replied. "It all looks good. Thanks for meeting me." She began to twist her hair around her index finger. "How's the investigation going?"

Hogan toyed with the edge of his menu. "It's not progressing as fast as my boss, Carla, would like and I can chart her satisfaction in expletives used per day; this morning was calmer, and the press coverage is relentless, too, so we must be careful what we say." The words tumbled from his mouth, like a nervous best man at a wedding.

"I can imagine. The conspiracy theories are outlandish—I saw one blaming aliens plotting to take over the country." Marissa emitted a small, throaty laugh.

"Most days, I feel that has already happened," he managed to joke back. She laughed harder this time, and this helped his jitters. He wanted to discover more about her, while remaining professional. He was glad she was talkative and jumped between subjects as he ate and nodded at the right points.

She wasn't one of the spoiled, vapid rich kids that LA churned out for fun. She was engaging and intelligent and ran her charity foundation from a Beverly Hills office. He surmised she was in her early thirties, and she alluded to being single. After the coffee arrived, she moved on to the information regarding her father.

"It might be nothing," Marissa continued in an absent tone, "but the foundation received several graphic threats about our immigration stance and support for refugees. They mentioned my father, too. We get this kind of thing now and then, but I thought it might be relevant now." She unfolded several sheets of paper from her bag and them to Hogan.

They were letters. Extreme right-wing vitriol dripped from the pages, and all were signed "AFAO." He pointed to the acronym.

"Do you know what this stands for?"

"'America for Americans Only.' I couldn't find out much about them. My father said to ignore it, that they'd be some crackpots out on a compound. But then these killings happened and…"

"He's probably right. Can I take these?"

"Of course. It's likely to be a waste of time, but I thought I should let you know."

"I'm glad you did. I'll check this out."

Brushing aside Marissa's protest, he picked up the check, and they headed outside.

"I better get going," Hogan said, wishing the opposite despite the fact he'd already been gone too long. He'd enjoyed spending time in this woman's company. "And I'll call you as soon as I have anything on this AFAO organization."

"That sounds good. Thanks again," Marissa replied, flashing a luminous smile that stayed with him for the rest of the day.

24

CARLA PACED HER office like a pushy realtor trying to pull off a deal, gripping her Friday-morning coffee. The catalyst for her anger was a Hugh Fairfax CNN segment that aired the previous evening. He'd been circumspect on the case but had boasted about the FBI visiting and offering advice on security and personnel.

"After this fucking interview, Director Sullivan insisted we treat other potential high-profile targets equally and provide senior investigator access. I mean, we still don't know who, if any of them, are at risk. Some of them had called the president to complain about preferential treatment. It's one big fucking boys' club!" Carla stopped pacing, met his eye, and slid two sheets of paper over her desk.

"You're taking Charles Lyle in Miami and Mark Fullerton in New York. I'm gonna go see Cole Sandzer in Vegas—that asshole demanded a personal briefing from me. Alson is taking Felix Moore in Seattle and Douglas Matterhorn in San Francisco—it's her turf. Miller is meeting with two local bigshots with political clout. If anything happens, we mitigate blame," she declared.

"Fairfax had already beefed up the security team before my visit." Hogan kept his tone measured; he didn't want to take the heat for this.

"I know. This isn't you. Start by flying to Miami on Monday evening and get back by Wednesday—okay? And try to shake up a new lead or two— We could do with more." Carla dug her fingers into her temples. "Fucking Fridays, always the bad news day."

Hogan did the *ain't that so* nod and escaped the office while he could.

The hunt for the suspect's Ford F-150 inched along. The California-focused search generated reams of data. It needed to be cross-referenced against the ALPR database that recorded license plates on major routes. Alson's team had shifted focus to Decker's HQ garage to investigate if his car was compromised there.

Hogan started reading up on Charles Lyle to prepare for his Tuesday morning meeting. Now in his seventies, the billionaire had amassed his fortune in oil and plastics. The EPA had sued his companies a record number of times, but the fines were a fraction of the profit made from their environmental transgressions. The parent company continued to lobby on Capitol Hill for lighter-touch regulation. Lyle was a favorite villain of the liberal left, a role he enjoyed. He counted both the Russian and Saudi Arabian leaders among his friends. According to *Forbes*, Lyle was the world's fifth richest man. *This is just great; Miller stays local, and I end up with the guy with dictators as buddies.* It was late—he needed a beer.

He'd exited the main doors to the parking lot when a figure jogged up next to him.

"Nicely done with the Sure-Park cameras."

Jared Miller wasn't here to dispense compliments, so Hogan stopped and waited.

"We were going to pull the footage Monday, as we figured the killer arrived at the property via the ocean, so likely parked near there," he continued.

"Of course you were." Hogan didn't hide his sarcasm.

"For a guy with such a good memory, you seem to have forgotten your fuckups. But I'm not sure everyone else has."

"They won't forget your Angels of Death case. You never shut up about it."

"And I'll be the next SAC because of it. You might be leading this case, but I wouldn't get too comfortable." Miller shot back and stalked off.

25

THE MORNING OF betting and trading English soccer had been a failure. Hogan's normal laser focus kept slipping away, leading to ill-considered decisions. The upshot—he lost a few hundred dollars, leaving him further away from the money required for Paradiso Care. As usual, he'd add three thousand bucks from his monthly paycheck, but that still left him way short. He'd send a chunk of cash this week to buy some time. He said goodbye to an unusually muted Amber and walked out of the rear exit while planning a detour to the La Isla Bonita taco truck. As he entered the parking lot, preppy Chad climbed from his blue Corvette. He couldn't pass up this opportunity.

"Hey, Chad." The blond marine-cut head swiveled in his direction and frown lines formed as a kernel of recognition reached his brain. This time, he wore a salmon-pink T-shirt with lemon shorts—the full Tommy Hilfiger.

"Hey, mister," he answered and walked toward Hogan, who now blocked his path. Chad stopped, puffing out his chest as his lips and eyes narrowed.

"I see another mark on Amber, our next encounter will be a lot less conducive for your health," Hogan stated in a level voice.

"Then let's skip the bullshit right now," Chad growled, taking another small step forward, his fists tightening. Hogan's confidence he'd see any punch coming a mile off meant he stayed where he was, his balance ready to shift. Chad relaxed a little like he planned to let the matter drop, but the eyes gave him away. Hogan had already started ducking as a massive right hook sliced through the air where his head had been.

He exploded upward with a heavy body shot to Chad's exposed ribs, doubling him over, and an overhand right sent him sprawling to the floor. Hogan glanced around to confirm they were still alone, stepped over the prostrate figure, and continued to Rose Avenue. He'd need ice for his hand to go with his fish tacos.

Hogan discovered his dad in the main room at Paradiso. Mentally debilitated residents occupied most of the seats, watching, of all things, *Columbo*. He sat to his dad's left, leaning over to hand him a pack of chocolate chip cookies.

"Hide those, or they'll want some." The elderly man waved his hand at no one in particular.

"I'll put them in the drawer in your room, then." They'd be a welcome surprise next time his dad opened it. Peter Falk announced 'just one more thing' as Hogan turned back to the TV. It could have been twenty-five years earlier, except with his mum sitting beside him.

"So, they always show us the killer at the start?" Hogan passed across the popcorn.

"They do."

"But why?"

"The joy of the show is seeing how clever Columbo is, and how he slowly pulls the pieces together. He's very smart, like you."

"He doesn't look it, in that jacket."

"That's the cleverest thing of all."

Hogan frowned as his mum passed the bowl back, but she smiled and nodded at the TV.

Watching *Columbo* became their thing. He grew to love the character as his mum did. Hogan hadn't realized then how it would shape his future.

He stayed holding his father's hand until the show's end—it was always worth the wait to see the trapped villain's face.

When Hogan rose to leave, his dad wobbled as he stood to embrace him and asked the question he always hoped to avoid: "Is your brother coming to see me soon?"

"He won't, I'm afraid. We haven't seen or spoken to him for over six years."

"Oh, that's too bad. You'll come again tomorrow?" Dementia had stripped away his emotions, too.

"Next week now, Dad." He didn't have the heart to lie this time.

Mrs. Malkin bustled into the hall as he left the lounge. "How was he today?" she inquired in a friendly tone. A genuine smile split her sunken cheeks.

"He was in good form and content for most of the visit."

"Well, isn't that great! Erm, I'm sorry to bother you with this, but next quarter's invoice is now overdue. I imagine it is an oversight on your behalf—I saw the press conference about those terrible murders, so I'm sure you have a lot on your plate." She clasped her hands together. Hogan had never mentioned he worked in law enforcement; with this discovery Mrs. Malkin was like a new person.

"Yes, I have been," Hogan said in his most authoritative voice. "I'll find time to get this sorted ASAP." He may as well play along.

"Oh, but of course. Sorry again for bothering you when you're so busy."

Once outside, he took a moment to enjoy the fresh air after the stale aromas of Paradiso. The irony that his dad's memory was so screwed, and Hogan had won a competition proving his was the opposite, wasn't lost on him. It was why he ensured his brain's one hundred billion neurons were put through their paces—the universe's most complex organ thrived on action—and why he eschewed a more traditional approach to Jay Chopra's Malibu death. Plus, memorizing crime scenes and evidence led to quick connections he would never have made.

He pulled out his phone and called his cousin in the UK. It connected after one ring.

"Well if it ain't my boy Hogan."

"Hey, Toby, is now a good time?"

"Definitely! I saw you on CNN—what's been going down? You any closer to catching the guy? I mean, I bet those other rich blokes are shitting themselves." Toby chuckled. "It's been playing havoc with the markets here in London. We took a bath on Amici."

"I can't really talk about the case, I'm afraid. But yeah, it's pretty crazy right now."

"I understand, mate. If anyone can get him, it'll be you. Is it transfer time again?"

"Yeah, I've withdrawn the sterling equivalent of sixteen thousand in dollars from Betfair, it should be in your account now. It's been a shitty last month because of work, so I've not had my head in the trading game or spare weekend time."

Hogan could use this betting account if it was registered in a UK resident's name. His cousin, a natural gambler at heart, had been happy to provide the service and send across the winnings. Each transaction needed to be below ten thousand dollars, anything above this would be flagged to the federal government.

"I bet it has. I can top it up a little if you want, and you can square away next quarter?"

"I appreciate that—but it's all cool. Things will hopefully work themselves out. If you could send it to the usual account, please, Toby." Hogan wasn't about to start receiving charity or loans now. That was a slippery slope he refused to take. He'd found a way so far, and he would again. "Everything all good with you, with work?"

"You know me, mate, navigating the markets like the barracuda I am. The fund is up double digits, so all hunky-dory here. When you coming over, we're overdue a good booze-up. Proper beer too, instead of that weak-as-piss lite stuff the Yanks serve up."

Hogan laughed. "Next year, fella. I'll let you know. Glad all is well, say hello to your old man, and give my love to Emily and the kids."

"Will do, mate. Speak soon, and take care."

Hogan hung up and climbed into his Jag. It was getting harder to pull the cash together every quarter. The alternative budget care homes were awful. His dad couldn't be stuck in one of those dives—most were miles away too. He'd pay Malkin two of the months owed next week. And between the case and sleep, he'd find a way to make the rest.

26

A PING ANNOUNCED the arrival of an email. Hogan's initial investigation into America For Americans Only led to posts on right-wing conspiracy sites 4chan and QAnon. The person behind them was deranged. It was getting harder to separate crackpots from the genuinely dangerous. He'd asked a cyber squad buddy to track down their origin, and now they'd come back. He scanned the information, picked up his phone to update Marissa, then stopped. He wanted to see her again; maybe this was the excuse. It was a little tenuous, sure, but plausible. He tapped out a quick message, and grinned when moments later, she replied, suggesting coffee that afternoon.

This time, Hogan arrived early. He balanced on one of La Colombe's fashionable wooden stools waiting for Marissa. He'd read earlier that she'd divorced five years ago and generally kept a low media profile. He'd also found photos of her in Africa and Central America with grateful locals celebrating new water supplies. Most news articles focused on her foundation work. After her marital problems, the gossip columns left her alone.

Marissa strode through the entrance and waved. He rose to shake her hand, and together, they surveyed the chalkboard of coffee choices. Hogan sneaked a sideways glance as they ordered. She looked terrific again in tight-fitting jeans and a pink cashmere V-neck sweater, a delicate pearl pendant necklace today's accessory choice.

Drinks in hand, they found a table.

"I'm convinced those uncomfortable stools is their subtle way of saying, *if you want free Wi-Fi all day, try Starbucks instead,*" Marissa commented.

Hogan laughed, immediately more at ease than when they'd last met.

His companion offered a coy smile in return. "So, Special Agent—what do you have for me?"

"Well, we found out who was behind the threats and AFAO in general."

"Should we be worried?"

"It's one guy in Tulsa, so something we can easily deal with."

Marissa smirked. "Not much of an organization."

"Exactly, even I thought it could be something a little bigger. Local PD will swing by anyway, warn him and mention the FBI. That kind of stuff usually works."

"That's great, and thanks for putting my mind at ease. How's the case going?"

"My pleasure. Slowly, so far. I'm flying to Miami later to meet with a concerned citizen."

"Anyone I'd know?"

Hogan paused, then decided they'd be little harm in sharing. "It's Charles Lyle." A look of distaste passed across Marissa's face. "Have you met him?" he asked.

"No, but he hit on one of my friends a few years back. He got insistent, and she had to leave dinner early. I mean, he's older than my dad, for Christ's sake!"

"I *could* bring it up tomorrow, if you want?"

She responded with a throaty laugh. "Imagine! It was a while ago, and who knows how many times he's pulled a stunt like that? When do you get back from your trip?"

He paused a moment, intrigued.

"Wednesday, most likely."

"So, you'd be free Friday night? You've bought me lunch *and* put my mind at rest. I owe you dinner in return."

"It's all good. I was just doing my job." Taken aback, he hadn't known what else to say.

"And if I insist?" Marissa cocked her head to one side, giving him a half smile.

He grinned. "I'd ask what time."

27

HOGAN CLIMBED INTO the black Ford Explorer idling outside his Brickell hotel and chucked his worn overnight bag onto the back seat. The suntanned driver rocked a pair of gold-framed aviators. A broad, friendly smile spread over his lined face as he pumped Hogan's hand.

"Special Agent Coleman, it's good to meet you. How was your flight?"

"Hogan—you too, thanks for collecting me. Not bad. I got some time to think, I suppose." He'd endured almost six hours cramped in economy before he reached the illuminated sprawl of Miami the previous night.

"Spurs fan?" Hogan asked, pointing to a Tottenham Hotspur air freshener dangling from the rearview mirror.

"Ever since the '82 FA Cup final. You?"

"I lived in London as a kid and caught the bug then. I still miss going to the matches."

"I'd like to go to one. Maybe when they next make a final."

Hogan laughed. "Could be a bit of a wait." They were going to get along.

Coleman adopted a faux tour guide persona as they merged into crawling traffic.

"Lyle lives over on Star Island, 'bout a ten-minute drive, traffic permitting. Lots of famous folks have places there—Ricky Martin, Gloria Estefan, and the Viagra guy." Coleman chuckled before continuing, "And there's the house from the end of *Scarface*."

Hogan nodded; everyone knew that scene. He took in his first daytime Miami views as they hit the entrance to a causeway across the bay. The city's buildings glistened in the sunshine—no LA smog here. The water on either side was a coruscation of turquoise—deep enough to moor the enormous cruise liners on Hogan's right. He squinted to read their names—*Norwegian Sky* and *Carnival Victory*. He'd never been on a cruise; the prospect of sailing into a vast ocean made his hands clammy.

As they passed a sign announcing "Star Island Next Signal," Coleman eased the Explorer into the left-hand lane. They turned to cross a short bridge across the shimmering water. On the other side, ostentatious floating trophies of wealth bookended immaculate gardens. These all led up to palatial properties. Coleman badged the security guard upon reaching the island's entrance. They continued past several impressive mansions then stopped outside a set of black-and-gold gates. Another flash of their credentials at the camera triggered them to open. They set off down a palm-lined driveway shaped like an elongated egg timer. A dazzling white Spanish Colonial-style property sat at the end. The Mars-red terra-cotta roof matched the octagonal tiles stretching out in front of them. Coleman gave a low whistle.

"Scarface should have got into the oil industry," he murmured.

"No kidding."

Two armed guards framed the doorway to the main property. A third, tall and athletic, marched toward them, the bulge of a gun visible under his tailored suit.

"Markus Vlok, Mr. Lyle's head of security," he announced in a clipped South African accent as they shook hands.

Both agents reached for their badges as Vlok waited. Hogan pegged him as ex-military.

"Thanks, gentlemen, I needed to double-check in the current environment," he said, palming the IDs back. "If you could follow me. Oh, and Mr. Lyle prefers visitors to avoid eye contact, so if you could bear that in mind," he added, pushing open a towering wooden door and beckoning them into the residence.

Charles Lyle sat at a circular table on a balustrade-lined terrace with views across the water and beyond. He had a thatch of impossibly black hair for a man his age, a tanned face, and an aquiline nose upon which circular steel glasses rested. His taste in linen jackets lay somewhere between extravagant and Liberace. On introductions, Hogan met Lyle's eyes, happy to set the meeting's tone, and to receive a frown. A maid hovered nearby with an ornate silver jug.

"Karak tea, gentlemen?" Lyle asked. "I acquired a taste for it in the Middle East."

They both nodded.

"And welcome to my humble home," he continued in a voice lacking sincerity. "I thought it was important that I knew all about the 'situation' so I could change security protocols. I believe that you can update me on the finer details."

Hogan ruminated on how two executions were best described as a "situation" as he sipped the creamy, sweet tea.

He started with comprehensive security advice and followed it with information already shared by the press. Lyle tried to delve deeper with some pointed questions over the next half hour. Hogan remained tight-lipped to the obvious annoyance of his host.

"So, you're going to catch the people responsible soon, right?" Lyle asked, after it became clear the briefing had finished. He clicked his fingers at the maid, who scuttled to top up his cup. His jaw tightened as he leaned back, arms folded, glaring at both agents.

"We hope so, sir. We have an experienced task force working through all the leads."

"Do you think the killings might be politically motivated?"

Hogan ignored this. "As I was saying, sir, there are multiple leads, both nuanced and obvious. We advise the most prominent billionaires, like you, to avoid routine, strengthen security, and report anything suspicious. We could have a clearer picture if another attempt is made on a target's life."

"Is that likely?" Lyle snapped.

Hogan suspected the temper hid the man's fear. "It's possible," he conceded. "Would you know of any connection between the two men that could have led to their deaths?"

"Nothing you haven't already thought of, I'd imagine. I barely knew Jay Chopra. Quinton Decker was an eco-blowhard who loved the sound of his own voice. He sued me once for defamation and won; despite my New York lawyers being the best that money could buy. I won't miss him. But I must say your progress appears limited. I'd have expected more."

Hogan took this slight as a cue to end the meeting and slid his card across the desk. "We need to get going. My details, should anything else come up."

"All that money, and I hear he's still mean." Coleman shook the forkful of chicken and waffle to highlight his point. "Only hiring illegals for his mansion here to save cash, despite a high-profile anti-immigration stance. Goddamn hypocrite."

They were in a Miami Beach restaurant called Yardbird. "*You'll love the fried chicken, and it's not too far,*" Coleman had insisted. Hogan hadn't counted on it coming with watermelon, cinnamon, and waffles, but the delicious combination worked. Coleman was proving to be excellent company.

"Do you know much else about him?"

"Not too much, except he has every major Florida politician in his pocket. They'd miss him if someone took him out. I know nobody fucks with Lyle, here or back in Houston."

Coleman made the universal hand signal for the check to a nearby waiter.

"No family to speak of?"

"One sister. He's never married. The rumor was he never wanted to risk a penny of his fortune, even with a prenup." Coleman sighed. "Having gone through a divorce myself, I can't blame him for that. C'mon, I'll take you to the airport. I'm bored of white-collar bullshit cases this month, so I'd love to hear more details of a proper one."

28

The silver Toyota Prius featured prominent Lyft and Uber signs on the windshield. It was the perfect choice for covert action around Manhattan, and you avoided assholes jumping out trying to flag you down. Kirov parked, engine off, opposite what was known as billionaires' row, just up from Columbus Circle on the south side of Central Park. He wanted to confirm his latest target had ended their routine. Kirov's backup plan involved switching to evening surveillance. He'd been trained to adapt from the beginning of his career. He wondered if the CIA still had their covert midtown office. Everything leading to this point had started with the Agency.

Lukas sat in the filthy cell, his head in his hands, wishing he'd stopped punching the dirty Russian, but he couldn't. He blamed them for everything. If not for those bastards, his grandmother would still be alive, and he'd have never had to set foot in that orphanage. It had been seven years since she'd died, and not a day had gone by when Lukas hadn't thought of revenge. Yesterday, yet again, he'd been seeking it, and when they'd dragged him off the soldier's lifeless body, it was already too late. He'd messed up real bad this time.

He heard the clunk of an outer door, and a dapper man in a fedora approached the bars of his cell and stopped as if weighing a decision.

"This him?" the man asked in English.

"Yes," replied the officious-looking man next to him.

"Good. Open the doors, and I'll take it from here."

After a bath and returning to discover new clothes in his size, Lukas walked with the man a short distance to a café on the edge of Vilnius old town. They ordered hot kibinai and cabbage soup.

"I'm told you speak English," Fedora Man said. Lukas caught a hint of an American accent.

"Yes. My grandmother taught me, and I read a lot of Western children's books, even some the Russians banned," he added, as the memories flooded back.

"Perfect." The man ignored the teenager's tortured look and continued. "The Russians are leaving soon, Lithuania will get its independence any day now, but the fight"—he paused, staring at Lukas—"is just beginning."

The man consulted the papers on the table in front of him. "We know you're intelligent and resourceful, but also full of rage. We can take these personality traits and teach you how to harness them. Russia will be a fractured, dangerous place in the coming years, and we need operatives from relinquished territories to help us influence the new order."

"Who's 'we'?" Lukas asked, looking up from his soup.

"All in good time. If you want real revenge for your grandmother and to help your country, this is your chance." The man fixed him with an intense stare.

Lukas tried to make it look like he was thinking, but his mind was made up. His only other option would be a long stretch in jail. He'd have to abandon his solitary life, for now. Plus, the promise of vengeance was enticing.

"Okay," he muttered, then added one more thing. "I'll need to pick up some books from my room." The man nodded, reached forward, and gave him a light pat on his back. They sat in silence until Lukas had devoured his remaining food.

The sharp honk of a horn jolted Kirov back into Manhattan street life. A red-and-white horse-drawn cart had eased into a gap in the traffic, its giant rear wheels grinding as the blinkered horse trotted forward. Kirov checked his watch—9:30 a.m., this man's previous daily routine remained non-existent. But there was one place the target couldn't resist visiting. Time for him to ditch this vehicle and prepare for that opportunity.

Kirov was about to leave his curbside spot when a stocky, well-dressed man exited the apartment block opposite. He began weaving toward him through the static West 59th Street traffic. As he got closer, Kirov recognized him from the Chopra and Decker press conference. It was the FBI agent with the intriguing British accent. Kirov's heart rate ticked up a few beats. Logic kicked in—he looked like any other Uber driver and had to act like it. Still, as a precaution, he reached down for the SIG Sauer P226 under his seat. The agent stared at his vehicle, holding his phone in his right hand. Kirov eased his finger over the double-action trigger and glanced at the park to pick a route if he had to act, then flee. The back door handle clicked, and Kirov shifted the SIG to his lap. Perhaps this was part of a covert operation against him, but how? He didn't intend to find out. If the agent climbed into the car, it would be the last thing he did.

29

IT WAS EIGHT blocks from Hogan's hotel to Mark Fullerton's apartment. He decided to walk. He loved the vibrancy of New York City streets, especially in the morning. People filed into soaring office towers carrying the caffeinated drinks that helped fuel this city. A bedraggled man shouted something unintelligible from his slumped position in a doorway. This was the other side of Manhattan; omnipresent but ignored by most. As he continued up Eighth Avenue, memories of his last trip here with Katie came swimming back.

She'd recently started as election campaign manager for Thomas Mitchell. He was a state senator fancied to win his run at Congress. Hogan had wrapped up another complex case and seemed assured of continued progress within the Bureau. He'd pretended the trip was to celebrate, but on their final day, he proposed on Brooklyn Bridge. He remembered his euphoria when a tearful Katie agreed.

"Hey, buddy, watch yourself," a man shouted.

Hogan jinked by a FedEx driver wheeling a trolley of parcels. He offered an apology and pushed the memories back down, deep inside. It was too painful. He checked the route to his upcoming meeting again and continued his stroll.

Mark Fullerton was the self-styled "King of Hedge Funds." He'd started with nothing and was the American Dream writ large, in pugnacious and loquacious form. Since the mid-nineties, his Babylon Fund had crushed rivals' returns. He'd foreseen and amassed profits from both the dot-com and the housing market meltdown in the noughties. He threw obscene money at a slew of Republican lawmakers to ensure the tax cuts required to increase his wealth. When his fund bought shares in a business, everyone stood up and took notice. He was the kind of guy who'd sell a ton of oil shares one day and buy a Botswanan dam the next. Like Fairfax, he could move markets with his decisions. His personal life often made the headlines for the wrong reasons, but he was thick-skinned and shook off any scandal. He had two sons and a long-suffering wife.

Hogan crossed West 59th Street, to an apartment building at the storied location of Central Park South. After badging the doorman, he signed in with the concierge and left his overnight bag. Security escorted him to the penthouse elevator. He'd read the Fullertons had bought the place last year for $280 million, making it the United States' most expensive residential property. It sounded like cock waving of the highest order, but he tried to reserve judgment as the elevator doors swished open.

The all-white vestibule contrasted with the black-suited close protection guys flanking a gilded entrance. After the tedious process of proving his identity again, the doors to the apartment swung apart. He walked into a room that, on arrival, threatened sensory overload. Fifteen feet-high windows ran across three of the four aspects with stunning views over Central Park. Antique mahogany chairs sat at precise angles around a matching table. A plush chaise longue occupied the far-left corner. A painting that suggested a paintbrush-wielding infant had been let loose dominated the back wall—no doubt a Pollock. Further on, plinths supported precarious, priceless vases, and a shiny red balloon-style rabbit graced the other far corner. An adjacent door swung open, and Fullerton stormed in.

"So what the fuck is going on? Am I in danger? Can you not just catch this psychopath?" The rapid-fire of questions like a maniacal quiz show host caught Hogan off guard. Stunned into silence, he searched for a suitable response.

"If we could, er...if we could take a seat, sir, that's what I'm here to explain."

"Okay, then keep it brief." Fullerton perched on a vermilion sofa as if getting more comfortable might prolong the conversation. His shoulders hunched in tension or anger. Hogan sat opposite and launched into his security recommendations and top-line investigation update. The hedge fund mogul's hooded eyes contracted, and he frowned several times before tightening his lips as the briefing ended.

"In short: no suspects, no real idea if the crimes are connected, security advice that a child coulda offered, and no accurate indication that anyone else is at risk. Do I have this right?" Fullerton fired back.

"Not exactly, sir. We're confident the crimes are linked, but as I said, we can't prove it yet. If the culprit decides to strike again, you could be at risk, and it would be remiss not to suggest this is a possibility."

"I'm not holin' up here, even with these views"—Fullerton threw his arm out toward the windows—"while waitin' on you guys to find a connection or suspect. Someone might have killed the other guys because they were irritatin' fuckers."

Then you're screwed.

Hogan waited for a beat before responding.

"That's your prerogative, sir, but please do remember if the suspect is responsible for both killings, he is adroit at establishing potential weak spots. I can only reiterate—retain a strong security team and choose locations wisely."

"And wait for the *FBI* to solve this? Great to see my tax dollars at work so efficiently." Fullerton's voice was laced with sarcasm. "What's that fuckin' accent as well—we can't recruit agents from this side of the pond?" He paused, then waved a hand. "Have you anythin' useful you wanna add?"

"No, that's all, sir—thanks for your time."

With a grunt, Fullerton stalked from the room.

Hogan rose and fought the temptation to knock over a vase. Instead, he drank in the views one last time and left.

Before he entered the elevator and his signal disappeared, Hogan tapped his location into Uber—adding JFK for his destination. After retrieving his bag, he wandered out onto the street. Traffic crawled as intermittent horns pierced the hum of background construction. New Yorkers were to patience, what sloths were to speed. Drivers only paused for milliseconds after light changes before frustration became audible. Central Park Tower soared into the sky, a few streets away. Manhattan land on these blocks was so expensive, even the air had its price. Checking his phone, he searched for a silver Prius and spotted one with Uber signage. It was slotted in behind a tourist-hunting horse and cart easing into traffic. As he approached the car, the driver stared at him with a puzzled frown. He had close-cropped dark hair with flecks of gray and an impenetrable gaze that gave Hogan pause. He reached for the handle to climb inside. As he began to pull the door, a flash of lights from behind caught his attention as he observed another silver Prius from which an Asian driver waved. Realizing that was his actual ride, Hogan shouted an apology through the open door, clicked it shut, and walked toward the other vehicle. He began the airport journey trying to decide if Fullerton was the biggest asshole he'd ever met.

30

WHILE IN GREEK mythology, Zeus cursed Sisyphus to endlessly push a rock up a hill before it rolled back down, Hogan figured his eternal damnation would be continual domestic flights. The dead-eyed flight attendants would fit right in with his vision of hell. He'd spent most of the cramped journey reading news reports speculating on the suspect and which billionaire might be next. These reinforced his determination to find the killer and bring him to justice. It was why he'd joined the Bureau in the first place. As the fasten-seat-belt sign announced their descent into LAX, he began flicking through a pack of cards, memorizing the order.

At Wilshire, Hogan discovered Carla was due back from Vegas later that evening, so he sought out his team. He found them cloistered in a conference room.

"How was the trip?" Ranger asked, leaning back in a chair that creaked in protest.

"It was okay. I know some people hate the rich, but I understand why after meeting Mark Fullerton and Charles Lyle. They were instantly dislikeable. It's no surprise people are so pissed at inequality." Since the high-profile killings, societal disquiet about the hyper-concentration of wealth had risen to new levels. Some people suggested the assassin was tackling an issue the government continued to avoid, albeit with brutal outcomes. The murders had galvanized protests and malicious commentary on social media platforms. Hogan reached back to close the door. "Who wants to update me first?"

Silence followed. Vance started shaking her head.

"You two are such pussies! So, I investigated the sunset philanthropy angle and there isn't much crossover with the charities that benefit from both deaths. I'm gonna stick my neck out here and say that motive is unlikely. I've also followed up with Miller's team on the vehicle, and they've identified sales and thefts of all black F-150s for the last six months. There's still a fair bit of data to get through, so they'll continue to eliminate where possible and share what's left. It should be any day now."

"How about the Imperium VX lead from Carmel?" Hogan asked.

"That's easier. Alson's team has traced new purchases across states within a day's drive along with those resold by private sellers. They're working these as we speak."

"How about the stolen ones?"

"That's why it is easier; they're almost impossible to boost. There was only one reported theft in the last four years."

"Yet the killer still got into Decker's?"

"He did, and it's why he'd require an Imperium to complete the job. You'd have needed to be intimately familiar with the features and interior to have pulled this off," Vance replied as she nudged Ranger. "You next, scooter boy."

"Oh, man! We've run into dead ends with the underwater scooter sale," he groaned. "Over fifty thousand are sold every year here in the US alone. I've tried numerous suppliers, and from the footage, they can only suggest a range of manufacturers. Then there is the secondary market. I'm working through logs of online sales in California, but damn, it's slow going."

"This guy isn't stupid. I hardly expect an order to lead to him," Hogan replied.

"We've got nowhere with the wetsuit too, with black ones so common that—"

"I get it. Any of the death threats lead anywhere?"

"Nope, wack jobs or anonymous losers. Either way, none alluded to how the murders would happen or suggested multiple killings."

Hogan turned to Chung. "Any joy?"

Lime-green and blue stripes was the analyst's shirt choice of the day.

"Well, to begin with, we discovered a few major shorts on Amici and Decker Battery stock placed just before Chopra's death."

"So the trader benefits if the price crashes?"

"Exactly. In this case, for a few hundred million dollars each time. One short profited by three billion. The company is based in Belize, but it's proving challenging to discover who is behind these monster trades. If there was a symbol for corruption, Belize might put it on their national flag. Unsurprisingly, investment banks are loath to share any details. My team will keep digging, and we still have a few tricks to try. It could be unrelated—they're heavily traded companies. We did have more joy on Democratic Party donors. Hugh Fairfax and Cole Sandzer are big contributors via multiple sources. Douglas Matterhorn also donates chunks. Charles Lyle and Mark Fullerton coordinate powerful Republican super PACs. But it still leaves us in the dark for motive."

Hogan rubbed his chin. "Thanks. I'd love to know who's behind that three-billion-dollar trade, so do everything you can. We'll find political connections everywhere, but this information could prove valuable. I appreciate all your efforts. Now we know Alson's and Miller's teams will chase down every crime scene lead and share that with us to review potential links. In the meantime, I want us to keep working motive. It could lead us to a connection and potentially identify the next target."

"If there is one," Ranger countered, shrugging.

"I don't think we're done yet. Anyway, there must be some link and motivation behind the deaths of Chopra and Decker, so we keep digging."

"I'll ensure we have all the vehicle data by Saturday, especially on the Imperium, as I've got a feeling that's gonna lead somewhere," Vance said.

"We'll all reconvene then and ideally share positive progress."

"No pressure, Vance," Ranger teased.

"Pffft, I eat pressure for breakfast."

Hogan laughed, only half sure she was joking.

31

THANKSGIVING ARRIVED WITH the task force hoping to grab some family time. This job chose your hours, not the other way around. Hogan stepped into Carla's office.

"Welcome back," she said, grabbing the phone, and making two quick calls.

Miller joined them with a sly smile, then Karyn Alson walked in, her keen brown eyes darting across the office. Her investigative feedback was always intelligent and concise, unlike Miller's circumlocution, which, in Hogan's experience, was a smoke screen for progress.

"Okay, let's hear about your meetings with this country's great and good," Carla said with a sardonic grin as they sat. "Hogan, you traveled farthest, so you get to go first."

He rifled through an overview of his two meetings, explaining they hadn't added much to the investigation. His description of the Fullerton meeting evoked the most reaction.

"He sounds like a piece of work," Carla offered once he finished. "Lyle also has the potential to make this case even more pressurized, so keep him at arm's length."

Alson was next up. She offered a natural warm smile that ran up to her high cheekbones and shuffled her small frame forward.

"Okay, right...Felix Moore, up in Seattle, stayed silent as I ran through the investigation. He just smiled throughout as if he was taking some"— she paused, looking for the right words—"malicious pleasure in their deaths. Pretty odd, I thought, but then again, he sat in a dressing gown stroking a cat the entire time, so it was already surreal."

"Like a Bond villain," Miller offered.

Alson laughed. "Yeah, that's exactly what I was thinking. He nibbled on Twinkies until he began firing questions about the circumstances behind the deaths. I deflected and offered little else. He even asked us to arrange additional security for his ranch outside Seattle. These guys hate spending money, huh? It makes you wonder why they work so hard to amass it."

"Did he know either of the men well?" Carla inquired.

"No. And he had no opinion or idea why they may have been killed."

"Okay, thanks. And Douglas Matterhorn?"

"He was the opposite. He appeared cut up about their deaths—he'd known Chopra for years. He's also a big Democratic Party donor and another sunset philanthropist, so he's convinced he'll be next should the killer strike again. He's flying with his family and sizeable security detail to Necker Island, insisting he'll remain there until all this is resolved."

Hogan found himself nodding. He'd always wondered why in movies, when people lived in a haunted house or were in danger from a deranged killer, they didn't disappear halfway around the world. (Aside from plot consequences, of course.) Alson eased back on her chair and indicated she'd finished.

Miller leaned forward. "Same for one of my guys. Terrence Fisher is leaving for New Zealand today. He's become a citizen and has arranged security on the north island. He wanted to know if his family was at risk, so I offered our standard advice. He was pleasant and appreciative of the visit.

"Simon Thorpe has a survival bunker outside of Palm Springs and will see out the 'murder apocalypse' as he referred to it, there. He knew Decker well, having crossed paths on many occasions. He was interested in connections indicating he would be next. I explained we didn't have a working hypothesis, and he seemed satisfied. It felt like he'd got us down there because he could." Miller spun a pen between his fingers as he leaned back.

"How was Vegas?" Hogan turned to his boss.

The corner of her lip curled down.

"Still there, unfortunately," she said. "Cole Sandzer has decided to run his streaming and media empire from his huge penthouse on the strip. He insisted it was safer than his mansion in Seattle, so he intends to remain there. He was sprightly for a septuagenarian—he hopped around from the moment I arrived. He suggested that a foreign power was behind the killings and feared he might be next. He explained that his newspapers constantly called out certain world leaders' transgressions, and that put him at risk. But he offered little when I asked about a connection between him and our two victims. If he stays put, he should be safe."

"Tight security?" Hogan asked.

"Fuck, yeah. Everywhere you turned there were ex-special forces guys. He boasted about his windows being bullet resistant against all calibers of rifle. For now, his life of luxury will be in this gilded cage."

Carla rose from her seat. "Thanks. We've ticked those boxes for Director Sullivan. I'm not sure we've learned much, but these chats may yet prove useful. You can go and enjoy what's left of Thanksgiving. But after that, let's get back to catching this fucker."

Celebrating today would remind Hogan of what he'd lost, so he'd turned down Nemo's dinner invitation. For the last few years, he'd ignored the festivities, and today would be no different. He worked late, his only concession to tradition, adding turkey to his pizza order.

32

HOGAN PACED HIS bedroom. His day had dragged with investigation progress scant. What would the evening hold? Dinner with a beautiful woman, sure, but was there an attraction for her too? He checked the mirror—tired eyes, exacerbated by the week of traveling, stared back. He ran some more wax through his unruly black hair. His mother often espoused the benefits of a good first impression and it was a mantra he'd carried through college and beyond. He'd been glad of it after his visit to Fairfax's mansion. Time and finances meant no new attire, so a newish white Saint Laurent shirt would have to do. He'd matched it with selvage jeans. He entered the living room and stood in front of the fish tank.

"What do you think, guys? Will I pass?" The starfish didn't move, but the seahorse raced up to the top of the tank—he was impressed. Or hungry. Hogan was sure he knew which.

He listened for the sound of a vehicle; Marissa had offered to pick him up.

Still nothing.

His stomach flipped again, so he grabbed a Pacifico.

He was draining the last drops when a horn tooted outside. He peeked through the blinds to see a black Lincoln pulling up. He took a deep breath, grabbed his keys, and trying to convey confidence he didn't feel, stepped outside.

Marissa, in a little black dress, stunned him into silence. Hogan remembered his manners.

"You look fabulous."

"Thank you," she beamed, cast an admiring glance in his direction, and waved her hand at the limo's extensive bar. "Can I get you a drink?"

"Sure, I'll take a beer," he replied, glad of the opportunity for a dose of extra courage. It helped, and the journey flew by as they fell into comfortable conversation.

Heads turned as they walked through Nobu Malibu. Hogan felt his cheeks heating up as the echoes of an incoherent Japanese welcome from the chefs behind the sushi counter trailed in their wake. Marissa tapped his arm as they arrived at an ocean-view table.

"You okay?"

"Yeah...I mean, this is vastly different from my usual Friday nights. I usually grab a burger after working late. A good one, though, don't get me wrong," he insisted as a waiter materialized and laid menus on the table.

After flicking through the cocktail pages, Hogan chose a Yuzuri Sour, and Marissa opted for the same. She started running through her favorite dishes while he tried to keep up. Rock shrimp tempura, black cod, dragon roll, yellowtail; they sounded like characters and moves from a kung fu flick more than food. He deferred to her choices.

"So, tell me more about the accent?" Marissa asked once she'd placed the order.

"I was born here but pretty much lived in the UK until I was nineteen. My dad is from Brentwood, but my mum was English," Hogan began, and to ward off the inevitable next question added, "she died just before we moved back."

"I'm sorry."

"It's okay, it was a long time ago now. When we returned to LA, I wanted to keep as much of my English side as possible; it helped me deal with everything in the year following her death." He reached for his cocktail and its reassuring clink of ice. "How old is Audrey?" he asked, shifting the conversation in a positive familial direction.

"She's eight and has the famous Fairfax stubbornness already, but she dealt brilliantly with the upheaval of her father leaving us. It helps, of course, that my dad dotes on her."

A waiter placed down two tempura bowls, announcing "ponzu" and "jalapeño" as he did. The food provided a hiatus from chatting, but they soon settled back into a natural rhythm of conversation. By dessert, they were tipsy and giggling away like naughty school kids. Hogan's account of his teenage weekend jobs was a revelation to his date, and she explained her biggest worry at that age was she looked gawky. A concept he found incomprehensible and said so.

"Honestly," she insisted, "they made fun of my walk." She caught his wide eyes and gave him a shy smile. "I was a late bloomer. So how does a Stanford graduate end up at the FBI?"

Hogan considered the question; one often asked after he finished college.

"I loved detective shows growing up. I found the notion of using your brainpower to solve crime resonated. My mum knew I wanted to do something that made a difference in the world. My dad, however, thought brains should lead to financial reward. After I won a scholarship to Stanford, he suggested careers in finance or tech. But after my mum's recent death, that career direction felt wrong. I wanted to do something that would have made her proud, even more so now she was gone. Who has ever heard of a commodities trader helping to make the world a better, safer place? By my second year, I knew I wanted to join the FBI when I graduated." He paused and sipped the excellent sake they'd moved on to. "Anyhow, tell me more about your foundation."

Marissa pushed a few errant strands of hair behind her ear.

"You can imagine it would be easy to live a listless life with my father's wealth, so I created a purpose. I, sorry…the foundation wants to bring clean drinking water to every corner of the globe. It's a mammoth task but an important one. It helps keep me grounded too. Well, most of the time." She laughed, panning across the emptying restaurant.

When the check arrived, Marissa ignored Hogan's attempts to pay. He tried to hide his relief; his bank account couldn't handle it, but he'd offered anyway.

"I appreciate the gentlemanly gallantry, but I wanted to return the favor after you got lunch," she insisted, signing away.

"About that. I was kind of surprised when you asked me for dinner."

"Why?" She gave him an intrigued half smile.

"Well, I was hardly the best lunch companion when we met up. I was quiet, and, I don't know, I suppose I came across a bit dull."

Marissa shook her head. "I remember a handsome English gentleman, interested in what I had to say, and despite what you may think, I found you charming. It made a refreshing change from boorish rich men boasting about wealth, privilege, or yachts. For once, it was nice to spend time with someone normal, doing a real job that matters. No offense."

"None taken." Hogan grinned.

"I wondered what dinner would be like, if, how do I say this, you were more relaxed? After we got coffee together, I decided why not and asked. I'm glad I did."

"Me too, although this river of alcohol helped tonight."

Marissa laughed. "That applies to both of us, then."

As the driver pulled up, Hogan cast a disbelieving glance at the beautiful, vivacious woman on his arm, who shared his sense of humor. The evening had exceeded his expectations. As the drive back began and emboldened by the final glass of sake still coursing through his veins, he tried to sound casual when he next spoke.

"Do you, erm...do you fancy getting together again?" he offered, his heart drumming a little faster as the seconds ticked down while he waited for a reply.

"I'd like that a lot," Marissa replied as her sleepy eyes met his. She rested her head on his shoulder with a soft sigh. They stayed that way until the car pulled up outside Hogan's apartment.

33

As he rode the office elevator, Hogan's nagging hangover began to ease. Marissa had responded immediately to his thank-you message that morning. He smiled at the thought.

Ranger handed him a much-welcome glass of water as he entered the main conference room. Vance had insisted they'd need the whiteboards inside there today.

"How's Gabriela? Not giving you too much headache with all the office time?" Hogan had met Ranger's fiancée a few times, and she could be fearsome but complemented his colleague's more laid-back personality.

"Man, she's finding further ways to spend money on the wedding. She knows I can't say shit as I'm not around that much. The longer this case goes, the more expensive it gets."

He forced a smile at Ranger's response—his canceled wedding plans a painful, buried memory. He was thankful when Vance rushed through the door.

"Sorry I'm a little late, I've been training. I wanted to get the hours in while I could."

"You got another fight coming up?" Ranger asked.

"Not 'til next month, but a girl's gotta take her workout time when she can."

A bright orange jacket hung on the edge of one chair.

"Where's Joseph?" Hogan inquired.

"Just wait," Ranger responded. A few moments later, Chung entered carrying a stacked tray of take-out boxes and eased it onto the table. A rich, sweet smell permeated the room.

"It's Korean food—all from my mum's restaurant. I know it's early, but I thought it would help kick-start the day."

"Works for me," Vance announced, snatching up some cutlery.

Once all were sated, Vance took up a position at the front of the room and after consulting a sheet from her open file, she began to stick tacks in a map of the West Coast and nearby locations. When she finished, she had five blue and three green tacks. They ranged from Seattle right down to San Bernardino. She turned back to face the group like a proud child beginning a class reading.

"Okay, guys. So Miller's team has finished chasing down all the sales and thefts of later-model black F-150s. We've ruled out people making the purchases, so we're left with the five thefts that haven't been junked or recovered. The locations they were boosted from are represented by the blue tacks." Vance spoke with her usual assurance. "Alson's team has done the same with Imperium sales, leaving three suspicious transactions." She pointed in turn at the three remaining locations tagged on the map.

"In what way are they suspicious?" Ranger asked.

"Well, if you give me a chance, I was *about* to get to that," Vance feigned annoyance. Her colleague raised both his palms.

"The purchase in Portland was completed in Bitcoin, leaving us with a fake name and IP. In Sacramento, an offshore Bermudian company executed a direct bank transfer. The dealership told Alson's agent it was unusual but not without precedent. Finally, a Bakersfield car salesman found nothing suspicious about an eighty-five grand cash sale. He was too busy counting his commission. In all three cases, no camera footage of buyers survived or was captured, and none have yet registered with the DLV." Vance finished the summary and grabbed a red marker with a dangling string. She tied the end around the pin stuck in Portland. In one swift motion she circled that city with a fixed radius. She did the same for Sacramento and Bakersfield.

"These are one-hundred-and-fifty-mile-radius circles from the Imperium sales locations. As you can see, they each also include a tack for the theft of a black F-150." Vance waved a finger at the red circles.

Hogan raised a hand.

"I'm going to play devil's advocate—what if he bought an Imperium in Portland and stole an F-150 in"—he searched the map for a location with a blue tack—"San Diego?"

"In a nutshell, we don't know he didn't. But we should assume the killer chose an accessible place for the theft. He would need to plan to change plates and drive a longer distance—increasing the risk of getting pulled over."

Vance had been as meticulous as ever.

"Nice work. I like where this is going. We need to get this narrowed down. The Imperium purchase is the best lead we've got. Miller's team will continue to work the F-150 angle, but it's almost exhausted. Let them continue chasing shadows," Hogan replied, turning to Chung.

"Can your team chase down the money transfer and Bitcoin? For now, we'll park the cash sale; it's too clumsy."

"Did the dealer selling the car for cash describe the guy—they must have seen him, right?" Ranger interjected.

Vance shook her head. "I asked the same. A woman paid—which apparently added legitimacy. I don't like this location for the Imperium, anyway."

"Which do you like?" Hogan asked.

"Sacramento. Its radius includes favorable locations for Carmel and LA. The corresponding F-150 could have been stolen from Stockton. The others don't fit as well."

"Then start there and ask local PD to trawl through ALPR data for the original and stolen plates. Ranger can go through information regarding the Stockton theft. The further we can narrow it down, the smaller the haystack for the needle of a suspect becomes."

Hogan rose and walked across to the whiteboard where potential motives were outlined. A number had already been crossed out, including family members, AFAO, and previous threats. A few remained. He turned back to Chung.

"Did you get any further on the stock shorts, and who profited on those transactions?"

Chung opened a file in front of him.

"The largest beneficiary in Belize has so far proved impenetrable. We're trying to trace who registered the company there. It's usually a law firm, but we'll still be several layers removed from the real owners. It's why they do this. Better news elsewhere, though. Two other companies benefited significantly. One was Mark Fullerton's hedge fund, and the other was the trading arm of the Fairfax Group. The positions had been in place for a few months. I spoke to the Securities and Exchange Commission, but they passed up investigating further."

Hogan reached for the file. Both companies traded millions of shares each year. Either could be involved in the killings. The Belize activity remained the most suspicious. He finished checking dates and turned back to the analyst.

"Thanks, Joseph. Keep pushing on Belize, and ask your team to monitor eye-catching short positions. If this theory has substance, it might provide a heads-up on the next target."

Chung bobbed his head in agreement.

"And we'll be the ones to stop the killer," Vance declared, reaching for a box of cold Korean food.

34

AFTER SIX CONSECUTIVE evenings, Kirov had grown tired of watching the apartment block opposite his hotel. He'd played the cycling-mad tourist since he checked in last Thursday. He left in biking gear each morning and returned mid-afternoon. A helmet and visor completed the fiction. It didn't help that East 61st Street was as dull as his adopted persona.

Of specific interest to Kirov was when the young lady in apartment 1209 would receive a particular visitor. A walking Chanel advert, Eliza Meyer had no job, a shopping habit to rival a dictator's wife, and lived in an eight-million-dollar home. With a figure that stopped traffic and looks that had bewitched Mark Fullerton, she was the key to eliminating him.

Kirov's phone vibrated, and he tapped the Signal icon for the unread message from Silver:

Are you any closer to completion? It's conducive that we remain within a specific timeline.

He tapped away:

I'm optimistic an opportunity will present itself in the coming days.

The reply came almost immediately:

Good, the next job will require all your ingenuity and take longer to complete.

Kirov allowed himself a small smile:

For what you will be paying me, I'd expect nothing less.

Kirov closed the app and imagined Silver doing the same. He'd been unable to identify the person or agency behind the messages. He only worked on a referral basis. After completing an assignment, he shared an anonymous encrypted email address. Each time this was different and allowed Kirov to identify the sender. He'd undertake comprehensive due diligence to ensure it wasn't a setup. His previous employers knew the consequences of selling him out. None of them ever had. This time, he'd waited six months, including extensive surveillance on the referee. The delay almost cost him the job, but people were prepared to wait for the best. Satisfied, he'd opened communication with Silver, who'd since proven discreet in all interactions. His paymaster's identity remained one of intrigue.

So far, it smacked of government or a well-resourced individual. Shit, he wouldn't rule out the Agency, especially as they might not know whom they were hiring, even if they were familiar with his work. They had trained him, after all.

Lukas held his hand out. It remained steady. After a grueling six months of training by the man in the fedora—or "Frank," as he'd become known to the program recruits—he was finally out on his first assignment. It was his seventeenth birthday. Lukas knew little about the target zigzagging down the cobbled back street in Vilnius. It wasn't his place to ask questions. He knew the man was a Russian who took monthly trips to see a notorious general in Kaliningrad, and that was enough. Taking the sharp blade from his pocket, he surveyed the street and ascertained they were alone. The Russian was unaware of the shadow of death approaching his rear. Adrenaline coursed through Lukas, lifting the winter chill from his body. He called out the last words the man ahead would ever hear, "Izvineeti, pazhalusta." Turning his bulky body to see who was asking to be excused, the target didn't get the chance to utter a sound because a blade stabbed into his throat. The shock on the Russian's face was frozen like the ground he crumpled onto. Despite warnings about his first kill, Lukas was surprised to feel nothing.

An SUV approaching the apartment block snapped Kirov forward three decades, but a cursory glance revealed it wasn't Fullerton's. He sighed, surveyed the array of operational items assembled across the bed, and did another silent checklist. A usable card key for the garage and elevator to the apartment had been an essential part of the planning. Eliza Meyer often enjoyed Frappuccino at the same establishment. Kirov followed her on one occasion and took a seat behind her. He scanned her apartment access card, sending the data to a cloning machine in his backpack. These radio-frequency identification tags interacted with readers throughout Meyer's building. Once Kirov added it onto his card, they would recognize this digital key as belonging to a resident. It was more straightforward than most people thought to copy and clone RFID tags. For a man of Kirov's talents, it had been a breeze.

Next had been sorting the right vehicle. Two residents drove black Land Rovers, so he'd acquired one six days ago. It was sitting in a rented garage space two blocks away with identical plates to one belonging to Mr. Oscar Hamilton III. He'd drive up and tap the card for entry—assuming the concierge didn't open the garage when the vehicle first appeared on camera. Upon accessing the premises, the next stage of the plan kicked in. A branded pizza box, jacket, and cycling helmet lay on the bed. Next to these, lay his SIG Sauer P226 with a suppressor and the midnight-blue book, open at chapter thirty-three. Kirov flipped his wrist to view the time on his Panerai Luminor; he doubted he'd work tonight. He'd remain invisible, as he had in the encounter with the FBI agent. He recalled the patience of the Count of Monte Cristo. This wait was nothing. Soon, Fullerton would visit his mistress for the final time.

35

WHILE HE WAITED alone for Jeff Bailey, the SAC of counterintelligence, Hogan flicked through playing cards again. People who stared into space on a plane or train freaked Hogan out. His mind craved action. The more you tested your brain, the stronger it got. Witnessing the terrible effects of his father's dementia made him determined to avoid the same fate. Fellow agents raised eyebrows when he memorized crime scenes and evidence lists, but the exhilaration of pushing your mental capacity was addictive.

Elephant footsteps announced Bailey's imminent arrival. Although his stomach was turning to fat, he retained that old lineman build from his college football days, which he often revisited. This earned him the nickname "Touchdown" around the office. His face was forgettable, but the earlobes attached were long, like stretched pieces of Silly Putty. Bailey flopped into a chair.

"I believe I owe you an update," he announced. Hogan had been pursuing a counterintelligence debrief for days now. For a man his size, Bailey had proved elusive. "So, we've been rustlin' some feathers and makin' some plays," he continued, never one to shy away from a clichéd or, indeed, football-based idiom. "The guys at each embassy say the same thing—this has nothing to do with them." Hogan's eyes began to drift to the man's ears. "Of course, we haven't taken them at face value. My team has been busy.

"We trawled through all diplomatic arrivals into the US from the limited number of nations who could've pulled this off but drew a blank. We examined all the data points we had on existing agents known to be on US soil—to exclude them. Also, bupkis!" Bailey raised his open palms.

"And if the killer entered on a normal passport and was previously unknown to us?"

The SAC nodded as he replied. "We're looking at this. The UK tracked the attempted murders in Salisbury, England, to Russian agents traveling on tourist visas. The profile of height and suspected age range helps, but that still leaves us reams of data to get through."

"Do you think the Russians could be a possibility?"

"The smart money would be something different entirely. A malign foreign power—even them—would be crazy to pull this."

"Even with the significant economic instability this has led to?"

"Even with that. The risk-reward ain't there."

"How about one of our allies?"

"That would make zero sense."

"Maybe not. How about Pakistan, India, or even the Saudis? You remember how many of the 9/11 terrorists came from there."

"Of course I do, but the government didn't control them," Bailey snapped. "If they had covert agents here, we'd know. The same goes for other countries. I'd keep speculation like that to yourself."

Hogan raised one hand. "Okay, okay."

"Are we done?" Bailey didn't wait for a reply and marched from the room.

Nemo had been a massive 49ers fan since childhood, so he'd twisted Hogan's arm to meet for Monday-night football in Busby's on Santa Monica Boulevard. The walnut walls had lost their battle against TV installation. The lingering smell of stale beer seeped up from the stained floor as he eased through the babbling crowd of college frat boys. He found Nemo draining a glass in a corner booth. His friend caught a waitress's eye and raised two fingers. The standard bear hug ensued—an action guaranteed to lift his spirits.

"I'm telling you, if we lose to this shower of shit today, I'm gonna spew," Nemo announced. The Rams were having a poor season, and the 49ers were expected to win at Levi's Stadium. In the background, Booger McFarland made an animated point as the game buildup continued. The waitress reappeared with the beers almost immediately, and Nemo grinned after she left.

"I tip very well. You gotta on game night, as it gets crazy in here. How's your old man?"

"Not so bad on my last visit. I try to keep his mind active when I see him. He's comfortable at Paradiso."

"Still asking about your brother?"

"Yup. Sometimes I want to tell Dad what he did to him and the business when he stole the money." Hogan sighed. "But he'd lack comprehension. Plus, his emotions have been stripped away these days."

"Scott still in the UK?"

"Yup. Last I heard, he was in London, but I stopped caring long ago. What he did is on him, and he's the one who'll have to live with it."

"I hear you." Nemo raised his glass and shouted, "Let's fucking go!" as the game started.

After Nemo finished celebrating an easy 49ers victory, Hogan brought him up to date with the case. He trusted him—plus his friend was no stranger to national security clearances. This led to an idea.

"You think anyone within our government could be behind all this?" he asked, lowering his head closer to Nemo.

"Shit, dude, I hadn't even thought about that. It's hard to imagine, though." He became serious as he grasped what else Hogan was alluding to. "Listen, I ain't seen anything from our data access that indicates state involvement, and I shouldn't even confirm that. Something like this would have to involve the top echelons of the security services, and they'd avoid any exposure to third parties."

"That's what I figured, too."

The sober look left Nemo's face as he changed the subject.

"So what's the latest with this chick, Marissa?"

"I'm not sure. She's cool, stunning, and entirely out of my league—"

"I dunno. You still have those looks so popular with the ladies at college."

"Mate, she's a billionaire's daughter and not just any billionaire."

"But you're seeing her again, right?"

"For sure. Friday night went very well. I want to see where it goes. I know this is weird coming from me, especially after one proper date."

"Seems fine. I think you deserve a bit of luck right now, dude, and a beautiful billionaire heiress sounds like that!" Nemo burst out laughing, and Hogan joined in—his friend did have a point.

36

KIROV'S LONGEST WAIT to eliminate someone was over. He'd needed to be patient and adaptable—something Cardinal Richelieu had always instilled into his agents.

Fifteen minutes before, Mark Fullerton had pulled up outside the grandiose building on East 61st Street. Two hard-faced men shadowed him through the baroque-style entrance. The driver remained stood by the armored Bentley Bentayga. There had been minimal fuss. Fullerton was keen to avoid drawing attention to his visit to his mistress. The resulting stripped-back team would play right into Kirov's hands. Security protocol meant the first close protection operative would wait by the lobby elevators and the second outside Eliza Meyer's apartment.

Kirov drove the Land Rover out of the parking garage and continued the two blocks to the building that by now featured in his dreams. The pizza box and cycle helmet sat on the passenger seat. The SIG Sauer P226 nestled in the zip pocket of his branded fleece jacket. Matching trousers replete with cycling clips completed the outfit. When he drove down the sharp ramp to the underground garage, he slowed to pull level with the entrance scanner and began to reach for the cloned card. The tinted windows protected him from the camera above the solid white slatted door, which had now started to rise. As he suspected, the concierge had recognized the vehicle and license plate and saved Kirov any effort. *I suppose this is what tens of thousands in annual service fees get you.* Once inside, he parked in the closest space to the anonymous white elevator door, stuck the cycle helmet on, and pulled the modified dark visor down. There were cameras, but the main desk's concierge only had the front door and garage entrance video feeds. Once in the elevator, he tapped the card on the oval sensor and hit seventeen. The button glowed red in acquiescence.

As he lifted the helmet's visor and unzipped his jacket pocket, Kirov checked the SIG Sauer and visualized his plan upon leaving the elevator. He'd prepared for the most likely scenarios. The guard on the door was a professional—he could even be exceptional. It didn't matter; Kirov was always better.

Upon reaching the seventeenth floor, Kirov didn't exit but held the doors. He waited for thirty seconds, then pushed the button marked sixteen. After a tiny drop, the doors slid open again, and with the posture of a weary delivery guy, he stepped into the hall, turning toward Eliza Meyer's apartment. The close protection operative stared in his direction, the elevator ping having announced Kirov's arrival. He edged down the corridor, pizza box in both hands. Four doors down, the barrel-chested man reached for the spiral cord dangling from his earpiece. He never got the chance to speak.

Kirov let go of the pizza box and human nature did the rest. The bodyguard's eyes flicked down as it hit the floor, and Kirov pulled out the SIG and shot him between the eyes. The guard's fingers were wrapped around his half-drawn weapon, but those last split seconds of his life had counted most, and he'd fallen short. Kirov strode to the body, removed the card key from the tailored suit pocket, and hovered it over the entrance pad until the door clicked. Once inside, the noises from the bedroom became more audible as he approached. When he entered, Meyer was grinding Fullerton on a gold-silk-sheet-covered bed like a live *Basic Instinct* audition. Kirov shot her twice in her beautiful back and continued to her panicked partner. Fear contorted his face as Eliza's body slumped to the side. He put another bullet in her head— you could never be too careful. This was unavoidable collateral damage.

"B-b-b-billion! I'll give you a billion…" Fullerton began in a shaky voice, his terrified eyes meeting those of the assassin, who responded with a double tap to the billionaire's temple.

He paused to snap a photo on his phone, then left the room.

In the lobby, the second close protection officer, Malev had observed the CCTV of the black Land Rover's arrival with professional curiosity.

"That's Mr. Hamilton's," the concierge offered as he lifted the gate.

Malev waited until the vehicle entered, then focused on the two elevators. A minute later, the bold LED numbers above one of these started climbing upward.

"What floor does he live on?" Malev inquired in a low growl.

"Oh, Mr. Hamilton, that would be the seventeenth."

The numbers climbed to seventeen and stopped. Malev waited, then, satisfied it had completed its journey, turned back to the front entrance. An elderly gentleman was cackling at a comment from the doorman.

"Good to see you, Mr. Horowitz," the concierge chimed as the tip-tap of the support stick edged closer to the desk.

Malev relaxed on the recognition and half listened as Mr. Horowitz related a family drama to the fawning employee.

When the long, banal tale ended, the old man tapped his way to the elevators. Malev reached to press the call button, glancing up when he did. The left elevator slid open, the other now in the basement.

"That's funny." Malev spun to see the concierge staring at the screen. "Mr. Hamilton is heading back out already."

Malev clicked the switch on the cord of his earpiece. "Basha, all good up there? Basha...?"

Nothing.

Fuck! He ran into the elevator and pounded sixteen, but as the elevator climbed upward, he knew it would be too late.

37

THE DAY HAD been going so well. They'd eliminated two unusual Imperium purchases. This left the vehicle acquired via the Bermudian shell company.

They had a solid lead at last.

Hogan had also arranged to see Marissa that Saturday, and when Jared Miller walked by earlier, his suit glowed with a luminous green stain. Someone was owed a beer. Then, at seven p.m. everything turned to shit.

Carla hurtled out of her office, tipped her head at Hogan, and without another word, stormed back inside. He sprinted over, closing the door behind him.

"Mark Fullerton is dead, along with one of his bodyguards and an unidentified female."

Hogan sat in stunned silence. He'd later recall that shameful schadenfreude flashed across his brain. Carla continued to let loose.

"Fuck, fuck, *fuck*! What a mess. I don't even know where to begin with Director Sullivan." She kneaded her temples. "And the press will crucify us." She fell silent for a moment, then regained her composure.

"You'd better get out to New York—take Vance with you too."

Hogan found himself back in the Big Apple for the second time in under a week. The red-eye flight had got them into LaGuardia at eight a.m. He'd managed to grab only an hour of sleep; Vance had slept like a baby the entire flight.

Until they pulled up in front of a majestic granite apartment block, Hogan assumed he'd be prepared for the press assembled outside the building.

He wasn't.

TV trucks lined the street, and countless reporters jostled behind uneven NYPD barriers opposite the entrance. Most shouted his name or questions as they passed.

In the lobby, an unsmiling gentleman with a salt-and-pepper beard and sporting a well-worn suit greeted them. His resigned look suggested his title before he even spoke.

"Detective Carlotti, Homicide—I'm the lucky guy who caught this in the pool," he replied, shuffling away. "There's a coupla your guys upstairs already. I'll take ya there."

As they rode the elevator up to the sixteenth floor, Hogan took the time to think. The killer would have taken part of this journey yet had evaded detection. How did he do this?

"CSI and your Evidence Response Team guys have just finished up," Carlotti said. "Fullerton's bodyguard"—he flicked pages in a note-book—"Basha Hasani was shot once in the head here." A bony finger pointed to a dried crimson stain on the cream carpet outside the open door of an apartment. "He had his weapon in his hand, but it hadn't been fired; we believe he mistook the killer for a pizza delivery guy."

They moved into a hallway lined with black-and-white photos of a woman in various tasteful poses. Each captured her undoubted beauty. A figure stepped out from the room ahead.

"Special Agent Shah, good to meet you both," announced a well-groomed man in his mid-thirties with a broad smile and intelligent eyes. Oaky cologne wafted into Hogan's nostrils as they entered the bedroom. Shah and Carlotti ran through the crime scene and where the bodies were discovered. Hogan tried to imagine the sequence of events as he stared at the bloodstained silk sheets. They appeared to have been "in flagrante delicto" when the killer struck. How would Fullerton's wife feel when the whole sullied story came out? The female had been shot three times, including twice in the back, and Fullerton likely executed immediately afterward. The provisional timeline before "Mr. Hamilton's" supposed Land Rover left the garage pointed to ruthless efficiency. Shah explained that only the elevator vestibule camera captured footage of the suspect, who was around six feet tall. He wore a cycle helmet with the visor down and was dressed in full pizza delivery garb. It all reinforced what they already knew: the killer was thorough, and this job, like the others, took meticulous planning. Hogan was sure crime scene evidence suggesting the perpetrator's identity would be non-existent. How he'd approached the execution and the preparation it entailed would be more valuable information. As a result, he decided against forming a memory palace.

He left Vance and Shah talking through finer ballistic points and walked to the plush living room. Edging past a sofa buried under an avalanche of shocking pink cushions to the window, he surveyed the busy street below. The married Fullerton would have arbitrarily grabbed time with his mistress. So the killer either followed him from his previous location or was surveilling this property, waiting to strike. From a planning perspective, the latter made way more sense. He squinted at the two sizeable buildings opposite. One appeared to be a similar-looking block to this one. The other featured rows of identical-looking rooms running down to the corner of Park Avenue. He called Carlotti over.

"That a hotel?" He gestured straight ahead.

"Uh-huh, Loews Regency."

"Thanks." He didn't want to waste any more time here. He hurried back to the bedroom. "Vance, we're leaving."

38

THE LOEWS REGENCY lobby buzzed with activity. Velvet sofas housed businessmen, tourists, and a huddle of Japanese girls perfecting selfies. Art deco features defined the entire space, and crystal chandeliers floated from the roof. Hogan and Vance marched across the marble floor to the reception.

They'd established the hotel had 378 rooms on their short drive over. They had to divert a few blocks to shake off any following press. Hogan wasn't sure how many of these faced onto East 61st Street, but the manager—"*Susan, how can I help you today?*"—promised a swift answer as they entered her office.

"Two hundred and twenty-four." The sleek black ponytail flicked from one shoulder to another as Susan announced this and turned from the computer to face them. They began an elaborate game of room *Guess Who?* Hogan removed many possibilities with his single male occupant parameter and, along with Vance, worked through further questions: only staying one night...over sixty years old...was the booking via a business they'd heard of...?

"Does he have a mustache?" Vance offered, and they both laughed. Susan didn't get the joke.

Once they'd exhausted the exclusions, nine potential rooms and guests remained. The killer would be long gone, but if Hogan's hunch was correct, he would have occupied one of these rooms, leaving something for the ERT to work with. They made straight for the elevators.

Starting on the second floor, Susan knocked on the dark mahogany door while calling, "Housekeeping," in the lilting voice every traveler had awoken to at some point. After enough time without response, they entered a stylish room featuring calming blossom tree photographs. Light streamed in from the window to which Hogan walked, checking the line of sight to the building opposite. Beneath it, a silver Rimowa suitcase lay open, clothes escaping from one half. On the nightstand sat a finger-smudged glass alongside two empty vodka miniatures. Vance shook her head and he concurred. The room was a treasure trove of evidence and still occupied—it wasn't their guy.

The next two rooms were similar, so not viable candidates. A man in a robe opened the next door, pointing to the "Do Not Disturb" sign as they proffered an apology. The next was empty and immaculate, as if ready for a new arrival. Hogan turned to Susan.

"Is someone still meant to be staying here?"

The manager tapped away on the tablet she held.

"Dumas Enterprises booked the room for a Mr. Richelieu." Hogan raised an eyebrow as Susan tapped away. "It was reserved for two weeks from…let me see…last Wednesday. All paid in advance from a corporate card—the guest checked in via our app."

Someone had stayed here—a chair faced the window, and faint impression marks remained on one corner of the bed.

"This is the room," Hogan announced. "Vance—can you request the ERT and wait for their arrival?" She pulled out her phone and stepped out of earshot. He turned to Susan again. "We'll need to seal off this room. Where do you keep this floor's camera feeds?"

"Down in security," she replied, having bought into the intrigue.

"Then that's where you and I are heading next."

It took under an hour to discover the first pieces of footage of the person suspected of staying in room 709. The guest had walked through the lobby at 8:01 p.m. the previous evening wearing full cycling gear. A helmet and visor obscured his face, and he carried a large messenger bag. This had to be the same figure captured on the garage camera in the building opposite. The same tactics had been employed to limit any chance of facial recognition. The height and confident, loose walk appeared to match the suspect from Malibu, but it wasn't a leap he could make yet. CJIS over in Clarksburg would help establish this for definite. He uploaded the last eight days of files from the lobby and seventh floor to the cloud. Then sent a quick message to Madeleine Peace, asking her to liaise with the Gait Recognition Team. They'd met on his trip to West Virginia, and she'd be pleased to help. After she confirmed receipt of the files, he asked her to alert the FACE Services Unit. His expectations were low but no harm in letting them pore over the footage. Hogan wanted to confirm one last thing.

"Where's the parking garage entrance?"

"Follow me. You can take the service elevator," Susan responded.

"Perfect. Thanks for all your help. We'll be out of your hair soon, I promise."

"My pleasure, Special Agent. My kids will be interested in my day for the first time."

They confirmed the Land Rover disguised as that belonging to Mr. Oscar Hamilton III had not parked at the Loews Regency the previous evening. Yet still, it must have been located nearby. Hogan called Special Agent Shah, asking him to pull agents together to figure out where. They agreed to work within an eight-block radius. Any farther, and the killer couldn't have made it to the vehicle and back to enter the apartment block garage in the time window. Shah promised to call the minute he had anything.

Hogan spent the journey down to Federal Plaza in Tribeca bringing Carla up to speed with the developments and preparing for the joint press conference the NYPD had called. When he arrived at the FBI's New York HQ, he located Vance and asked her to find some decent food—something she excelled at. She returned shortly afterward carrying two subs, each the size of a newborn child.

"Pastrami or meatball?" she asked, shaking each hand. The smell of rich marinara sauce filled the room, so he pointed to the left baby. They ate in silence—the supersized delis of Manhattan were no match for Vance's voracious appetite.

"So CJIS is sure it's him, the guy from the Malibu Lagoon parking lot?" she asked, folding the empty wrapping and searching for a trash can.

Madeleine Peace had pulled out all the stops and sent through email confirmation as Hogan had walked into the building.

"It's him, alright. The press is going to lose their shit when they find out."

"What time's the conference?"

"Seven p.m."

"It's going to get even crazier for us, right?"

"It is. We need to find a way to stop this guy." Hogan paused to wipe away sauce from his chin. "Because something tells me he isn't done yet."

39

FROM A RAISED platform, Hogan surveyed the rows of journalists. They contained faces from all the major twenty-four-hour news channels. The tardy fought for a position crammed against the back wall. Hogan dabbed the sweat from his brow, the air too stuffy. Conversations calmed to a hush as the police commissioner stepped onto the platform. He raised his hand, waited for the photography flashes to subside, then began speaking.

"Welcome, everyone." He had a booming voice to match his imposing figure. "I'll speak first, followed by Assistant Director in Charge Thomas Lewis. At 8:29 p.m. last night, officers attended a scene at an East 61st Street apartment. There they discovered multiple fatalities, all the result of gunshot wounds. The victims have been confirmed as Basha Hasani, Eliza Meyer, and Mark Fullerton; all were Manhattan residents."

On this announcement, murmurs and gasps rang out across the room. Given the scandal, Hogan was surprised they'd announced Meyer's name. Mind you, New York high society would love it. Commissioner Jowell waited for a moment and continued.

"On behalf of the NYPD, I would like to pass on our condolences to the families of the deceased. Early indications are all three were killed by the same individual." Jowell turned to his left. "Now I know after recent events in California, there will be significant speculation on links to this crime and those already under investigation by the FBI's Los Angeles office. So, with that in mind, I'd like to pass over to ADIC Lewis." Jowell took two steps back from the jutting array of microphones to allow a gangly gentleman with a pointed chin to step forward. Lewis took a deep breath to compose himself, eased his round glasses up the bridge of his nose, and began to speak to the rapt audience.

"Thank you, Commissioner. We will compare surveillance footage of the suspected perpetrator of this crime to that of an individual sought for the murder of Jay Chopra on October twenty-eight. Our CJIS Division in Clarksburg will establish any matching attributes. If these deaths are connected, the task force in Los Angeles will update accordingly." Lewis looked over at Hogan, who offered a polite nod. They'd agreed to keep the identity development to themselves for now. Earlier, Director Sullivan had also confirmed the current investigation structure would continue. He'd known at this juncture a change of personnel wouldn't play well in the media, despite the perceived failure to apprehend the suspect before Fullerton's death. It was smart, but the pressure gauge would hit maximum.

Lewis called for witnesses who'd stayed at the Loews Regency between the twenty-third and thirtieth of November to get in touch. He finished his summary with a description and the license plate of the black Land Rover.

Jowell returned and opened the floor to questions. He ignored the unfettered shouting until journalists understood he'd pick from those with raised hands. The first one selected was a woman from the *New York Post* with a forehead that didn't move but a quickfire mouth.

"Can you tell us more about the relationship between Mark Fullerton and Eliza Meyer?"

So much for the important questions.

"I'm afraid we can't comment on that." Jowell spat his response, his disdain at the question clear. He pointed to a well-known face from CNN.

"Is the FBI task force any closer to identifying the individual, and if not, how can we have any confidence they'll be able to stop him from striking again?"

Jowell chose to direct this question elsewhere and invited Hogan forward, who began with a diplomatic reply.

"We're making daily progress in establishing data points that will significantly narrow the search for the suspect. We remain confident we will apprehend the perpetrator. This is the first time he has struck since coming to our attention, and as a result, we have several new leads to follow. In the interim, we continue to liaise with potential targets to ensure they minimize risk to their well-being." Hogan kept his voice level as one or two journalists' heads tilted on hearing his accent.

"The S&P 500 Index of shares is down two hundred points today alone. Are you worried about the economic effects these murders are having and could this be a motive for the attacks?" A pinstripe-suited gent asked before Hogan could retreat from the firing line. But he enjoyed thinking on his feet, so he answered once again.

"We're more concerned about how these terrible killings have devastated the families of those involved. Regarding motive, we're exploring multiple theories on why these individuals were killed. Of course, given their standing in the business community and economic influence, we can't rule out a financial angle to these nefarious acts." Hogan kept his dialogue crisp and noticed a few nods of agreement. He fielded a couple more questions before one on Bureau jurisdiction brought Lewis back in his stead. The conference dragged on a little longer before he escaped the stifling room. Vance joined him by the exit.

"Nicely done up there. You'll be getting your own talk show next. After all, the viewers love an English accent," she proclaimed, punching him on the arm.

"Cheers, but I'm not sure I'd be diplomatic enough. I'll settle for solving this case," he responded, stepping into the bracing New York winter air. It complemented his cold, hard determination to bring the killer to justice.

40

RETURNING FROM NEW York, Hogan wanted nothing more than to rest—but stirred early, ruminating on the case. He rose and started working on the heavy punching bag, changing angles and striking accurate raking shots. He enjoyed the discipline and fitness of training, but he missed fighting. Boxing had been a key part of his college life and beyond, but after he met Katie, he'd fought less. She'd argued it wasn't fair to worry about the dangers in the ring and at work. In the end, Hogan should have worried more about her. Considering any return felt like a betrayal. This wasn't logical, but grief skewed all rational thinking.

After he'd returned from the rehabilitation retreat and begun tackling his grief, Vance had suggested he start his day with a freezing shower. She'd insisted it energized the mind and reduced stress. The idea was named after some Dutch dude. The routine had stuck. As the water pounded his back, he ran through his case updates for Director Sullivan later that day.

The most significant was Chung's discovery that a Land Rover sold in Brooklyn was to some Bermudian company that bought the Imperium in Sacramento. They could prove the same person had ended the lives of Chopra, Decker, and Fullerton. The killer was anything but sloppy, so he must not care they'd make this connection. It suggested supreme confidence in his ability to avoid capture, which was troubling. Or perhaps he wanted to ensure credit for the killings?

Secondly, the ERT team assigned to the Loews Regency room had reported back. The killer had stayed there almost a week. They'd run all the usable prints through the Next Generation Identification program but received no matches. They did add a slew of new DNA profiles for comparison but, unfortunately, only got two hits from CODIS that led nowhere. The killer was unfazed that they had likely obtained his DNA. He knew he wasn't in CODIS. Most of the room had been wiped down, suggesting concern about prints. This offered a glimmer of hope for the future.

The third update was the lamest—the task force had ruled out a political angle. Fullerton had been a prominent Republican, so the killings were about something else. He also had zero interest in sunset philanthropy, unlike those killed previously. His entire estate was set to be divided between his two sons; his widow must be apoplectic. Fullerton was so different from the previous victims: much older, less benevolent, and part of the New York establishment. From what Hogan had learned, Chopra and Decker hadn't been friends with the brash hedge fund boss and, if anything, shared a mutual dislike. He reached for a towel. He hoped all this would be enough to placate Sullivan.

Hogan tapped Carla's open office door and held up coffee and bagels. She grunted a thank-you and grabbed the cup with "Logan" scrawled in marker down one side.

"Sullivan is expected here at eleven. So, talk a good game like you did at the New York press conference." Carla hated preamble. "He's been pretty pissed the times we have spoken this week, so you can imagine how excited I am." However, she enjoyed sarcasm. "I'll let you know when to join us."

Hogan's early morning confidence in his updates began to ebb away. He might need to embellish them. He hoped Alson or Miller would offer some supportive progress.

Bang on eleven, Director Harvey Sullivan marched from the elevator lobby across a hushed floor to Carla's corner office. He famously made a point of being as punctual as a Tokyo train driver, and reamed out agents who weren't. Sullivan always wore a crisp white shirt, this time with a bottle-green suit and muted tie. Around average height and size, his aura made him seem taller and broader. As the office door closed, a susurration of intrigue began between cubicles.

At midday, Karyn Alson appeared at Hogan's desk, and they fell into an easy conversation. Miller lurked outside Carla's office, from which she stepped grim-faced and beckoned them all in. Sullivan's thick-set features remained unmoved, but his body language suggested a fraught last hour. They settled into chairs positioned to make the angles work for everyone. Tension hung in the air as Carla introduced them. On Miller's intro, the director's nod was a little too familiar.

"Can you each brief Director Sullivan on the positive threads of the investigation," Carla continued, all business now.

Alson explained Decker's Imperium had been compromised at his company's Mountain View HQ. The cameras tracked a vehicle with cloned plates entering the underground garage. Unfortunately, no footage covering the period the vehicle was interfered with existed. It left them with more questions than answers.

Miller spoke next. His version contained considerable embellishments on his team's achievements right down to discovering the security camera footage at the Malibu Lagoon State Beach parking lot. Hogan's face reddened as Miller took credit for most of his work on the Chopra investigation. He took a moment to compose himself before running through the update he'd rehearsed that morning.

Sullivan remained silent throughout, drinking in the information. Once the briefing had finished, he shifted in his seat and cleared his throat.

"There's some good progress here, Agents, but we need work so brilliant the superlatives haven't been invented yet." His tone foreboding, he continued, "Three of this country's most powerful people have been snatched away in their prime. Others remain virtual prisoners afraid to attend public engagements or meetings. The economy and stock market are hurting, and you'd better believe the president is passing that hurt on to me. We must bring this killer to justice before he strikes again. I'm assured you have all the necessary resources, but if not, I'll make it happen. The reputation of the Bureau is on the line here, so don't let me down."

They all responded with hums of affirmation as the director rose, nodded once at Carla, and marched out the door.

Karyn Alson let out an audible sigh as Hogan turned to his right, furious.

"What the fuck, Jared?"

Miller sneered, "What?" As he scuttled backward from the room. Alson also hurried from the suffocating atmosphere.

"I get it, he's a devious shit," Carla began, closing the door, "but I spent ten minutes arguing with Sullivan why Miller shouldn't take your investigative role, so park this fight."

Shell-shocked, Hogan processed this comment.

"Why would he want that? I mean, why him instead of me, what did I do wrong?"

"Nothing. Look, Miller's golden boy status hasn't gone unnoticed. Sullivan also mentioned your botched cases after"—Carla paused, her features taking on a rare softer look—"after Katie's death. He'd done his homework. I explained the exceptional circumstances and that it was all behind you."

This, at least, Hogan understood. That first year after her death remained hazy.

"I referred back to the whole host of achievements you racked up previously and your stellar work in leading the task force to this point," Carla said. "So he demurred, for now."

"Thanks for going to bat for me," he replied, with feeling.

Carla offered a wry smile in return. "Of course, but don't let me down, okay? Now get the fuck out of here!"

41

ABANDONING HIS USUAL Saturday routine, Hogan headed to the office first thing. After yesterday, he wanted to demonstrate his dedication to the case. The prospect of dinner with Marissa later lightened his mood on the drive in. They'd exchanged messages daily since their evening at Nobu. He'd picked a local spot called Gjelina on Abbot Kinney Boulevard. It offered flavorsome quality food that wouldn't hurt his wallet.

Hogan returned to DNA profile updates recovered from the suspect's room at the Loews Regency. Two had been flagged by CODIS. One, an ex-lawyer previously convicted of money laundering, the other a high-class call girl. He remained sure one remaining unidentified profile belonged to the killer. They were comparing these DNA samples with those from Decker's Imperium wreckage. Most doubted they'd get a match.

Fullerton's death confirmed one more thing: the suspicious trading by his hedge fund after Chopra's and Decker's deaths was a coincidence—it made no sense otherwise. Hogan may have to reappraise his belief in them. The Fairfax Group trades still warranted a closer look, but they still had nothing on the Belize-based business that gleaned huge profits. Carla was considering sending an agent down to the Central American country if they had no alternative. Whoever went would need cash if they wanted a helpful welcome.

As the afternoon turned to evening, Hogan suggested his team take some time to unwind. The sighs of relief were audible. It had been an exhausting few days. Plus, he had an ulterior motive, although he hadn't yet told Vance or Ranger about his new love interest.

"Different Class" by Pulp provided the soundtrack for Hogan's drive home. It had been his brother's favorite album back when they were thick as thieves. Like most siblings, he looked up to his big brother, Scott, and copied his interests. Once, he'd even donned thick black glasses, pretending to be Jarvis Cocker, much to his mum's amusement. The opening guitar riff of "Disco 2000" echoed around his Jag as his phone lit up with a message from Marissa:

Slight change of plan. Will still be at your place around 7 but bringing Audrey along. I'm thinking take-out. Hope that is ok? Will explain when I see you. X

He sighed. This would temper his plans for a romantic evening. The night wouldn't end in the way he'd spent his morning drive imagining it could.

A purchase of yellow roses helped brighten up Hogan's apartment and made it look less sparse. And groceries now provided company to the lonely row of chilled Pacificos. The cheerful assistant at Lincoln Fine Wine had helped sort a quality bottle of white and child-friendly soft drinks. As he bobbed between rooms, the doorbell rang.

As he opened the door, Audrey thrust forward a bunch of daisies.

"These are for you—from our garden." She tipped her head, waiting for a reply.

"Thank you ever so much. They're lovely," Hogan responded, taking the flowers, and stepping back so they could enter. Audrey gave him a wide grin as she walked by. He leaned forward and dropped a kiss on Marissa's smooth cheek. She'd dressed in tight-fitting jeans again. He couldn't keep the grin off his face.

"Come look, Mom, it's a fish tank!"

Audrey stood with her hands and nose pressed up against its glass.

"*What's that?*" She asked, pointing to the seahorse. "Ooooh, you also have a starfish! Does it have a name?" She spun around with an expectant look.

"Actually, no," Hogan replied, in a voice tinged with sadness, "I never got around to naming it or the seahorse."

"I *love* them. Mom, can we get some?" Audrey looked up with full doll eyes.

"Maybe, sweetheart."

"Pleeeeease!"

"It's still a maybe, for now."

"The new aquarium in Santa Monica should have more, and I hear it is great," Hogan offered, gaining an appreciative look from Marissa.

"Really! Do they have jellyfish there?" Audrey cried. "I love them too."

"I'm sure they do, honey—perhaps Hogan could take us sometime?"

"Um, yeah...sure," he muttered and retreated to the kitchen to fix drinks.

He had begun pouring the wine when Marissa appeared in the doorway frowning.

"Hey! I mean...if you don't want to hang out with Audrey and me..." She tailed off.

Hogan started shaking his head. "No...no, it's not that—" He began. "I have a fear of water, long story, but the short version involves a swimming pool at a holiday park and a briefly unsupervised seven-year-old. Let's just say I got out of my depth, and by the time my dad noticed, I'd almost drowned. I've been petrified of the water ever since."

Marissa smiled, relieved.

"Sorry, I thought—"

"You weren't to know. I'm probably one of the few people keeping aquatic animals who hates the water," he interjected, smiling. "The fish

144

tank was an idea to help, but I'm not keen to go boating or be under millions of gallons of water yet. I'd love to do something else together another day, though." He finished sorting the drinks, handing one to Marissa.

She clinked his wineglass. "That sounds like a plan."

The connection they had shared at Nobu was still there. They only paused talking when the Thai takeout from Siamese Garden arrived. Audrey remained oblivious to their presence. She'd become engrossed by a teenage YouTuber on the tablet brought for that precise purpose.

"Hope it's okay Audrey came along." Marissa glanced over at her daughter. "She was acting out earlier today, and I didn't want to leave her. She's frustrated days out with Grandpapa have been curtailed while this ominous threat hangs over all of us. Sorry, that's not a dig—I know you're all doing everything you can." She touched Hogan's arm.

"It's fine. It has been fun meeting her again; she's a great kid," he responded as Marissa's face lit up again, and an idea came to him. "Anyone fancy ice cream?" Audrey's head snapped up, the two magical words cutting through the YouTuber's maniacal nonsense.

"I do!"

The looping line for Salt & Straw was standard for 9:30 p.m. on a Saturday night, but it advanced in no time. Audrey wolfed down her chocolate gooey brownie ice cream as Marissa nodded throughout.

"This is realllly good," she said. "It would be dangerous if I had this on my doorstep."

"Happy to be of service," Hogan replied, mock bowing as they finished up. A black Escalade pulled up to the curb alongside them as they walked outside.

Marissa glanced at the car, pulled a sad face, and helped the waving Audrey into the vehicle.

"I need to get her home; I already feel like a bad mom letting her stay up this late."

"I totally get it. Do this again soon?"

"You better believe it." She leaned forward, giving him a soft kiss before adding, "Very soon."

Hogan watched various cable news channels to distract him from the emptiness of his apartment. The first one covered the latest transgressions from Russia and criticized the tacit support from the Chinese and Saudi Arabian leaders. Oil and money always seemed to skew meaningful action. The next channel was rotating through speculation about the assassin dubbed "Richelieu." Someone from the Loew's Regency had leaked the room booking details, and now the killer had a name. One which the media had embraced with gusto. Copies of *The Three Musketeers* had been flying off the shelves. Reporters and online sleuths searched for connections to the story and sought comparisons with the scheming cardinal. They'd done the same at Wilshire but found nothing meaningful so far. After an hour, he'd had enough. He opened his laptop and read more about Fullerton. His only commonality with the other dead men was untold riches. If this was the connection and motivation for the killings, the task force was screwed. Anyone could be next. The doorbell interrupted his dejected musings. He eased open the door to a seductive grin from Marissa.

"I told you it would be very soon."

His imagination on the drive to work that morning didn't even get close.

42

CHALLENGES WITH THE "Richelieu" case, as everyone was now refer-
ring to it, and elsewhere in Hogan's life were stacking up. His Sunday
trip to Paradiso had presented issues. His dad had shuffled into the
main room wearing a baggy yellow Lakers jersey, procured via an unannounced late-night visit to one resident's room. Paradiso didn't want
to curtail his dad's freedom yet and promised to monitor the situation. A brief reminder of the remaining quarterly invoice balance didn't
help either. Hogan picked up the brown envelope on his desk and slid
it into his top drawer. Out of sight, out of mind—which was more
than he could say about Marissa. Not all the distractions this week were
unwelcome. As Saturday night received another mental replay, a flushed
Joseph Chung snapped him from his reverie.

"I think I've got something. It could be big!"

"Okay, not here. Get the guys together in conference room five."

Chung squirmed as all eyes shifted to him, but his excitement took over
almost immediately.

"So my team has followed the money to the bank that originally
funded the Bermudian business account used to buy the Imperium and
the Land Rover. It took a fair amount of pressure, but they ultimately
decided to assist us. Oh, and a well-timed call from a friend at the treasury also helped." Chung flashed a wicked smile.

"From there," he continued, "we traced the account funding that one
to a Russian bank called Archangel International. At this point, you can

imagine how helpful the Russians were, and we figured we'd hit another brick wall." He became more serious. "So we hacked them."

Ranger and Vance gasped—this was their kind of analyst.

Hogan gripped the table and nodded.

"Go on."

"The Archangel account funding came via a Bitcoin exchange. The total credit was for two hundred thousand dollars in two separate amounts of one hundred thousand each. We sifted through exchange transactions on the blockchain ledger for Bitcoin across previous weeks, eliminating similar larger ones using various criteria."

"Such as?"

"Location—there was significant traffic from South Korea and China and IP addresses of major institutions. Bear in mind the person funding the account could never have suspected we'd get the information to track this back to the ledger and this exchange." With Chung in full flow, Hogan stayed silent. "We found two Bitcoin sales—both for one hundred thousand dollars—recorded to an IP address here in the US." The analyst paused for a moment for effect. "You want to know where?" Chung received collective affirmative head movements. "San José, California!"

"That totally works for funding the Sacramento Imperium purchase, and it's convenient for Carmel!" Vance blurted out.

Hope surged inside Hogan. This could be the breakthrough they needed.

"Okay..." He waited for the initial frisson of excitement to subside. "So, first up, nothing leaves this room. It will take more evidence to move on whoever uses this IP address. But this is very interesting. I want every piece of information on this IP by the end of play. In the interim, we can start scoping out surveillance options."

"Does this mean there is a Russian angle?" Ranger asked.

"It's concerning. I mean, it could be their banking system was an obvious choice to shift the money through. But yeah, there could be more to it. I'll pass this on to Touchdown and see if he knows of any connections between the FSB and Archangel." Hogan moved his attention back to Chung. "This is excellent work, Joseph. But, um… tweak the official version on how the trail allowed us to locate the IP address—best we avoid any undue oversight. We'll reconvene around four p.m. and share what we've found." Everyone hustled out of the room. At last, the hunt for Richelieu had a location.

When shit needed to get done, there was no better ally than Carla. A few quick calls sorted a good portion of what they needed. The initial first chunk of data from the IP address catalyzed action. There had been a gap in traffic for ten days, which covered the period their suspect would have been in New York, a red flag on its own. There had also been previous Google searches on Mark Fullerton, his Manhattan apartment and company addresses, and for flights between San José and Newark. On the night of Jay Chopra's death, there was no web traffic from four p.m. for twenty-four hours. Chung continued to sift through data. Hogan left Carla's office with growing anticipation.

By the time the smell of late-evening pizzas engulfed the office, surveillance on the property had been confirmed. It would begin early the following morning—and a SWAT team from San Francisco would be on standby later that day. Miller suspected a breakthrough, but Hogan reveled in keeping him out of the loop; at least until the task force briefing first thing the following morning. After delivering that, he'd join Ranger and Vance to fly straight to San José and Richelieu's location.

43

KIROV SAVORED ANOTHER glass of Macallan 1946 Select Reserve. He enjoyed the indulgence and not caring about the crazy price. He scrolled down an article about the first edition copy of *Alice's Adventures in Wonderland* up for sale at Christie's New York. The rumors were true. He pictured walking through his Montenegro retreat and adding this to the special cabinet in his fortified library. It was an auction he would win. Three million dollars or more would be a small price to pay for the holy grail of children's books. His grandmother's novels would sit next to this final purchase and other first editions. It would be a reminder of the memories of reading them for the first time and how he felt. It was something you couldn't recapture, like those moments of happiness. He glanced upwards, raised his glass, then drained it.

His thoughts switched to Silver. He was still no closer to figuring out who was behind the terse exchanges on Signal. This most lucrative of referrals had come via a big-pharma executive who'd had a persistent blackmailer eliminated. He considered hacking into that individual's network to see with whom he communicated—but this would take time and effort and even risk the next payday. Discovering the identity of Silver could wait. He typed a quick message:

Any update on the next target?

He didn't have to wait long for a reply.

By the end of the week, the decision will be with you by then.

Still nothing.

I'll await your next message.

He tossed the phone back onto the sofa. Waiting for new assignments was a game he was used to; he'd spent most of the nineties doing it.

Lukas was awaiting another target when they came. The last seven years had followed a now-familiar pattern: he'd be handed a new file from his handler at one of the prearranged meeting points. Frank had returned to Washington after Lukas completed his first year in the program, so these were now an array of nameless operatives. Just how he eliminated the person inside was up to him. Sometimes the targets would be well guarded, but Lukas loved the challenge and had always found a solution. His skills had continued to develop. But now, there had been nothing for the last two months. He had an inkling why. His previous job in Moscow hadn't completely gone to plan, and he'd killed a wannabe oligarch who was building a power base in the steel industry. The situation had got messy, and he'd been fortunate to escape intact. Not hearing from his paymasters since was concerning. He wondered what his grandmother would have made of his new occupation. He'd hoped it would feed his vengeance for her death. But it didn't—no matter how many Russian lives he ended.

He was heading out into the freezing winter night when three large men bundled him into the back of a van. He thought he was a dead man, but as the doors slammed behind him, he recognized the features of one of his previous handlers. An older gentleman with a thin smile and black goatee shuffled onto the bench opposite and offered him a cigarette. Lukas took one, his hands still shaking.

"Sorry to drag you off the street like that. We don't have much time. There are two FSB operatives on their way to kill you. Your cover is blown, so your time here is done."

"In Vilnius?"
"In Europe."

Kirov's stomach growled. San José was full of decent restaurants—but he decided to stay home; the pizza in the freezer would do. He smiled. No one else on the planet would be eating a four-dollar pizza and drinking a thirty-thousand-dollar bottle of single malt tonight. He thumbed on the TV and found coverage of his exploits. It was everywhere. For the first time, others, aside from whoever had hired him, celebrated his killings. It was an odd concept. The news report focused on Reddit message boards celebrating the murder of Chopra, Fullerton, and Decker. It wasn't only legacy hatred but also that the rich could suffer like the masses, and not even money could save them. He'd become an unlikely hero for those protesting the country's gross inequality. Trickle-down capitalism was questioned, as the rich hoarded their money. Kirov wondered if he might have set in motion a chain reaction that could transform society. He wasn't bothered but found the premise intriguing. He hadn't expected remorse from all quarters when he'd killed these guys, but he'd not predicted this reaction. The world was one fucked-up place.

44

RAISING THE KOWA binoculars, Hogan focused on the target's apartment window. The blinds had been down for the previous thirty-six hours. Below, a furniture shop began to close. It was part of the three-story building that ran the block's length, the buff sandstone facade an inoffensive design. Some properties had balconies, although the one that interested them did not. He sat with Vance around three football fields away on the edge of a featureless concrete parking lot. It continued to empty as rush hour wound down.

"You think he'll head out tonight?" she asked.

"Hard to say. Ideally, he stays put, but we'll wait and see." Since they'd joined the surveillance team on the property late the previous morning, the suspect hadn't left. Heat signatures indicated one person within the apartment. The past few days, IP traffic had been streaming sites, random websites, and late-night pregnancy porn. This discovery left Vance queasy, but it could be worse.

"How's your dad doing over at Paradiso?"

"He's comfortable, and they care for him so well. Aside from that, the slow decline continues. I feel like I'm losing him, piece by piece."

Vance placed a hand on Hogan's arm. "I'm sorry, that must be tough."

"It is. Increasingly it's like visiting a person you barely know." He shook his head, and they sat in silence until he broke it. "How about your folks, still going to all your fights?"

Vance smiled. "Oh yes. My dad is convinced he is a good luck charm now, so refuses to miss one. Although I think he is secretly glad this case keeps me too busy to fight."

The parking lot continued to thin out, so Hogan gunned the engine to tailgate an Impala. He continued six blocks west from Japantown to the operation staging post and an anonymous panel van. They climbed in the back and greeted Ranger, hunched over a screen. Cameras covered the entrance and exit to the building. Everything was in place for the planned early-morning raid should nothing change. Vance and Ranger teased each other as they waited for any shift in circumstances.

None came.

At 1 a.m., Hogan called it, and they drove the mile back to their downtown chain hotel.

After a few hours of restless sleep, Hogan gave up and opened the curtains to the orange streetlight glow below. The combination of anticipation and nervousness that an operation brought dominated his emotions. Today could change everything. With a cold shower pounding his back, he clicked through his mental gears, examining all they'd learned by late the previous evening.

A shyster landlord named Kenneth Hallows owned the suspect's apartment. After a fraud conviction, he'd kept his nose clean and had rental properties dotted across San José. They'd decided an approach could risk a tip-off, and as the utility bills for this particular one were in his name. It appeared he rented out the property for one flat rate. Even more damning IP traffic had come to light as Chung combed through more data. This included Google searches for Malibu Lagoon State Beach and its surroundings. It had to be their guy.

As caffeine gave way to adrenaline, Hogan strapped on the standard-issue bullet-resistant vest and checked his Glock 9 mm. He'd recently switched from a Glock 22. Since then, he'd bested Ranger and Vance down the range but didn't expect to use his new piece today. That's why they had SWAT.

Hogan climbed into the waiting vehicle and received a steely-eyed nod from Ranger. Vance fumbled the key into the ignition, and they set off in silence. A minute in, she began squirming in her seat, then turned to the passenger seat.

"Don't you think we're rushing in a little here? We should wait for a potential ID or to get eyes on the suspect. I'm worried it appears too simple."

"And risk him slipping away or a gunfight with a professional on the street? I don't see how it isn't our guy. Everything points to the fact he is," Hogan argued.

They settled back into a more uncomfortable silence. The raid was happening.

Two blocks short of their eventual destination, they rendezvoused with SWAT. Early rays of sunlight cut through the crisp air as agents approached the target building's rear. Four snipers were in place on a rooftop farther down the street. The breach team leader crept to a door next to the furniture store's entrance. He punched in the door code for the apartment lobby, and five other team members followed him through. Hogan, Vance, and Ranger eased in behind. Once on the second floor, they hung back as SWAT fanned out either side of the third apartment along. The suspect's door shattered as agents moved in, guns arcing in narrow angles as they did. Hogan tightened the grip on his Glock as he edged down the hall, waiting for gunshots, but none came. Thirty seconds later, the voice of the SWAT team leader came over the radio: "*All clear, one suspect in custody.*"

Hogan sucked in a breath and hurried toward the apartment. They had him! But on arrival to the bedroom, his elation tumbled to the pit of his stomach. A young man sat cuffed on the bed, no more than twenty-five years of age. He'd soiled himself, and tears streamed down his face. *Shit!* This wasn't right at all. This couldn't be Richelieu. They'd fucked up—he just couldn't figure out how.

As Hogan perched on the rear edge of the staging van, the shame of failure burned through him. He'd wanted it to be their man so much that he'd not rationalized alternatives. The "suspect" was a twenty-two-year-old student named Todd Connors. He'd recently spent ten days at his parents' home in Minnesota, not stalking a victim in New York City. Yet the other data showed they'd been duped, but how? He turned back to Ranger, who tapped away on his laptop. Vance was slumped in the other corner. She hadn't said, *I told you so*; she didn't need to—they should have waited.

Hogan wanted to check one thing.

"Can you look at the IP traffic for the evening of Thursday, October the fifth?" he asked. Ranger began to read URLs from the screen.

"That's fine. Connors was home. That's the first date we captured images of the suspect on the Malibu Lagoon State Beach parking lot cameras." Hogan wrapped his hands around the back of his head. "If I'd waited and checked this date, we'd have known something was wrong."

"That still doesn't explain the searches made for that same parking lot from this address," Vance replied, with a valid point.

Hogan smiled, grateful for her support.

"Do we have the information on the other apartments in the block?" he asked.

A minute or so later, Ranger handed over two sheets of paper for his colleague to scan.

"Apartments seven and nine have no resident information. Are they vacant?"

"Number seven should be, as it has no internet or utilities registered. We didn't get a chance to confirm personnel at the other, especially as we'd already established where the supposed suspect was," Vance replied.

Hogan leaped off the back of the van. "Strap your vests back on and follow me." For the second time that day, they would obliterate a front door. He only hoped this time, his theory would make it worthwhile.

Apartment seven was two doors down from Todd Connors' place. The ERT was filtering back through the door as they passed; no need to waste their valuable time now. Neither Hogan nor Vance could recall activity from this unit during their surveillance. They stood on either side of the entrance as Ranger's chunky arms drove the enforcer through the door. It didn't stand a chance.

They entered the gloomy hallway, weapons drawn. The apartment contained no furniture, leading to a quick confirmation of no occupants. But it wasn't empty. In the center of the front room sat a silver MacBook, and a long white cable trailed from the socket. Hogan shook his head as Vance stretched to flick the light switch; wary of a booby trap, he checked and raised the blinds instead.

They all bent down to take a closer look at the computer. Hogan suspected it was connected to Todd Connors' Wi-Fi and someone had been controlling it remotely. The screen lit up from its slumber, and the Google home page opened. All three stared as the cursor formed words in the search bar: "Who in the world am I? Ah, that's the great puzzle."

The screen began to fade to black, then a countdown clock appeared starting at five. It hit four, and Hogan shouted, "run!" as they scrambled to escape.

45

SHOCK REGISTERED ON the FBI agents' faces as Kirov finished typing. His favorite *Alice's Adventures in Wonderland* quote was perfect. He'd often imagined law enforcement across the globe asking the same question. He couldn't resist baiting them with it. He watched shock turn to terror as the countdown clock started—an extra bit of fun he'd added. They'd assume it would end with an explosion, but there was nothing to be gained by that. At zero, a self-destruct instruction wiped the MacBook and closed the remote-access tool allowing him control. This RAT ensured complete anonymity. Law enforcement would find this device useless now it had served its purpose. He wasn't surprised to see the agent named Hogan again—first New York and now San José. One coincidence, the next misdirection. Would there be a third?

Kirov had rented the apartment for a whole year a few months earlier, paid over the odds in a bank transfer, and had the keys sent to a PO box for a little extra. It had taken minutes to hack the Wi-Fi of the college kid two doors down and set up the MacBook. The remote set up allowed him to visit specific incriminating sites and maps. All would support suspicions if law enforcement got this far down the false trail. It had now served its purpose as a trip wire. He'd sent the FBI bumbling into a blind alley—sacrificing time and resources while making them look foolish. It was why he'd left crumbs of evidence. It let him evaluate the team on his trail. He'd give them a little credit for cracking the previously secure Archangel Bank, but now they'd be back to square one, searching anew for financial footprints they would never find. They hadn't considered he would have used Tor as a browser and a remote server to hide the real IP address of the cryptocurrency owner before crediting the Archangel account. This kind of oversight only a team rushing for results would make. That was an excellent sign. He took malicious joy that they were a few miles away while he relaxed.

He flicked on the news, but it was too early for anything concerning the raid. A sour-faced woman with square blue glasses made an animated point to the anchor. She argued the killings were part of God's plan to rebalance equality in the world and that a few dead billionaires might be a good thing. Richelieu was doing His work. Kirov smiled upon hearing his moniker once again. When he'd selected that name for the hotel booking, it had been a private joke. He hadn't counted upon the press adopting it. It had a much better ring than "suspect," and he liked the choice. Cunning, ruthless, and deceptive; Cardinal Richelieu's traits ran through Kirov's blood. The childhood days of imagining he was d'Artagnan were long gone. Those dreams had died back in the orphanage.

This new name had only accelerated his global notoriety. Speculation on who might die next had reached fever pitch, but only one person knew. Although he was still waiting for his next assignment from his unknown paymaster, it wasn't the Almighty.

46

HOGAN TOOK THE brunt of the botched raid fallout. Carla had tried to mitigate the situation with Director Sullivan.

"There were enough things that didn't add up; we should have waited." Hogan clasped his hands together opposite his glaring boss.

"You're damn fucking right you should. Sometimes I think you want this too much."

Despite helping with the aftermath, she was still furious. Everyone's nerves were stretched thin, and the crumbs of information they had, were destined for the trash. The realization of failure had burnt away any positive momentum.

"It does confirm some suspect theories," Hogan argued, attempting to deflect the accusation. "He's focused on this series of assassinations and nothing else. He could have booby-trapped the apartment."

"We still had to send the bomb squad in, didn't we?"

"It was all a test, and he feels invincible. Maybe he'll catch some hubris. Plus, the message he sent was another classic book reference. It ties into the hotel booking in New York—it's something."

"*Alice in Wonderland*? Forgive me if I don't throw a tea party!" Carla snapped back. "We're on borrowed time with Quantico, so come back with progress, not theories."

The team was downbeat. Even the irrepressible Vance was silent in the corner. It had taken all her charm to convince Todd Connors not to pursue a lawsuit. The small amount of MDMA they found in his apartment helped too. Chung apologized again.

"It's all my fault. I was the one who started all this." But Hogan wasn't having any of it.

"This is on me, Joseph. We're dealing with a brilliant individual with significant resources. You were right—the accounts and companies did belong to him, yet he didn't care. He's cocky, and we need to exploit that. It will make it that much sweeter when we get him."

It was early evening in the office as Hogan sought a caffeine top-up. He passed one of the meeting rooms where Vance crouched, sheets of paper scattered around her.

"What's this all about?"

She spun around to face him.

"I wanted to work up new ideas and angles. When you fight, you're always looking to deceive your opponent and set them up for a move they don't see coming. It's an important part of the discipline. The better you get at this, the more success you have. I thought I'd adapt the process here."

He crouched down next to her. "Go on."

"So, the behavioral unit's reports on Richelieu are useless. A bit like throwing a leg kick at an opponent who can't wait to take the fight to the ground. What applies to serial killers doesn't to a man with an agenda we don't understand."

"I can see where you're coming from. The pursuit of motive is getting us nowhere."

"Exactly. Why don't we start thinking more about who this guy is, what he's good at, and how this narrows down potential avenues for suspects. If he's too good at some things, that's more valuable information than if he's sloppy elsewhere. Tons of killers make errors; few are this efficient." Vance shifted papers in Hogan's direction. "Don't just crouch there. Get a marker and get started. I'm working through his technical knowledge and what it means." She held up a sheet of paper with "an expert in coding, creates sophisticated custom malware" written on it.

In the zone, they began working in tandem. By midnight, the floor was covered with pieces of the puzzle, and a picture of the suspect became clearer. From now on, his team would change direction. Let Jared Miller handle the trickle of information from the previous murders and wild-goose chase calls. Richelieu's unparalleled skills could provide the key to his identity and to catching him.

47

From his usual spot in The Rose, Hogan attempted to make money for the looming Paradiso payment. But he was distracted, the magnitude of trying to stop Richelieu lingered. Despite their recent work, the killer remained a ghost who didn't care about DNA or even newer ID technologies. They'd have to rip up the playbook. They'd had composite sketches, and it still took forty years to nail the Golden State Killer. By finding another way to identify the assassin, they could gain the upper hand—or at least level the playing field.

By the end of the soccer games, he'd only made a few hundred dollars, which wouldn't make a dent in the outstanding invoice. Time was getting short, too short. He might scrape the money together this time, but it would likely be the last. Getting the SAC role and the healthy increase in his paycheck could be a possible panacea. But that wouldn't happen unless he solved this case, and the last week showed how difficult this would be. Downcast, he closed the laptop as Amber approached, her brow furrowed. Had her boyfriend mentioned their altercation? He figured not—Chad would want to maintain the tough-guy image.

"You okay, Hogan? Anything else I can get you?" Her green eyes flashed with concern at his defeated posture. Hogan looked up and smiled for the first time that morning.

"I'm fine, thanks, Amber." He paused, weighing an explanation. "Tough week at work."

"Which is why you need another almond croissant, on the house, of course." She produced a plate from behind her back and put it down with a flourish.

She's a good kid. He offered thanks and got a broad grin in return.

"How's Chad?" The name caused a flicker of annoyance across her freckled face.

"He's good… We're good, I suppose."

"For what it is worth, I think you can do better—much better."

Amber twisted her curls and looked down. "I know," she replied and walked away.

48

A KALEIDOSCOPE OF neon tripped across the calm ocean opposite Nemo and Francesca's sumptuous apartment block. The early evening crowds on Santa Monica Pier added to the ambience of the picture-postcard view. As Hogan admired it, a black Escalade pulled up, and he helped Marissa climb out, waving away the advancing driver. She wore a figure-hugging black dress and red-soled high heels and greeted him with a kiss. The same blonde concierge met them as they entered.

The penthouse elevator doors slid open to the light hum of conversation. Nemo had predicted about twenty guests, and most already appeared to be here. Hogan recognized many and offered polite hellos. Francesca glided over from a small group.

"Hogan! And you must be Marissa." She dropped kisses on their cheeks. "So lovely to meet you. Let me get you champagne." She beckoned a server holding a tray of flutes.

"Beautiful place you have here," Marissa offered.

"Thanks, that means a lot, especially coming from you." Francesca put her hand to her mouth in horror. "Sorry, that came out all wrong."

"It's absolutely fine."

"You sure?" their host responded, crestfallen.

"Of course. You fancy showing me around?"

"Most definitely," she replied, taking Marissa's arm. "Nemo's out on the terrace," Francesca called over her shoulder as they walked away.

Nemo bounded over to swallow Hogan in his customary bear hug, then his eyes shifted left and right.

"Did you bring your fine lady?"

"She's off on the grand tour with your better half."

"The closet could be one on its own," Nemo groaned. "Here—take this, dude," he added, swapping the glass for a Pacifico. "Unless you're getting a taste for the champagne lifestyle?" He arched an eyebrow.

Hogan wrinkled his nose. "Not yet. Cheers!" They tapped the beer bottles together.

"Rough week, huh?"

"Yeah, it sucked."

Nemo placed a hand on his shoulder. "You'll get him, dude—if anyone can, it's you."

"I'm not sure this time—he's really fucking good." Hogan brought Nemo up to speed with the developments in the case. When he'd finished, his friend pursed his lips.

"I think you might be right about Richelieu. His skills reek of government training."

"That's one avenue we need to push harder. Counterintelligence can only give us so much. They doubt it's a foreign operative based in the US. Only a recently activated long-term sleeper agent would make sense. And to be fair, no one likes that theory."

"Or an existing one who has never hit their radar and arrived here recently. Your guy could be a freelance operative. Ex-FSB, MOIS, or Mossad, even," Nemo offered. "So you're asking the wrong people. You should be speaking to an agency that might know about similar killings outside of this country. An international footprint seems likely for such a talented killer. You need to speak to the CIA."

Nemo could be right. It had always been unlikely this was Richelieu's first foray into eliminating high-profile and well-guarded targets—he was too good. Having honed his skills at a government agency made sense. A host of nations had trained assassins over the previous decades, although you wouldn't read about it in your morning paper. A self-taught lone wolf theory held way less water.

"You could be on to something, but the CIA…"

Nemo thrust a business card into his hand. It was embossed with only a name and number.

"Maybe I can help. Start with this guy—Warren Fisk, at Langley. He's my liaison for our projects with them. Once I give him a quick call, he'll point you in the right direction."

"Thanks, this could be super helpful." An existing contact could give him way more leverage than a cold approach. He turned to see Marissa moseying toward them.

"You must be Nemo. It's great to meet you. Are you two staying out of trouble?" She asked with a wry smile. He'd related some of the less salacious college stories to her last week. Most of them involved his best friend.

Nemo laughed. "With this guy? Never!"

The evening had been a success, Hogan reflected. Marissa slept, her head resting on his chest, errant wisps of hair tickling at his face. He hadn't felt this comfortable so fast with anyone except Katie. He'd always been protective of his emotions, even before what happened. Once back from Nemo's, they'd worn each other out, then spent hours chatting. He discovered Marissa's mum had left and moved to Rome when she was at college, and they rarely saw each other now. Hogan talked about his mother, and the aftermath of her death. They had strengthened their bond, but he couldn't sleep—thoughts continued to swirl around his mind. After battling through the grief of losing Katie, his father was slipping away. If his feelings for Marissa grew, he'd open himself up for further heartache if this didn't work out. He wasn't sure he was ready to risk it. This brought more doubts; it had been amazing so far, but was she this into him? It was almost too good to be true. He needed a dose of Vance's optimism to change his mindset—and perhaps Nemo was right; he deserved some luck in life now. He tried to calm his negative thoughts as he stroked Marissa's hair and stared into the shadowy darkness until he succumbed to exhaustion.

49

NEMO STUCK TO his word. Hogan's call to Warren Fisk received a swift response—which was why now, only two days later, he sat in the lobby at Langley. A cleaner polished the floor's CIA crest as the gentle tip-tap of shoes announced the arrival of his liaison. Perry Wolgomott's thin lips formed a cursory smile as they shook hands. Hogan pegged him as more bureaucrat than field agent as they passed through the toughened glass security gates to the elevators.

After several turns down the fifth-floor corridor, they reached an office—all eggshell and frosted glass. A bottle of water and two tumblers sat on the desk separating them.

"So, how do you think we can help today?" Wolgomott asked, emphasizing "think," like a bank manager who'd already decided to reject your loan request.

"I assume you're familiar with the Richelieu case, as it has become known?" Hogan flipped open his navy-blue briefcase and extracted a file.

"Of course. But I'm not sure how this domestic problem pertains to us."

"We're working on a hypothesis this killer has previously operated internationally. Assuming he has, you may have attributed previous assassinations to him. This profile lists the key characteristics across his MO so far."

Wolgomott stroked his weak chin while reading the similarities they'd identified. Upon finishing, he leaned back, arms folded.

"This is pretty broad. I'd point to the differences in MO across the three crime scenes. I'm not sure we can be of much help here."

"Can you at least circulate this to station chiefs and see if it jogs any memories?"

"That may be possible, but between North Korea, Russia, and global terrorists, we have a fair bit on our plate." Wolgomott's supercilious tone irked Hogan.

"If it is not *too much* trouble—*please* try to make it possible," he responded, laying on the sarcasm. "We're talking about some victims who were personal friends of the president, after all." The implied threat hung heavy in the silence that followed.

Wolgomott frowned before he framed his reply with equal sarcasm.

"I'm sure we can dig a little deeper for *our friends* at the Bureau. Maybe you should ask MI6 over in the UK. You sound just like them. They're always asking for our help too."

"That's a good idea," Hogan responded, convinced it would annoy Wolgomott. Only after their strained goodbyes did he conclude it actually was.

After returning his pass, Hogan walked outside, figuring he'd grab an Uber and kill time at the airport bar. As he opened the app, someone called his name. He spun around to find a breathless, well-dressed grizzly bear smiling at him.

"I'm Warren Fisk. Glad I caught you." He offered a hand as hairy as the rest of him. "Apologies, I'm a little out of shape," he added between pants.

"Thanks for sorting the meeting."

"No problem. Although I'm sorry they chose Wolgomott—the guy is a massive dick."

"I'm not sure he buys into the idea of Bureau-Agency cooperation."

Fisk laughed. "He doesn't buy into *internal Agency* cooperation." He pointed at Hogan's briefcase. "You got a spare copy of that profile you mentioned?"

"Sure." Hogan fished one out and handed it to him.

Fisk rolled it up and tapped it in his palm. "I'll run it by a few people, see if anyone knows anythin'. I owe Nemo a favor or two, so it is the least I can do."

"Thanks, Warren."

"No worries, my friend. I hope you get him."

50

WHILE HOGAN REMAINED pessimistic that his Langley trip would bear fruit, Warren Fisk's offer to follow up meant it wasn't a complete bust. Carla had also contacted the commissioner of New Scotland Yard, who'd engineered a call with MI6.

At 11 a.m., he picked up a secure line and dialed the number provided.

"Campbell Agnew," announced the cultured voice.

"Hi, this is Special Agent Hogan. You're expecting my call."

"Indeed, I am. How can I help this evening?"

Hogan started to object, then remembered the time difference—it was seven p.m. in London. He outlined what he needed. Once he finished, the officer stayed silent for a moment before responding.

"I presume you've asked the same of your people."

"I have. However, we believe he could also have operated in Europe, even the UK," Hogan lied. "You guys might know more or provide a different perspective."

"Interesting," Agnew replied. An extended silence followed. "Do I detect an English accent?"

"You do. I grew up and went to school in London."

"Harrow?"

"Woodside High School."

"Ah, can't say I know it. Well, listen, I'll dig around a little here and feedback on anything relevant, provided it isn't classified."

"Of course, and thanks for your time." Hogan replaced the receiver.

Lunch with Marissa had provided a release from the pressure building across the office. His grin from seeing her was still evident. She'd pressed for info on the case's progress, but he'd remained professional and changed the subject.

On his return, he'd found a quiet spot to read about Mark Fullerton's hedge fund positions when he died. The list of companies was long, and Hogan memorized them all. He still enjoyed this process, even after so many years. It allowed him to make rapid connections that could otherwise elude him when presented with other information. One notable point of curiosity was that Fullerton held no investments in fossil fuel companies. He hadn't struck Hogan as someone with the planet's best interests at heart, but perhaps greater profits lay elsewhere. He needed Chung's help dissecting the more complex data, and overviews of the companies behind the lesser-known names.

"I reckon two million, then five million, then eight million?" Vance announced, indicating each number like a growing stack of actual cash.

They were in The Nickel Mine again. The mixed Friday night clientele contained plenty of familiar faces. Jared Miller leaned on the end of the bar, staring in Hogan's direction. His nemesis appeared to come to a decision and stormed across.

"You need to start sharing information as soon as you get it," Miller shouted, jabbing a finger as he did. "You're fucking this case up—San José was a shit show. I argued it wouldn't be our guy, but no one listened."

"Well, not very fucking loud, Jared. Did anyone else hear this?" Hogan turned to his colleagues and received firm shakes of heads. It smacked of Miller's usual opportunism.

"You think you're so smart, but you won't be so smug when you're off the case." Miller's spittle caught Hogan's suit lapel. The furious agent barged past and headed to the exit.

"Man, you're really getting to him," Ranger said, eyebrows raised.

But were these Miller's usual empty threats or something more?

"Hogan, it's your turn," Vance announced. They'd been guessing Richelieu's fees and possible employer.

"Maybe he works for a foreign government and is off the books," he speculated. "Although I still can't figure out which country would significantly gain from these deaths, they're harming not only ours but the global economy. Have you seen oil prices?"

"If it's not a country paying him, then it must be a well-resourced organization or individual," Vance replied.

"Like a billionaire?"

"Exactly. They could ship tens of millions over to an assassin no problem."

"There's over seven hundred in the US alone. Where would we start?" Chung interjected.

"We could try to figure out who else benefited from the killings so far, but quietly? After San José, I'm not sure Carla will be receptive to unsubstantiated theories. Joseph, if you could pick this up, that would be great," Hogan replied.

"Sure, but only if I get a share of the reward if we catch the guy!"

"Shit, imagine?" Vance poured another glass of wine from the bottle resting on the bar, festooned with Christmas decorations. The victim's families had gotten together. The current reward for information that led to Richelieu's capture was sixty million dollars. It had generated a deluge of tips currently being fielded by LAPD officers assigned to the task force. They'd received nothing concrete so far.

"Another beer?" Ranger offered.

"Yeah!" Chung shouted, already a little tipsy.

Hogan took another cold one, enjoying unwinding. He told himself everything would improve next week.

He couldn't have been more wrong.

51

HOGAN SPENT THE first half hour of his morning with the classic hang-over conundrum. The idea of moving for water filling him with horror. He had sketchy recollections of leaving the dive bar on Sunset that Vance had dragged them to for more unnecessary drinks. She'd wanted to discover more about Marissa after he'd let slip they were dating. They'd consumed a ton of booze, and he was paying the price. Thirst won, so he plodded to the fridge and gulped down ice-cold water, receiving brain freeze for his trouble. A bracing shower would be the first in several steps to begin to feel human again. After this, once dressed and starting to function, he set off for coffee and as many carbs as he could stomach.

Mid-morning at The Rose was busy, but he needed food and every-where would be packed this time on a Saturday morning—and he had a table reserved. He'd missed all the UK soccer, so he wouldn't make any money today. He cursed his lack of self-control, but the night had been fun and valuable in building team spirit, especially after the events in San José. They'd formed a determined drunken pact to discover a way to find Richelieu.

There was no sign of Amber. With an understanding smile, her colleague eased a breakfast burrito onto the table. He surveyed it through puffed-up eyes and summoned the will to eat.

An hour later, he wasn't exactly back in the game but could at least function now. He'd head back to his apartment, freshen up, and attempt to drag himself to Wilshire.

Outside, he sucked in deep breaths of cooler fresh air as the cloud cover began to lessen, allowing patches of winter sunshine to punch through. He still retained some of the drunken optimism Vance had fostered in him the night before—somehow, they'd solve the case. He quickened his pace, albeit from a slow to almost steady stroll. He didn't hear the rapid footsteps behind him until the last moment, his senses still deadened. The part of his brain registering this, translated it to fear too late. As he began to turn, a crashing blow struck the back of his head, sending him sprawling to the ground. He smacked his temple on the curb, hard. A sharp kick to the ribs followed as the world tilted.

His attacker snarled, "You're not so fucking tough now."

Hogan tried to turn his head, but it wouldn't obey. He lay there for another twenty seconds, staring at a sideways world becoming foggy. As he began to drift out of consciousness, the last thing he remembered was a blue Corvette speeding by.

52

HIS EYES FLICKERED open, then closed again. A numb pain enveloped Hogan's entire head, and his left side throbbed. He blinked into view the jarring brightness of a hospital room.

"I think he's awake," someone said to his right. Vance's face appeared with Marissa's alongside it—concern in their eyes.

"That bad?" he managed to croak.

"You've looked better," Ranger called from his small hospital seat. Hogan moved, receiving another dose of pain for his trouble.

"What happened?" Marissa asked the question first. He closed his eyes, dragging back his memories.

He remembered walking, being struck as he was about to turn, the sidewalk approaching at speed, and then the kick. His temples pounded as he tried to focus.

"Back to my apartment...whacked over the head...something hard." He wasn't keen on the effort of forming coherent sentences.

"Did you see who did it? Did they say anything?" Vance demanded.

He closed his eyes again. The voice and the blue Corvette eased into this mind.

"...just the blow...and hitting the sidewalk." The clarity came with a resolution not to share everything.

"A dog-walker found you on Hampton Drive, a few blocks from your apartment. They called nine-one-one. They've got patrol officers canvassing homes," Vance explained.

Marissa leaned in and dropped a light kiss on his forehead.

"I'm fetching the doctor. Shall we let him rest?" She smiled at the two agents.

"We'll come by again tomorrow," Ranger agreed and headed out. Vance tipped her head toward the distracted Marissa, gave a vigorous nod and a thumbs-up, and followed her colleague out of the door.

When Hogan awoke, it was early evening. Marissa reached over and poured him some water. The throbbing had lessened, and he shuffled to a more comfortable position.

"Thank you," he said, "and thanks for being here."

"Of course, I was so worried. I'm glad it's not serious. The doctor said you have a concussion, but the swelling is coming down. The MRI scan showed no further damaged. They'll be monitoring you for a few days to be sure."

Hogan gave a light nod and looked at his bandaged side.

"Three badly bruised ribs, but they aren't broken." Marissa offered an encouraging smile.

"I guess we're missing the dinner reservation."

She peered at her watch. "We've still got twenty minutes to make it." They both started laughing, and Hogan's entire left side objected.

"Audrey wanted to come to the hospital too, but I wasn't sure about your condition. I'll bring her here tomorrow if that is okay?"

"Sure. Where is here, by the way?"

"UCLA Santa Monica." Marissa picked up the TV remote. "Let's see what's on while you relax, hey?" She began flipping through the channels.

"No news about billionaire deaths and nothing funny; it hurts too much when I laugh."

She stopped on a channel showing *Two and a Half Men*.

"This should be perfect, then."

53

HOGAN'S FOLLOW-UP MRI scan confirmed no lasting damage, and he was to be discharged Wednesday morning and advised to rest. But he couldn't, not with Richelieu still out there. He looked up at the TV—another ad break. He'd love to know the commercial-to-news ratio on this channel. A suburban fifty-something hawked medicine for an ailment he didn't know existed. One of the possible side effects was death, which didn't sound ideal.

Work colleague visits had punctuated his boredom, and even Carla swung by. Marissa called in for a few hours each day—the only real upside of the attack. Not working the case was frustrating. He moved from the bed to sit on the guest chair and began memorizing a pack of cards he'd requested from Vance. He wanted to check there was no lasting damage. As always, he used the PAO system, which stood for person, action, object. Each card symbolized an image he'd previously created reflecting these three things. It meant you could memorize three cards in one crazy amalgam of imagery, taking the element from each that worked for the new memory. He flipped over the queen of diamonds: the person for that card, Beyoncé, ten of clubs: the object for that—a trombone, four of hearts: the action waterskiing. In the memory palace of his childhood school, he stored the image of Beyoncé playing the trombone and waterskiing down the hallway. Mentally filed and difficult to forget, he moved on to the next three cards. When he'd finished, he put the cards to one side and stopped his phone timer. Now he needed to run back through the images and recite the deck. To his relief, they flowed back, and he got all fifty-two cards correctly in order. He'd spent one minute and forty-five seconds memorizing them, a respectable time, and his mind was as sharp as ever. The US memory championship had moved on light-years since he competed. The record for this challenge now an insane 18.65 seconds.

Placing the deck to one side, he considered his decision to hide from the police the knowledge of his attacker. He didn't need the headache of their history. It may have been a sucker shot, but Chad had got the drop on him—there wouldn't be a second time. Amber's boyfriend didn't know his victim was law enforcement, either. Once Hogan was fully fit, Mr. Preppy would pay for his mistake.

54

COLLEAGUES HAD POPPED by Hogan's desk most of the morning to wish him well and to fish for information on his attack. All left disappointed on the latter. One had even suggested Richelieu could be behind the attack. He couldn't have been, Vance pointed out; Hogan wouldn't still be breathing if he had. The hospital discharge had been seamless, although they repeated the advice on rushing back before Christmas. He was back in the office within hours.

Hogan was savoring his coffee, trying to forget the hospital cups of tar, when he received a formal email from Carla asking to meet in ten minutes. He reread the message, puzzled. Nothing like this had happened before; her tone was terse, the wording tight. She usually opened her door to beckon him in. His discomfort grew as the minutes ticked by until the wait was finally over, and he tapped on the corner office door.

Carla's lips formed a thin slash. Two males in identical dark-navy suits sporting close-cut hairstyles and emotionless faces sat to her right.

Internal affairs.

He took the chair opposite and focused on remaining calm for the inevitable questions. It couldn't be a trivial matter; Quantico-based IA agents were only required for a non-designated inquiry. Local ADICs had to accommodate their presence.

"Thanks for joining us, Special Agent," Carla said, the usual familiarity lacking. "This is Special Agent Tate and Special Agent Monroe from the Internal Affairs division." The men opposite fixed matching stares on Hogan. He wanted to shrug and say, *So what?* But instead chose to remain still and composed. It was essential not to look ruffled. He glanced across the desk but divined nothing from his boss's expression.

"I hope we can clear this up quickly, then we can all get back to more pressing matters," Carla continued, hinting she wasn't comfortable with proceedings.

"Clear up what?"

Tate smirked and reached down to produce the brown envelope Hogan had placed in his desk drawer days earlier.

"We've received information that leads us to believe you may be using illicitly gained funds to pay a care home provider. We say 'illicit' because we can trace back payments made by you for two years to Paradiso Care LLC for $247,566." Tate paused after the figure to ratchet up the tension. "Now Monroe and I also both receive comparable agent-grade salaries, which makes us wonder how you found all this cash."

Hogan cursed his naivety in not ensuring his desk was secure. Jared Miller must be behind this. He kept his eyes locked on Tate and waited for him to continue.

"This prolonged period recently includes an invoice requesting payment for $31,333 for this quarter. With some funds still significantly overdue, I might add." Tate pulled the invoice from the envelope with a dramatic flourish. They'd already been in touch with Paradiso.

"What happened? Your paymaster not getting the information he required?" Monroe leaned forward, a mean snarl forming on his pockmarked face. Tate shot his colleague a look, who eased back, eyeing Hogan all the way.

Carla shuffled in her seat and placed her hand under her chin.

"This is a good time for an explanation." She stated, her voice softer than usual.

Hogan had used every available second to process the questions. He doubted the agents had traced the source of his funds back to his cousin yet, but he couldn't be sure. He intended to remain circumspect.

"You're right when you say I haven't been paying all these fees from my salary."

"No shit," Tate exclaimed.

"Although I do add a chunk of it to each quarterly payment."

"Then you have a mysterious trust fund to pay most of it, right?" Monroe sneered.

"No, I don't. I did have savings back when I started paying—"

"Which you exhausted quickly. A recent inheritance, perhaps?"

Hogan shook his head. They already knew the answer to these questions. They wouldn't be here if they hadn't pulled all his accounts.

"So…" Tate began, then paused like a trial lawyer about to deliver a stunning piece of evidence. "The 247,000-dollar question is"—air quotes now—"*where have these funds come from?*"

Hogan considered his next steps. The investigation wouldn't shut down even if he did talk. He needed to speak to Toby and ensure they were on the same page. He'd raised the faint possibility of something like this happening, so he expected his cousin to be partly prepared. If they sent over local agents unannounced in London, the optics would be bad. Any sniff of impropriety could damage Toby's hedge fund.

"I need to consult my FAA representative before I speak further," he replied after a long pause. "I'm willing to offer a full explanation after seeking advice."

Tate's expression turned sour. "Why am I not surprised."

Carla's look of disappointment filled him with shame.

"Special Agent Hogan, you can consider yourself suspended from this moment on."

55

KIROV STILL HADN'T received his next target. He wouldn't be operational again now until after Christmas. He could walk away and enjoy his retirement, but he'd never failed to see a job through and wouldn't this time. All the best villains of his favorite books kept going until the end.

The winter sun warmed his back as he approached Philz Coffee in downtown San José. Okay coffee, shit name. A kaleidoscope of Christmas tree lights reflected through the window as he sat outdoors. For Kirov, the festive period was anything but.

Lukas was happy for the first time since his tenth birthday. He'd begun to believe happiness was possible after celebrating his first year with Isobel. He'd spent five years in the United States by then. "A few more jobs," his handler at the CIA had promised, "then you can get on with your life." What choice did he have? Trips to Mexico, Venezuela, Guyana, and Brazil followed. Important people died. But his role lacked the purpose of the early years, and he became listless and disillusioned. He'd given the Agency an ultimatum— the next job would be his last. They'd fought hard but acquiesced.

He moved to start a new life in Florida, choosing the sedate location of Fort Lauderdale. He'd met Isobel at a start-up drinks event not too long after. His fledgling software company already had a good reputation. The new digital age provided many opportunities for quick learners like himself. He was a natural with technical problems and studied coding and online security. He wanted to keep the business lean but still make a comfortable living and build a life he could share with someone. Over the next two years, Isobel became that someone.

In retrospect, Lukas had been foolish to think he could leave the past behind forever. The beautiful house, pregnant fiancée, new name, and successful business didn't erase what he had done. However, he welcomed these distractions. But men like him weren't allowed to walk away and enjoy everyday life. And one day, the past came for Lukas

It was an early December weekend that his life changed forever. He'd bought the most expensive tree he could find and loaded it onto his truck. Although it was still a few weeks until Christmas, the friendly couple enjoyed a brisk Saturday trade on the sidewalk. He drove to the marina, hoping to finish the last bits of work on the boat.

By midnight, he was exhausted. Everything had taken longer than planned since he'd started this project nine months earlier. It was Isobel's birthday next weekend, and he wouldn't let her down. He grabbed his phone and pressed one.

"Hi honey, sorry, time kinda got away from me," he began.

"That's okay. I've got Friends DVDs for company," Isobel replied. Lukas was not a fan.

"I'm thinking of staying on the boat and finishing everything by lunch tomorrow. You'll be alright?"

"A little lonely, mister, but yeah, that's fine. I'll sort food for when you get back—you'll have earned it."

"Thanks, honey, and sleep well—you're sleeping for two, remember."

"You too, babe, and yes—I do. I get the occasional kick to remind me!"

The shrill phone ringtone jolted Lukas awake.

"Is that Mr. Shaw?" The unknown voice was solemn.

"Err, yeah. Who's this?"

"I'm Police Detective Blaine Hollins, and we're at your house on Hathersage Street. Could you head over here right away?"

"What is it? What's going on?" Lukas started to panic.

"We can explain when you get here, sir," Hollins answered and hung up.

Lukas dashed to his truck, throwing his shirt on as he ran. His heart pounded in his chest as he peeled out, repeating, "Let her be okay, let her be okay, let her be okay."

"Can I get you another?" The question brought him back to the present. A waitress hovered over Kirov, moving his empty cup away.

"If I want another, I'll head inside," he snapped as she edged back.

Isobel wasn't okay. That's what the detective explained to Lukas, although the words made no sense. They'd taken her to the hospital suffering from multiple stab wounds, but neither she nor the baby had survived. He slumped to his knees on the curb. Neighbors peered from behind the police tape, concerned. He knew he'd been the real target. His old life had returned to haunt him, and he should have protected them. They were dead because of him. He'd leave Fort Lauderdale immediately. There was nothing left here for him now.

A car blasting out "All I Want for Christmas" pulled up at the lights outside Philz, and Kirov glared at the driver, who fumbled to raise the window. He fucking hated this time of year. Since that day in Florida, Kirov hadn't cared for anyone again. The hatred and anger he'd first experienced when his grandmother died flooded back after the deaths of Isobel and his unborn child. He remembered that boy who'd left the orphanage—callous, vengeful, and determined to shun human connection. He became him again.

He delved into his pocket and pulled out his phone to discover a new message:

The decision on the next target has been made. Apologies it took longer than expected.

Kirov voiced his frustration, exacerbated by his mood:

No fucking kidding.

Silver either ignored the profanity or had already written the reply:

Cole Sandzer. Las Vegas.

Kirov didn't respond. Silver followed up:

He's holed up in a penthouse, Howard Hughes style. It will present a significant challenge. I hope this is ok?

No shit, it will, thought Kirov. Then he tapped out a reply:

I'll advise once I'm on the ground in Vegas.

Silver had been contrite in this communication. This behavior led him to speculate more than one person could be behind the messages. As for the target, he supposed he should have expected something like this next. The richest men on earth, already among the most well guarded, were even more so. All because of his recent killings. While everyone else would enjoy Christmas and stuff their faces, he'd do the only thing that mattered—plan death.

56

AFTER SEVERAL REPEAT left-hand turns to shake any tail, Hogan made for Westfield Century City Mall. He visited two stores to buy burner phones and entered a UK number into one. Once he'd noted the other phone's digits—he made a call. Toby answered after a few long rings.

"Hello?" He had that polite, inquiring tone you used for numbers you didn't recognize.

"Hi, Toby. It's Hogan."

"My boy! How are you doing? You got a new number?"

"No mate, but listen, we might have a problem." Toby was razor sharp, so would grasp what he meant.

"Ah, that's unfortunate."

"I'll WhatsApp you a number. Get a burner phone, and buzz me back, okay?"

This way, in the unlikely event IA had surveillance on Toby's cell phone, they'd be covered. The next call would be between two unconnected, unused numbers.

"Sure thing, mate. I'll get on that right away."

Hogan had begun negotiating the crowds of Christmas shoppers when his new phone rang with an irritating generic tone. He answered and walked out into the expansive parking lot.

"Thanks for this, Toby."

"No worries, mate. I like the spy stuff—proper cloak and dagger! What's going down?"

"IA pulled me on the cash for…well, you know. They want information on its origin."

"I get you. Nothing else on the actual source, though, right?"

"Nope, I'm pretty sure there is no way they can know about that."

"Okay, so it's all good. I'm a concerned rich nephew paying for his uncle's care like you've always said—and that's perfectly legitimate."

"I've stonewalled them for now, but when I talk, or even before, they'll be coming after you for details—I want to double-check we're covered?"

"Don't sweat it, fella. The cash comes over from an assigned account funded by the business. The other cash from Betfair goes into a rainy-day account for Tilly and Posey."

"That's a lot of rainy days."

Toby chuckled. "It's the UK, mate."

"They may look at your hedge fund as a result. You'll want to chat with them away from the office when they call you. They may send over agents on the ground in the UK, so get ahead of them and suggest meeting up."

"Let them look. We're as clean as a whistle—at least for this industry. I'll check tomorrow to ensure all is shipshape. We can keep a lid on this. I'll loop in my lawyer too."

"Perfect. I didn't want them to reach out and snoop around without a heads-up."

"Appreciate it, mate. It'll be fine. Hope it gets sorted for you too."

"Me too. They're about to hit a succession of dead ends, but they'll still think no smoke without fire. Once IA gets a hard-on for something, they keep digging for a while."

"They ain't got the smarts to come at you, mate. Let me know if you need anything else, okay? And take care."

"Will do, fella, and thanks again—you're a legend." Hogan hung up the phone, smiling at slipping back into British slang after all these years. He removed the SIM, walked a few yards, and dropped the cheap phone in the nearest trash receptacle—it had served its purpose. His normal cell was blowing up with missed calls and messages. He'd hurried from the office without a word to anyone. Vance had sent the first saying: *"What the fuck is going on? Call me!"* He'd respond later. As for now, he'd covered everything he needed to. Let IA take their best shot.

57

"So why didn't you tell them Toby pays for your father's care?" Marissa asked a legitimate question once Hogan finished his story. She joined him on the sofa, rested her feet on his lap, and ran a finger around the edge of her lipstick-smudged wineglass.

"These guys are already convinced I'm dirty. They were smirking like they'd caught me red-handed with a suitcase of dodgy cash. I was getting suspended whatever happened, it's better I give Toby a heads-up first."

"But if you told them straight away, it could have gone differently?"

"They'd still investigate, and I'd be on the bench while they did. The fact Quantico sent them shows this is serious. Toby has done a lot for my dad; I don't want his life affected by this."

He disliked lying but had little choice.

"Yeah, I suppose; it sucks, though." Marissa pulled a face. "This guy at work must really have it in for you!"

"He does. He found an opportunity and took it—he's been angling to get me off the case. Of course, I can't prove it's him, and his plan might work." Hogan cast his eyes downward. For the first time since he proved Chopra was murdered, he prayed the case would remain unsolved until his exoneration and return.

"I'm sure it's going to work out. Once IA realizes they've messed up, you'll be back on the case sharpish. Any new leads on Richelieu? My dad asked how it was all going."

She moved her legs and shuffled up next to Hogan, who frowned. Marissa's questions about the case had become more frequent. He'd prefer to avoid discussing work with her, and to switch off. She knew he wouldn't share much but asked anyway. Was this genuine innocent interest, or was Hugh Fairfax pushing for more information for other reasons?

"None, I'm afraid." The last thing he needed was for her dad to give another TV interview.

Marissa looked like she was about to reply but then rested her head on his shoulder. He caught a pleasant waft of jasmine and vanilla.

"So, I'll need to be careful around you if we ever argue." She announced after a few moments of silence.

"What do you mean?"

"Well, you never forget anything, right?"

"I see you've been talking to Vance."

"You were out for quite a while at the hospital."

"You don't need to worry—I still forget everyday things like the next person."

"That's a relief, then!" Marissa laughed. "It's very cool you won the championship—I'm surprised you hadn't mentioned it already. Are you always so modest?"

Hogan shrugged, "I was raised never to brag. The memory stuff was something I learned to do, and I got extremely good at it. I have techniques for remembering decks of cards, faces, names, crime scenes, long strings of numbers, and even entire poems. Of course, some are more useful than others." He grinned.

"You'll have to show me one time. It sounds incredible."

"I will. But after I've reeled off a whole deck of cards, I can still forget where I put my car keys. The human brain is crazy like that."

Marissa sat back up, facing him. "You sure you can't come to spend Christmas with us, now, well, you know?" she asked, eyes bright and hopeful. He shook his head.

"A private island sounds awesome, but my dad will be alone. I want to spend time with him at Christmas while I still can. Plus, with IA breathing down my neck…disappearing until we next meet will look bad. I mean, you understand, right?"

"I do. Can't blame a girl for trying, though."

Hogan smiled, then fell silent. His thoughts oscillated between the happiness of having Marissa here and his doubts and fears. Guys like him didn't end up with girls like her, which still bothered him. It must have shown.

"What's on your mind?" she asked.

"It's…it's all going so well. I wanted to check you're not getting bored with the normal guy with the normal job?"

"Quite the opposite. I feel like there is still plenty to learn about you, I want to peel those layers back. Most guys boast about their achievements, you don't, and I like it. Don't forget I tried the eligible-bachelor route and got a cheating, conniving husband for my trouble. It's nice to be with someone who understands and challenges me."

He smiled. "Great. I didn't want to be some experiment—"

"You're not, okay? I'd say hunting down Richelieu is pretty far from a regular job."

"Not right now, though."

"You'll be back soon enough. You sure you don't want to take a few days off with me?"

"I wish. Next time, for sure."

"I better show you what you'll miss over Christmas, then." She leaned forward and, careful not to bump his left side, began kissing him.

By the end of the night, he'd almost changed his mind.

58

Marissa left early, and although movement came with jolts of pain, it had been worth it.

Christmas was only two days away and gave IA an excuse to continue to drag their heels to meet up. Although Hogan was detached from the Richelieu investigation, it dominated his thoughts. But this was worse than his time in the hospital. Grabbing his phone, he messaged Vance, asking her to call. He'd explained the suspension the day before and sworn her to secrecy. She replied with the thumbs-up emoticon, and ten minutes later, she rang.

"Any developments?" he fired immediately.

"Well, hello to you too."

"Sorry, I'm going stir-crazy here."

"Nothing to report of note. Miller demanded we keep you out of the loop—standard procedure, yada, yada, yada. I feigned agreement, but he can swivel—especially after what's happened. We still lack notable connections between Fullerton—and Chopra and Decker. And Miller's theories are pure crap. IA still riding you hard?"

"They're still fucking me about on the meet. It's going to be next week now. They'll stretch this out. I look forward to seeing their faces when it comes to nothing."

"Keep calm and carry on, old chap." Vance gave the best approximation of his accent.

He laughed. "I'll try. Have a good Christmas. Call me if anything significant breaks."

"Of course! You too, and stay out of trouble."

After four beers and bored of trying to find connections in the murders, Hogan decided on an evening diet of Domino's and TV. He'd joined Fox News mid-segment broadcasting from a familiar Miami location. Charles Lyle's taste in linen jackets had not improved.

"Law enforcement's incompetence means that I won't spend Christmas at my home in Houston," Lyle sneered. "If they'd caught this Richelieu character, I wouldn't be stuck here."

Hogan shook his head. How much sympathy could viewers have for a billionaire forced to spend the holidays in his current mansion instead of his Texan one?

"The stress and untold difficulties of heading up there while my life is at risk mean I'll continue to wait right here for the FBI to…*do their job*." Lyle emphasized these last three words. He wasn't alone. Billionaires nationwide had changed their schedules and ramped up security. Many feared that with no discernible pattern to the assassinations, they could be next. If Richelieu's aim was to disrupt the nation's business community, it had worked.

"Do you have any viable theories about who could be behind the killings?" the interviewer asked, her spectacular platinum-blonde hair unmoved as she tilted her head.

Well, do you?

"It could be some damned commies trying to bring down corporate America. God knows they've tried everything else," Lyle offered.

That's a no, then.

"I'm surprised the *Washington Tribune* hasn't discovered who is behind the killings. If Cole Sandzer's mouthpiece put as much effort into finding the assassin as writing untruthful articles about my business dealings, this would be over already."

"And how is business?"

"Oil is going through the roof, so that's good. These woke liberals calling for clean energy forget how much they need guys like me. And as for those people calling for more billionaires to die…"

What a piece of work. *Happy Christmas!* People across the country are struggling to put food on their plates, yet this guy, wealthier than some nations, was getting coverage to air his grievances. No wonder the average Joe was pissed. The doorbell rang, making him glad of the respite from this nonsense.

He sat back down with his pizza. If Richelieu did strike again, he could do worse than pick Charles Lyle.

59

A RAPPING ON the door woke Hogan. He grabbed his phone and squinted at the time. Cursing, he shuffled to the door and found Tate and Monroe on the other side.

"Really, seven a.m.? What the fuck do you want?"

"We have a warrant to search the address and remove any electronic items, including your cell phone." Monroe thrust a piece of paper into his hand.

"You got nowhere else to be on Christmas Eve?" Examining the warrant, Hogan saw Judge Ramirez's name under a familiar signature.

Well, isn't payback a bitch.

He stood aside and let them enter.

"Party for one?" Monroe snarked, gesturing at the bottles on the table.

Hogan gave him the finger and settled back on the sofa—annoyed they'd called on the rare occasion his apartment wasn't tidy. Beer bottles kept the empty pizza box company on the coffee table.

"Shit, this is gonna take no time at all," Tate announced as he returned from the bedroom, his eyes panning across the sparse living room.

Hogan turned to the fish tank.

"Sorry about the disturbance. These two boneheads shouldn't be long."

The seahorse bobbed across the tank with what might have been excitement. The starfish peeled a leg off the glass, then reattached it in a wave of solidarity.

Tate laid out a MacBook, phone, and several files, as Monroe focused on writing out evidence bags. There hadn't been much to take and the resulting search was brief.

"When will I get my stuff back?"

"Once we're done," Tate growled. "Oh, and we request your appearance at Wilshire on Thursday, December thirtieth at midday." *

At least he had a date now.

"Can you let me copy a number from my phone?"

The agents looked at each other, unsure how to proceed now this was in their possession.

"Whose?" Tate asked, narrowing his eyes.

"My girlfriend's, you can watch me do it."

"Thought you were the memory guy. I don't think so."

"I guess I got lazy. How do you dumb fucks plan to break the key lock?" Hogan asked, confident their impatience would get him what he wanted.

Monroe's face turned an ugly shade of red; he stepped forward, but Tate, the more pragmatic of the two, raised his hand to stop him.

"You'll leave it open after?"

"Sure, I've nothing to hide, and the quicker you confirm exactly that, the sooner I get it back."

Tate handed it over.

Hogan memorized Marissa's number to prove a point, set the auto-lock screen to never, and held it out like a petulant teenager to an angry parent.

Tate took it, dropped it in a clear bag, and joined his partner by the entrance.

"Your ass is ours!" Monroe called back as he marched outside.

60

Colorful vendors hawked tarot readings, iron sculptures, and eclectic artwork as Hogan strolled down Venice Beach Boulevard. There was limited passing trade—but given the pervasive aroma of pot—everyone should get through the day just fine.

As the winter sunshine warmed his face, he messaged Marissa. He imagined her reading it, tight red bikini contrasting with a white sandy beach, azure waters lapping in from the ocean. It wasn't difficult, as they'd FaceTimed yesterday—another brief insight into a different life, one of luxury. Hogan had even installed his old Instagram account onto his burner phone. Marissa had explained she'd update it with her days in paradise.

Christmas Day at Paradiso had been pleasant enough. If the staff begrudged working, they hadn't shown it. Bing Crosby and Dean Martin had provided a festive soundtrack—his dad sang along. Another miracle of the mind was that song lyrics endured, but memories of friends or family did not. The Christmas dinner there had saved Hogan from a lonely takeaway. He'd declined Nemo's invite but suggested they meet today.

Yet another electric scooter zipped past Hogan as he walked. Like most locals, he hated them and hoped the company's bankruptcy would come soon.

IA's visit a few days earlier made Hogan thankful he'd been so careful—everything at The Rose should be safe. His exoneration would take time—the first step toward that was due later that week. His frustration of being away from his team and the case continued to fester.

With worries an ongoing companion, he couldn't wait to chat with the smartest guy he knew.

Hogan walked into the Ye Olde King's Head at the bottom end of Santa Monica Boulevard. It sat next to a store of the same name, which had the addition of the word "Shoppe." No doubt they hoped this throwback to Chaucer would add further medieval authenticity. He'd driven by but had never set foot inside. He sneaked up behind Nemo's stool and slapped his broad shoulders; his friend jumped—and spun around with an excited grin.

"Hey! You like the place? It's like an English pub, right?"

Hogan surveyed the establishment. A jumble of plaques ran across the bar's wooden beams, and the menus were emblazoned with Union Jacks and London Underground roundels. Signs for Boddingtons and Newcastle Brown Ale called out to you from behind the bar. He dredged up memories of the English pubs of his late teens but wasn't sure they had looked like this. Regardless, it triggered his love of nostalgia as he pulled up a barstool.

"Kinda. It's subtle."

Nemo snickered and beckoned over the barmaid.

"Two Guinnesses, please."

After a few beers at the bar, they moved to a booth for more privacy. Scotch eggs, shepherd's pie, and bangers and mash followed as Hogan enjoyed dishes from his childhood. He wished he could be transported back to when his mum eased dinner in front of him, with a warning dessert required an empty plate.

Nemo's chunky fingers waved across his vision.

"Hey, anyone home...you okay?"

"Sorry, mate, I was miles away."

"A couple of decades away too, right?

Hogan nodded. "Another beer?"

"Damn straight."

They discussed the case for hours, throwing out theories and discounting most. The comfortable leather squeaked as Nemo leaned forward with his latest point.

"Richelieu isn't going to make a mistake, so it's gonna take a chunk of luck to catch him. Time for you to make your own fortune."

"Meaning what exactly?"

"Well, it's time to get more proactive. We know Richelieu surveils his targets in advance. I'm also guessing now more comprehensively with the new security in place."

"Agreed."

"So let's assume that is happening again right now. How about hunting the hunter?"

"The next target could be any billionaire or even someone else."

"True, but let's assume it's the former. Maybe stick to the top twenty or even ten richest. Pick one, then figure out how you would surveil them if they were your target."

Hogan paused—his beer shy of his mouth. Nemo was right—he needed to be proactive. He had spare time. He'd be doing something useful. Sure, the odds were against him, but way better than kicking his heels at home powerless, brooding—waiting for Vance's snippets of info. He scribbled down the possible choices on the back of a beer mat. Miami was far and expensive this time of year, and rushing back to LA would be tough. They ruled out New York for the same reasons. Fairfax would be a convenient choice but didn't feel right. Douglas Matterhorn was cocooned on a private island, and Terrence Fisher safe in New Zealand. He could head up to Seattle, and Felix Moore or down to Palm Springs, but the most obvious option was Cole Sandzer in Vegas. He circled his name.

"Why am I not surprised?" Nemo laughed.

"It makes sense, though, yeah?"

"It does. Perfectly legal sports-book for soccer betting, too, while IA is on your case."

"That never crossed my mind."

61

TATE AND MONROE kept Hogan and his FAA rep, Pete Butler, waiting half an hour.

"Sorry for the delay," Monroe began, "lots of data to get through." Tate joined him at the table, tie askew, eyes tired.

"You ready?" Butler asked, his broad shoulders and jaw set firm.

Hogan indicated he was. He had a prepared statement a couple of days prior. He relaxed and fixed his stare on Monroe as he read it.

"On the twenty-first of December, we had a meeting where you requested an explanation of the origination of funds that pay for my father's ongoing care at Paradiso in Culver City. I'm now happy to share that information…"

"Why not share it last week?" Monroe interjected. Hogan ignored him and continued.

"My father's nephew, my cousin, funds much of the care. He owns a successful London hedge fund. I can share his contact details with you to verify this and close this charade of an investigation. He'll be happy to answer any questions you should have. Given his standing in the London business community, I would appreciate it if any interview could be discreet. I hope this clarifies the source of funds and proves no wrongdoing on my behalf."

Tate and Monroe looked at each other and back at him. They'd not expected this level of cooperation. He didn't expect it to shift their conviction he was receiving illicit cash, but he caught the momentary doubt in their eyes.

"Oh, we know about the London bank transfers. You knew where the electronic payment trail would lead and have concocted this story." Tate wafted his hand in dismissal.

"You can believe whatever you like. It is the truth."

"Why are you behind on payments if he's so rich?" Monroe shot back.

"He's a busy man, or maybe I forgot to remind him the invoice was due. We have quite the case going on that we need to—"

"Bullshit."

Tate reached over, resting his hand on his irate colleague's arm.

"You understand we won't take your word for this; it all seems a little convenient."

"Of course, which is why I have all the details for Toby and his lawyer here." Hogan slid a piece of paper across the desk. "I hope this will speed up proceedings, and you can clear me for proper investigation work." He left the *unlike this* off the end of the sentence, but the implication was clear. Monroe shoved his chair back and stormed out of the room, but Tate lingered—frozen as if weighing up his next move on a chessboard. He sighed and rose from his seat.

"We'll be in touch."

As Hogan left the elevator, he came face to face with Carla.

"We're getting coffee," she announced and walked out of the building; he followed.

After grabbing two triple-shot Americanos, they sat in the corner of their local joint.

"There is a good explanation, right?" she asked.

"There is."

"Because you had me questioning my judgment. Why the fuck did you not explain everything to IA last week, then?" The added deep frown lines weren't needed to convey her annoyance. Hogan ran through the same story and rationale he had with Marissa, finding a more understanding audience. Carla had been around long enough to know that IA wouldn't have dropped the inquiry at this. She nodded as he finished.

"Sounds like a good guy, your cousin. Kinda tough he's been dragged into this."

"That's why I wanted to give him a heads-up. They'll dig more, but there is nothing to find." Hogan turned over his empty palms to illustrate the point. "How long do you think?"

"I won't lie, it could be weeks, months even."

Hogan froze, stunned. He might as well be off the case for good.

"That's bullshit. Is there nothing you can do?" he pleaded.

"I have no jurisdiction over IA, you know that. Only a deputy-director or above could intervene."

"So, I have to sit on my hands while they drag this out?"

"I'm sorry, but yeah."

"And I hear Miller's taken over from me." Hogan didn't hide his distaste. "You know he's behind this phony investigation, right? He wants me off the case and to claim the glory if we get Richelieu," he added. This time, when Carla answered, she was defensive.

"Hey, I got a solid nudge from above. I already told you he's a golden boy to many. His dad is connected in Washington, so who knows what's gone on behind closed doors." She sighed. "I'm guessing you can't prove it's Miller who passed on the invoice?"

Hogan shook his head. "And if I get back before the investigation gets wrapped up?"

"Let's see where we are when you're back, okay?"

"*Let's see* was my parents' response when I asked for something they knew we wouldn't do."

"Hey! I'm on your side here." Her voice was firm now. "If we haven't got him, you'll come back refreshed, and you can go again at nailing this fucker—that's the most important thing here, however it happens."

She was right, only he had no intention of waiting. He'd be hunting Richelieu.

62

Without friends, the drive to Vegas dragged. On the first Monday of the new year, Hogan was heading there with more hope than expectation. He'd used the days since meeting with IA to research Cole Sandzer and explore connections suggesting he could be the next target.

The billionaire bought his first newspaper in 1975 and built one of the largest media empires in the world. Their editorial was liberal, and articles attacked the Russian, Chinese, and Saudi Arabian governments. This made him powerful enemies. In recent years he'd led the streaming revolution. His platform, Watchable, had over three hundred million subscribers globally. The dynamics of movie production and distribution were changing, and despite his advancing years, Sandzer was at the forefront.

The previous evening, Vance had called around with an update. There hadn't been much progress. The ballistics from the Fullerton killings were a dead end. Despite the San José setback, Chung and his team were still working the finance angle, convinced it was their best chance of a breakthrough. Vance and Ranger continued to refine Richelieu's profile. His friends had promised to keep in touch while he was away.

The sprawling Primm Valley casino announced the Nevada state line. The neon lights told degenerate gamblers arriving from California they need head no further. He had an hour's drive left. He thumbed out a reply to Marissa's earlier message as "Roll With It" started on his nineties playlist. Maybe it was a sign he should hit the craps tables.

The new year had come and gone without incident—not hard when you had six beers and a starfish and seahorse for company. Marissa had been in touch every day and had called at midnight, sounding a little drunk. She expressed excitement about her return at the end of the week, which he'd reciprocated. He'd kept his Vegas trip from her for now.

Las Vegas Boulevard was broader than most highways, and the surrounding gargantuan hotels skewed your perspective. Nothing was as close as it seemed. Hogan turned left off Tropicana Avenue onto "the Strip," and then by a giant Chili's, swung a right into the Travelodge.

Nothing to shout about here; this wasn't a high-roller establishment.

Opposite, numerous colossal glass structures made up the City Center development. In the middle and atop a shimmering tower sat Cole Sandzer's penthouse.

Once he'd checked into his uninspiring ground-floor room, he left the lingering smell of nicotine and despair, walked by a tattoo parlor called Vegas Inc., and onto the Strip. What happened in Vegas stayed in Vegas—aside from a tattoo. Across the street, the Aria's ten stories-high screen played scenes from Jewel nightclub. The crowd bounced to a fist-pumping DJ, and groups of model-grade couples enjoyed bottle service. Vegas's entertainment side was now as essential and competitive as the gambling choices in this ever-evolving city. The contrast to Hogan's side of the Strip was stark. There, shops offered four T-shirts for ten bucks and tacky souvenirs as country music blasted out. He headed to the nearest bridge over Las Vegas Boulevard to cross to where the real money was spent.

A doorman performed his specific duty, and Hogan walked into a compact ornate entrance with a compact concierge desk. He turned down the offer of assistance. This towering building was split between luxury condos and the Waldorf Astoria Las Vegas. The WA's lobby was twenty-three floors up—rooms beginning from that floor and running almost to the top. Cole Sandzer's penthouse covered the highest floor. Carla had mentioned the only access was via two hidden elevators close to where he now sat messing with his phone. Two capable-looking close-protection guys flanked the doors to these. Both were alert and unsmiling, their back-suited arms bulging. He continued to play the part of a tourist waiting for a friend, on occasion glancing in expectation across the room, including surveying both men.

A few minutes later, the doors to the private elevators parted, revealing two more guards as a sharp-suited man strode toward him.

"Can I help at all, sir?"

"Oh, I'm waiting for a friend."

"Then I'm sure the hotel lobby will be more comfortable." The man waited until Hogan rose, walked him to the elevator, and punched number twenty-three. He stood expressionless until the doors closed.

Hogan stepped out opposite a champagne vending machine with Moët & Chandon signage. Potato chips and Dr Pepper didn't cut it in this establishment. He continued through the plush surroundings to the bar, paid for an overpriced drink, and took a seat facing out over the Strip. Taillights flashed as traffic edged north. Savoring the expensive beer, he considered what he'd learned. Gaining entrance to Sandzer's penthouse via the elevator lobby would be near impossible. He'd need to plot alternate routes and methods the following morning. To catch the assassin, he'd need to think like one.

63

Two miles north of the Waldorf Astoria, Kirov selected yet another seventeen-dollar bottle of Fiji water from the mini-bar. He'd opted for comfort a suitable distance away from the impending scene of carnage. This time, an anonymous shell company had booked this room at the Wynn—one of the hundred and fifty thousand available in this city. These numbers helped justify this low-risk indulgence. He'd spent the last two nights here, having switched from the less desirable Paris Hotel. Both had offered online check-in, a must in his situation. After his next killing, the FBI would search for long-term single male occupants, so moving ensured an arduous hunt.

It had taken Kirov eleven days to perfect his plan. and, satisfied he had covered every eventuality, he was almost ready to go. Vegas would reach full capacity later in the week. The annual Consumer Electronics Show began Thursday and attracted swarms of tech-loving nerds, journalists, and media companies. The city would be full of men wearing branded baseball caps and carrying goodie bags of shitty merchandise. The timing could not be more perfect. It would be easy to blend right in. He even had a fake beard for that extra realism.

Kirov hopped from the bed. After all this was over, and he settled down in Montenegro, he'd acquire one this comfy—giant square pillows and all, although five was excessive. He walked over to the window and opened the Signal app on his phone. The evening sky offered a gradation of moody blues as Kirov surveyed the jagged mountains below in the distance. Roads snaked back to the Vegas sprawl from the darkness of the foothills. A century before, this had been nothing but desert.

Flashes from the direction of the Treasure Island Hotel caught his attention. A little down the Strip, crowds had congregated to watch a simulated pirate ship battle. It appeared a little too good-natured, even at this distance. He felt a pang of nostalgia for the night he first read the book of the same name. If his grandmother hadn't been killed his path could have been so different, but it was too late to dwell on what might have been. His life, with rare exception, had been one of violence and anger since that day. The phone remained lit up in his hand, and he typed a quick message for Silver:

Thursday should be the delivery day. As before, you'll know when the job is complete.

He gazed back out of the window. What would Robert Louis Stevenson have made of the themed hotel?
The phone vibrated with the reply:

Excellent. Will be in touch after.

The final leaps of performers through the smoke ended the battle scene. Stevenson would have hated it as much as he did.

64

THE FOLLOWING DAY Hogan returned to the Waldorf Astoria under the premise of wanting to book a conference for Nemo's company. The friendly receptionist agreed to show him a room on the highest floor.

The elevator opened onto a tasteful corridor, and Debbie, his companion, tapped her card on a sensor a few doors down. The room offered up a subtle scent of jasmine as they entered.

The Travelodge this was not.

"So, this is our one-bedroom suite, popular with executives," she announced in her lilting southern accent as Hogan headed to the window.

The Strip views were badass.

"How many rooms may you require?"

"I'm not exactly sure yet, quite a few."

"Okay, cool. There's a deep soak bath, a control panel by the bed, and blackout blind. Also, these rooms are soundproof—you could have a party, and your neighbors wouldn't know. But, of course, we don't encourage that kind of behavior."

"Of course." Hogan gave the desk a quick once-over for added effect. "It's just what we need." As they stepped out of the doorway, he stopped, brow furrowed. "One last thing. My CEO is a bit of a safety nut. Where is the fire escape located?" This was the real reason for his subterfuge. He wanted to check potential entry to the penthouse floor and Sandzer.

His companion pointed to the universal green exit sign at the end of the corridor.

"Could we open it?"

When Debbie paused, he added, "Sorry, he insists I ensure it all works. These crazy tech guys, *huh*?" And threw out his palms.

"Okay…I suppose," she tapped a code into a keypad by the door. It clicked open, and she pushed it, explaining, "It sets off an alarm otherwise."

They entered a stairwell with steps leading down—all normal. But if you wanted to head up, you wouldn't get far. A steel door and fitted frame lay seven steps up on the first landing. Sandzer *definitely* wasn't taking any chances. Hogan turned, eyebrows raised.

"Oh, our very top floor is being refurbished."

He offered an understanding nod; Sandzer must have closed that too, worried about an attack from below his penthouse.

Arriving in reception, he thanked Debbie with suitable effusion. Her manager hovered in the background, so he promised Selantio would book soon.

Hogan stepped onto the Strip. As he walked, he encountered Transformers, half-naked girl cops, and, of course, Alan from *The Hangover*, baby sling included.

Here, the grift never stopped.

He crossed the street to the Miracle Mile Shops to find binoculars for the next part of his reconnoiter. Straight after he entered the mall, a bar called The Tipsy Robot caught his attention. Rows of iPads sat behind industrial-looking robotic arms shaking cocktails. A group of junk-food-loving onlookers in NASCAR T-shirts stood enthralled. When the AI and robot revolution came, his job should be safe; if he could get back to it.

As Hogan completed his purchase, his phone rang. No number showed, but he recognized Monroe's angry tone immediately.

"We spoke with your cousin in London and know he's lying."

Hogan remained silent, letting this play out.

"There's no way he's that fucking generous. Something else is going on. I know you're dirty, and we're gonna find out exactly how. I could smell the fear of a guilty man the first day we met."

"You finished?"

"Not with you. Don't think your boss can put pressure on mine. That shit isn't gonna fly—we'll keep coming at you till we find what we're looking for."

"Then you're going to be searching for a long time. There's nothing to find, never was."

"We'll decide—"

He hung up before Monroe could continue. He wasn't going to give him the pleasure. IA's Viagra hadn't yet worn off, and they'd keep pushing. He approached a crosswalk as traffic built up at the lengthy red lights. One driver at the front gripped his steering wheel. Hogan could empathize—IA had nothing, but he'd have to wait for their green light.

For the rest of the cloudless afternoon, Hogan used his new purchase to pan across Sandzer's penthouse, then back to surrounding buildings. He looked at rooftops and angles, hypothesizing on locations for a potential attack. Any exterior assassination attempt stood little chance. Sandzer's windows were UL Level 8 bullet resistant, designed to take 7.62 mm caliber rounds without any immediate risk to the occupants. Bulletproof was only a phrase for the movies and Joe public, and suppliers always avoided using this term, probably to avoid being sued if things went wrong. The surveillance didn't improve his mood and fostered a growing conviction this was all a waste of time. A long-distance shot at Lyle on Star Island or beating Felix Moore's ranch security would be more doable.

Hogan flopped onto the bed in his miserable room. Right now, Miller and countless other agents were working the case hard. Any slight bit of luck could bring a breakthrough, and where would he be? Staring at faded curtains in this shitty motel. He grabbed his wallet and resolved to find one-dollar beers and cheap blackjack. He could get drunk, make a little cash, and do what this city was built for—escape reality.

65

THE COSMOPOLITAN SPORTS-BOOK ensured a captive audience. The curved wall of screens a morass of sport and betting opportunities available to patrons slouched in deep leather seats. Hogan had several bets on evening UK Premier League matches, and two games were live. He never got a chance to trade matches midweek because of work, and without a laptop, he still couldn't now. Acquiring another would risk it ending up in the hands of IA.

Several drinks and two hours later, he rose from his chair, satisfied. He'd made a few hundred bucks toward the trip costs. He'd make up for lost time once he could return to The Rose. The clock was ticking—any day now, he expected an awkward call from Mrs. Malkin about the remaining Paradiso balance.

Fucking Internal Affairs.

As he stepped outside, blinking at the aggressive sunlight, his cell phone rang, and he fished it out of his jeans pocket. He figured it would be Marissa or the long shot of Carla with unlikely news of reinstatement. He frowned at the *unknown* description on the screen; only a few people had this temporary number. He hit the green button and waited.

"Hogan?"

"Who's this?"

"Nemo gave me your number."

"Ah, okay—"

"It's Warren Fisk. You're a hard man to get hold of."

"Sorry. Internal Affairs have my phone."

"Figured somethin' was off. I called you a few times and got no response. Then Nemo explained what had gone down."

"You have some news?" Hogan replied, buoyed by the officer's efforts to reach him.

"'Fraid not, though that's the reason for the call."

There must be more, so he waited for Fisk to continue.

"After you passed me the profile, I asked a few people here and there, coupla station chiefs I go way back with, you get the idea. Next thing I get Wolgomott up my ass, asking what the hell I'm doin'. I tell him to go to hell, but then Deputy Director Kline drags me into his office and tells me to leave this alone. It's a federal problem—blah, blah, blah, and that sources could be compromised. So, I've had to back off. Hope you understand, my friend."

"Of course. Feels a little odd, though. This case is a big deal for everyone. You think this is the same old Bureau-Agency bullshit?"

"I'm not so sure, but I can't push it further. I wanted to let you know. Sounds like you have enough on your plate."

"I appreciate the call, Warren. Thanks for trying—I owe you."

"No worries, sorry it was a bust. Take care."

Hogan slipped the phone back into his pocket. Another avenue had closed, but this didn't mean the CIA had nothing to hide. He longed for a beer with Nemo to talk this through.

He spent what remained of the afternoon scanning across the top of the Waldorf Astoria and adjacent buildings.

Nothing suspicious stood out.

If this was all a waste of time—he might as well spend the evening in a bar. He resolved to stay two more days, then head to LA. Marissa would be back on Saturday too. He still hadn't mentioned he was in Vegas, only that he was pursuing a lead. But he wasn't to know that a few miles down the strip, Kirov was ready to change everything.

66

From the Aria roof, Kirov gazed up from his book as the sun began its daily climb. His eyes tracked back to the Waldorf Astoria. The building's exterior screamed expense—ostentatious gold panels clad its side. *The Hangover* had got it wrong: getting off the roof would never have been the issue; getting on there would have taken more effort. He'd followed a window cleaner to a downtown bar and scanned his access card to clone it. The process he'd used in New York proved useful again. Then he'd needed an Aria room key to flash at security when he approached the elevators. He'd booked a night and checked in the week before but never set foot in a room.

The empty lanes of the Strip stretched into the distance. Occasional cabs trundled by, taking workers to or from casino shifts or call girls home. This roof gave the ideal vantage point from which to launch his attack. Every element of the equipment before him had required careful acquisition. This included the two assembled DJI Matrice 200 V2 drones, delivered to a vacant house in Henderson the previous week. Online delivery made life so much easier to achieve complete anonymity. Both were fitted with three kilos of plastic explosive from his private, untraceable supply. If CubeSmart could see what sat in his San José storage unit, they'd have to evacuate several blocks. The drones wouldn't be able to fly for long carrying this weight, but he only needed them to make it the six hundred yards to Cole Sandzer's penthouse. After that, it was a matter of timing.

Kirov checked the light, deemed it okay, and launched into action. He stood at the roof's edge and panned his FLIR thermal-imaging camera across the penthouse windows. There was only one static heat signature in the room. He picked up the drones and rested them on the ledge. Both were preprogrammed to fly to the same GPS location. Once they left the roof, it would take them less than forty seconds to reach Sandzer's bedroom. Setting them off twelve seconds apart would be optimal. The first would decimate the bullet-resistant glass but would be unlikely to cause a fatality. The next drone would fly straight into the room and dispatch its deadly payload. The timing would be too quick for the target to react, but the slight gap was essential to avoid damage to the second drone from the first explosion. He folded the bag that had held them both, added it to his branded backpack, visualized his escape route from the Aria again, and edged forward.

He had death to deliver.

67

THE AMOROUS COUPLE next door ended Hogan's fractured sleep. He showered gingerly—his ribs still sensitive to touch. On leaving his room, a blast of weed-filled air hit him; the guy next door stood outside enjoying a postcoital joint. He eyed Hogan and held it out. *Why not?* He didn't have a badge, after all. But he shook his head and turned to walk to the Strip, bathed in the first rays of sunlight from the east. At this early hour, the Aria buffet presented the most enticing option.

After stopping in Walgreens for a bottle of water, he crossed to the other side of the Strip and meandered up the sidewalk to the Aria, killing time. He'd checked, and the buffet didn't open until seven a.m. If Vegas had a downtime—it was around now. Too early for most and too late for many. Panhandlers had even retreated to whichever storm drain they called home. By normal standards the streets were deadly quiet. He craned his neck, the angle up to Sandzer's penthouse oblique from where he stood. Then, born out of habit from the last few days, he switched his view to the latticelike roof of the Aria.

Nothing.

As he reached the far end, a reflection of sunlight and movement snapped his eyes back left. He reached for his budget binoculars and trained them on the spot where the flash of light had come from. A figure dressed in black and sporting a green cap bent over, working on something. The person continued to the roof's edge and placed an item down. Hogan's view wasn't clear, and he wished he had a pair of Kowas.

He panned to the empty window-cleaning rig a few floors down to rule out workers starting early and back across to the Waldorf Astoria building. The Aria roof provided a vantage point from which to launch an attack, and if this figure was Richelieu, it appeared imminent. Hogan glanced toward Sandzer's apartment building, but what would he say? He had no badge and nothing concrete—they'd peg him as a threat, and then it would be too late. He turned back to the Aria and began sprinting toward the entrance.

Kirov ran through the final checks of the drones and placed them back on the ledge.

It was time.

He set the first on its way, counting, "One billionaire, two billionaires, three billionaires." On twelve, he launched the second. Glad of his sunglasses, he tracked their inexorable path to death.

Hogan sprinted across the casino floor, zigzagging between chiming slot machines toward the Sky Loft elevators. He'd stayed here four years ago, so he had a good idea of the direction. The guard staffing the wooden security desk shouted as he flew by. He'd started hitting the call button when a figure appeared next to him.

"Hey, buddy, where's the fire? I need to see your room key."

"FBI, it's an emergency. I need to get up to your roof."

The guard eyed Hogan's casual attire.

"You got some ID?"

"Yeah, no, wait...not on me..." The light pinged—he didn't have time for this. The guard, not buying the story, stepped toward him as the doors slid open. Hogan turned and struck him in the kidneys. The man doubled over and fell to the ground. Stepping into the elevator, Hogan hit the button for the top floor, but nothing happened, and realizing why, he hurried back to the prone guard. Grabbing the key card clipped to his cheap blue blazer, he evaded the gasping man's grasping hands. Hopping back in the elevator, he tapped it on the sensor, and to his relief, the number fifty-nine lit up when he hit it. The doors closed as the guard panted into his radio for help.

After what felt like an age, the doors opened on the top floor. Bursting out, Hogan ran down the main hallway, then turned down a smaller one leading to the fire-escape doors. Flying through these, he scrambled up a ladder to the hatch to the roof. Ignoring the alarm warnings, he flung it open and clambered into the bright sunlight.

Even though he knew it was coming, Kirov flinched when the first drone collided with the window and exploded. Glass and debris tumbled to the ground below as a smoke cloud blossomed in all directions. The second drone continued on the same path, passing through the smoke before exploding with a duller thud. The lessened explosive sound told Kirov all he needed to know; it had detonated inside the bedroom. Sandzer couldn't have survived. He grabbed the backpack and began to sprint across the roof. The farthest exit from the rooftop was closest to the elevators, and it was wiser to cover the ground here than through the corridors. He'd mapped out every step of the escaped route. Confusion would reign for a while, giving him time to disappear. As he reached the open hatch, he observed a figure climbing onto the roof three hundred yards away. He paused to draw his brand-new SIG and jumped onto the ladder.

As Hogan emerged onto the roof, smoke billowed from Sandzer's penthouse. He was too late. Scouring the expanse, he shouted at the figure on the opposite side to stop.

He didn't expect him to.

The man wore the same green cap he'd spotted from below. He spun in Hogan's direction, reached into his jacket, then disappeared downward. It must be the route to the other fire escape, and this guy had to be Richelieu. Hogan turned back and slid down the ladder, cursing that he was unarmed. How he would stop the assailant hadn't yet crossed his mind.

He flung open the fire exit door and ran down the first shorter hallway before turning onto the main corridor. Richelieu stood in front of the bank of elevators, weapon drawn, head flipping from side to side. The assassin swung the gun and fired in one swift motion. Hogan had already begun to throw himself to safety but wasn't quick enough. Searing pain tore through the top of his arm even before he hit the floor. He rolled over once and sprang to his feet, ducking into a recess between rooms. An elderly woman emerged opposite—he shooed her back inside, the desperation in his eyes enough to convey the danger. Edging back toward the main hallway, Hogan crouched down and stole a glance. Richelieu was gone. He got up and sprinted for the elevators. His arm throbbed, but still had movement. At first look, it appeared to be a through and through—he might have got lucky. He banged on the call button, and when the elevator arrived, he stepped forward to enter it, only to find a gun pointed at his head.

68

HOGAN WAS STILL alive because the gun belonged to an overweight hotel security guard flanked by one of similar girth and a skinnier younger one. As he raised his hands, he was spun around, and his face crushed into the elevator's mirrored wall. One guard cuffed him while another punched the lobby button.

"I'm an FBI Special Agent, and I'm pursuing a fugitive who just blew up Cole Sandzer's penthouse," Hogan announced as the elevator began to descend. The guards exchanged surprised glances; the explosion was still news to them. "You need to radio all security now to apprehend an individual, around six-foot, green cap, beard, and carrying a black bag."

The skinny guard's eyes darted to the bloody droplets accumulating near his colleague's feet.

"He fucking shot me! It's Richelieu. I'm guessing the name means something!" Hogan was less calm now as he arched his head back further.

"The radios don't work in the elevator, pal, but all I know is you slugged Donald pretty good. I mean, you could be this Richelieu fella," the tubby security guard drawled, pushing Hogan's head back into the glass for good measure. The elevator pinged, and the doors slid open on the first level. "We'll wait for the police, and I suppose a paramedic too—then we can see what's what." They began marching Hogan toward a door marked "Private." He tried to scan across the casino as they did, but it was too late.

The arrival of two police officers provided a rapid resolution to Hogan's immediate situation. One recognized him from press conferences on

Richelieu, and a few calls later, they had reassurances on his identity. They, in turn, confirmed what he already suspected—that Cole Sandzer had been killed. A sharp-eyed paramedic had worked on his injury in the interim. The bullet had torn through the edge of his arm, taking a chunk of flesh with it, but nothing more. It could have been way worse. She had dressed his wound and given him antibiotics after he'd turned down a trip to the ER. Time was of the essence.

With the police's help, Hogan gained access to a stuffy security room. He reviewed the security footage from the fifty-ninth floor and elevators, trying to trace Richelieu's movements. His phone buzzed in his pocket—news traveled fast.

"Do I have this right—you're on the scene in Vegas? How the actual fuck, Hogan?"

Carla sounded more surprised than angry.

"Happy to share the whole story, but I need back in, Carla. You have to get IA to wrap their shit up." For once, there was silence on the other end of the line, so he pushed on. "I can help with the crime scenes here, all of them. I know this guy better than anyone—he just shot me, for Christ's sake!"

"Okay, okay. Woah, hang on…you hurt?"

"No, I'm good. The bullet passed straight through. I got lucky."

"No shit. Listen, I got pushback from Monroe and Tate's boss already."

"They intimated as much. Circumstances have changed now. Do you want to explain why an agent had to chase down Richelieu with no weapon?"

"Of course, I fucking don't," she snapped before falling silent for a few seconds. Then sounding more collected, she said, "I'll make the case to the director himself and see if he can get this put on ice."

"Thanks, I don't mean to be—"

"Okay, Hogan, another time. Miller and a team of agents are traveling to join those from the Las Vegas field office. Stay put and do nothing until they arrive."

Hogan couldn't let Miller sweep in and take over. He had the jump on everyone and intended to keep it that way.

He turned his attention to the screen before him and rewound the elevator footage. Richelieu came into the frame making good his escape and, despite rushing in, kept his bearded face hidden from the camera. He held a SIG Sauer P226 in his hand. The same type of weapon used to kill Fullerton. The green cap had "Moliff Technology" emblazoned on it. The black bag was adorned with an inverted pyramid logo and a strap-line saying: "Turning History Upside Down." It sounded like tech company bullshit. The outfit would blend right in with CES in town. He made a note to follow up on these companies anyway. He continued the footage until Richelieu exited the elevators. Then paused it. Confident of what he had missed, he returned to the beginning. He stopped the footage when the promenade-level button lit up. He'd been trying to figure out why that floor and not the first on initial viewing—when he should have focused on something way more important. Hogan's unexpected arrival and pursuit of the killer had caused him to make a mistake.

The frozen image proved it.

When Richelieu had tapped the button with his right finger, he hadn't been wearing gloves.

69

KIROV KEPT THE white Nissan Sentra at a steady sixty. The I-15 heading away from Vegas was quiet. The cap, fake beard, bag, and SIG Sauer P226 had all been buried fifteen miles back. One of the advantages of driving through a featureless desert was infinite hiding places. He was more than a little rattled. How the hell had the FBI agent turned up on the roof at that exact time? How come he was on his own and unarmed? It made no sense at all. If they'd known about the attack, he'd be in custody or likely dead. This was something else—a riddle he couldn't solve right now. For the first time since he became Kirov after leaving Florida all those years ago, he'd been close to getting caught. Special Agent Hogan was a loose end and would have to be dealt with.

Despite the unexpected events after the drone strike, he kept to his plan and left the elevator on the second floor. This route was the best to avoid security on the short walk to the Aria's rear exit. Once outside, he'd strolled into the Vdara Hotel, continuing straight to the walkway leading to the Bellagio, making the parking garage there within minutes. His silver Prius had been charging at the convenient spots reserved for electric vehicles. He'd swapped caps, slipped gloves on, and jumped into the car. As he'd eased onto the Strip, the first emergency vehicles had streamed by, leaving a cacophony of noise in their wake. Light traffic meant he'd swung left over the bridge across I-15 and pulled into the vast Rio Hotel parking lot, all within minutes. His vehicle became one of the thousands already there. The Sentra had pulled onto the I-15 bound for LA before the police reached the Waldorf Astoria lobby. Only once Kirov passed South Point Hotel and Casino, did his heart rate slow to its usual fifty beats per minute.

The radio buzzed with his work. Sandzer and a bodyguard had been confirmed as deceased. Police and the FBI were keeping an open mind, but with another billionaire dead, speculation was only heading one way. Richelieu was name-checked everywhere.

Not long into the journey, Silver had sent him a message of praise for exceeding his expectations. Kirov hated being underestimated; it was a mistake a few people had made, and all of them were dead. Their exchange had yielded further information. Silver had one last assignment and promised to help ensure it happened. But before that, Kirov decided he would need to pay a certain special agent a visit.

70

ONE HUNDRED MILES back down the highway in the Aria, Hogan stood in the elevator Richelieu had used to escape. The forensics team began pulling prints from the second-floor button. One LVPD crime scene technician turned to him and eased down her mask.

"We're gonna have a load of partials. I can't guarantee we'll pull anything usable."

Hogan had another thought—maybe the panicked assassin had made the same mistake twice.

"When you're done, can we head up to the fifty-ninth floor? If we're lucky, we'll get a second shot at a partial."

This elevator ride felt quicker than earlier. After leaving the technician with another cop, Hogan caught a glimpse of himself in the mirrored steel. His hair was wild, and purple bruising had formed around his right eye. The Aria security guards could call it a tie—everyone had more pressing issues right now. He retraced his route onto the roof, now a hive of activity, and surveyed the Waldorf Astoria tower. Jagged glass formed a frame around the devastation inside Sandzer's penthouse opposite as police moved to erect sheeting. The bullet-resistant glass proved no match for the explosives Richelieu had sent across. He had to admire the ingenuity. LVPD technicians continued to comb the area from which the drones of death were launched. The FBI's ERT team had joined them. He couldn't get near Sandzer's apartment until his status changed. For now, and despite being cold, Richelieu's trail might offer more.

Camera footage had picked up Richelieu on the second floor of the Aria, known as the promenade. The killer had traversed this to a down escalator that led straight to the rear exit. It was a smart route. The green-capped assassin had continued around the curved walkway leading to the Vdara Hotel's lobby, where Hogan now stood. He looked right to left, then at a sign indicating a route to the Bellagio. There was no direct easy exit from here, but if Richelieu had walked to the neighboring hotel, he could've headed out onto the Strip by foot or in a vehicle. He flinched as a monorail train rumbled over his head. The day's events had left him jumpy. He quickened his pace down the glass-covered walkway, and within a few minutes, entered the Bellagio lobby. He negotiated his way through a throng of Chinese tourists snapping the multicolored glass flower ceiling to the security desk. After a quick call for verification, they agreed to offer access to the hotel video recordings. He hoped it would support his escape theory.

The Bellagio fountains began their twice-hourly climb into the sky as Hogan wandered down the pathway from the hotel to the Strip. "Time to Say Goodbye" blared from the speakers built into the walls and gardens. The water soared in time with Bocelli's voice while a gaggle of phones tried to record that perfect social media clip. The last two hours reviewing the security footage had proven fruitful. The compliant Bellagio staff helped him to track Richelieu until he turned left onto Las Vegas Boulevard. He'd alerted the police to be on the lookout for a silver Prius and provided the license plate. Next up, he wanted to get the Strip traffic camera feeds. He called Vance.

"Tell me you're already on your way out here?"

"We're an hour away. Miller isn't happy."

"I bet. Listen, I need your help. Can you peel off from the group and meet me at LVPD HQ?"

"Hell yeah, I can. I wanna know *everything!*"

Hogan laughed, hung up, and stared ahead as the music and fountains continued their duet to a crescendo.

71

"THIRTY BUCKS FOR three coffees!" Vance eased a cup in front of an empty chair and Hogan.

"Welcome to Vegas prices," he responded. It was eight p.m., and he needed a caffeine focus boost.

With LVPD's help, they'd tracked Richelieu to the Rio Hotel parking lot. Ranger had headed to plot the killer's trail from there. Miller and his team were still at Sandzer's wrecked penthouse. Hogan was sure they'd find little. Everything pointed to meticulous planning.

The third chair at their table sat empty because Carla was embroiled in an animated conversation out of earshot. She'd been on the phone with Director Sullivan since she arrived. Every available screen in the casino hosted 24/7 coverage of events. Helicopters hovered near the penthouse, and serious anchors spoke to solemn experts. A chyron of sensationalism slid across the screen: explosive drones suspected of ending Sandzer's life, and Richelieu was the chief suspect. Carla joined them and snatched up her cup.

"How was Sullivan?" Hogan asked.

"In three words?" she answered. "Pretty fucking unhappy." She took another gulp and continued. "He started by relaying the president's anger that another big supporter was dead, and he wanted the FBI to know it. Although I don't recall him being as unhappy when Fullerton was bumped off," she scowled.

Hogan and Vance offered empathetic nods.

"Then we spoke about you." She fixed Hogan with her steely eyes. "IA were raising a stink about autonomy, and they have a point. But

I argued we need to put something positive in front of the press. And you being shot while almost apprehending the villain provides a strong narrative.

"What does that mean?" Hogan's spirits lifted.

"It means that, for now, the investigation is suspended, and you're reinstated. IA will reserve the right to reopen it after this case ends."

"Thanks for going to bat for me, Carla. Really, it means a lot. So, I guess the task force is still on the case, too?"

She harrumphed.

"Just. We have two weeks—if we haven't apprehended Richelieu by then, Sullivan will overhaul the task force, and we all know what that means."

Even if he hadn't consumed three Americanos, there was no danger of Hogan sleeping. He stood with Vance in the LVPD crime lab over-looking the CSI technician comparing prints. Despite the late hour, the place was still full, with focused officers collating evidence.

"Okay, so I have two sets of multiple partial prints. One from the fifty-ninth-floor call button and one from the second-floor button in the elevator itself. The first bunch has the clearest examples, so I'd say that's your best shot of a match," the technician offered.

Hogan had provided his prints for elimination.

"I'll scan these prints and email them to you. You can run them back at your field office."

"Let's get out of here," Vance announced.

The two of them huddled over a computer in a back corner of the Las Vegas FBI field office. They'd retreated there; Miller was due back at the LVPD as they left. Hogan didn't trust himself near him. They also wanted privacy if they got a hit. Vance signed in and waited. Hogan doubted IT had reinstated his access yet. His gun and badge were waiting back at Wilshire. A few days as a civilian had only confirmed how much this job meant to him. He had to solve this case. A future outside the Bureau was one he couldn't countenance.

Vance uploaded all the partial prints to the NGI program. They hoped Richelieu's recent print would be clearer. They had no way of knowing for sure. If the prints found a match, they could get a response in less than a minute. However, including searches of civil fingerprints, it could take the program up to twenty minutes to work through the eighty million records.

After around forty seconds, they got a match. Hogan's heart hammered inside his chest as he clicked open the file. They had the bastard!

Except they didn't. He stared at the police record of a thirty-four-year-old call girl named Casey Hillcrest and pounded the table in frustration. A few surprised officers looked over. He clicked out. The call button partial prints were still running.

"There's time yet," Vance proclaimed as they returned with focused stares that would rival Audrey on her favorite YouTube channel.

But there wasn't. It took only eight minutes for their hopes to be shattered. Hogan eyed the "No Match Found" overlay on the screen with bitterness. He slumped in the leather swivel chair, resting his head in one hand.

"He'd been so careful to never leave a print anywhere—I figured he'd be in the system."

"Perhaps the partial wasn't clear enough to match? It's better than not having these at all."

Yet something still didn't add up.

"He wasn't concerned we might obtain his DNA from the Loews Regency. Yet he didn't leave a single print there. Why would you care if you knew you weren't in the systems for either? They both nail you the same."

Vance's brow wrinkled.

"We could've got unlucky…" She let the sentence trail off.

Hogan tried to blink away his brain fog.

"I know we're missing a piece of the puzzle, but what?"

72

Hogan opened the fish tank and added shrimp to the timer-activated feeding station. It had dispensed its last delivery yesterday before he'd returned from Vegas.

"Sorry for the wait, guys; I nearly didn't make it back this time."

The starfish raced across the rocky bed as two small pieces of mussel landed next to it.

Carla had faced the baying press the day after the fingerprint failure. He'd stood in the background, his arm in a sling. More for show than necessity. His experienced boss navigated the barrage of questions well.

Over the last few days, they'd identified the vehicle Richelieu had switched to before heading out on the I-15. They'd picked him up on cameras farther down the highway, but the trail ran cold in the labyrinthine LA interchanges. They'd still released vehicle details for the moonshot that anyone, anywhere, had seen something. Identifying where the killer spent time before Sandzer's killing had so far proved fruitless. Las Vegas had been swarming with single male CES attendees matching the description of a six-foot male with an average build and a beard (they assumed was fake). It could be anyone. The timing had been perfect, and if Hogan hadn't spotted Richelieu immediately before the attack, they'd have even less to go on. With Vegas leads scant, he'd driven back earlier that day.

Hogan grabbed a beer and eased himself onto the sofa. His exertions in Vegas had aggravated his previous injuries, and his arm remained bandaged. He circled back to the few positives from his trip. Without the partial matching, Richelieu had neither been arrested nor served in the armed forces. Yet the lab experts who'd watched the elevator footage suggested he'd likely have left a usable partial print. This felt like an error but had still led nowhere. At least sifting through the daily deluge of the public's proposed suspects should now be more manageable. And Richelieu no longer seemed infallible. If Hogan had been armed, he might have stopped him. Also, if another killing was planned, and they guessed it was—the assassin should find it almost impossible to get near his quarry. A significant law enforcement presence was supporting those guarding Members of Congress and the existing security teams of numerous billionaires. The unprecedented killings were considered a matter of national security, and the global economy continued to falter as oil prices climbed. They had to be prepared for the unexpected. This should all be enough protection but might not help them catch their adversary. Teams of agents continued combing through security footage from Vegas, sharing pertinent images with the FACE Services Unit in Clarksburg. They had more to work with this time, even with the disguise.

Meanwhile, the press continued their relentless coverage. Serial murders—and billionaires at that—equaled blockbuster ratings. Of course, certain networks made political currency out of law enforcement's failure to capture Richelieu, while some liberal media commentators continued to fuel the theory that inequality could be the motive for the killings. The president was more vocal in his White House briefings, promising unlimited resources to bring the killer to justice. The pressure from the top had permeated throughout the Bureau. Cracking the case would take a decent chunk of luck. Hogan hoped he hadn't used his up when the bullet passed through the flesh of his arm. Had he moved a few fractions of a second slower, he wouldn't be here at all.

When Marissa arrived, suntanned and relaxed, she made for a contrasting figure to Hogan, bruised and bandaged. She brushed his hair away from his forehead and kissed it.

"You okay?"

He nodded. "I'm glad you're back. I promise you it isn't always like this."

"What, being hospitalized and then *shot*? I'm guessing not." She laughed. "I'm just happy you're in one piece."

"It could have been worse. And I'm back on the case; IA is no longer chasing me. And you're here." He reached over to kiss her.

"How come you were in Vegas anyway? You never mentioned that?" Her tone suggested she was a little put out.

"I felt foolish being there, I thought it would lead nowhere, and people would think I was crazy—randomly surveilling billionaires."

"But you got so close. You can still get this guy—he slipped up once; he can again. Next time take a SWAT team or something, okay?"

"That may have been our only opportunity." Hogan winced as he moved his arm. "But yeah, *if* we get another chance, I'm hoping not to be alone!"

"Do you think he'll strike again?"

"We have to assume so."

Marissa's look shifted to one of concern as she rose from the sofa.

"How bad does it hurt?" she asked and raised an eyebrow, looking back to the bedroom.

Hogan reached for her hand. "Not *that* bad."

73

HOGAN LEFT THE late morning meeting with Touchdown feeling like a player who'd just missed an attempted field goal. The burly SAC explained that counterintelligence had no trace of relevant chatter from foreign agents, evidence of untracked operatives on US soil, or intelligence to suggest any nation could be behind the killings. Hogan regretted not pressing on if this included "friendlier" countries, or whether the burly SAC still discounted this. No one in the department had flagged any notable communications following Sandzer's death.

A rap on the glass broke Hogan's concentration as he pored over months of drone purchase records matching those used in the attack. Vance and Ranger were in the room doing the same, focusing on tracing those bought by businesses. A pair delivered to Henderson in Las Vegas before the attack warranted the most interest. LVPD was sending officers to scope out the address later that day. They were already halfway through the week, and the pressure of Director Sullivan's task force deadline had started to show. When he raised his head, he was surprised to see the weak chin and calculating eyes of Perry Wolgomott from Langley. Easing himself up, he strolled to the door.

"Special Agent, sorry to drop by uninvited like this. Do you have a moment?" Wolgomott offered a sickly smile, oozing forced friendliness as they shook hands.

"Of course, Percy." Hogan matched his tone, the wrong name designed to annoy.

"Perry," the officer responded, nostrils flaring. The smile returned. "Don't worry, it happens all the time."

The two men headed down the corridor, searching for an empty office. Hogan appreciated the extra time to speculate why Wolgomott had turned up today.

"I was in Los Angeles for an unrelated matter," Wolgomott began, with a dismissive wave of his hand, "and with all the recent drama, thought I'd come by to see you. I hope you don't mind?" He leaned back in the chair—relaxed as if they were grabbing a beer together.

Hogan remained wary but professional. "No problem. I'm a little surprised, that's all, given I've not heard from you since we met."

"Yes. I'm afraid we didn't have anything to update you on. Still don't, actually."

"So why are you here?"

"To offer our assistance in the investigation." The sickly smile returned.

"You don't have *too much* on your plate now?" The niceties were over. Wolgomott kept his languid pose.

"Let's just say we've had pressure exerted from above, so we're offering cooperation. With more data and updated information, we can help."

"Forgive me if I don't get excited right now."

"We can offer more focus and resources this time." Wolgomott didn't miss a beat. Hogan was no less suspicious than when the meeting started but played along.

"So, what do you want from us to make this happen?" This wasn't an altruistic visit.

Wolgomott paused for a moment, calculating.

"You to keep us in the loop. We could start by circulating your updated profile on the gentleman the media have branded Richelieu. Our assets may know something."

Hogan wanted to call bullshit, but politics ensured the CIA would get what it wanted. They'd argue help was offered but rebuffed, and the fallout would escalate.

"Then I'd want regular updates. It's a two-way street, Perry."

"That isn't a problem. We want this guy caught too—domestic weakness negatively reflects itself on the international stage."

Hogan suspected the officer was telling him what he wanted him to hear. He could play along too, for now.

"I'll have a summary across by tomorrow. Weekly joint status updates work for me."

"Agreed. I look forward to working with you more closely." As Wolgomott rose and they shook hands, he stared at Hogan's wrist. "I think your watch has stopped, Special Agent."

"And it will stay that way."

The officer frowned, forced a final smile, and slid out of the room.

Hogan stayed put and replayed the conversation. He was a confirmed coincidence skeptic, especially when the CIA was involved. It was the timing, more than anything, that set the alarm bells ringing. They'd received no help from Wolgomott. In fact, from what he heard from Fisk, quite the opposite. Then the Bureau ran the prints through the NGI, and the next thing he swings by the office? Was this a connection to Richelieu's earlier caution? Or had something else that happened in Vegas precipitated the visit? He'd wager there was no unrelated matter that required Wolgomott's presence in LA. Of course, he could be reaching—and Wolgomott had been instructed by his superiors to help after Sandzer's death. But that didn't explain a senior officer making a nine-hour round trip for a ten-minute meeting. A message had been sent, but what exactly? There was something significant, even sinister, behind this, and he resolved to be careful in his communications. He could speak to Carla, but her inquiries would receive the same bullshit story. Wolgomott had spent a few decades practicing subterfuge, and he'd be prepared.

Then again, maybe not.

Hogan developed a theory for the unexpected visit. Once he fleshed it out, he decided on a plan of action. It was dangerous—reckless, even—and if they got caught, the consequences didn't bear thinking about. It didn't matter—it was a play he would try to make. He pulled out his phone and called Nemo.

74

BACK IN THE Ye Olde King's Head in Santa Monica, Hogan sat in an isolated booth. Nemo returned from the bar, two Guinnesses in hand.

"Is it true it tastes better in Ireland?" he asked, placing them on the stained wooden table.

"I never made it over there. Doubt it, though—it all comes from the same place, right?"

"But I heard it travels as well as the 49ers!" Nemo leaned forward with a conspiratorial look. "So, what's going down, dude?"

Hogan ran through the full events in Vegas, his friend looking on in astonishment as he received the unedited story. He moved on to his call from Warren Fisk and brought him up to date on the case—from the fingerprint evidence to the mysterious visit from Wolgomott earlier that day and his suspicions. Once finished, he waited as Nemo took a few moments to assimilate all the information. He finally replied.

"Crazy shit. Glad you still have those boxing reflexes; otherwise, you may not be here!" Nemo placed a meaty arm around Hogan's good shoulder. "As for the CIA, I agree—something else is going on here. I'm not buying this Wolgomott's story either. Not least because they had already shut Fisk down. That's the weird part. Why not pretend they were trying to help? What changed their minds? Was it the print, though, or something else? That's the real question."

"Which brings me on to what I propose to do next." Hogan looked around to ensure nobody was in earshot and continued in a low voice. "Would you be able to access communications from Wolgomott, recently viewed files, and so on?"

He'd had rarely seen his friend look as grave as he did now.

"Shit, dude, I dunno." Nemo's eyes darted from side to side. "This is serious stuff. If we were to get caught, we'd both be royally screwed."

"I know. If the risk is too great, I understand." Hogan paused, then with a renewed intensity, said, "But I think I'm right, and if I am, this could be the only way to get Richelieu. If I could think of another way, I wouldn't be asking."

His friend's jaw clenched tighter, and he shook his head. "You could be wrong…I can't, I'm sorry. And if you are, I'm risking everything; you are too—for nothing."

Hogan nodded; he didn't want to apply more pressure. Nemo's tormented face told him all he needed. "It's fine. Really. I shouldn't have asked. I didn't know what else to do…"

"Fucking spooks," Nemo replied, breaking the tension. "Look, I'll have a quiet word with Fisk again, see if he can ask a few trusted sources this time without it getting flagged. It's safer that way."

"Thanks, and sorry for putting you on the spot like that."

"It's okay, I get it. Shit, part of me still wants to backdoor Wolgomott so I can see if you're right. If you get something more concrete…" His friend was still uncomfortable about not helping.

"It's cool, honestly."

"Another beer?"

Hogan raised his empty glass in response but got a shake of the head from his best friend. "Off you go, then. It's your round."

Hogan scrolled through Watchable, seeking late-night distraction. Too much choice led to more indecision. Shit, as a kid there were only four UK channels, and people survived. He tossed the remote onto the sofa. He had two non-work-related problems to solve. The first by far the most serious.

To pay Paradiso, Hogan needed another eight thousand dollars. He'd put aside all he could from his most recent paycheck. He'd have to return to The Rose early Saturday and risk his entire Betfair account trading float to garner enough profit. If this didn't pay off, he'd have to seek new accommodation for his father and still settle his debt. Some of the potential new abodes were awful. He'd considered asking Nemo or even Marissa for a loan, but he hated relying on others. Plus, how could he pay them back, his situation unlikely to improve anytime soon? Family took care of each other, and with his brother out of the picture, the responsibility fell to him alone. He'd find a way as he had done so far. If he could get through the next month, somehow apprehend Richelieu, then make SAC, he might be okay, but in the short term, he needed that money. He sighed. What was that saying: Man plans, and God laughs? Frustrated, he switched to his other problem—what to do about Chad. He mulled over a few options, including elaborate revenge scenarios. They were tempting, but he resolved to retain his discipline until the case ended.

Marissa interrupted his pondering, checking in and confirming they were still good for Sunday. He'd promised Audrey a trip to Santa Monica Pier and planned to grab a few hours with them away from the madness at work.

Hogan began to pace the room. Most men would kill for Marissa, yet darker thoughts still pushed through. He battled to ignore them and pretend everything was okay. His mum would have known what to do, but she was gone, like Katie. His dad—a shadow of the man he used to be, languishing in Paradiso. Each one hurt so much in a different way. Could he leave himself open to that pain again? The only way to protect himself was to never care. If he fell for Marissa even more and it didn't work out, he'd find a way through it. He could manage a break-up but not more grief. If he opened his heart and something happened to her... He didn't think he'd get through that. He wasn't strong enough. Last time, he'd managed to pull himself from the precipice, but it was a close-run thing.

Was he better off alone, fragile but safe? He cracked open the first of many beers that evening. They might help him find temporary solace, but later, the nightmares would come.

75

"THE BIGGEST INVESTIGATION in the FBI's history." This line was trotted out in response to the barrage of daily press inquiries. It was true, as well. Hundreds of agents worked across numerous field offices throughout the country. Every level from ADIC and below was involved in the quest to bring Richelieu to justice. The investigation's scope required significant delegation. Agents everywhere hoped to find the career-defining breakthrough and to restore the public's waning faith in the Bureau. The original Wilshire task force remained the fulcrum for all promising leads. Everyone felt the pressure, not only from Director Sullivan and his deadline but also because Richelieu could be about to kill again.

Without discovering what the CIA may be hiding, the only way they would stop the killing would be to capture Richelieu in action. This was great in theory but, in practice, unlikely. The steps taken by law enforcement were designed to deter the assassin. Paranoia had spread through high society and government. Some targets' homes were under police surveillance, and their prominent owners cloistered inside. But without an opportunity, Richelieu might disappear for good and leave everyone in limbo. They'd have no way of knowing. The killing spree could even be already over.

With a link between the deaths elusive, Hogan began scrolling through the late Cole Sandzer's largest news property—the *Washington Tribune*. He focused on commentary around Richelieu's assassinations, but then a homepage story caught his eye. It concerned the sale of a first edition of *Alice's Adventures in Wonderland* in New York a few days earlier. The final price had been a record-setting $3.4m, an insane amount for a book, and the bidding described as intense. Following the quotation on the screen in San José, the team had gone down that rabbit hole and found nothing. No previous quotes from that book or Lewis Carroll's other work had correlated with similar crimes or led anywhere. It had been the same with Alexandre Dumas and *The Three Musketeers*. With other leads scant, was it worth checking this story out? If Richelieu was a huge fan of the author, could he even be the buyer? He'd have the resources to purchase this rare copy after the last few months. They needed a break, and sometimes the long shots paid off. Hogan hurried to find Vance, Ranger, and Chung to check if they thought he was crazy.

They didn't and set to work devouring everything they could about the sale and purchaser.

An hour later, they reconvened with progress.

The auctioned book hadn't been just any first edition. Macmillan & Co. originally printed two thousand copies and advanced fifty for Carroll to give to friends. However, when the book's illustrator—John Tenniel—saw the printing of his drawings, he hated them. He persuaded Carroll to pay for a full reprint, and those original copies got pulped. But some of the advance books had already been sent out. Twenty-two were known to have survived—the majority residing in institutional libraries worldwide. Six or so remained in private hands, and one had sold at Christie's, New York. It had been described as a once-in-a-generation event.

With charming threats, Vance persuaded Christie's to share the purchase information. The transaction was conducted via an offshore company registered in the British Virgin Islands. This wasn't unusual; rich people loved their privacy and avoiding taxes. Chung had called his friend at the Department of the Treasury and received assurances they'd exert pressure to obtain an anonymized statement from the account. This way the bank afforded their client protection and got to keep the full force of the US Treasury off their backs. It was now a waiting game.

Hogan had paced the boxy conference room for the last hour, his initial optimism waning. Vance had popped out and brought back a smorgasbord of deli options, but he'd eaten little. Finally, Chung's cell phone rang. The analyst listened, smiled, then ended the call.

"What did they say?" Hogan's patience had long since disappeared.

Chung smiled. "They obtained a full statement. It should be with me...' he checked his laptop, "about now."

The three-year-old account had regular inflows of between one hundred thousand to three hundred thousand dollars. It also showed seven recent transactions from auction houses in the UK and the US. Hogan turned to Ranger.

"Can you track down which lots these payments relate to?"

"On it," the big guy replied.

In the last few months, large transfers originating from a different bank located in the Cayman Islands had credited the account. These had all been in the low to high seven figures. Major debits included one to a law firm in Kotor, Montenegro, for $3 million and most recently to Christie's, New York. There was one other payment sandwiched in-between to a company called Elcano for seven hundred dollars. Vance Googled it.

"It's a shipping company, and do you want to know where it's based?"

Hogan tipped his head but didn't smile.

"Okay, I'm guessing you're not in the mood for suspense—San Francisco Airport."

"Looks like someone is planning to leave the country," Chung said.

"Yeah, and to a place with no US extradition treaty," Hogan replied.

The team worked late into the evening. The matching lot prices at the auctions were all for rare children's books but nothing by Alexandre Dumas. This gave Hogan pause. Yet one positive was that if Richelieu was their buyer, he'd assume this account would never be discovered by the FBI. They had located a property in Kotor that matched the sale price for the transfer to the lawyer and formulated a plan for the shipping company. Ranger and Vance would pose as customs officers to visit the premises of Elcano. That way, they could examine a bunch of planned shipments without alerting the staff to this particular one. It might take a day or two to set up with the Customs and Border Protection agency. A sudden CBP inspection could raise suspicion, so they needed to provide notice. They'd have to take the risk the shipment wouldn't be happening before this weekend. If it did, surveillance would need to help delay it at the eleventh hour. The problem of action in Kotor required assistance at a much higher level. Once they'd cleared the plan with the CBP, Hogan intended to take everything to Carla. International missions were above his pay grade.

Around midnight, as he walked to his car, Hogan's cell phone rang.

"Hello?" he asked, suspicious of who would be calling at this hour.

"Good morning, Special Agent. Can you confirm which high school you attended?"

He recognized the rounded vowels of MI6 officer Campbell Agnew.

"Woodside High School."

"Excellent. I'll keep it brief on this open line. We received feedback on your questions. Of the possible foreign intelligence agencies that could have more knowledge of this individual, I would suggest beginning with your own."

Hogan gripped his phone tighter.

"Thanks for letting me know."

"No problem at all. You understand I can't share anything further."

"Of course, I appreciate the heads-up."

"Well, goodbye, and good luck, then." Hogan leaned on the roof of his car. Agnew was pointing him back to the Agency. It meant he had been right; they were hiding something or could even be orchestrating the murders. He needed to persuade Nemo to hack the CIA.

76

HOGAN CROSSED THE open-plan floor of Selantio past well-spaced uncluttered desks. The workplace was gamified with foosball, pool tables, and a PS5 hooked up to a giant screen. He stood out in his smart suit—it was Supreme and Veja for the employees here. These workers were some of the most intelligent around. Expensive, but necessary for success. The views across Marina del Rey beat staring down over the 405. He almost regretted not taking one of Nemo's job offers over the years. Although he wasn't sure he belonged here and however difficult work was right now—he was doing what he loved.

Nemo approached and enveloped him in a bear hug. As they entered his office, he gestured to a comfortable leather sofa below a shelf full of trophies.

"It's great to see you so early, dude, but why am I apprehensive?"

Hogan ran through the evening call from Campbell Agnew, including the startling implications. He waited as his friend tapped the desk, his brow furrowed.

"How sure are you about this?"

"I'm positive they're hiding information that will lead us to Richelieu. If I can't make something happen, my career in the FBI is as good as done. A shitty posting and zero chance of promotion may be the best I can hope for."

Nemo clasped his hands together, then, after a while, appeared to reach a decision.

"If *we* do this, and I'm emphasizing that we're in this together, and it remains an *if*, I've got conditions." All the usual levity was absent from his voice. "Firstly, I choose the best time to obtain the data. Secondly, we view what we find in this office, and immediately after, we'll remove it from whichever staging server we use. The final one is the most important. If you act on this information, you can't share it, allude to its provenance, or acknowledge its existence to explain your actions." His eyes fixed on Hogan, awaiting a response.

He didn't have to wait long.

"You have my word on all the conditions. I would never jeopardize your company or our friendship. If you want to walk away, I understand. I know this is a huge ask."

"I mean, I do. I'm crazy for considering it. But I asked myself if the situation were reversed, what would you say? And that helped make up my mind." His best friend circled out from behind the desk as Hogan rose. "I also think you're right. And it will be a hell of a challenge—even considering our integration and access to selected Agency systems. I can't risk leaving even the slightest trail, so I'll need to proceed with both stealth and caution. I'll call you once I have something. And when I ask if you fancy catching a movie, then head here."

"Thanks. I owe you big-time for this."

"You're damn fucking right, you do."

Hogan pulled open the office door and peered back to his co-conspirator—who raised his hand with a wide grin, but also a flicker of fear in his eyes.

77

At first, the CBP had proved unhelpful.

Chung had demanded an urgent inspection, but one instigated without attracting suspicion. Their contact's response was sluggish, but after veiled threats, he agreed to Monday—when an agent could accompany a genuine CBP officer. Vance got the gig, and Hogan headed to bring Carla up to speed.

Jared Miller stood with a fellow agent, blocking the direct route to the corner office. He called out. "How's the bullet wound? If you'd been armed in Vegas—you might have been the hero."

Hogan got up in his colleague's grill.

"And why the fuck was that, eh? I know it was you who spoke to IA."

"No idea what you're talking about." Miller stepped aside, hands raised, and tipped his eyes at the other agent as if to say, *This guy!*

Hogan regained his composure and left the pair behind, whispering. The sweetest revenge would come if his team found a way to stop and apprehend Richelieu.

"You'd better be bringing me a development," Carla announced as Hogan closed the door and sat.

"Okay, I'm going to bring you up to speed on a potential lead on Richelieu. Please let me get to the end before you dismiss it. This isn't going to be another San José clusterfuck." He waited as Carla scowled, then sighed. He took that as his cue and ran through the whole story, ending with the planned inspection after the weekend. The lines on his boss's forehead deepened at numerous points, but by the end, she bobbed her head in what passed for agreement."

"If this does pan out as expected, what next?"

"I don't know; it depends on what's in the shipment and if that helps us find Richelieu or prove that it belongs to him. If it does and we can't get him in the US, we know where he'll pop up next."

"In a country with no extradition treaty."

"But we both know when it reaches that point, it won't matter. Only this time, the Navy SEAL team will bring him back alive, not dropping his body in the sea like bin Laden."

They chatted a few more operational points and formulated an outline of a plan. They now needed to establish it was Richelieu heading to Montenegro.

Hogan got up to leave, but Carla called him back.

"One more thing. Special Agent in Charge Peterson took early retirement yesterday."

"So, when are you choosing whom to appoint as his replacement?" He tried to sound indifferent, but he doubted it worked. As if the pressure wasn't already ratcheted up to the highest level.

Another sigh. "Soon, Hogan, but we've got bigger fish to fry. If we don't stop Richelieu, I doubt *I'll* be appointing anyone."

78

IT WAS OVER a week since Sandzer's assassination, and all appeared fine. On the drive back into LA, Kirov had replayed all events in his head. The agent appearing on the roof had resulted in a minimal error. He now assumed they'd pulled partial prints from his right index finger. Under pressure to get into the elevator and down to the promenade before the agent got closer, he'd punched two buttons. Had he known his pursuer was unarmed, he'd have been calmer and more careful. It shouldn't matter. He'd never been arrested, so he knew neither his DNA nor prints were on any domestic law enforcement computer. The CIA was a different story. They had his fingerprints from when he became an asset. After everything he'd done, he was sure they wouldn't be in the NGI, at least not for a nosey police officer or agent to identify him. If anyone needed to keep his previous work buried, it was the Agency.

All major news outlets still showed the same security footage from the Aria and asked witnesses to come forward. But nothing about prints or a former operative known as Lukas. The images of him on camera could have been anyone in a green cap and shades.

He rose from the sofa in his San José apartment and poured around two thousand dollars' worth of Macallan 1946 into his glass. He didn't trust the shipping company not to break this new bottle, so he'd kept it to finish it.

Earlier that day, Silver had informed him of his final mission and reiterated the promise to create favorable conditions for success. Kirov gave a little snort and wondered how. If law enforcement wasn't enough, close protection agents covered most other options. He couldn't get close to the new target's property. But it would be the final part of the job, and he'd never failed to deliver. It wasn't even about the money now; it was his reputation, his legacy. He wanted people to know his name in centuries to come, like Cardinal Richelieu's. In *The Three Musketeers*, his assassin, Milady, had found someone to kill the Duke of Buckingham, even after she was caught and imprisoned. Kirov wouldn't falter and would take whatever action was necessary. This would be the grand finale in a series of murders that would immortalize him. If circumstances fell right for him to escape in one piece, he would risk it all one last time. He was to travel to the required location on Tuesday. Now he had the final target and timeline, he had a narrow window of opportunity to deal with Special Agent Hogan. He'd been unable to explain the events of the previous week, and his arrival on that rooftop. Kirov hated unknowns, and considered whether the agent was operating independently that day, and if so, what information he had. You had to be ruthless with loose ends. He'd learned that with Isobel. He'd drive to LA tomorrow, and the agent's address. En route he'd work on a suitable cover, and plan. But first, he wanted to arrange the safe passage of all his books to Montenegro.

He'd fallen in love with Kotor seventeen years previously. He became Kirov there. He'd chosen a Russian name for his future clients. He liked the irony it suggested he was ex-KGB or FSB. Back in the 1930s, Sergei Kirov had been assassinated on Stalin's orders and triggered the first great purge. In a way, that was what Kirov had spent his time doing since he'd left Florida—purging clients' enemies. But before that he'd started with his own.

After Isobel's death, his previous life became a footnote. One which he fled immediately. A period of happiness a man like him hadn't deserved. The rage of his youth burnt again. It took him two years to track down the last living killer from the three-man team that came to his Fort Lauderdale home that fateful night in December. Kirov had ended his life with a shot through each eyeball after hours torturing the Russian

FSB agent who squealed like a pig throughout. He'd dropped the body, or at least what remained, in the Adriatic off the Croatian coast before continuing down to the Bay of Kotor in Montenegro. He'd found the tranquility there soothed the anger that had powered his vengeance. His future lay as a sole contractor, killing. He had no interest in building a life or getting close to anyone again. He'd decided back then that when he had the resources and was ready to disappear into secluded retirement, this would be the perfect place.

That time was almost here.

Kirov tapped away on his MacBook, checking his shipment details again. He'd arranged for his books and a few other items he valued to be shipped from two locations. The schedules were provisional, as the address on the valuable New York shipment wasn't even its eventual destination. He'd need to be alive to change it after his last job was complete. If he wasn't— that package would be going to the perfect new home. Everything was in order. First, he'd deal with Hogan, then Richelieu would strike one more time. After that, he would disappear forever.

79

FUELED BY TWO extra-shot Rose coffees, Hogan was ready to go. His previous best day trading Premier League soccer resulted in three thousand dollars of profit. Today, he needed to make a minimum of eight thousand; to do so, he would have to put every dollar he had on the line.

It was a bad start. After twenty-three seconds, one of the games had a goal. It wiped out his chance to trade out his initial 0-0 bet on that game and put him one thousand dollars behind. He brushed it off and by halftime had locked in one and a half thousand profit from one of the other five games.

He was in the zone for the second half, but the potential profit positions he had created began to slip away with goals. He was left with two big remaining chances. He'd bet sizeable wagers on one—nil on two teams at 10-1 odds and taken bets, after a period of the score remaining the same, at 5-1 for five hundred dollars per point. This created a potential profit of up to two and a half thousand per game, but only if there were no more goals. Eschewing the chance to cash out gains, he held firm. He needed the full amount from each position. Then, just like that, the away team equalized in each game, knocking out his unrealized profit in both with only twenty minutes of play left. He stared at the screen in despair, his head in his hands. A few patrons that had filled the nearby table gave him a concerned look. He was almost out of options. He checked the total balance left in his account and found he had five thousand dollars remaining. In the Everton versus Manchester City match, the correct score of 1-1 traded at 1.8.

It was all-or-nothing time.

He stuck the entire remaining balance on the score remaining the same until the end of the match—if it did, he'd end the day with over fourteen thousand bucks. This would be enough to pay Paradiso and leave the bankroll in the account he always needed to trade. If it didn't, he'd have lost everything and wouldn't even have money to trade in the future.

The next nineteen minutes were the longest of Hogan's life. He winced at every attack and eyeballed the clock in the corner. The tension of praying for Spurs to hang on to a winning score didn't compare to this. His dad couldn't leave Paradiso. Then, as the clock ticked past the ninety-minute mark, Manchester City got a penalty. It was over, the market suspended, so he couldn't trade out, and he'd have to watch as a simple finish from twelve yards wiped his account out. He muttered, "Miss it, miss it, miss it," between gritted teeth as Kevin De Bruyne shaped up to take the penalty kick. He stuck it clean to the right, and the keeper dived the correct way, but it didn't matter. The penalty thumped off the post to an Everton defender who hoofed it out of play. Hogan leaped in the air; this time, everyone in the café looked his way as he upended his coffee. He didn't care. A remaining minute of stoic defending kept the ball out before the glorious sound of the final whistle.

He'd done it!

Hogan slumped in relief, sweat trickling down his back as he puffed his cheeks and blew out the tension.

An hour later, he'd recovered from going through the emotional wringer, and his appetite had returned. Amber arrived for her shift as the tables filled up. She rushed over, slid into the seat opposite and arched an eyebrow.

"It's the enigma that is Hogan. I haven't seen you here in weeks. I thought you found a new spot." She pulled a sad face. "But then I checked, and you still had your stuff here, so I guessed at a long holiday. Where *have* you been?" Her green eyes shone.

He hadn't ever told Amber what he did for a living, deflecting the question whenever it came up. She mustn't watch the news, although, with the competing options for a millennial's screen time, it wasn't a surprise.

"Well, first it was Christmas, then I had a work trip away."

"Oh, cool. Was it fun?"

"Uneventful. How are things with you?" Hogan asked, keen to change the subject.

"Usual. Too much college work I can't be bothered doing."

"And Chad?"

"Oh…yeah…Chad…" she answered, looking worried. "I better go start my shift. Good to have you back, Hogan. I missed you." Her eyes shone again, and after a lingering look that suggested she wanted to add something, she hurried away.

He would deal with Mr. Preppy soon enough.

For once, when he visited his dad today, he wouldn't have to sneak in or out.

Eight steps. That's how many Hogan managed down Paradiso's main corridor before Mrs. Malkin appeared in the reception. He suspected she'd be awaiting his arrival.

"Sorry to bother you, but I have left a few voicemails." She fidgeted with her beaded necklace. He put her out of her misery.

"I'll be transferring the remaining money owed Tuesday. I'll also try to make an advance payment on the next invoice due at the end of the month if you need…" he lied before he let the sentence trail off. It worked.

"Oh, no, no, no, I felt so bad chasing—it's the rules…" She moved closer, looking conspiratorial now. "Even for FBI agents." She stepped back and opened the connecting door. "Your father is in the main lounge; he seems to be in a social mood today."

Hogan stepped across his dad's view of the TV; it did the trick.

"Lovely to see you. Thanks so much for coming to visit."

"How've you been?" He sat and grasped his father's hand.

"Okay…I think."

"You've not been wandering into rooms that aren't yours?"

"I…I…don't think so… I can't remember."

"That's alright. Try to do what the nurses ask."

"I'll try. Is your brother coming to visit?"

Hogan sighed—he hated this question, usually deflecting it, but today opted for the truth.

"We haven't seen Scott for six years, Dad. He stole everything from your business and left you bankrupt. I'm sorry, he won't be coming now or ever." He kept his tone soothing.

"Oh, that's a shame. I would like to see him again."

He might as well have told his father lunch would be late; dementia had stripped away his memories. And without memories, what are we? Although, with his brother, this was for the best. He could no longer remember or grasp the damage inflicted by his other son.

"So would I, but for different reasons."

He wasn't sure the comment had sunk in, so he grasped his dad's hand tighter and spent the rest of the visit recounting tales about his mum.

80

WITH THE WEIGHT of the Paradiso bill lifted from his mind, Hogan bounded into the office. He spent the next hour on Google Earth surveying the property and surrounding area in Kotor. Three million dollars went far in Montenegro. He'd zoned out the office hum, where even tenuous leads were being chased down. Another one had hit a brick wall. They'd linked the drones used to kill Sandzer to a Henderson delivery. Unfortunately, this rental property was vacant, and the package left in a parcel box. The signatures of the explosives had led nowhere either. The shipping agent lead and whatever Nemo discovered could be their last hope of a break-through. They'd know more after Vance's trip on Monday. The jangle of his ringtone broke his concentration, and he tapped to answer Marissa's call.

"Hey."

"Hey, you. What you up to?"

"Looking at property in Montenegro."

"*Huh?*"

"Just some work stuff. We still good for tomorrow?"

"Yeah, definitely, I was wondering…erm…well, we were wondering if you'd like to come over for dinner tonight too?"

"Who's 'we' here?"

"My father and me. He's been nagging me to invite you."

"Sounds good, providing nothing breaks here."

"Great. See you around eight."

He hung up and mused. Was this a father vetting his daughter's suitor or was the invitation motivated by the opportunity to ask Hogan questions about Richelieu?

And was there something more to them?

81

FROM THE BACK of his white panel van, Kirov watched Special Agent Hogan climb into his red Jaguar and drive off. It was a little after seven p.m. and already dark.

He'd been there for a couple of hours. In that time, he'd completed a full reconnoiter for cameras in the area. New video doorbells added complexity to any suburban targets. You had to assume you would be picked up on camera and take suitable countermeasures.

He wore khaki overalls with two patches attached stating "pest control." A white mask, clear goggles, and a cap completed the outfit. There would be nothing unusual about an early evening visit to an address. When people had this kind of problem, they wanted solutions, whatever the hour.

He approached the Westminster Avenue apartment and climbed the steps. He started up the next set, then stopped. He clipped a small camera to one of the many cactuses on the terrace above and positioned it to overlook the door to Hogan's home.

With this in place, he headed down to finesse entry to the target's residence. After decades of practice, he made short work of this. Having checked there was no alarm, he slipped inside, closed the door, and headed to the bedroom. Once there, he got his setup ready. His phone displayed a video feed of the apartment entrance. In the other hand, he held a SIG Sauer P226 with a suppressor.

It was now a waiting game. He assumed Hogan would return that evening. And when he did, it would be for the last time.

82

THE JOURNEY UP the Fairfax mansion driveway proved no less awe-inspiring the second time around. After several security layers, two capable-looking guards flanked the same butler who'd greeted Hogan on his previous visit.

"Welcome back, sir, if you would like to follow me." The servant marched down a hallway and into a cavernous sitting room. Fairfax sat in the corner in a worn port-red Chesterfield armchair. He swirled his glass and rose to greet his guest.

"Welcome back. It's great to see you again." He clasped Hogan's hand in both of his and squeezed it. "I'm pleased you took us up on the invite for dinner on such short notice," he continued. He was the picture of health; if his current living circumstances were stressing him out, it didn't show. He had the poise and vigor of a man at least ten years younger.

"Great to meet you again too, sir..."

"Oh, come now, call me Hugh. Marissa should be down any moment; she's putting Audrey to bed. Drink?" Fairfax walked over to the array of decanters fighting for space on a Gatsbyesque art deco stand in the corner.

"Sure. Bourbon?"

"I have just the thing." Fairfax poured a healthy measure, then placed a heavy crystal glass on the side table. "Pappy Van Winkle, twenty-three-year-old."

"Great, thanks." Hogan took a sip—it was rich, flavorsome, and downright delicious. Figuring this may be the only chance he ever got to try this fêted bourbon, he took another moment to savor it. "Damn, that's good," he announced, shaking his head.

"The best." Fairfax flopped back into the chair, the leather squeaking as he did.

"So, how's the case? Are you any closer to capturing this Richelieu character? Delightful as this house is, I miss trips for dinner, the variety of life, and most of all, days out with my granddaughter. When this is over, taking her out will be the first thing I do."

"I'd like to think we're getting closer—"

"Really? In what way?"

Hogan weighed how much to reveal to the keen-eyed gentleman across from him. He decided to give him a tidbit of information to test his reaction.

"Well, we have a print we're confident is from the suspect."

"Yet he remains an enigma?"

"He does. We're convinced a third party is providing the extensive finance required to pull off these killings." Hogan stared at the billionaire; did he imagine that facial twitch after this statement?

"A foreign power, perhaps?"

"Or an individual."

This time, the older man's face was a mask. "Indeed."

"I believe we're closer than ever to apprehending the killer."

"No doubt, I have every confidence." Fairfax's look belied his conviction as he leaned forward. "Now tell me more about your English heritage. I must admit I am fascinated."

Hogan was deep into his lineage by the time Marissa hurried into the room. She hugged him, and soft lips touched his cheek.

"Sorry, Audrey insisted we finish the latest chapter of *Harry Potter*. Have you boys been getting along okay without me?"

"It's been enlightening," Fairfax answered, then looked at his watch. "Come, let's head to the dining room. Amuse-bouche will be served shortly."

The next few hours were a blur of delicious dishes and head-shakingly excellent wine. The names like "Pétrus" and "Latour" even sounded expensive. Fairfax had a magnetic personality. Yet, at moments, he could seem guarded and watchful. Stories of high-stakes financial gambits and battles with other business titans soon flowed like the bottles of red.

Fairfax became most passionate when describing the planned April launch of his secret new venture—Aeolus. He was convinced the low-cost wind power company would one day provide enough clean energy for the entire country. It was a huge undertaking that required multiple investment partners—a first for him—but he insisted this would be his legacy. From how he spoke, Hogan believed Fairfax had a great chance of succeeding.

Marissa appeared pleased by the chemistry between the two men. Despite the wine, Hogan remained guarded whenever the conversation turned to his work. At midnight they retired for a drawing room nightcap. A flushed Fairfax bade them good night soon after.

Marissa left him alone as she went to freshen up. That's when the familiar doubts and worries came rushing back. He was falling in love with this woman, and the possibility of heartbreak triggered his greatest fears. He couldn't control these feelings. And although the alcohol helped, it wasn't enough. Wracked with panic, he even considered leaving, but he sucked in deep breaths until it passed and summoned a smile as Marissa returned.

"You okay?" she asked.

Unable to think of anything else to say, he mumbled, "Too much wine. How did I do?"

Marissa tipped her head. "Pretty good—I can tell he likes you."

"I'm not sure, but I think the accent helps," Hogan replied, his composure returning.

Marissa laughed. "I know it does. It worked on me.

83

HOGAN PUSHED HIS cup away, rested his hand on his brow, and stared at the floor. He'd enjoyed most of the night before, and by any measure, his relationship with Marissa had deepened. Yet after that moment of panic, a gnawing sense of unease had developed as he drove to the office from Fairfax Mansion. He'd had way too much wine the night before to drive home.

"Are you okay?" Vance asked as she entered the office kitchen.

"Yeah, I was elsewhere," he replied. Vance began to respond, but he got in first. "When do you leave for San Fran?"

"Flight is around seven am. I'm excited we're on the cusp of the breakthrough we've been looking for, but also fear it will come to nothing. Still, you know me—I think it's gonna be good, and this time tomorrow, we'll be much closer to nailing Richelieu." Her optimism remained undimmed, but Hogan couldn't muster that emotion right now.

"It's got to lead somewhere," he snapped, then, even though they both knew it was broken, looked at his watch and said, "Sorry, I've got to go." When he walked from the kitchen, Vance's look of concern followed him.

Hogan waited by the pier on Ocean Avenue, alone with his spiraling negative thoughts. Through the throng of the Sunday crowds, he saw a Lincoln pull up and the door open. Audrey hopped out, then Marissa appeared, the late-afternoon sun catching her sunglasses as she raised a hand, waving.

Hogan reached to grab a railing to steady himself. Flashbacks to Katie's final moments came rushing back. He braced for an explosion. Inside, his buried pain began to fracture.

Marissa planted a kiss on his cheek.

"Are you alright, you look a little pale?" she asked, stepping back. He bobbed his head in response but could see she didn't believe him.

Audrey tugged at her mum's arm and pointed to the pier. "Can I go and play *Dance Revolution*?"

The color had returned to Hogan's cheeks as they watched Audrey throw herself around on the neon dance platform. He gave monosyllabic answers to Marissa's questions.

"What is wrong with you today?" she demanded.

"Nothing, sorry—it's just the case," he lied.

She appeared mollified and they stood silent for a moment, watching Audrey mimic the flashing moves.

"So, I was thinking"—Marissa took his hand, her eyes brighter—"we should all go away for Easter. What do you think?"

"That's if we're still together by then," he replied before he could stop himself, his fears manifesting aloud. Marissa's mouth formed a small O, then came confusion.

"What do you mean?"

"I'm not sure we should be making plans, you know, for the future right now."

Marissa's expression moved from hurt to anger.

"Actually, *I don't know.* What did you think this is—just some fun? It isn't for me." She raised her voice even as it wavered a little.

"It's not that—I need a little space. Everything that's happened over the last few months with the case and then us." Hogan tried to deflect, but he'd opened the door, and there was no going back.

"Look, I know you're under pressure—"

"I need time—" He dropped eye contact, his mouth dry. An awful silence followed.

"Then I'll give you some," Marissa responded in a small, sad voice. She turned away and walked over to take Audrey's hand. Her shoulders slackened, then she pulled herself upright again. A few steps farther down the pier, she stopped and looked back. Hogan wanted to call out to her and try to explain, but the moment passed, and Marissa continued into the distance.

After his second pint in Ye Olde King's Head of all places, he checked his phone to see if Marissa had messaged, but there was nothing. His rationalization ended back at regret. It would have been easier if she'd gotten angry, pushed him away—but she'd been, what? Understanding? He'd tried so hard to bury the hurt from the past, but today when it came rushing back, he'd dealt with it in the worst possible way. He was considering returning to work when Nemo's name appeared on his screen.

"Hey, do you want to catch a movie?" His friend's serious tone belied the question.

"I'm on my way to you now." His relationship turmoil would have to wait—Nemo had completed his mission, and it could change everything.

84

KIROV SAT ON his bed in his motel, considering his next move. He'd waited until dawn until he left Hogan's apartment, preferring the cover of darkness for what he had planned. He was surprised when Hogan didn't come home, especially as he'd been driving. Returning later to repeat the process was the logical decision. Even though it was unlikely, what if Hogan didn't return tonight? This job had felt rushed from the outset. He could do with an extra day to be sure. But he had to be in place Tuesday for the final killing, and he'd need to head back to San José before that. He opened Signal.

Could I delay my arrival until Wednesday for the final project?

He waited. A few minutes later, the reply arrived.

Could I ask why?

Kirov weighed the question. This should be of benefit to them both. And whatever Silver had planned to help, this would be an extra distraction for the FBI.

I want to eliminate Special Agent Hogan. He's got a habit of appearing in unexpected places. It would also provide a diversion for later this week.

The answer was swift.

Special Agent Hogan is off-limits. You need to focus on what I'm paying you for. I expect you in place as planned on Tuesday. I expect no unwelcome surprises before that.

Kirov stared at his phone. He disliked Silver's tone but conceded his point was valid. He was paying for his services, and more time for this final challenge would be beneficial. Leaving today could be the lesser of two evils.

Understood, I'll stand down. I'll be in place Tuesday as agreed.

New York, Las Vegas, then last night; Hogan's luck had held again. Kirov hoped it wouldn't come back to haunt him.

85

THE TANG OF stale sweat and crumpled shirt suggested Nemo had slept in his office. Hogan's friend's hand hovered over the touch pad of his laptop.

"It's been a stressful weekend, but I have what you need."

"How did you do it?"

"You're better off not knowing all the details. Let's just say that without our current Agency access to seed the zero-day exploit in Warren Fisk's email, it would have been almost impossible."

"And they can't trace this?"

Nemo shook his head and clicked open a screen in Tor. "I'm almost certain they can't. I've collated the data on this staging server to summarize it for you. There is still a fair bit to get through. After we finish tonight, it'll be like this never existed."

"Okay, I'm ready."

Nemo placed a hand on his friend's forearm. "And some of it will be hard reading. I want to make sure you're prepared."

Hogan bowed his head once, pursed his lips, and opened the first document.

For the next few hours, Hogan sifted through retrieved deleted emails between Perry Wolgomott and Agency deputy director, Stirling Kline. The interesting interaction began after Hogan's Langley visit. They feared an individual they only referred to as "L" was the assassin known as Richelieu. Suspicious of a link, they decided to take no chances. Any internal inquiries, such as those initiated by Warren Fisk, would be shut down. Kline mooted the idea that Wolgomott got closer to the FBI investigation, but they decided against it and remained in the shadows. All that changed the day after Sandzer's murder.

Hogan paused, reached for a glass of water, and turned to Nemo, who remained tense.

What else is in here?

"So they suspected his real identity all along. Is he ex-Agency…current Agency?" he asked.

Nemo sat stock-still and responded, "Keep reading."

What followed was panicked individuals coming to a shocking realization: Richelieu had been one of their own. The NGI check had been the trigger. The Agency had built a back door into the system. It provided them with alerts on specific prints without notifying the person running them. Hogan enjoyed the moment of vindication. When they'd run his partial from the Aria, the CIA had received confirmation of their fears. Richelieu was the individual referred to as L, who'd spent over a decade in the Agency's employ. Stirling Kline panicked Richelieu would be apprehended and talk. The consequences for the Agency would be severe. So they planned for Wolgomott to re-engage with Hogan and the investigation. They needed to get closer, so, if possible, they could kill Richelieu before he was captured.

Wolgomott emailed regular updates on the investigation, but nothing about Montenegro. Hogan clicked the close icon and leaned back. Nemo shifted over and reached to open another file with four asterisks as its name, offering a heads-up as he did.

"I dug deeper into Wolgomott's Agency database search history, trying to shed light on the identity of L. After a while, I found this." He clicked another file. "I'm sorry," he whispered.

Confused, Hogan began to read:

TOP SECRET
Ref: LV/EE91.225548
Lukas Vilkas

Asset recruitment and major activity summary:

Following Lithuania's declaration of independence, officer Frank Smith identified several candidates to work with Karol Motieka's new government and ourselves. They'd be targeted against rogue elements of the fragmenting Soviet Union. From the selection of recruits, Lukas Vilkas stood out as an individual of high intelligence who responded well to training. The subject remained emotionally detached during the arduous program. He was selected for field work when the right target presented itself.

In June 1992, Lukas killed an ex-naval commander selling Soviet munitions to questionable sources. Despite his age, he became one of our most valuable Eastern Europe assets. He continued to liquidate targets over the next six years, with numerous successful Russian missions. His contributions exceeded expectations. He was an ideal weapon over this period allowing us full deniability if the mission failed. On his last assignment in the region, he eliminated oligarch Ivan Sokolov but was almost apprehended by two bodyguards. One survived the encounter and provided a detailed description. The FSB became confident they'd identified the killer and dispatched two agents to Vilnius. With intercepts revealing Lukas's life was in immediate danger, we acted to retain the asset and relocated him to the US with a new legend.

We continued to use the asset for operations across Central and South America pink tide countries. He removed high-ranking political figures to nullify the shift toward extreme left-wing policies.

By 2002, Lukas expressed disillusionment at operating in these countries and questioned the politics driving the killings. His hatred of Russia had been the motivator for action in the nineties; now, he voiced concerns about the legitimacy of our work. We presented other operational options to retain the asset. He turned them down, determined to start a new life. Faced with no alternative, we agreed, and Lukas moved to Florida with the new identity of Mr. Andrew Shaw. Periodic checks followed, as is protocol with all ex-assets of his standing. In the next two years, he built a small but successful software company and rebuffed all our approaches for ad hoc work. He wanted to leave his past behind.

Soon after the last of these, in December 2005, his fiancée, Isobel Parker, was slaughtered at their home. Lukas had stayed elsewhere that evening, returning to the carnage and suspicious police officers. We suspected foreign agent involvement and made steps to locate him. Lukas would have assumed this too and disappeared. Police had marked him a person of interest, but security footage showed three masked gentlemen entering the home shortly after two a.m. Our inquiries pointed to Russian involvement, but we lacked proof, and the investigation wound down. And Lukas became a ghost. We couldn't even establish whether he was still alive. All this changed a few years later. Please refer to the complimentary file K.05/3448 "KIROV."

Hogan looked up at Nemo, who remained somber as he leaned forward and opened another file marked with five asterisks.

TOP SECRET
Ref: LV/EE91.225548
Associated File: K.05/3448
"Kirov"

In 2007, a new operator eliminated an Indonesian businessman in Hong Kong. The same person was suspected of other high-profile killings in the Far East. One of the deceased had connections to several US senators, so we received political pressure for information. We concluded we were dealing with a dangerous and proficient killer. The assassin had appeared from nowhere. Other nations' security services denied responsibility. A freelancer had committed the killings, and we were keen to establish his identity. We discovered a code name—Kirov, but nothing further.

Over the coming years, we tracked several murders that bore the same hallmarks across Europe and the Middle East. Two station chiefs in those regions noted similarities to the brutal killings of three FSB officers between 2006–2007. The Russian government threatened to retaliate, despite our assurances we were not involved. Our investigation discovered all three individuals entered the US in December 2005. They stayed for only four days, flying in and out of Miami International. Officer Howard Snyder, who'd handled Lukas previously, identified a link to the killing of Isobel Parker within that time frame. His hypothesis: Lukas Vilkas was the man code-named Kirov. This theory had sufficient support and credence to be elevated to the deputy director. He ordered the destruction of existing files on Vilkas. This file is the amalgamation of retained critical information.

In the years that followed we became convinced Lukas, under his adopted alias of Kirov, was also operating here in the US. His work for us would be harmful if discovered. We remain on the alert for any opportunity to eliminate him. A standing kill order exists. We have attributed to him the following high-profile killings on US soil since 2014. (Please consult the separate files on each.)

Peyton Wallis and Arnold Kobach, Washington, July 2014

Ronald Timmerton, Chicago, May 2015

State Senator Thomas Mitchell, Katie Conlan & Tony Morales, Los Angeles, January 2020

Hogan stopped reading. Blood rushed to his head as he shook it from side to side. Nemo placed a hand on his shoulder, but he sat, frozen.

Richelieu had murdered Katie.

86

HOGAN RETURNED HOME at dawn, his mind still swirling with emotion. After the shock of discovering the identity of the person behind Katie's murder, he'd reread the relevant documents several times, is ability to memorize chunks of information key. After years of hunting, it was surreal to have answers. However, the files offered no intel on why State Senator Mitchell was targeted or who'd ordered the killing. Nemo then deleted everything. This new knowledge of Richelieu and his identity was one thing, but using it without attracting attention was a different animal altogether. While Nemo remained certain he'd left no trail— Hogan couldn't make inquiries precipitated by these files.

The last twenty-four hours had been draining on many levels, but his brain was racing, and he had no chance of sleep. He showered and fixed a coffee.

He couldn't shake the image of Richelieu at eighteen years of age. The picture attached to one file featured a young man with piercing gray eyes and a high brow. His button nose and thin lips seemed out of place on the same face. It had triggered familiarity, but he dismissed this as wishful thinking. His only view of the killer had been from a distance— decades on—when he'd been disguised.

Hogan battled his baser senses; part of him wanted to find Richelieu and end his life. The assassin had to pay for what he'd done to Katie and others—who knew how many. But this would be a short-lived and empty high, a betrayal of who Hogan was; he'd sworn to uphold the law. Instead, he vowed to capture the killer alive and discover answers about that terrible day his world came crashing down.

For now, Richelieu remained elusive. They'd have to keep hunting. It meant the shipping company lead had to pay off; it would be the first step in what, to Hogan, bordered upon an obsession. His knowledge would remain secret—to act on it would be too dangerous. But how long could he ignore his discovery? And how much self-control did he have?

Hogan paced the office, waiting for Vance to report in. Ranger was also absent. He was down in Belize at Carla's behest. If the big guy's presence didn't persuade officials, some cash might. They needed to identify the law firm that registered the trading business. The entity would need to avoid money laundering restrictions, so required a veil of legitimacy. If they could discover this, they'd be a small step closer to discovering who'd shorted the Amici and Decker Batteries shares.

Finally, at midday, his new burner phone rang. Hogan had become paranoid that Wolgomott would tap calls with close contacts, so he'd bought Vance one too. She'd trusted him without question. After last night's discovery, it had proven a wise move.

"Sorry it took so long. Herman, the CBP guy, insisted we check ten different boxes and packages to ensure it looked like a real visit," Vance explained. A male voice grunted concurrence in the background.

"And the one we were interested in?" Hogan couldn't hide his impatience.

"Woah, someone needs to ease up on the coffee! Anyway, the suspect's shipping box contained a few clothes and around twenty children's books."

"First editions?"

"Maybe a couple, but most were old and battered bookshop paperbacks."

"Is that all?"

"No, also one shoebox with two old photographs. One of a smiling older woman and one of a younger woman in her late twenties. I dusted both frames for prints, took pictures of each on my phone—then cleaned them back up to ensure nothing was disturbed."

"What's your gut feeling—does this belong to Richelieu?"

"Well, it kinda fits, don't you think? *Alice in Wonderland*, and now more children's books."

Hogan agreed. They could dissect the psychology later. Right now, they needed to compare the prints to those taken at the Aria.

"How quick can you get back?"

"I'm waiting for a cab to the airport. I'll send the images now."

"Sounds good. You sure the manager of the shipping company didn't suspect anything?" They had to avoid any chance of a tip-off now they were making progress.

"Nah. I'm sure he thought it was a routine inspection. He was shooting the shit with Herman for a little while after, too. It was all relaxed."

"Nice work. Speak in a bit." He hung up and waited for the images. Would any resemble Richelieu's photo from yesterday? His phone lit up with Vance's message, and he downloaded the pictures.

The first featured a pretty female in her late twenties. The second, a solitary older lady in woolen knits, stood outside a dilapidated barn. Her eyes reminded him of the picture of the teenage Lukas Vilkas. Or was that more wishful thinking? He scrolled through the key contacts he'd added to this phone. He'd run the prints if they didn't match those from the Aria, but he needed help to compare. He hit the call button to make the arrangements.

Hogan waited in the LA County forensics lab. Bob McCourt stood next to him, more relaxed than the last time they'd spoken. Vance came bouncing in, and they all headed straight to a nearby desk. The screen there showed enlarged copies of the prints recovered from the Aria. As McCourt adjusted the microscope's focus, Vance slid over a clear evidence bag containing the prints she had lifted. He scanned the copy, then began examining the original with a loupe.

He looked up less than a minute later.

"I see a lot of similarities."

"You think it's a match?" Hogan asked.

"We can let the computer confirm, but yeah, I reckon, buddy. I'll have a closer look too." McCourt switched back to the microscope.

"Great. Don't run these through the system, okay? I need a more covert comparison."

Hogan stepped back to let the technician work. He didn't want to jump the gun and celebrate yet. Vance produced her phone and selected the image of the pretty blonde girl in her late twenties.

"Who do you think she is?"

If they had the correct shipment, this could be Richelieu's fiancée, whom the Russians had slaughtered.

"An old girlfriend? There weren't any others or more recent ones?"

"No, only this, and from the look of her clothes, it's from a while back. Either that or she doesn't update her wardrobe."

They turned their impatient stares to the huddled figure of Bob McCourt. He remained focused, so Vance offered Herman impressions to pass the time. After a while, the technician beckoned them over.

"It's a match." McCourt beamed, pointing to the confirmed points of comparison. "Whomever these items belong to also tapped the call button on that elevator at the Aria."

Carla looked at Vance, then Hogan, and for the first time in a long time, she didn't frown. She considered the information for a few more seconds, then came to a decision.

"Do you think further investigation via the shipping company could tip him off?"

"It's too much of a risk. Questions attract attention and could blow our only lead," Hogan answered, shaking his head. "We could look at upcoming flight manifests with connections ending in Montenegro?"

"That alone would be thousands of passengers, and he could fly to a nearby country like Croatia and drive. Or even somewhere different first. This won't help stop an upcoming attack," Carla moaned. "Our best option will be apprehension at the Montenegro property in... where was it again?"

"Kotor," Vance offered.

"Right, Kotor. I'll start conversations to put a Navy SEAL team in place. This is gonna have to go right up to the president for approval. We can't trust notifying the Montenegrin government—our relationship is fraught. It could cause another shitstorm like when we killed bin Laden, but we'll have to risk it."

"Can we keep the CIA out of the loop?" Hogan asked.

Carla arched an eyebrow. "Any particular reason why? I'll need a good explanation when I run it up the chain."

He'd have to obfuscate. He couldn't share anything risking last night's activity.

"I'm not sure they've been straight with us and think they may even be hiding something. They could have another agenda regarding Richelieu. I can't prove any of this, but can we keep them in the dark? It could jeopardize the mission to capture him."

"What are you not telling me?"

"Nothing. It's just after chatting with Perry Wolgomott—they suddenly appear a little too interested in the case. That makes me suspicious. Call it another one of my gut feelings. I know it isn't much."

Carla rested her hand on her chin, the cogs turning. He hoped he had enough credit banked from his previous intuition in this case and others for her to trust him.

"Okay," she replied after a long pause. "I'll ask to keep them out of the loop. If we can't, I'll need to brief my liaison, regardless of what you suspect."

"Could you let me know if you do?"

Carla frowned. "I suppose."

Hogan moved the conversation on to exact timelines to avoid further grilling. Once details were agreed, they went to brief the team.

"What's going on with the CIA, Hogan?" Vance wasn't buying his bullshit.

"Like I said, I don't trust them."

"It's more than that." She stopped and placed her hands on her hips. "Is this what was wrong yesterday in the kitchen?"

"Look, I wish I could share more. I really do. Can you trust me on this?"

"I thought we were partners in this? Maybe you should trust me," Vance replied and stalked away.

87

It had been three days, and so far, Marissa had stayed true to her promise. Hogan threw his phone back onto his desk. He'd tried to frame a message several times but struggled to find the right words. He missed her, and his regrets about Sunday continued to grow. If pushing her away was the best way to protect himself, he didn't feel better for it.

The office hummed with frustration and anticipation. Yet the task force was almost powerless until the assassin's next move. Even the most tenuous leads left agents scrambling, hoping for a breakthrough. Meanwhile, Hogan wrestled with his demons. The knowledge of Richelieu's real identity was a secret he couldn't share, and it gnawed away at him. After years of dead ends and false leads in a matter of days, he might get the chance to look into the murderer's eyes and get the truth about Katie's death. But the wait could be much longer. The added tension of Director Sullivan's deadline had ratcheted the fractious office atmosphere. If he stuck to his word, the task force would see major changes or be disbanded. Hogan hoped the discoveries earlier that week would buy them time.

The Montenegro mission had been greenlit, and only a select few briefed. This didn't include the CIA. An entire SEAL team was due to fly across to Croatia on Saturday to a location a few miles north of the Montenegro border. An FBI agent from Rome already had eyes on the Kotor property. So far, all was quiet. Richelieu could be planning to arrive at any point over the next few weeks. On confirmation the target had arrived, the operation would swing into action. Hogan and Vance would fly over to join the SEALs. Once Richelieu was apprehended, they'd escort him over the border to a waiting plane in Dubrovnik. The US carrying out another piece of extraordinary rendition would cause an international stink, but it would be worth it. Until then, they'd play a waiting game, praying that Richelieu showed up with no more blood on his hands.

Late afternoon, Hogan sought out Chung to see if he'd discovered anything further from the money trails linked to Richelieu. He found the analyst cloistered with Ranger in an unused office. The latter had returned from Belize with the name of a US law firm and an empty briefcase. It was a welcome lead. Carla was investigating what legal power they could bring to bear against them.

"Any progress with the Grand Cayman account?"

Chung shook his head. "I'm afraid not. We've tried the carrot and the stick, but the bank won't play ball. Their reputation for secrecy is more valuable to them than anything we can offer or threaten to take away."

"I could fly over?" Ranger offered, cracking his knuckles.

Hogan smiled. "I would like to see that. But we need to try more conventional channels."

"I've also got the latest breakdown from Forbes.com." Chung slid a pile of paper across the desk. Ever since Mark Fullerton's death, he'd monitored which billionaire's wealth had notably increased. If one of them funded the killings, avarice could be a compelling motive. The online site now updated the changes in real time. Most were dictated by share price or asset sales.

"How many do we have with increased wealth?"

"Sixteen. I've marked them on the list."

Hogan began scanning the names, the total wealth increasing with each one. Many had gained places because of the killings. And some had lost money with the economic fallout from the murders, pushing them down the list and elevating others. He was most interested in those at the top.

It read as follows:

1. Hugh Fairfax	$210 billion	+ $2 billion
2. Charles Lyle	$121 billion	+ $14 billion
3. Douglas Matterhorn	$109 billion	+ $3 billion
4. Felix Moore	$104 billion	- $4.4 billion
5. Terrence Fisher	$102 billion	+ $2.6 billion

He stopped at the second name from the top. "Charles Lyle is fourteen billion richer?"

"Yeah, he sold his Russian assets for a favorable price, and Lyoil, his oil company, is on the up following the chaos at Decker Batteries, and skyrocketing crude prices."

Hogan imagined the obnoxious billionaire enjoying his strange Middle Eastern tea on his terrace on Star Island. As memories of his meeting there sharpened, he shifted in his chair and turned to Ranger. "That law firm connected to the Belize entity was called Cohn and Berenson?"

"Yup, they're based in New York and are huge. Overseas company registration is only a small part of their business."

"So they have civil defense lawyers?"

Ranger took a moment to think. "They must do as they have a strapline: *Expense gets the best defense*. I assume it appeals to the wealthy."

Hogan pounded his laptop keys. He searched for the case when Quinton Decker had sued Charles Lyle. That event continued to rankle Lyle when Hogan met him in Miami. He opened an article about the dispute, and several paragraphs down, it was right there. He spun his computer around to face his two colleagues and pointed to the screen.

"Cohn and Berenson represented Charles Lyle in a civil defamation case." It was a connection they couldn't ignore. Hogan pushed the printed Forbes.com breakdown into the center of the table and jammed his finger on the second name down. "Let's get everything we can on this guy."

Empty food wrappers and soda cans littered the large conference room table where Hogan, Ranger, and Vance had spent the last six hours. The door creaked as Chung returned to join them. They'd been collating connections and motives supporting the hypothesis that Lyle had hired Richelieu.

Hogan joined his hands and pushed them out. "Okay, let's share what we have."

Vance looked up from her laptop, pointed at herself, and received an affirmative.

"I couldn't discover any clear financial motive for Lyle to have Cole Sandzer killed. Joseph checked out a few half-assed leads, but they came to nothing. However, there was plenty of animosity between them. Sandzer's *Washington Tribune* has run countless negative stories about Lyle and investigative pieces into his connections to the Russian President and the Saudi Crown Prince."

"He did make a bundle of cash from the asset sale in Russia," Hogan interjected.

"Yup. Lyoil reaped vast profits in the region over several years, even during US sanctions. But the most scathing articles followed the death of the *Washington Tribune* journalist Zayn Kahn. Intelligence agencies confirmed the Saudi government's involvement."

"Shit, yeah. Didn't they chop him up then deny everything?" Ranger asked.

"Exactly, it was horrific. Lyle has numerous Saudi assets, so unsurprisingly came out in support of the Crown Prince and his claims of innocence, despite proof to the contrary. This only intensified the attacks by the newspaper on Lyle and the Saudis."

"Would this be a strong enough motivator to have Sandzer killed?" Hogan asked Vance with a questioning gaze.

"Well, there are several documentaries on both Lyle and the journalist's death on Sandzer's streaming behemoth, Watchable, too. It's further motive, and if you'd hired the world's most deadly assassin to kill for you, I'd imagine Lyle could have been tempted to add Sandzer's name."

"Then it's a workable connection for one death, but we need more."

"I'll send through sources for you to review."

The room fell silent, so Ranger moved his bulk forward, tapped his laptop once, and looked up.

"The main interactions between Jay Chopra and Charles Lyle related to disagreements on climate change. Several posts by the latter had been deleted from Chopra's social media platforms, mainly because they lacked any substance of truth. Chopra criticized oil and gas companies and their attempts to slow shifts to greener energy, but nothing too incendiary. At least not enough for Lyle to have him killed."

"So, we're only left with the significant profits made in Belize?"

Ranger shrugged. "It seems that way, and while it is a big chunk of change, I'm not sure."

Hogan nodded. "I agree, but that company profited from the death of Quinton Decker in the same way—so there is a connection there. We keep digging."

Chung took this as his cue and cleared his throat before speaking.

"Lyle had plenty of reasons to want Decker dead. The defamation suit was one incident in an ongoing spat between the two men. Most of what I found attributed this to Decker's revolutionization of the car market and the danger this posed to the oil industry. We know he could be abrasive at the best of times, so this escalated fast. There was a fear across the petroleum industry that Decker's aviation battery solution would send oil prices tumbling to unsustainable lows."

"Good old-fashioned greed mixed with hatred, then?" Hogan asked.

"Pretty much. Add in the money Lyle may have made shorting Decker Batteries, and we have plenty of motive."

"Thanks, Joseph. I'm afraid I had less joy with Fullerton. The only connection I could find was his decision to move all his traditional energy assets into renewable companies. This was an unfortunate market mover for Lyle and other oil company executives—but it also happened eighteen months ago. Why kill Fullerton so long after? Any damage had already been done—unless there is something I'm missing?" Hogan stared at the wall, exhausted. It was two a.m. already.

"It's only been a day—we can go back at it tomorrow. I can start running more granular financial checks," Chung replied, offering an encouraging smile.

"We'll have to, but we're running short on time." Hogan feared the task force could be off the case soon. They might not get the chance to move on Lyle. Even then, it may get them no closer to Richelieu. He was desperate to find a way to get to the assassin and take him alive. If the lead in Montenegro didn't pan out as expected, or another killing happened before, he could be forced to change career. He'd need to find a way to support his dad whatever it took. These could be his final days at the Bureau.

———

88

SINCE DAWN, HOGAN had been hunched at his desk, building out the Charles Lyle dossier. Any next steps would take time and caution. Several connections for motive weren't strong enough, and the evidence still circumstantial. The phone rang. He grabbed the receiver.

"Hogan."

"Hi, Special Agent, it's Perry Wolgomott. Is now a good time?"

"Hi Percy, I suppose so," he responded, needling the officer, then paused. Did they know? Nemo's work should be untraceable. And they wouldn't call. No, this was something else.

"I was following up to see if there were any further developments in the case. One we could help with?" Wolgomott's fishing lacked subtlety. He couldn't be sure how much the officer knew, if anything, about the plans for Montenegro. He might have heard whispers. He'd tell the officer a half-truth to divert attention and explain these.

"There have been a few but nothing concrete. We're investigating suspicious money trails tied to certain accounts. They show large deposits immediately after the killings began and some funded property purchases in Europe."

"You think this is tied to...ah...Richelieu, then?"

"It's a long shot, but possible. We're still trying to corroborate the intel."

"And which countries were the property purchases? We could help there?"

"Unfortunately, we don't know yet. We have transactions routed to property agents that cover most of Europe. Of course, once we find a way to establish locations without attracting attention, I'll be in touch." Hogan stayed professional despite wanting to scream down the phone: *I know what you're hiding, you snake!*

"Hmm. We would appreciate that. Any other promising leads, Special Agent?"

Hogan caught the suspicion in his voice—enjoyed it, even.

"Nope, that's the best we've got for now. Speak soon, Percy." He hung up before Wolgomott could reply.

"Sorry about the other day," Vance offered as they perused the menu board in Fat Sal's.

Hogan turned to his friend. "It's okay. We're all under pressure. I wish I could explain, and in time, I will."

She'd dragged him there for lunch, insisting he eat something substantial. It would be unavoidable here as the menu appeared designed to feed Olympic swimmers. He settled on a Phenomenal Philly Cheesesteak, and Vance plumped for a Fat Texas.

"I also wanted to check you're okay. You know, with the anniversary tomorrow and everything else we're dealing with." Vance took a pull on her soda and met Hogan's gaze.

"Thanks, I appreciate it." It would be three years since Katie's death, and he dreaded the pain. Only this time it would be different—he knew who was responsible, and he could be on the cusp of vengeance. But would that bring any closure? Perhaps if he put Richelieu behind bars, he could move on.

A waitress slid two plates onto their table. The pictures hadn't lied. Hogan doubted he could finish his but had no such concerns for his lunch partner.

"Nailing Lyle for this is going to be tough," Vance said between bites.

"I agree. We need a money trail between him and Richelieu. That won't be a quick process. Or maybe we apprehend the assassin in Kotor, and he talks. Either way, we're back to a waiting game." Hogan waved his giant sandwich. "This is great."

"Of course, it is. Well, the plans are robust. All potential targets have tight security and patrol cars outside their properties. Let's hope Richelieu has decided to leave or is already on his way to Montenegro. The pieces can still fall into place."

"Or remain shattered." Hogan raised his hand. "Sorry, I want to remain positive, and spending time with you is the best medicine. I'll try to be more upbeat."

"Well, that and melted cheese steak," Vance responded, laughing.

With sleep elusive, Hogan headed to the sofa and pondered Richelieu's next move. Could it be possible Hugh Fairfax was the final target? He mentally opened the door to his memory palace on Mark Fullerton's hedge fund assets. There had been no connection with the other dead men, but how about Fairfax? He began flipping through each investment and its accompanying image. He expected to find nothing, but then came upon a giant purple owl perched on a doll's house. This took him back to the previous Saturday evening and Fairfax's proud announcement about Aeolus. It was right there, in Fullerton's assets. One among a slew of companies, bonds, and share names. Fairfax had mentioned the venture's secrecy when he shared his vision. His wind-powered clean energy revolution would change the nation and be his legacy. And this would hurt Charles Lyle. He'd check in with Fullerton's son tomorrow for context. Could this have been the motive for the New Yorker's murder? But it hadn't derailed Fairfax's plans, so could he be next?

89

TIME DID HEAL, or it could be the raft of distractions. Either way, today was a modicum less painful than the previous two years. After a restless sleep, Hogan welcomed the warm embrace of caffeine and spent the morning following up on Aeolus. Paul Fullerton had confirmed his father had made a $12bn investment in the company, his largest ever for one venture. The patriarch had expected it to be a game changer—he shared his business partner's view of the financial multiplier of a clean energy revolution. Fullerton was all about the dollars. The amount invested and details had been left off the company's asset report after Fairfax's request for secrecy until the announcement.

Ranger approached Hogan's desk and pulled up a chair. "I've spoken to the guards at Fairfax Mansion. With LAPD outside, the layers of security, and now the agents you requested, we're good. If he is the next target for Richelieu, the assassin should have no opportunity to strike. It could increase our chances he'll head to Kotor—if he hasn't already."

"Perfect, thanks, Ranger. This and our other measures elsewhere should accelerate that timeline."

Hogan remained stoic in his team interactions throughout the morning; only Vance knew about the anniversary. He focused on the positives. They could be confident Richelieu would head to Montenegro and had a theory on who had hired him. The motives for this still needed more substance. And he'd uncovered a crucial part of the puzzle that had haunted him for so long—Katie's killer had a name and face.

Hogan prayed he could capture Richelieu alive and get more answers. Meanwhile, the dossier on Charles Lyle grew thicker. The team would add to it over the weekend and take it to Carla on Monday.

After engineering alone time, Hogan researched Mr. Andrew Shaw from Fort Lauderdale. He wasn't surprised to find no matches to Richelieu's previous identity. He dredged up the name of the assassin's fiancée from his memory and tapped it into Google. There were several news articles about Isobel Parker's murder. He found one with a picture. The clarity wasn't brilliant, but the likeness was enough to suggest the woman in the photo at the shipping company was the same person. He couldn't share this information, but it did at least validate the plans for Montenegro. Richelieu also had a tragic anniversary, and a wave of empathy surprised Hogan, but anger crushed it. His fiancée might have been as innocent as Katie, but Richelieu had chosen his dark path leading to Isobel's murder.

"How you doing?" Vance asked, only steps from his desk. Hogan hit his touchpad and turned to face her.

"Not too bad, managed to keep busy all day."

"If you fancy a drink later, I can grab Ranger too?"

"I do, but on my own."

Vance rested her hand on his arm. "I understand. Give me a call if you need to talk."

He bowed his head once. "I will."

Hogan paced the elevator vestibule, waiting to escape the suffocating office.

The metal doors slid open, and Monroe and Tate stepped out. The latter's resigned look told him they weren't here for him.

"Found another innocent guy to harass?"

"Nice tactic getting shot, shitbird, and putting the investigation on ice. We'll be back for you in the future, and not even Sullivan will save you then." Monroe thrust his face so close his garlic-laden lunch invaded Hogan's nostrils.

"I'm pretty sure it ended because there was nothing to find; you guys chose this blind alley. If you wanna waste your time again—"

"Just 'cause we found nothing doesn't mean we believe your story. As soon as this Richelieu shit is over, we'll be back monitoring your case. You'll fuck up in the future, the corrupt guys always do, and we'll be waiting."

"How will I sleep at night knowing the A-Team is still after me?" Hogan held eye contact until Monroe began to fidget, then stepped aside. Tate nudged his partner, who swore as they trudged down the corridor.

In the grimiest bar in Venice—Hogan had one goal for the evening: get as drunk as possible and blunt today's pain. As he finished another drink, memories from three years ago pushed through. Katie turning and waving, then the explosion. Had Richelieu been there, watching? These memories carved out a special kind of hollowness. He could train his brain to remember, but it didn't mean he could force himself to forget. He waved at the barman for mental salve and scanned the room. Most fellow patrons perched on similar tall stools, elbows resting on the dirty bar countertop, facing downward. The kind of people who drank because they knew no different. Life had fucked them too, harder. He parked his pity; tonight, they were his brethren.

He staggered home in the early hours—the short journey taking way longer than it should. Even thinking hurt. The weight of greasy bar food churned his stomach as he swayed on his apartment steps. He swallowed the bile and stumbled through the door, slamming it behind him. He welcomed the sofa's embrace and passed out.

90

THE HAMMERING WOULDN'T stop, and Hogan couldn't understand why. He waited, telling himself it would end at any moment.

It didn't.

He forced his head to turn toward the noise as someone called his name. The moisture levels in his mouth suggested he'd chewed a stack of breadsticks in his sleep. He dragged himself up to a sitting position, the room swaying through his blurry eyes.

"Okay. Hang on!" he tried to shout, but it came out more of a rasp. When he opened the door, Vance rushed inside.

"I've been banging for ages. Jesus, Hogan, you smell awful." She wrinkled her nose and pulled a face. "And I've been trying to call you—are you okay?"

He had a vague recollection of trying to frame an apology to Marissa. Then his phone battery died, and he focused on drinking away the pain.

"What's going on?" he murmured, sitting back down with his head in his hands.

"Wait, I'll show you."

Vance scanned the room, located the TV remote, and went straight to a news channel.

She turned back to Hogan, pointing to the screen.

"This!" she exclaimed. "Richelieu is dead! He was shot in Miami this morning attempting to assassinate Charles Lyle."

91

WHEN THEY ARRIVED at Wilshire, Hogan ran straight from Vance's car to Carla's office. He burst in to find his boss conducting an animated phone conversation.

"Where the fuck have you been?" she demanded, covering the receiver with her hand.

"I need to get out to Miami right now," he panted, alcohol sweat seeping out of him.

"Forget it, Hogan—Miller and Kowalski flew out over an hour ago. He can liaise with the Bureau on the ground there. I need you here to help coordinate incoming intel. We can decide on next steps once we confirm it's Richelieu in the Miami morgue."

"Is there a chance it's not? If I could just head—"

"I don't think so. If we could've gotten hold of you, you'd have been on that flight. We couldn't, and you're here. Now deal with it and be professional." Carla's tone brooked no argument. She returned to her call. He marched out and continued to the conference room, where agents had congregated around the TV. Vance joined him—she'd not sprinted into the office. Hogan wished he hadn't too.

After she dropped the bombshell in his apartment, Vance had relayed the scant details they'd received from Miami. He chugged water and Tylenol to prepare for the office, and adrenaline did the rest. He'd cursed having been uncontactable for most of the ride in. And now, Jared Miller was bound for Florida to become the face of any perceived success.

Information continued to flow from the Miami field office. Hogan wanted to absorb this and analyze incoming footage of the attack along with on-camera witness reports. He recognized the location—it was the bridge from Star Island to the causeway. Charles Lyle had been traveling in an armored limousine, accompanied by two SUVs full of close protection officers. A Kenworth truck had crashed into the lead security vehicle as it turned onto the causeway, separating it from the limousine. The screen showed the wrecked Escalade getting loaded onto a tow truck. The attacker had jumped from the cabin and fired bursts from an AR15 at the tail vehicle. As those inside dived for cover, he trained his weapon on the limousine's back windows and unloaded the clip. From eyewitness accounts, at this point, the assassin was shot multiple times from a location at the island's exit and continued to be struck even once he'd hit the ground. There were unconfirmed reports the limousine had belonged to an ex-president. Either way, it had absorbed the gunfire. Lyle and the driver were described as shaken but unharmed. Aside from minor injuries, his security detail was unharmed.

Hogan tapped the seated Ranger on the shoulder and asked him to follow him to a quieter location. Vance and Chung joined them.

"Where the fuck was Lyle going? Wasn't the instruction to stay in a secure location—especially this weekend!" he complained once the office door closed. Ranger held up a finger, ducked back out, and returned shortly after carrying a stack of reports. He flipped through the pages of one, then stopped.

"He was heading to the airport. He needed to attend an emergency board meeting in Houston, something to do with a hostile takeover attempt. The police stationed outside were caught flat-footed."

"Why would he put his life at risk at the most dangerous time? What else do we know?"

Ranger slid the top file over, and Hogan began flicking through the latest summary. The close protection officer, Markus Vlok had shot the assassin. He'd not traveled in any of the vehicles but instead been stationed alongside the island's security booth. He'd trailed the convoy through the lens of a high-powered rifle as it approached the gate and causeway.

Convenient. And odd.

Nothing about this attack made sense. Lyle had looked so good to be their guy, but not so much now. Their suspicions would be dismissed. He glanced up from the paperwork.

"Do you guys think this is adding up? That this was Richelieu, and he's dead?" After discovering the killer's real identity, he thought he would be the one to capture him or, if this wasn't possible, take revenge by ending his life.

"What if we were all wrong on Lyle? He does fit as a target in the pattern of assassinations," Ranger said. "He might have succeeded if it weren't for the vehicle spec."

"And Markus Vlok," Hogan added, rubbing the back of his neck as he continued. "It all seems way too inept compared to the previous killings. The chances of success were slim; surely, he'd have accounted for the limousine to be armored. He found a way through the bullet-resistant glass at Sandzer's apartment—how could he be so unprepared this time? Richelieu was or is too smart to be behind this." He could see Vance nodding in agreement.

"Something isn't right."

"I'm with you, too," Chung added.

He could find out for sure. "Where are we with identification?" Hogan asked.

"The body is with the Miami-Dade County ME. It was shot up pretty bad. A couple of agents used the word 'overkill.' His possessions are now at the Miami PD crime lab," Ranger replied.

"Which were?"

"Cash, keys to the super-bike he had waiting as a getaway vehicle on the causeway, extra ammunition, and a motel card key."

"Where's the motel?"

"It's one out by Miami Airport." Ranger checked his watch. "There should be a team tossing it as we speak."

Hogan wished he could be there to search that room, but the main priority would be fingerprint comparison.

"Have they rolled his right fingers yet?"

"We've had no confirmation, but the ERT could've. They know it is a priority. They're checking the other items they found for prints too."

He jumped up from the desk. He needed someone in Miami who could help him cut through the bullshit and delays to get him real-time updates. He grabbed his phone and made the call.

92

HOGAN HAD EXPLAINED to Special Agent Coleman what he needed. They'd swapped messages a few times since his Miami trip, and he was confident his friend would help. Back at his cubicle, he continued coordinating the inflowing information from the attempted assassination. The attacker's weapon had stood no chance against the limousine's defenses. He questioned how the assassin could have known Lyle would leave the property, for the first time in months, at that exact time. If he'd been smart enough to plan this, he'd have known an attack on the vehicle would fail. These mistakes Richelieu wouldn't make. He was Agency trained, and no one had put a glove on him in two decades. While he wrestled with these significant doubts, the office jubilance continued—most agents believed they'd got their man. Less than an hour later, Coleman called back.

"What do you have for me?" Hogan skipped any pleasantries.

"I'm guessing we'll save the soccer chat for later—so, okay, here goes. The assailant was shot up *bad*. There won't be an open casket at his funeral. One bullet hit his right hand, pretty much obliterating it. We're talking .223 Remington rounds here. Another two almost split his leg in half; he was struck eleven times and dead before hitting the ground."

"And prints?"

"Yeah, they took them from the three remaining fingers on his left hand. A bullet hit his shoulder and exited via that wrist."

"Shit, have they run them through the NGI yet?"

"Not yet. Miami PD is still focusing on ensuring he didn't have an accomplice. They said the prints are not their number-one priority at this moment."

It didn't matter. Without the right index fingerprint, they couldn't confirm it was Richelieu. But the NGI could prove it was someone else. Only nobody wanted that.

"You managed to see the body?"

"Yeah, the ME is a friend. From what I saw, he was around six feet tall, dark hair—age would be hard to say with no face—not young by the looks of the rest of what was left."

"And the DNA sample?"

"Not been taken yet, but they're gonna. Most of the big guns are at the Ramona Motel, near the airport. One of your task force guys is meeting them there. Thought you may have come out here."

"I wanted to. Instead, I'm tied up at my desk; but I'm not buying this so far."

"Well, most people here are, I can tell you. Everyone wants a piece of the pie. You need anything else, just holler, okay?"

"I will, and thanks, Coleman."

"No worries, I'll drop you a message if any major shit changes."

Hogan's shoulders slumped. Vance caught the vibe.

"No use, then?"

"The prints from the body are a bust. We'll have to see if they pull any elsewhere. We still have no identification, and DNA is backed up," Hogan replied, pushing back his chair. He needed to be closer to the action. Time for one more try to get out to Florida.

If anything, Carla was more emphatic than before—his presence in Miami would change nothing. He had no choice but to sit tight. He headed over to Vance again. He found her in the conference room watching news reports.

"Why would he be planning to return to his room this time if the job went down as expected?" he asked her. "After the other killings, he disappeared immediately without a trace."

She shrugged. "I don't have answers, same as you. If you want to argue them with Carla, I've got your back. The rest of the guys too."

"Not yet, but I appreciate that. Let's wait and see what the motel room throws up and if it's as spotless as the one in New York."

It turned out it wasn't. Not even close.

Mid-afternoon, Carla bounded into the conference room.

"It looks like it's him, alright. I just got off a call with Miller. Thank Christ!" she exclaimed.

"How...how do they know?" Hogan demanded.

"They found a phone in the room. It's got photos from previous crime scenes that only the killer could have taken. Chopra and Fullerton are both on there," Carla responded.

Hogan had been so convinced it wasn't Richelieu.

"That's great news," he muttered. "What else did they find?"

"All kinds of incriminating stuff—close to half a million in cash, a couple more weapons, maps of Star Island and Miami. Plus, photos on the phone of the causeway and bridge where the attack took place."

"Do we have an ID?" He still wanted to see an image of the suspect—to compare the resemblance to a young Lukas Vilkas now etched in his mind.

"Not yet. There is no ID in the room, at least not that they've found, but they're still taking it apart now, and the name on the booking sounds phony. We'll get a full breakdown when the team is done." Carla frowned. "Look, this is great fucking news, I know you wanted to be the one to nail this guy, Hogan, but he's dead now. We can finally get back to something close to normality. We've worked hard to get here, even if this isn't how we expected the case to end. Once we're certain he's our man, we can celebrate."

Other agents in the room were high-fiving and slapping each other on the back. They were ready to celebrate now. Hogan wanted to voice his concerns. If anything, they had grown with this news, but Carla had gone. He turned back to Vance.

"The room is a fucking treasure trove?"

"I mean, the pictures on the phone, I can't explain, but I remember that room in New York. The occupier had been professional, ultra-careful, and neat. This can't be the same guy," she replied.

"And why has he got so much cash in the room? He led us on a merry trail to San José, moves money like a professional, without a trace, and suddenly, he's lugging around a suitcase of dough?" Hogan snapped. "It's bullshit."

Vance placed her hand on his arm.

"So what can we do about it?"

"Nothing right now; nobody wants to listen to us." He shook his head, stalked out of the room, and didn't stop until he reached the far corner of the office. He looked out over the 405, watching traffic build. Why couldn't Carla and the others see it? At least Vance and the team helped keep him sane. Until he saw absolute proof, he refused to believe Katie's killer was dead.

93

THE ALL-IMPORTANT news conference from Miami drew closer. As it did, Hogan urged Carla to call the investigators to suggest caution. They needed to match prints from the room or, at the bare minimum, a DNA sample with one from the Loews Regency. At first, she was reluctant, questioning his motives. After relenting, she called Miller to advise they didn't confirm Richelieu had been the dead assassin. It would leave them flexibility in the unlikely event he wasn't. The press would form their own opinions and stories regardless. The news cycle had to be fed.

Information from the Miami Bureau had flowed throughout the day. The motel room had been occupied since early that week, suggesting the assassin had arrived in town then. The examination of security footage from the motel continued while other agents focused on the Kawasaki Ninja ZX-11. The planned escape vehicle was presumed stolen. Facial reconstruction experts were flying into Miami to start working up a likeness of Richelieu from his shattered face. It would be the first step in identifying the man behind the moniker.

The countdown to the press conference ended. A collective hush settled over the assembled task force members as the TV camera panned over to the packed rows of media. It came to rest on the podium of law enforcement behind the usual jumble of branded microphones. Hogan recognized the SAC from the Miami Bureau and, alongside him, Miller. He gritted his teeth at the injustice. He'd believed in the case from the start.

Once a suitable level of decorum was reached, SAC Mason stepped forward. He maneuvered a few microphones that were too high, then began.

"Good evening, everyone. I'm Special Agent in Charge John Mason. I'll run through today's events and what we know so far. As this is an ongoing and fluid investigation, we'll update information as and when we receive it. They'll be a time for questions after the following statements."

With a confident stare, Mason summarized the attempted assassination, including the shooting of the suspect by Charles Lyle's security head. National news outlets had covered some of this already, but the press scribbled in notebooks and tapped on their phones to fill in the gaps. Once he'd finished, to Hogan's horror, he turned to Jared Miller, whose smug features filled the screen.

"One of the lead investigators from the LA task force, Special Agent Miller, arrived in Miami this afternoon. He joined the investigation at a critical time as we searched the suspect's airport motel room. I'll let him update you on what this yielded—particularly in the broader context of the existing investigation. Special Agent Miller, if you could—" The SAC stepped back on the podium.

You must be fucking kidding me. If Hogan had been hoping the dead attacker wasn't Richelieu before, he prayed now.

"Thank you, sir. As you know, this investigation has been the largest in the Bureau's history. I've been proud to help lead the world's most talented law enforcement officers in trying to identify and stop the assassin we know as Richelieu." Miller stared into the camera, loving the attention. "In the suspect's motel room, we discovered evidence that unequivocally proves he was the killer behind the high-profile murders that have blighted our fine country." Hogan couldn't believe this. He spun to face Carla as her face reddened. Miller couldn't help himself; the opportunity to burnish his profile was too tempting.

"Added to other key pieces of supplementary evidence, we can say"—Miller threw in a dramatic pause for good measure—"we've got him, folks!"

A round of spontaneous applause followed as the grinning agent stepped back and waited for it to die down.

"Our exceptional agents have worked tirelessly to apprehend the killer, and this relentless pursuit has forced a fatal mistake. Today, Richelieu reached the end of the road. In the coming days, we expect we'll have a name to go with the body in the Miami-Dade morgue. After this, the investigation into motive and any potential accomplices will continue. We'll update further in due course." Miller edged back, and a city PR representative stepped forward and opened the floor to questions. Hogan couldn't watch Miller's smug features anymore and stormed out of the room. Optics were everything. Jared Miller was now the face of the successful end to Richelieu's reign of terror, even if it wasn't the direct result of the Bureau's work. After all, they'd hardly captured or indeed stopped the killer. This didn't matter; they had to make it look like a win. It would be the final push Miller needed to lock up the SAC position, regardless of Carla's anger—she wouldn't have a choice. And where did that leave him?

Vance caught up with Hogan in the hallway.

"I thought we weren't going to announce it was him yet?" she asked, looking confused.

"I guess that fucker couldn't help himself. Carla will tear him a new one, but it will be worth it now he looks like the golden boy. Plus, if the body is Richelieu, the fact he spoke prematurely will become redundant. I bet Director Sullivan lapped up his performance too." Hogan shook his head in disgust. He'd had enough of this day, and its bullshit. Grabbing his suit jacket, he left a grim-faced Vance and headed for the exit. As he rode the elevator down, he came to a difficult decision that had been percolating all day. If tomorrow they received confirmation the dead man in Miami was Richelieu, he would resign. The SAC job would be out of reach, and without the extra money, he wouldn't be able to keep his dad at Paradiso much longer. Life with Miller in that position would be intolerable. A position in Nemo's company should be possible, or he could command a decent salary elsewhere and spend his free time investigating Katie's death. He'd have to give up his dream job, but life had never been fair. He walked to his car and called Nemo.

94

IN HIS STUDY on Star Island, Charles Lyle flicked off the Miami press conference. The police had insisted everyone stay put while the investigation continued. He didn't mind. The alleged takeover attempt had been a ruse to leave his residence so the assassin he'd hired could attack. Everything had gone like clockwork. The FBI had rushed to the conclusion that Vlok had gunned down Richelieu, the smug face of an agent announcing that looping on Fox News. He could give the green light for tomorrow. He picked up his phone and opened the Signal app, messaging Kirov:

As planned—today's events have convinced the world Richelieu is dead. Fairfax should buy this too. I trust you can adapt to opportunities tomorrow to carry out this final mission. I remain confident he'll leave his home, very possibly with his granddaughter. After all this time cooped up, the chance to do so will be irresistible.

Fairfax was a workaholic, but in several news articles, he mentioned spending Sundays with his granddaughter was sacrosanct. These trips had been curtailed for months, and now they had a window of a day or two. After this, and despite the events of these last few hours, the FBI might start forming doubts Richelieu was the assassin shot in Miami. Tomorrow, Fairfax would be vulnerable—providing the opportunity Kirov would require. He needed to overcome one last hurdle. The phone vibrated, announcing a reply:

I'm not sure how you've done it, but I think you've created the opening I need. I'm ready for tomorrow but will only proceed if I can complete the mission successfully. The target will have to leave the property.

Lyle smiled and typed a reply.

He will. Keep me updated on any major developments.

Kirov came back immediately.

Understood.

Lyle placed his phone down. He had every faith in Kirov; he'd delivered each time. His rogue plan to kill the FBI agent the only misstep. Despite everything, Lyle still considered himself a patriot and drew the line at killing law enforcement. He'd be happy to settle the fee for this last murder—this time next month, he expected to be the richest man on the planet.

When Charles Lyle had turned seventy-four, he'd come to a stark conclusion: his last and enduring goal in life wasn't going to happen. For decades, he'd bought companies, added to his empire, and trampled everything that got in his way, only to never reach the zenith of wealth. He could buy houses, yachts, and wine, but so could all billionaires. There were no bragging rights for this kind of affluence. One thing mattered to him—becoming wealthier than everyone else on the planet. Before he'd died, Charles's father had pushed him every day of his life. He would throw each new *Forbes 400* release at him—bemoaning whichever position he'd climbed to, that it wasn't enough. It became an obsession for Charles and drove him to accumulate more and more, whatever the cost. If people died from polluted air released by his factories or from explosions on his oil rigs, he didn't care. It was the cost of doing business and the fines a fraction of the profits; that was how corporate America worked. Then everything changed. Fossil fuels became the new tobacco and faced an existential crisis.

His main business partners had the most to lose. Saudi Arabia's entire economy depended on oil, and the Crown Prince had tried to diversify, but traction had slowed. It turns out you can't recreate Dubai overnight. The stock exchange debut of Aramco—the nation's oil business—had met with a muted market response. Back in February, over a private dinner at Al Yamamah Palace, Crown Prince Khalid Hussain Al Saud outlined the parlous threats facing the Kingdom.

And his radical solution.

The battery revolution led by Quinton Decker presented the single biggest problem. The combustion engine would have been consigned to history decades ago if it wasn't for big oil. Now, however, he was pioneering a change that at best, the industry could only hope to slow. Once he launched a viable solution for the aviation industry, the price of oil would plummet. But without Decker as a talisman and driving force, his company would flounder.

Cole Sandzer had a specific stance on climate change, and his media outlets reflected this. Fossil fuel multinationals, oil-rich nations like Saudi Arabia, disastrous spillages, and fracking—all received criticism, and public opinion had begun to shift. This only intensified after one of the *Washington Tribune*'s journalists was killed and dismembered. The dissension he'd sowed within the Kingdom couldn't be tolerated. The Crown Prince denied involvement, and the US and other allies had given him a pass.

Meanwhile, Sandzer's streaming platform, Watchable, became the world's most popular. Residents of Saudi Arabia found ways to view and share its content, despite government barriers. They needed someone more amenable in charge of that business.

More challenges existed elsewhere. The ubiquitous Amici social platforms continued to galvanize change across Saudi Arabia. The government had been forced to make concessions like allowing women to drive—unthinkable a few years ago. Too much power and influence were concentrated in the hands of Jay Chopra's properties. A company board not controlled and outvoted by him offered more sway for Saudi government investment and influence.

However, the catalyst for immediate action was the initial Aeolus consultation between Fairfax and Fullerton. The Crown Prince had previously exchanged WhatsApp messages with the hedge fund boss that contained customized spyware. This allowed the Saudis' expert cyber team access to this secret information. Khalid outlined the duo's game-changing plans to Lyle, who immediately grasped the danger. A world without gas-guzzling cars or planes, but with universal cheap renewable energy, was a financially dystopian vision they shared.

Their interests aligned, so they thrashed out an arrangement. Lyle would run and fund the operation from the US. There would be no conversation or communication between him and the Kingdom. Even their public business dealings would take a back seat. Lyle would be on his own. It gave the Saudis complete deniability, crucial given the gravity of what they were orchestrating. They'd gotten away with the events of 9/11; they might not again. In return, Lyle could short the share price of the first two victim's companies via an obscure offshore company and bank huge, anonymous profits. In addition, on completion of the operation, the Saudis would buy his assets in the Kingdom for $14bn. This was around $12bn over market price. This windfall would come with one other condition: he'd use a portion of it to lobby the US government, especially while a vacuum in business leadership existed. If everything went to plan, Crown Prince Khalid would get the time needed for structural change in Saudi Arabia, and Lyle's businesses would be protected from decline for years to come. With his increase in wealth and the redistribution of billions following the targets' deaths, he should become the world's richest man. Lyle had agreed in a heartbeat, his dream now within reach.

It had taken months to find the assassin. You couldn't make casual inquiries for this specific requirement. Then Lyle's close friend had intimated at having used an exceptional gentleman to solve a particular problem. This turned out to be Kirov, and Lyle received an encrypted email and protocol guide to reach him. That and the first million down-payment was how the operation got started. Chopra died not too long after.

Lyle rose from his desk and poured himself a celebratory glass of 1982 Pétrus, savoring the bouquet of blackcurrant and vanilla.

The occupants of Al Yamamah Palace would be satisfied. Each death had already benefited him and his partners in increasing increments. At some point, Lyle expected scrutiny from the FBI, but he'd been careful. They'd have no proof, and he needed to continue to play the game. Now, only the elimination of Fairfax remained. The smug prick would have spent the rest of his days hiding in his eponymous mansion, untouchable unless something changed. He'd need to be convinced the danger was over, and that Richelieu was dead. Lyle couldn't do this alone, and his plan came with risks. He'd chosen to loop in his head of security, Markus Vlok, without sharing any motivations. The South African was en route from giving statements to the FBI, now much richer than a week before. It was a further two million well spent.

Vlok had been crucial in the planning and finding them a patsy. An old ex-mercenary acquaintance from Zimbabwe took the bait. Karl Bekker had an ill daughter who needed urgent surgery at eye-watering costs. Vlok believed this man had the right combination of arrogance and desperation to think he could pull the job off. Vlok had acted the part of a disgruntled security chief who'd been approached by a wealthy adversary of Charles Lyle's to betray his boss. It had taken time and limousine misinformation to convince Bekker. That, a bag of cash, and the promise of an additional five million dollars he'd never live to collect.

A knock at the door jolted Lyle from his recollections. After he murmured for the person to enter, Vlok walked in and poured himself a glass of the Pétrus. Lyle frowned at the impertinence but then relaxed. His security chief deserved this today, and the plan had been masterful. Lyle began to speak in a hushed tone.

"Excellent work, Markus. Especially on the motel and planted phone." Lyle insisted from the beginning Kirov send him crime scene images. Then it had been a case of loading them onto a burner phone to leave at the Ramona Motel. Karl Bekker hadn't been anywhere near the motel room at any point. Vlok had booked it with an anonymous prepaid credit card and checked in via their app earlier in the week. He planted the phone and other incriminating evidence before taking the card key and leaving the way he came in, via the fire escape.

"Yeah, they're pretty fucking dumb," Vlok replied, "and jumped right in. They wanted it to be him real bad."

"That was some pretty fancy shooting too."

"My location made it easy. I obliterated his face as you asked, took one of his hands, and almost got them both. Thought it would slow them down. I slipped the motel card key into his pocket while checking his pulse. Not that I needed to."

"The FBI is in for a shock when Fairfax dies, and they realize their mistake."

Vlok laughed. "Be too late by then."

"Are you sure there'll be no trail leading back to you from Karl?"

Vlok shook his head. "We're good. It's been twenty years since I last saw him before this week. No one will make the connection when his real identity comes to light. All our communication was encrypted, and his real devices destroyed. Eventually, the feds will blame a copycat."

Charles allowed himself a satisfied smile. Later this year, his destiny would be complete. His face would finally grace the cover of the *Forbes 400* edition.

95

KIROV FINISHED TYPING his reply to Silver, tossed his phone on the hotel bed, and walked to the window. A plane cut through the smoggy dusk on its way to nearby LAX. Silver had to be Charles Lyle—he didn't see how else everything could have fallen into place. The billionaire fit the profile he'd formed of his employer—rich, ruthless, and calculating.

The botched assassination attempt stunk of a setup. It was embarrassing they were attributing it to him and reporting his demise. He wouldn't have pulled off anything so amateur, even as a teenager. Lyle must have hired this shitty assassin. Otherwise, how else could Silver have known the window of opportunity to kill Fairfax would open? Kirov had been surprised at the speed at which the FBI had bought it and publicly announced his death. The agent called Hogan had been absent from the coverage. Had he jumped to conclusions like his colleagues? He'd never know how lucky he was to be alive. Still, Kirov would have the chance to complete the impossible job if Fairfax let his guard down. He had to hope circumstances allowed him to pull it off. Eventually, the FBI would realize they'd made a mistake, but not by tomorrow, or at least until Fairfax died.

Kirov had spent the last few days familiarizing himself with the surrounding areas of the Fairfax mansion. He'd stolen long-distance views because of the police and agents outside. While he remained secure behind the wrought-iron gates, any attempt on Fairfax's life would have been a death wish. Kirov had been intrigued by how Silver would manufacture an opening but now understood. On his first day out with his granddaughter in months, Fairfax would likely retain some security. But with the apparent threat eliminated, it should revert to standard close-protection protocol. Kirov was confident he could deal with that. The main challenge would be getting ahead of where Fairfax was going, to have time to set up favorable conditions to end his life.

He picked up his phone and clicked on the Instagram profile for Fairfax's grandchild, Audrey. There had been no update. She'd uploaded their Sunday adventures before her grandfather locked down his home. Instagram stories of them riding roller coasters at Six Flags and Universal Studios were pinned on her profile. Kirov had gained access after hacking the account of a girl from Audrey's school, and he'd done the same to Marissa Fairfax's work colleague. He logged out and into this profile. He'd been surprised to learn Fairfax's daughter appeared to be dating Special Agent Hogan. His grudging respect grew. He guessed the agent would be busy celebrating "Richelieu's" bloody end. In the last week, Marissa Fairfax had posted nothing new, so he shut the app down.

The images of happy families took Kirov back. In different circumstances, he'd have grown up to lead a normal life in Lithuania. Or after he'd met Isobel, and if his past hadn't caught up with him, he could be watching his child graduate high school this year. He could have been the parent his never were. Alcohol was their priority long before they abandoned him at his grandmother's. But his path had been decided over that bowl of cabbage soup all those years ago. Or even earlier when he entered that soulless orphanage. Tomorrow would be his last day as Kirov and Richelieu. After that, would he get the ending he wanted or the one he deserved?

Kirov tossed his napkin on the half-eaten room service, pulled a sizeable black backpack from the closet, and unloaded its contents. He'd acquired a selection of weapons ready for tomorrow, allowing him to prepare for many potential scenarios. He was doing his best to keep SIG Sauer in business, with his third P226 in as many months. The weapon hadn't failed him yet. He had a backup Glock 22 and two FN SCAR assault rifles. He didn't expect to use these but would have them on hand anyway. You never wanted to be outgunned. Unsheathing his

Ontario MK-3 knife, he slid his thumb along the razor-sharp edge of the black-oxide blade until he drew blood. Next to this, he placed his final backup weapon—a Gerber Ghoststrike—this blade the perfect size to strap to his ankle. Ready for the unpredictability of this last job, he returned the items to the backpack. He unzipped another bag that sat next to his bed, counted the books inside, then closed it. Prepare, kill, disappear.

Kirov had booked three flights out of LA over the next thirty-six hours, all to Europe. He'd be one of fifty-thousand souls passing through the airport in that period. He planned to leave the crime scene, switch vehicles, and park on the sprawling lot at LAX. There would be chaos after Fairfax's death. He would slip away and enjoy ice-cold beers in first class at thirty-six thousand feet before they began to figure out what the fuck had happened.

Kirov flicked on the TV to watch the rolling news coverage of his death. He glanced at his bag and thought of his well-thumbed copy of *The Adventures of Tom Sawyer*. This situation reminded him of that scene when they thought Tom was dead, and he appeared at his own funeral. He also had a pristine first edition in his precious New York shipment due for dispatch later next week. He made a mental note to ensure he rerouted this from its current destination to Kotor if everything proceeded as planned tomorrow. After an hour, bored with the repetition and incessant commercial breaks, he turned in. He planned an early start and would need to be prepared to follow Fairfax to any destination. After which, he'd have to break his rule on intricate planning and eliminate the target on the fly. It would be his first time doing so. The operation would run much smoother if he had the location in advance. Either way, Hugh Fairfax should become his final victim tomorrow.

96

SPENDING THE PREVIOUS evening with Nemo had been the perfect tonic. They both knew more than anyone about Richelieu, and neither could reconcile he was the deceased assassin in Miami. Hogan argued none of the DNA profiles recovered in New York would match the dead guy, but Nemo had countered. Despite his extended stay in the Loews Regency, the FBI couldn't be certain they had Richelieu's DNA.

Hogan revisited their conversations while a cold shower helped revive him. His despondency yesterday evening as he left Wilshire had ebbed, but he agreed with his friend. He needed clear security footage images of the Miami killer before the attack to compare his mental one of Lukas Vilkas at eighteen. And, although less useful, to the man he'd seen in the Aria hallway.

But then what?

He could hardly chime in and say: *Hey, I've viewed a top-secret file my friend and I hacked from the CIA, and the image doesn't match.* It left him in a bind. Maybe his refusal to accept the official version of events was an act of self-delusion, and Katie's killer died yesterday. And if proven—how would he feel, his quest for justice not over, but closer to completion. He still needed to identify who'd ordered State Senator Mitchell's killing.

He toweled himself off and checked his charging phone. After typing out a quick message to Coleman chasing any updates from Miami, he dressed and trudged to the kitchen to make a four-egg omelet. Wilshire could wait, the prospect of compiling the incoming evidence from the East Coast unpalatable. If they confirmed Richelieu as the dead assassin,

Miller would have won, and Hogan's time as an agent would, in effect, be over. He grabbed his keys; he could pay his father an early visit while waiting for news. It might be the most enjoyable part of his day.

Hogan parked his Jag and tapped out a reply to Vance. She'd suggested the four of them take their doubts to Carla later that morning, with Ranger and Chung also skeptical. He expressed gratitude for their solidarity and agreed they'd give it a shot.

The lounge at Paradiso could sap a visitor of joy. So many residents faced daily struggles. For many, it was not a life; it was an existence. Hogan approached his father, who offered a carefree smile. One advantage of his condition was that nothing bothered him anymore. After the usual greeting, his dad asked about his week.

"It's gone from bad to worse. I thought I was on the right track; then everything started falling apart," Hogan replied. His pent-up emotions caused him to respond with a frank honesty that he'd long since avoided with his father.

His dad's eyes took on a rare lucidity, and he leaned forward. "You'll get through it. You've always made me proud."

Hogan sat there for a moment, stunned. These days, any clarity was rare, and the words yanked at his heartstrings. He embraced his father and felt rough stubble against his cheek.

When they separated, his dad stared at the TV. The moment had passed.

He chatted about Marissa and Audrey, hoping to get a further reaction, but his dad's attention wandered, and his eyes were dull once more. Talking about this only served to swell the feeling he'd fucked up. They'd still not spoken. Would he push anyone he fell for away indefinitely, and to what end—to become a broken old man in a place like this? It was time to face his issues head-on, starting with work. He kissed his dad's forehead, told him he loved him, and he would visit again soon.

Hogan's burner phone rang as he approached his Jag. Coleman's name lit up the screen.

"Hey, mate."

"Hey, Hogan, now a good time?"

"For sure, any joy on the images?"

"Yup. So, the dude from whom Richelieu stole the Kawasaki Ninja, was a little paranoid. Turns out he'd hooked up two cameras to watch his bike. The thief had angled the first camera away. The second one, hidden in a tree, was a different story."

"You've got an image… Is it clear?" Hogan gripped his car key fob.

"We have, and yes, we have several from different angles."

"Is it the same guy in the morgue? Can you send me them?"

"He's wearing the same jacket he died in, and his build is the same, so I'm confident it is. I shouldn't share these yet, but that's never stopped me from helping a fellow agent. You think you'll recognize him? I asked a few guys here, but they don't know him."

"Thanks. I dunno, I'm one of the few people to see him in person, albeit disguised…"

"I'm gonna send them now. Lemme know if it leads anywhere."

Hogan stared at his phone in anticipation. Seconds later the first image arrived, and he clicked it open. The photo showed a man cutting a thick bike chain. He pinched the screen to zoom in. This guy had dark hair but a prominent curved nose, narrow eyes, and a flattish face. He compared it to the photo of Lukas Vilkas he pulled up from memory. It wasn't him, not even close. Almost everything about this man's features was different. The man Hogan chased in the Aria had been less built too. This hapless assassin, who'd been shot on the causeway in Miami, wasn't Richelieu. Hogan leaned on his car to steady himself. He checked the pictures again to be positive, the gravity of the situation beginning to dawn on him. If Richelieu wasn't dead, he was free to strike again. All his doubts about the Miami attack came rushing back. They made even more sense now. Yet he couldn't reconcile one inconsistency—

the images on the phone found in the hotel near Miami Airport. He climbed into his vehicle and began rapping his knuckles on the walnut dashboard—harder and harder, as he worked through the problem.

The pieces fell into place. The whole attack must have been a setup, even including those images. That's why it all made no sense and was a spectacular failure. But by who and to what end?

His sudden panic answered the question; the fake ambush gave Richelieu the opportunity to strike one last time. He'd set the whole thing up. It would allow him to attack another now relaxed target who no longer had extensive police surveillance.

Shit! He needed to get hold of Marissa and Hugh Fairfax right now.

Marissa's phone went straight to voice mail. He tried again and again—with the same result. He slammed his hand on the steering wheel and swore, then typed—*call me, urgently!* He added: *and I mean urgently!* Where was she, and where was her father? He opened Instagram praying for an update—and found a new story waiting—he tapped Marissa's profile icon to watch it. The video featured Audrey and Hugh Fairfax beaming into the camera with the Santa Monica aquarium sign in the background.

Hogan peeled out onto the street, calculating the quickest route. He hit the call button again, praying he'd got this all wrong, and if not, he could get to them in time.

97

AT SUNRISE, KIROV sat in a pull-off on Mulholland Drive, north of the Fairfax residence, looking like the everyday tourist. A patterned black man-bag was slung over his shoulder, and binoculars sat around his neck. A map lay open on the passenger seat of the anonymous blue Nissan Altima. Over the last few hours, he'd taken occasional strolls to snap pictures of the city through the haze below. After the most recent walk, he checked his phone to find Audrey Fairfax had uploaded a short story to Instagram. She expressed extreme excitement about a private Santa Monica aquarium tour with her grandfather later that morning. GIFs of fishes had danced across the screen as she'd spoken. He played it again to ensure he'd noted all the details and jumped back in the Altima.

From a distance, Kirov scoped out the aquarium reception area, ascertained where the two cameras were, and the angles to avoid them. He pulled his cap down and put on shades. He'd have to risk showing up on footage that might give authorities more to work with, but it wouldn't matter after this. He added the Ontario MK-3 knife and SIG P226 to his man-bag and left the backpack with the other weaponry in the trunk. To a separate bag, he added the midnight-blue hardback. It nestled next to his other grandmother's books which he'd carry on the flight in a few hours. He couldn't spare the time to read it, so he'd have to break his traditional preparation. Ensuring his car was positioned for a swift getaway, he set off toward the entrance.

The droopy-eyed teenager behind the reception looked up at the clock, then back at him.

"We close in under an hour, private event. Probably best to try another day," he announced in a bored tone. Kirov passed a twenty across the desk.

"My wife and kid are already here—I'm catching up with them. Seen one fish, seen 'em all, right?" He played the goofy dad role. It worked.

"Okay, it's your choice." The kid slid across the change and ticket. Kirov responded with his dumbest smile, then disappeared into the relative darkness and removed his shades.

He'd walked the entire aquarium in under thirty minutes and decided upon the ideal kill zone. The tour would be private, so he expected to deal with at least one, if not two, close protection guys before he got to Hugh Fairfax himself. On a more positive note, no members of the public could get in the way, and he had the opportunity to set up. It was as good as he could have hoped for. But it would take a bit more work, and time was not his friend. He hurried back to the perfect killing location, one with a direct way back to reception.

The aquarium centerpiece involved heading downstairs to an underwater tunnel. This led to a great glass dome where fish and even sharks swam above and all around you. This would be where Kirov would wait. There was an identical route out, which took visitors onward and upward to more aquatic delights. The Ontario MK-3 knife would be his weapon of choice. He wasn't keen on firing a gun in an area surrounded by glass and millions of gallons of water. Next, he needed a reason to be at this spot when the Fairfax party arrived.

He walked straight to the gent's restrooms located twenty yards from the main entrance and shoved paper towels down one of the toilets. With each flush, it flooded. After a few efforts, water had pooled out across the floor. With this sorted, he entered the gift shop, keeping his back to the camera, and approached the middle-aged lady behind the counter.

"Sorry to bother you, but the restroom seems to be flooding a little. Like there isn't enough water here already," he joked, playing the helpful visitor. The woman smiled.

"Ohhhh, thanks for letting us know, dear," she replied and reached to pick up the phone. Kirov waved and strode back out the door to wait.

The next part of his plan took a little longer than expected, and at least two other patrons hit the head before a cleaner arrived. In ten minutes, the place shut for the tour. The indulgences money offered knew no bounds—even closing a state-of-the-art place like this. Finally, the door clicked open, and a tired-eyed cleaner in green overalls with a matching cap pushing a mop and bucket entered. He looked at Kirov, who'd started washing his hands, flicked his head once in acknowledgment, and turned to the toilet cubicle with a heavy sigh. Kirov opened the exit door, from which an "Out of Order" sign hung, then let it close without leaving. He waited out of sight, hoping Fairfax wouldn't be late.

The cleaner finished his unpleasant task, and Kirov could wait no longer. He stepped out of the shadows, grabbed the cleaner around the neck, and dragged him back into a stall. The man's eyes bulged as he kicked out his legs, clawing at the strong arm lowering him to the floor. He passed out, leaving a dilemma: When eliminating a target, those with them and guarding them were fair game. This guy was neither. He could raise the alarm if he came around before Kirov completed the job. With a silent apology, he continued the choke hold until the unfortunate cleaner expired. He'd never experienced a moment of weakness and indecision before, and he couldn't afford another. He closed the door to the stall, locked it, and undressed the limp body. Once it was balanced on the toilet, he climbed over the top of the cubicle. He walked over to the mirror, checked the cleaner overalls he'd pulled on looked the part, and clipped the identity lanyard to his chest.

Kirov waited for fifteen minutes, ear to the door listening for a sign Fairfax had arrived. He was confident no one would try to enter the faulty restroom in the deserted aquarium. After a while, he heard a young girl laughing and other voices as they passed within feet of where he stood. He tried to count footsteps and estimated no more than four in the party. He stood a few minutes longer, then walked out of the door, his head bowed. He pushed the mop and bucket down the left-hand corridor, which led to his planned destination—Fairfax would have taken the opposite route. He reached his desired point without incident and stood to the left of the domed area's far entrance. Retrieving the gun and knife from the bag beneath his overalls, he placed them in either pocket and waited for his target to arrive.

98

HOGAN SCREECHED TO a halt outside the aquarium. He'd tried to get hold of Marissa on the journey, but to no avail, and figured any signal would be blocked by thousands of tons of water. The thought of which made him shudder.

He'd tried to rationalize the situation on his journey. Richelieu shouldn't know they'd be at this location. But what if the killer was a step ahead again? Once he'd secured Fairfax, he'd have to call Carla and tell her the assassin was still out there. He'd have to do whatever it took to ensure she believed him and deal with the consequences alone. If they apprehended Richelieu before he struck again, or stopped his plan, it would be worth it. If he didn't act, the next death would be on his conscience.

Hogan leaped from his Jag, turning to where a man in a dark suit leaned against the door of a limousine, his hand already sliding inside his jacket. It was one of the close protection officers he encountered on his last Fairfax mansion visit.

"Good to see you again, sir. Can I help with anything?" he asked in a flat monotone. The guy remained wary, appraising the wide-eyed agent standing before him.

"Where is Marissa, Audrey, Hugh?"

"They're inside on a private tour—my colleague, Jack, is with them too. Is there a problem?" The guard's eyes darted left and right.

"I hope it is nothing. I'm going to head inside to check. Can you cover the entrance?"

"Of course, but—"

"Thanks, I'll be back out shortly—keep an eye out for anything suspicious," Hogan replied, and sprinted to the aquarium's door.

Hogan pulled his badge out and called out to the youth behind the counter as he burst in. "What's the quickest way to catch up with the Fairfax party?" The teenager flipped his head one way, then another in confusion. "Come on, which way?" He waved his hands at the two corridors. "Left or right?"

The boy paused, glancing at the clock on the wall, "Head left. They'll be nearer the exit by now—"

He hadn't finished the sentence before Hogan ran toward the left corridor, drawing his gun in a swift motion.

Hogan blinked as his eyes adjusted to the murky darkness as he advanced through the first room of tanks teeming with marine life. He tried to ignore the sheet walls of water in the next as he listened for any sign of trouble ahead, scanning with the gun as he advanced. Claustrophobia and fear built as he continued deeper into the aquarium, but he pushed on.

After several rooms and narrow hallways, he approached a downward staircase marked with a sign announcing: "Shark Experience." He paused when he reached the bottom of the dimly lit stairway. Shafts of eerie light illuminated the curved glass ceiling and walls of the walkway ahead. He battled nausea; water framed him on every side except below. He stopped momentarily, leaving a smudged palm print on the cool glass, fighting the panic—not wanting to carry on. Then, on hearing the murmur of sounds ahead, he steeled himself, and edged forward, eyes focused over the barrel of his weapon.

99

A GIRL CRIED out in delight from back down the glass walkway.

They were almost here.

Kirov wanted to sneak a look but instead waited, mop in one hand and the other around the knife in his pocket. After a minute or so, he heard heavy steps approaching the area. His eyes never left the spot where the walkway opened into the cavernous room. A rangy man in a neat charcoal suit stepped into view and eyed Kirov with suspicion.

"Who are you?" the guy asked, his neck muscles tightening as he edged forward. Kirov looked like a cleaner going about his duties. He adopted a deferential tone.

"I was just finishing cleaning here; some kid dropped a drink earlier. Sorry, I'll get out of your way now, sir," he responded. The bodyguard stepped closer, looking at the mop and the man holding it before his eyes dropped to the ID tag. At this moment, Kirov let the mop slide back and, in a rapid, accurate motion, plunged the knife into the guard's jugular—grabbing his gun arm and dragging him forward and downward as he did. This action tore a ragged hole in the man's throat. Kirov pivoted, pushed the dying guard against the wall of toughened glass, knelt on his legs, and pinned his arms as the life drained from him. Kirov glanced back to the entrance, dragged the body farther to the corner and waited, listening. No one called out or voiced any concern from down the walkway. He'd managed to reduce the noise to a minimum. He wiped his right hand and the knife so it wouldn't slip when he used it next and closed his left around the butt of his gun—he couldn't discount needing it too. His heart rate ticked up a few notches, but his breathing remained slow and even. Kirov edged to the walkway exit. Calmness personified, he waited to end Hugh Fairfax's life.

100

Watchful, Hogan moved forward, fighting to control the panic, his breathing ragged. As he reached the end of the tube of glass, it opened up to steep curved edges resembling a giant fishbowl but with the water outside. As his line of vision panned left, it came to rest on a man covered in blood, staring at a frozen Audrey.

"Don't move," Hogan cried, stepping forward, training his gun on the bloodied man.

Kirov waited to the left of the entrance as a girl bundled into the dome. Fairfax's granddaughter stopped dead, her startling blue eyes growing wide with fear. He'd need to grab her now, and then the old man would do whatever he asked. But at this crucial moment and for the first time in action, he froze—aware he would shatter this girl's innocence. Thoughts of Alice on the edge of that rabbit hole pushed through his consciousness. They were interrupted by an order. He turned to see a gun trained on him. The FBI agent named Hogan held it, and instructed him to drop the knife. Alice stumbled back as her mother appeared behind her and screamed as Hugh Fairfax entered the dome. The tall man immediately stepped in front of his companions. Kirov imagined the angle the knife could travel if he turned and threw it. But his opportunity had gone, and his hesitancy could yet prove fatal. Survival could be his best possible outcome. The agent called for the trio to leave, and after more encouragement, the footsteps of retreat followed. Kirov turned completely to face the figure opposite.

"Drop the weapon," the agent called as he closed the distance. Kirov shook his head. This provided his only leverage. The special agent hadn't shot yet for a reason, one they both knew; it surrounded them. Kirov couldn't let him get much closer. His resolve returned as he tightened his grip around the knife. Would he be quick enough?

Hogan slowed his steps forward when Richelieu didn't comply. In his peripheral vision, Hugh Fairfax stepped across Marissa and her daughter. They were all Hogan's priority. He kept his eyes on his target and shouted, "Get out of here!"

The three figures didn't move. Richelieu's eyes darted left, then back to him. He called out again. "Just go, *now!*" This time, they listened, and he heard footsteps, slow at first, then faster. He still fought against the panic as he observed the assassin staring, awaiting his next move. The metallic tang of adrenaline engulfed the back of his throat. He steadied himself to shoot Richelieu if necessary, despite wanting him alive to pay for what he'd done to Katie and to ask why.

"Glock 9 mm. The bullets will go through me and the glass." The assassin sounded almost casual. Hogan could see his face now. It was older, lined, but him—Lukas, Kirov, or most recently, Richelieu. The cold, dead eyes triggered a memory, swimming through his fear. It hit home: this had been the Uber driver in New York, outside the Fullertons'. If he'd entered that car, he wouldn't have left alive. He needed answers, the first, the most important.

"Who paid you to kill Senator Thomas Mitchell?"

Richelieu frowned, then shook his head. Hogan's finger remained tight to the trigger. "Tell me, Lukas, and I'll let you live," he tried again. This brought a flicker of surprise in the killer's eyes before they turned cold again. They both knew this wasn't how this ended. "How about Chopra, Decker?" Hogan demanded, but the frozen figure remained silent.

The agent's opening question intrigued Kirov. What did a bombing a few years back have to do with now? He shook his head. If he died here, his secrets would follow him to the grave. Then he heard his real name for the first time in decades, which shocked him. He respected this man who'd not only discovered his identity but had gotten closer than anyone before.

He should have killed him as planned.

Special Agent Hogan asked one more question, then observed him with a steely determination. This was personal and meant nothing would stop this man from firing his weapon. Finally, that angry teenager named Lukas Vilkas would have to answer for all he'd done since he chose this path. He'd spent all these years living and plotting like villains from his childhood stories and overlooked they often got what they deserved. It was time to discover his ending. He threw himself left in one explosive motion, the knife flashing from one hand as he did, the other pulling out his weapon. This time, too slow. *So, this is how that feels.* The knife's trajectory faltered, and the bullets tore into Kirov before he hit the ground. As his mouth formed the word "Isobel," the final bullet exploded his skull.

The seconds crawled by, but Hogan got no response. If he were to get answers, they would have to come from elsewhere. The eyes of Richelieu focused, then the assassin began to move. Hogan's concentration didn't waver as he fired three times before the knife buried itself deep in his thigh. He staggered forward, emptying the clip until the body on the floor stopped jerking.

A jarring, splintering sound announced a spider's web of cracks, which began to rise up the curved glass. Hogan remained rooted to the spot in terror. He looked down at the bullet-riddled body of Richelieu. If he were going to die here, at least now, he wouldn't be the only one. Yet he still had a chance. He began to limp in the same direction Marissa had fled, blood pouring down his leg as he neared the stairs and safety. A violent crash announced a roar of rushing water. After two steps, it enveloped him, and everything turned black.

101

HOGAN REGAINED CONSCIOUSNESS. His last fragmented memories were terror as the water smashed into him, a brief snapshot of a paramedic's face in an ambulance, then nothing. He eased his eyes open to jarring hospital lights. As his focus sharpened, he began to register a sizeable number of figures in the room.

"He's awake," he heard someone cry before arms wrapped themselves around his shoulders and placed several soft kisses on his face and lips. Marissa moved back to reveal Hugh Fairfax observing him, gripping Audrey's hand.

Hogan only cared about one thing. "Is he dead?" he rasped, feeling the irony that he now needed water.

"Yes, very," Carla said from the other corner of the room. "The fifteen bullet wounds would have done it, even before the tank shattered."

Hogan closed his eyes and thought of Katie; retribution had been delivered. It would take time, but maybe now the nightmares would end.

"How are you feeling?" Vance asked, passing him a bottle of water before stepping back to stand with Ranger and Chung.

Hogan grimaced as he moved his leg; he hoped there was no lasting damage. His mouth tasted of salt, and his throat had the consistency of sandpaper. The first mouthful of water was bliss.

"Like I should stop getting beaten, shot, and stabbed," he said, emotional and grateful to be alive, surrounded by people who cared about him. A ripple of nervous laughter ran across the room. "How did I get out?"

"Mr. Fairfax plunged into the water to drag you out just in time."

Hogan turned to where his rescuer stood.

"Thanks," he croaked. The older man smiled and tipped an imaginary hat.

Carla walked to the end of his bed.

"We've got a lot to talk about, but it can wait. Get some more rest, Hogan—you've earned it. I need to go and make a statement. The press hyenas are braying outside—don't worry, we've LAPD officers stationed at every door. They won't get anywhere near here."

Vance offered a broad smile from behind his boss and nudged Ranger.

"We need to go too. We'll be back tomorrow."

Hogan responded, "I know you will." Then turned his gaze to Carla. "We got him together, as a team. Make sure everyone knows that, okay?"

"Of course," she replied.

Vance stepped forward and threw a playful punch, stopping short of his arm, then laughed. "I'll save that for when you're back. Call if you need us to bring anything."

Hogan managed a grin in return.

After they all left, Hugh Fairfax approached the bed.

"I may have pulled you out, but I only could because you saved all of us. I owe you a debt I can never truly repay—for the first time in my life. So—thank you, Hogan." He rested his hand on his arm, then moved back. Audrey looked up with her wide blue eyes.

"I think you broke the aquarium," she said, "but it's okay—I already saw most of it."

Hogan couldn't help but smile. "I think I did." Audrey took her grandfather's hand and walked toward the door.

"I'm going nowhere," Marissa began stroking his head.

"I've been a fool—" he began, but she interrupted him.

"Shsssh, not now. You should rest."

He closed his eyes and drifted back into a welcome sleep.

102

AFTER FOUR DAYS in the hospital, Hogan had gained enough strength to leave. He could see lines of TV vans and a throng of reporters below, waiting to grab a word with the man who'd ended Richelieu's life. Not that he had any intention of giving them that opportunity. Nemo had arranged for him to be smuggled out in an ambulance. The next stop would be his friend's penthouse, where he could change before continuing to Wilshire. By all accounts, his apartment in Venice was under siege. He'd been kept abreast of developments over the last few days, both by Vance and via the media frenzy on TV, but he needed to get into the office for a full debrief. Carla would have multiple questions, including some he couldn't or wouldn't answer. At least now, his secrets were safe.

As he hobbled on his crutches into the office, people rose from their desks and applauded him. His modest British side hated it, so he hurried as much as possible to where Carla stood, holding her door open. She had coffee waiting as he eased into a chair.

"How you doing?" she asked.

"Much better, thanks. My leg will take time to heal, but aside from that, pretty good considering."

"Well, yes, you're one lucky fucker, Fairfax too. We'll get to that, though," Carla responded with her usual forthrightness.

"So what's the latest from Miami?" He intended to deflect questions for a little while.

"They've identified the dead would-be assassin as Karl Bekker. An unnamed source who recruited for Blackwater in the late nineties recognized Bekker from the images on TV. We've contacted the Zimbabwe government, and they've confirmed it. Seems like the whole job was a setup to allow Richelieu's attempt on Fairfax's life. Lyle was never the real target." Carla paused for more coffee.

"And the images on his phone from the crime scene?"

"We assume Richelieu, or the man that hired him, sent them to Bekker when arranging the assassination attempt as a diversion. We fell for it. I should have listened to you."

Hogan appreciated the small mea culpa from Carla.

"And it makes sense that Lyle commissioned Richelieu, right?"

"It does, and we're still working on that. I buy into the idea he was behind the attacks, but we'll have to be cautious and prepared before we make any kind of move against him. We'll need compelling proof to get a warrant, as we only get one shot at this."

He wasn't confident they'd get it any time soon. But his team wouldn't stop until they did. The person who hired Richelieu to kill State Senator Mitchell mattered most to Hogan. He'd looked forward to asking his next question.

"How much shit is Miller in?"

"It's pretty fucking deep; his superstar status back at Quantico is in ruins. If he'd waited for print and DNA comparison and one more day for more evidence, he wouldn't have jumped the gun as badly as he did. Besides your loyal team, everyone else believed the dead man was Richelieu, but we didn't announce that in front of the world media." Carla ran a hand through her hair and sighed. "The FACE Services Unit came back Monday to say it wasn't our guy after they'd reviewed the bike theft security footage. We also know Karl Bekker wasn't even in the country when Jay Chopra died. Director Sullivan was pretty pissed at first, but Fairfax is so thankful to you, and by extension, the Bureau, that we're coming out of it okay. It helps you got the guy, and we have a bona fide hero as the task force lead." Carla fixed him with a full-watt smile.

Hogan took a moment to savor this and Miller's downfall.

"Now my questions," Carla began, the frown lines back to twitching in her forehead. "How the fuck were you so sure Bekker wasn't Richelieu? And how did you end up, and there is no other way to put this, in the right place at exactly the right fucking time?"

Hogan had taken days to think of the answer to this inevitable question. He proceeded with the best one he'd been able to muster.

"Special Agent Coleman from Miami sent through the images and raw video of Bekker Sunday morning." The video lie was designed to help his story. "Something about how he looked and moved didn't mesh with the footage of the real Richelieu and what I had seen of the suspect at the Aria. The build was different, for starters. Adding this to my doubts about the amateurish and reckless attempt on Lyle's life, I figured we had the wrong guy," Hogan explained. "I did urge caution on Saturday, remember?" Carla nodded. "So I realized Fairfax could still be at risk and drove to alert him straight away."

"At the aquarium?"

"Well, yes, I knew from Marissa's Instagram they were there."

"Marissa, your girlfriend?" She arched one eyebrow.

He smiled but ignored the question. "I rushed there to warn them—as a precaution. I wasn't actually expecting...well, the rest, you know."

"That's some instinct, Hogan." Carla's eyes narrowed, but what else could she say?

"Thanks," he replied. They sat in silence before he broke it. "Any leads on the identity of Richelieu?" He figured she'd expect him to ask this question, even if it was redundant.

"Not yet. We matched his DNA profile to one from the room at the Loews Regency New York to tie him to all the killings. The print from his right index finger matched the one taken from the Aria too. We ran all his prints through the NGI but received no hits. His body was a mess when we pulled it from the water—the sharks didn't help, but experts will model out his likeness, and we can release that to the public. We're going through the items from the shipping company for any clues to his identity. He has a few valuable books, but there is no sign of *Alice in Wonderland* or other first editions Vance identified that he bought at auction. Perhaps they're already on their way to Kotor? We may release the photos of people we found in the shipment to the press. It hasn't been decided yet. We discovered his vehicle outside. It contained a bag with battered old books, some with Russian written inside. Someone must know him—he can't be a ghost," Carla added.

At least one guy did. Hogan supposed Wolgomott would retreat again into the shadows and work on keeping a cap on information flow from their side. For now, at least, the CIA was in the clear.

"Have FLEA been sniffing about?" Hogan asked. They were the team tasked with following up on agent-involved shootings.

"I told them to wait a couple more days."

"Thanks. Once I know the prognosis on recovery for my leg—"

Carla batted his comments away with her hand. "No rush, Hogan. Director Sullivan himself sends a get-well-soon message. We're all good here—finally."

Mentioning the SAC position could wait. The outlook must be positive.

"I suppose we are." He reached for his crutches.

"Now go and find your team. They're desperate to head for lunch and hear all the juicy details from that Sunday. Tell them to take their time; it's the least they deserve." Carla gave him a final smile and opened the door for him to leave.

103

Charles Lyle stepped off his Gulfstream G700 into the cooling desert air. A limousine sat waiting on the tarmac, as it had on all his previous visits here. The Saudis treated their guests well. The ride into Riyadh would take less than thirty minutes.

The Kingdom Centre skyscraper loomed on his left, as they travelled to his destination. It was as if a colossal bottle opener had been placed in the city's center. But developments were planned elsewhere that would dwarf this. These included a sustainable city that would be one hundred and seventy-kilometers long and only two hundred meters wide. It was another reason the Crown Prince wanted to buy time for revenues for change.

The sweeping driveway leading up to the Ritz Carlton was lined by palms and flag poles, with pristine forest-green gardens on either side. As the driver pulled up, staff hurried from the palatial entrance, a foretaste of the grandeur within. Lyle received an escort to the Royal Suite. He had an hour to freshen up before meeting with the Crown Prince.

Four members of the Royal Guard marched into the suite at nine p.m. and swept the entire place for listening devices. Lyle found this odd but didn't comment. Once they had taken his phone, the men fanned out on either side of Lyle, and Crown Prince Khalid Hussain Al Saud glided into the room. He wore a black *thobe* trimmed in gold, and a red and white *keffiyeh*, with a black *agal*.

"I trust your flight was agreeable," Khalid said in his soft, structured English.

"Very smooth, Your Highness."

"Our business together has been pleasing. It was unfortunate it wasn't concluded."

"Circumstances conspired against us, but we could revisit this in the future?"

"That won't be required, it is now too big a risk, and we're seeing the benefits for the Kingdom already."

"As you wish, Your Highness."

"I trust you spoke to nobody about our arrangement?" Khalid's eyes flashed, then his dull stare returned.

"I gave you my word." Lyle shifted in his seat, disconcerted by the Crown Prince's demeanor.

"Excellent," Khalid announced, rising from his seat. "We shall dine at the palace tomorrow."

"And finalize our deal on my assets here, Your Highness?" Lyle's discomfort remained. He wanted confirmation he'd still be receiving his billions.

"Of course," Khalid replied, offering a thin smile. After a quick nod to the leader of his protective detail, he swept from the room.

Lyle sighed, threaded his hands together, and looked at the ceiling. When he focused back on his surroundings, two men remained next to where he sat, and the other members of the Royal Guard were striding toward him. They wore dispassionate expressions. He started to panic. Men on either side pinned him to the chair while the head of the detail produced a long needle from his jacket. As his bowels began to loosen, Lyle realized the Crown Prince had planned this all along. It ensured silence. The cool metal eased into the skin behind his ear, and seconds later, darkness as black as oil swallowed him.

104

IT HAD BEEN a few weeks since Hogan left the hospital. He couldn't wait to return to work. He occupied his regular table in The Rose, waiting for Nemo to join him for brunch. It was his first visit since the incident that turned him into a celebrity hero, at least for a week or two. He looked up from his phone to see Amber hurrying toward him.

"Why didn't you tell me you were an FBI agent—it's so cool. I've been telling anyone who'll listen that I know you. I mean, you've been all over social media."

Hogan smiled. "Hey, Amber."

"I still can't believe what you did. Hogan, the hero." She beamed and sat in the chair opposite.

"I did what any other agent would have done," he replied. Amber leaned in.

"I'm not talking about Richelieu."

"I don't follow."

"I know you had something to do with Chad suddenly leaving town, and I wanted to say thank you." She leaned even closer and dropped a kiss on his cheek. "I mean it, thanks." She got up before he snapped out of his silent surprise and started back toward the counter, then turned. "You don't have a younger brother, by any chance?" she asked.

Hogan laughed. "I'm afraid not. I think you'll be fine, though." Amber pulled a sad face, dipped her head, then walked away.

So, Chad had been watching the news too. He could imagine the panic when he'd discovered whom he'd attacked. Hogan allowed himself another smile at this image as the bulky figure of Nemo sat opposite and arched his head in Amber's direction.

"What's all that about? Dude, she's cute, but aren't you kinda taken?"

Hogan laughed. "It isn't like that. I did her a favor—that's all."

"Ah, I thought it might be a fan—now you're a crime-fighting celebrity!"

They caught up on the ten days since they'd last seen each other. Nemo had been away at a conference in Vegas and stayed at the Waldorf Astoria, racking up a decent bill. There had been no repercussions on their CIA file incursion, and they were both confident that would remain the case. Richelieu was still unidentified. Leads continued to come in due to the images and likeness released, but the Bureau remained no closer to finding out who he was. They only had a selection of pseudonyms so far. With the CIA working in the background, Hogan suspected the truth about his real identity would never come out.

Amber arrived with more coffee and pastries.

After she'd gone, Nemo cried, "So, Charles Lyle—what the fuck!"

Hogan looked from side to side, then lowered his voice.

"His body arrived back from Riyadh at the start of the week. The autopsy here found the same thing as the Saudis. A massive heart attack killed him."

"Convenient."

"Definitely—but no one is pushing this. The extended Lyle family just became fabulously wealthy, so they don't give a shit. Everyone back at Wilshire is convinced he hired Richelieu. There's no other way the attack in Miami and the opportunity that it created happens without his involvement. Plus, we had many other connections. Finding the proof would be tough, but we would have gotten there eventually."

"So, what now?"

"Nothing. The investigation will be wound down. We can't convict a dead man, and there is no mileage in releasing our theories to the public. Better to have a faceless assassin as a perpetrator than admit a high-profile billionaire funded the killings. The case will officially continue but will be little more than lip service. People will move on."

"But how about you, dude?"

"I'll never stop searching for the person who hired Richelieu to blow up Mitchell's car. I still owe Katie that much. But the rest, I can let slide, for now. I want to keep my job."

"One which would make your old man proud if he could comprehend what you've done. You've made a real difference, and how many of us can say that?"

"Thanks. I can believe that now." Hogan glanced up at the clock. "On that subject, I'd better head off soon. I'm meeting Marissa over at my dad's place."

Nemo smiled at the mention of her name; it was infectious—and Hogan did too. His fear of anything happening to Marissa or Audrey that day in the aquarium made him realize he couldn't run away from the specter of hurt and ignore his feelings. He'd begin a new chapter where he dictated his destiny and happiness. He needed to break out from the protective shell he'd formed and move on.

Nemo stared at Hogan's empty wrist, then into his eyes. They sat in silence for a few seconds.

"It was time," Hogan said, nodding. His friend smiled, and they both rose and embraced.

Hogan pulled up outside Paradiso. Marissa's beauty shone as she bounded over. An idiotic grin formed as he eased from the Jaguar. She stepped closer and kissed him.

"You ready for this?" he asked her.

"I can't wait to meet him," she answered. As they walked up toward the door, Hogan glanced up at the signage. It still said: "Paradiso Care," but underneath, an extra line had been added: "Part of the Fairfax Group of Companies." He looked back to Marissa, who'd watched him as he read it. She flashed a conspiratorial smile, took his arm, and they headed inside.

Epilogue

The head of the Foundation for Vilnius Orphans looked up from her computer in wonder; she had finished her calculations. She'd spent the last week researching the value of the mysterious crate of children's books, which had arrived two weeks prior. She shook her head at the figure on the spreadsheet in front of her. The total value was fourteen million euros. One book alone was worth more than three million. Not for the first time, she speculated on who the mystery benefactor was but remained none the wiser. The books had come with a simple note. It said:

"For the children, so they can have the future I never had."

Acknowledgements

I underestimated the gravity of the task of writing this book, but thankfully I had a stellar support network over that five-year period. Huge thanks to Dorie from The Dorie Simmonds Agency for her reviews of the manuscript, belief, and reliably sage advice. Thanks to all my friends, family, and associates who read the book's various iterations and offered suggestions greatly improving it, and, of course, to everyone at Simonstone Publishing. I was lucky enough to have two brilliant editors- Michelle Hope, and Robin Seavill, whose eagle eyes found and corrected my errors and offered feedback elevating the story. I also owe a debt of gratitude to Amie McCracken for the typesetting, Mr. X for the advice on hacking and other dark arts, and to the FBI's Press Office for being generous with their time. I want to give a special shout out to my dad for his unerring support, and to my amazing wider family. Finally, and most importantly, I couldn't have done this without my wife, Daiva, in my corner. She truly is one of a kind.